KU-265-436

Lisa Gardner is a *New York Times* and *Sunday Times* bestselling author. Her FBI Profiler novels include *Say Goodbye*, *Gone* and *The Killing Hour*. Her Detective D.D. Warren series includes *The Neighbour*, which won the International Thriller Writers' Award in 2010, *Catch Me*, *Crash & Burn* and *Find Her*. She lives with her family in New England.

Praise for *Find Her*:

'Fast-paced with edge-of-the-seat writing, you won't be able to put it down' *Daily Express*

'An absolute master of the psychological suspense novel. This story proceeds at a breathless pace, springing surprises at every turn and building up the tension to an almost unbearable level' Sharon Bolton

'The heroine of Gardner's latest blockbuster is one of the most nuanced of the many she has created' *Daily Mail*

'Original, chilling and so gripping I had to remind myself to take a breath. Lisa Gardner's *Find Her* is a sure-fire bestseller' Clare Mackintosh

'Lisa Gardner at her all time best . . . Innovative and unique as well as brilliantly crafted. Mark this one down as a "must read"!' *Huffington Post*

'An exceptional novel . . . You've had *Gone Girl* . . . now read *Find Her*' *CrimeSquad*

'Truly a contender for "Book of the Year"' *Postcard Reviews*

'A very clever story . . . one of the best thrillers I've read in 2015' *Compelling Reads*

'The quality of crime writing on offer today ranges from the indifferent through the workmanlike to the genuinely inventive, and Gardner is firmly in the upper echelons of the last category' *Crime Scene* magazine

Praise for *Crash & Burn*:

'Astonishingly gripping, heartbreaking, and as vivid as if you're living the heroine's nightmare yourself' Sophie Hannah

'Expertly crafted' *Publishers Weekly*

Praise for *Fear Nothing*:

'With heart-racing suspense and compelling characters, expect Gardner to hold you captive from beginning to end' *Hunts Post*

'Gardner continues to show why she is on the short list of top thriller writers today' *Suspense Magazine*

Praise for *Touch & Go*:

'Gardner keeps the suspense high and the unforeseen twists coming right until the last page' *Sunday Mirror*

'Even readers who figure out the ringleader long before Tessa and Wyatt will get behind on their sleep turning pages to make sure they're right' *Kirkus Reviews*

Praise for *Catch Me*:

'Well-wrought suspense . . . Gardner skillfully tacks back and forth . . . Fans should enjoy the numerous cameos by characters from other Gardner novels' *Publishers Weekly*

'Gardner brings the ingredients to a rolling boil . . . Irresistible high-wire melodrama' *Kirkus Reviews*

Praise for *Love You More*:

'An amazing writer. Her characters are multi-dimensional and believable, and they tell the kinds of stories that grip you right from the first page' Karin Slaughter

'This book had me at the author's name. Lisa Gardner . . . No one owns this corner of the genre the way she does' Lee Child

Praise for *Live to Tell*:

'Gardner has another hit on her hands' *Kirkus Reviews*

'An utterly gripping if profoundly uncomfortable story that could cause sleepless nights' *Irish Independent*

Praise for *The Neighbour*:

'Full of inventive twists, this highly entertaining novel delivers a shocking solution as well as a perfectly realized sense of justice' *Publishers Weekly*

'Suspenseful and stylish . . . A definite treat for her fans' *Booklist*

Praise for *Say Goodbye*:

'Suspense of the highest order' *Daily Mirror*

'Some of this novel gave me shivers up my spine. It is definitely not one for arachnophobes, but everyone else should love it' *Independent on Sunday*

Praise for *Hide*:

'A brilliant book, not to be missed under any circumstances' *Independent on Sunday*

'Gripping, the protagonists earn quick sympathy, and the pages turn with speed' *Wall Street Journal*

Praise for *Gone*:

'Good news: There are no damsels in distress here – the wife, their daughter and a female sheriff all kick butt. It's a whodunit until the very end' *Glamour*

Praise for *Alone*:

'There is an impressive air of gathering menace . . . This is not a book you'd want to read alone in a dimly lit place' *Guardian*

'Fast-moving . . . Makes [Gardner] a match for many of her best-selling compatriots' *Sunday Telegraph*

Praise for *The Killing Hour*:

'With tight plotting, an ear for forensic detail and a dash of romance, this is a truly satisfying sizzler in the tradition of Tess Gerritsen and Tami Hoag' *Publishers Weekly*

'Gardner keeps us guessing . . . She also keeps us on edge' *LA Times*

Praise for *The Survivors Club*:

'A high-octane, nerve-jangling tale of suspense' Harlan Coben

'Starts fast and never stops moving. The plot is clever, complex and original' Phillip Margolin

Praise for *The Next Accident*:

'A fiendishly well choreographed dance of death' *Booklist*

'Accomplished' *Kirkus Reviews*

Praise for *The Third Victim*:

'Riveting, hold-your-breath suspense' Iris Johansen

'A suspenseful, curl-up winter read, this thriller teems with crisp, realistic dialogue and engaging characters' *Publishers Weekly*

Praise for *The Other Daughter*:

'Sheer terror . . . A great read' *Booklist*

'Once again, Gardner serves up suspense at a furious pace' *Publishers Weekly*

Praise for *The Perfect Husband*:

'A dark, powerful tale of nerve-shattering suspense' Tami Hoag

'An unforgettably evil villain and a throat-gripping climax make *The Perfect Husband* a real page-turner!' Tess Gerritsen

LISA GARDNER

FIND HER

headline

Copyright © 2016 Lisa Gardner, Inc.

The right of Lisa Gardner to be identified as the Author of
the Work has been asserted by her in accordance with the
Copyright, Designs and Patents Act 1988.

First published in 2016 by
HEADLINE PUBLISHING GROUP

First published in paperback in 2016 by
HEADLINE PUBLISHING GROUP

11

Apart from any use permitted under UK copyright law, this publication
may only be reproduced, stored, or transmitted, in any form, or by any
means, with prior permission in writing of the publishers or, in the case
of reprographic production, in accordance with the terms of licences
issued by the Copyright Licensing Agency.

All characters in this publication are fictitious and any resemblance
to real persons, living or dead, is purely coincidental.

Cataloguing in Publication Data is available from the British Library

ISBN 978 1 4722 2031 8 (B-format)
ISBN 978 1 4722 3237 3 (A-format)

Typeset in Sabon by Avon DataSet Ltd, Bidford-on-Avon, Warwickshire

Printed and bound in Great Britain by Clays Ltd, St Ives plc

Headline's policy is to use papers that are natural, renewable and
recyclable products and made from wood grown in well-managed
forests and other controlled sources. The logging and manufacturing
processes are expected to conform to the environmental regulations of
the country of origin.

HEADLINE PUBLISHING GROUP
An Hachette UK Company
Carmelite House
50 Victoria Embankment
London EC4Y 0DZ

www.headline.co.uk
www.hachette.co.uk

FIND HER

For survivors everywhere

1

These are the things I didn't know:

When you first wake up in a dark wooden box, you'll tell yourself this isn't happening. You'll push against the lid, of course. No surprise there. You'll beat at the sides with your fists, pummel your heels against the bottom. You'll bang your head, again and again, even though it hurts. And you'll scream. You'll scream and scream and scream. Snot will run from your nose. Tears will stream from your eyes. Until your screams grow rough, hiccuppy. Then, you'll hear sounds that are strange and sad and pathetic, and you'll understand the box, truly get, hey, I'm trapped in a dark wooden box, when you realize those sounds come from you.

Pine boxes aren't composed entirely of smooth surfaces. Air holes, for example, can be crudely drilled. When you run your finger around them, when you poke your fingertip into them, desperately seeking . . . something . . . you'll get splinters. You'll chew out the wooden shards best you can. Then you'll suck on your injured digit, lick the blood beading the tip, and make more hurt puppy dog sounds.

You're alone in the box. It's frightening. Overwhelming. Awful. Mostly because you don't yet understand how much you have to fear.

You'll get to know the box well, this home away from home. You'll wiggle against it with your shoulders to determine the width. You'll trace the length with your hands, attempt to bring up your feet. Not enough room to bend your knees. Not enough room to roll over. It's exactly your size. As if it's been made just for you. Your very own pine coffin, straining your lower back, bruising your shoulder blades, paining the back of your head.

One convenience: newspapers lining the bottom. You don't notice this detail in the beginning. Don't understand it once you do. Until the first time you wet yourself. Then spend days lying in your own filth. Like an animal, you'll think. Except most animals are treated better than this.

Your mouth will grow parched, your lips chapped. You'll start jamming your fingers into those air holes, ripping apart your own skin, just so you have something to taste, swallow, suck. You'll know yourself in a way you've never known yourself before. Broken down. Elemental. The stink of your own urine. The salt of your own blood.

But you still don't know anything yet.

When you finally hear footsteps, you won't believe it. You're delirious, you'll tell yourself. You're dreaming. You're a lost, pathetic waste of human skin. A stupid, stupid girl who should've known better and now just look at you. And yet, the sound of a metal lock jangling on the other side of the box wall, inches from your ear . . .

Maybe you cry again. Or would if you had any moisture left.

When you first see his face, the man who has done this to you, you're relieved. Happy even. You gaze upon his puffy cheeks, his beady eyes, his gaping mouth, yellow-stained teeth, and you think, thank God. Thank God, thank God, thank God.

He lets you out of the box. Lifts you up, actually, because your legs don't work, and your muscles lack all strength, and your head lolls. Which makes you giggle. Head lolling. One of those words from English class that never made any sense. But there you have it. Heads loll. Your head lolls.

God, the smell. Garlic and BO and unwashed clothes and skanky hair. Is it you? Is it him? You gag, helplessly. And that makes him laugh. As he holds up the bottle of water. As he spells out exactly what you'll have to do in order to earn it. He's fat. Old. Disgusting. Repulsive. The unkempt beard, the greasy hair, the ketchup stains splotching the front of his cheap checkered shirt.

You're supposed to be too good for him. Young, fresh, beautiful. The kind of girl who could have her pick of the litter at a frat party. You have moves. Had moves?

You cry for your mother. You beg him to let you go as you lie in a crumpled heap at his feet. Then, finally, ultimately, with the last of your strength, you remove your clothes. You let him do what he's going to do. You scream, but your throat is too dry to make a sound. You vomit, but your stomach is too empty to yield any contents.

You survive.

And later, when he finally offers up that bottle of water, only to dump it over your head, you lift your hands shamelessly to capture as much of the moisture as you can. You lick it from your palms. Chew it from your oily, filthy hair. You wait till he's distracted, then suck that spot of ketchup from his now discarded shirt.

Back to the box. The box. The Box.

The lid hammers now. The lock snaps shut. The repulsive man walks away. Leaves you once again all alone. Naked. Bruised. Bloody. Knowing things you never wanted to know.

'Mommy,' you whisper.

But this monster's real. And there's nothing anyone can do to save you anymore.

This is what I do know:

There's not much to do day after day trapped in a coffin-size box. In fact, there's really only one thing worth imagining, obsessing, contemplating minute by minute, hour after terrible hour. One thought that keeps you going. One focus that gives you strength. You'll find it. You'll hone it. Then, if you're anything like me, you'll never let it go.

Revenge.

But be careful what you wish for, especially if you're just a stupid girl trapped in a coffin-size box.

2

She started with a pomegranate martini. Paid too much, of course. Boston bars being very expensive. Pomegranate juice being very trendy. But it was Friday night. Another week survived, and by God she deserved at least an overpriced fruity cocktail.

Besides, she had some faith in herself. Loosen another button of her white fitted shirt, pull a few clips from her shoulder-length blond hair. She was twenty-seven, fit, and with the kind of ass that brought notice. She might buy her first drink. But odds were, she wouldn't be buying the second.

She took a sip. Cool. Sweet. Biting. She warmed it on her tongue, then let the vodka slide down her throat. Worth every penny of the fourteen bucks.

For a moment she closed her eyes. The bar disappeared. The sticky floor, the strobing lights, the high-pitched squeal of the opening band, still warming up.

She stood in a void of silence. In a place that was solely hers.

When she opened her eyes again, he was standing there.

He bought her a second drink. Then a third, even offered a fourth. But by then the vodka and the dance-floor lights were starting to mix in a way that didn't make for a great morning after. Besides, she wasn't an idiot. Whole time Mr Haven't I Seen You Around Here Before was plying her with martinis, he stuck to beer.

He was nice enough looking, she decided somewhere near the end of martini number two. Muscular, clearly a guy who worked out. Uninspired taste in clothing, though, with his tan slacks, button-up blue-striped shirt. Going for young professional, she supposed, but she noticed his pants were frayed at the hems, his shirt faded from too many washings. When she asked what he did for a living, he tried for charm. Oh, a little of this, a little of that, he said, going with a wink and a grin. But his eyes remained flat, even distant, and she felt the first pinprick of unease.

He recovered quickly. Produced martini number three. Wasn't wearing a watch, she noticed, as he tried to catch the bartender with a twenty, then failed, as the other patrons were flashing hundreds. Not a wedding ring either. Unattached. Well built. Maybe her night was looking up.

She smiled, but it wasn't a happy look. Something moved across her face, that void again, that realization that all these hours, days, weeks later, she still felt alone. Would always feel alone. Even in a crowded room.

It was just as well he didn't turn around.

He finally snagged the bartender – white shirt, black tie, the kind of pecs that produced big tips – and got her a fresh drink.

She was ready for the fourth martini by then. Why not? It enabled her to talk about her little bit of this and little bit of that with a wink and a grin that matched the gleam in her eyes. And when his gaze lingered on the front of her shirt, the extra button that she might've slipped just moments before, she didn't back away. She let him stare

at the lacy hint of her hot-pink bra. She let him admire her
tits.

Why not? Friday night. End of the week. She'd earned
this.

He wanted to leave the bar at midnight. She made him wait
till close. Band was surprisingly good. She liked the way the
music made her feel, as if her blood were still alive, her
heart still beating in her chest. He was clearly uncomfortable
on the dance floor, but it didn't matter; she had moves good
enough for both of them.

Her white fitted shirt was now tied beneath her breasts
Daisy Duke-style. Her low-riding black dress jeans clung to
every curve, her tall leather boots stomping out each rhythmic
beat. After a while, he didn't even bother with dancing but
simply swayed in place, watching her. Her arms flung overhead, lifting her breasts. Her hips swinging round and round,
taut bare abdomen glistening with sweat.

He had brown eyes, she noted. Dark. Flat. Watchful.
Predatory, she thought. But this time around, instead of
being spooked, she felt a fresh spike of adrenaline. The
well-chiseled bartender was staring at her now too. She did
a tour of the dance floor for both of them. Having accepted
that fourth martini, her mouth now felt sweet and purple
while her limbs were liquid ice.

She could dance all night. Take over this floor, take over
this bar, take over this town.

Except that wasn't what Mr Haven't I Seen You Around
Here Before wanted. No guy bought a girl three overpriced
drinks merely for the privilege of watching her dance.

Band wrapped up, started putting away their instruments.
She missed the music acutely. Felt it like a pang to her soul.
No more driving bass to power her feet, mask her pain.

Now it was just her, Mr Haven't I Seen You Around Here Before, and the promise of a killer hangover.

He suggested they head outside for some fresh air. She wanted to laugh. To tell him he had no idea.

Instead, she followed him to the narrow side street covered in littered cigarette butts. He asked her if she wanted to smoke. She declined. He took her hand. Then, he pinned her to the side of a blue-painted dumpster, left hand already squeezing her breast, palming her nipple.

His eyes weren't flat anymore. They were molten. Predator having secured prey.

'Your place or mine,' he demanded.

She couldn't help herself. She started to laugh.

Which was when the evening really took a turn for the worse.

Mr Haven't I Seen You Around Here Before didn't care for being laughed at. He struck quickly. Right hand connecting open-palmed against the side of her face. Her head rocked back into the metal dumpster. She heard the crash. Registered the pain. But courtesy of four martinis, it all felt distant, a bad night happening to someone else.

'You a tease?' he yelled at her, hand squeezing her breast, face screaming just inches from hers.

This close, she smelled the beer on his breath, noted the distinct webbing of red veins around his nose. Closet drinker. She should've realized that sooner. Kind of guy who liquored up before coming to the bar because it was cheaper that way. Meaning he wasn't there for the booze at all but to hook up. To find a girl like her and take her home.

In other words, he was perfect for her.

She should say something. Or stomp her heel on the

instep of his foot. Or grab his pinky – not his whole hand, just the pinky finger – and wrench it back till it touched his wrist.

He'd scream. He'd let her go.

He'd look into her eyes and realize his mistake. Because big cities such as Boston were filled with guys like him.

But also with girls like her.

She never got a chance.

He was shouting. She was smiling. Maybe even still laughing. With her head ringing and the taste of blood salting her tongue. Then Mr Haven't I Seen You Here Before ceased to exist.

He was there. Then he was gone. Replaced by the body-conscious bartender with the amazing pecs and now a very concerned look on his face.

'Are you okay?' he asked. 'Did he hurt you? Do you need help? Do you want to call the cops?'

He offered his arm. She took it, stepping over the body of Mr Haven't I Seen You Around Here Before, who was knocked, slack-jawed, to the ground.

'He shouldn't have touched you like that,' the bartender informed her soberly. Leading her away from the gawkers gathering around. Leading her deeper into the shadows beyond the perimeter of the bar's flashing lights.

'It's okay. I'll take care of you now.'

As she realized for the first time that the bartender was gripping her arm harder than necessary. Not letting go.

She tried to talk her way out of it. Even when you knew better, it was a natural place to start. Hey, big boy, what's your hurry? Can't we just slow down? Hey, you're hurting me. But of course he never broke his stride, nor relaxed his bruising grip above her elbow.

He was walking funny, keeping her tucked against his side, like two lovers out on a very fast stroll, but his head was tucked down and tilted to the side. Keeping his face in the shadows, she realized. So no one could see him.

Then, it came to her. The line of his posture, the way he moved. She'd seen him before. Not his face, not his features, but the hunch of his shoulders, the rounded bend of his neck. Three or four months ago, summertime, on the evening news, when a Boston College student went out drinking and never came home again. The local stations had repeatedly aired a video clip from a nearby security camera, capturing the girl's last known moments as she was hustled away by an unknown male, head twisted from view.

'No,' she breathed.

He didn't acknowledge her protest. They'd come to an intersection. Without hesitation, he yanked her left, down a darker, skinnier street that already smelled of urine and dumpster trash and dark things never spoken of again.

She dug in her heels, sobering up quickly now, doing her best to resist. At 110 pounds to his 190, her efforts hardly made a difference. He jerked her tighter against him, right arm clamped around her waist, and continued on.

'Stop!' she tried to scream.

But no sound came out. Her voice was locked in her throat. She was breathless, lungs too constricted to scream. Instead, a faint whimper, a sound she was embarrassed to admit was her own but knew from past experience had to be.

'I have a family,' she panted at last.

He didn't respond. Fresh intersection, new turn. Skittering between tall brick buildings, out of public view. She already had no idea where they were.

'Please . . . stop . . .' she squeezed out. His arm was too

tight around her waist, bruising her ribs. She was going to vomit. Willed it to happen as maybe that would gross him out, convince him to let her go.

No such luck. She heaved abruptly, purple liquid spewing from her mouth, spraying her feet, the side of his pants. He grimaced, jerked reflexively away, then quickly recovered and yanked her once again forward, pulling her by the elbow.

'I'm gonna be sick again,' she moaned, feet tangling, finally slowing his momentum.

'Drank too much.' His voice was filled with scorn.

'You don't understand. You don't know who I am.'

He paused long enough to adjust his grip on her arm. 'Shouldn't have come to the bar alone.'

'But I'm always alone.'

He didn't get it. Or maybe he didn't care. He stared at her, gaze flat, face expressionless. Then, his arm shot forward, and he socked her in the eye.

Her neck snapped back.

Her cheek exploded. Her eyes welled with tears.

She had a thought. Fleeting. Faint. Maybe the secret to understanding the universe. But then it was gone.

And much like Mr Haven't I Seen You Around Here Before, she ceased to exist.

Friday night. End of a long week. She'd earned this.

He moved her. By foot, by car, she didn't know. But when she regained consciousness, she was no longer on the mean streets of Boston, but tucked somewhere dark and dank. The floor beneath her bare feet felt cold. Concrete. Cracked and uneven. A basement, she thought, or maybe a garage.

She could see faintly. Enough light from three small windows placed high on one wall. Not letting in daylight, but a dim yellow haze. As if a streetlight was outside those windows, permitting an ambient glow.

She used the wash of illumination to determine several things at once: Her hands were bound in front of her with plastic zip ties; she'd been stripped completely naked; and at the moment, at least, she was alone.

Her heart rate accelerated. Her head hurt, her skin prickling with goose bumps, and odds were she'd miss this state of relative safety soon enough. The kind of guy who knocked out his date and removed every stitch of her clothing wasn't the kind that was going to leave her untouched for long. Even now, he was most likely preparing for the rest of the evening's festivities. Humming away to himself. Contemplating games he could indulge in with his new toy. Feeling like he was the biggest, baddest asshole in town.

She smiled then. Though once again, it wasn't a happy expression on her face.

First off, inventory. Basement or garage inevitably meant storage, and as the saying went, one person's trash was another person's treasure.

He'd been stupid not to bind her ankles as well. Not as experienced as he thought. Not as clever as he was about to wish he'd been. But then, people saw what they wanted to see. She'd been taken in by his pecs. He'd no doubt assessed her as an easy blonde. Turned out, they were both in for some surprises this evening.

She found a heavy worktable. Raising her bound wrists, she skimmed her fingers across the wooden surface. She identified a thick metal vise built into one corner. Moved on more quickly in search of what she hoped might be an assortment of tools. But no, he wasn't that stupid and she wasn't that lucky.

No abandoned sharp objects, pliers, hammer. She searched the room's perimeter next, almost tripping over a metal can, then reaching out quickly to grab it before it fell. No sense in alerting him to her conscious state any sooner than necessary. Lid steady, nerves still shaky, she forced herself to continue.

The metal can yielded a filled plastic garbage bag. She set it aside in the short term, then paced the remaining two walls. She identified a collection of empty gas cans, as well as two plastic jugs. Based on smell, one gallon jug held the remains of windshield wiper fluid, the other anti-freeze. So she was most likely in a garage. Being Boston, probably a detached unit, allowing the bartender even more privacy.

She didn't dwell on what might happen next, why a man like him required such privacy. For that matter, she refused to get caught up in the stickiness of the floor in the rear corner. Or the smell that was becoming nearly impossible to ignore. An odor that matched the taste of blood on her tongue.

She took the jug of antifreeze and moved it to the bare wooden worktable. His first mistake. Her first victory.

She found a shovel propped up against the wall. With renewed vigor, she placed her plastic bindings against the blade and rubbed vigorously. After a minute or two, she was breathing heavily, sweat stinging her swollen eye. Yet to judge by the feel of the zip tie . . . Nothing. The edge of the spade was too dull, or the plastic too durable. She tried for another moment, then forced herself to abandon the effort.

Zip ties were tough. Frankly, she would've preferred metal cuffs. But at least he'd done the courtesy of binding her hands in front of her, where she still had considerable use of them, while not pulling the plastic so tight she lost all feeling in her fingertips.

She could move her feet; she could move her arms.

She could hold herself perfectly still and feel the void, right there. Dark. Comforting. Silent.

Alone in a crowded room, she thought, and for a moment, her body swayed, listening to music only she could hear.

Then she grew serious again. Trash. It was time.

She tore through the thin plastic bag using her fingers. First thing that hit her was the stench. Rotten food, rotted flesh, something worse. She gagged, felt tears well in her eyes and forced down a flood of bile. Now was not the time to be squeamish as she forced her fingers into oozing garbage she could feel but not see. Paper towels. Wet piles of God knows what. Discarded food containers. Takeout. From inside the home, or food he'd brought out here to share with his catch or munch on himself when taking a break from his entertainment. Halfway through the bag she came upon a new batch of rotten, more organic smelling this time. Her fingers moved quicker. Paper-dry petals. Squishy green stems. Flowers. A tossed bouquet. Because in addition to food, he plied his playthings with treats?

More likely, she decided, the last ruse he'd used to lure an unsuspecting victim. Then, in the next instant, it occurred to her: Where there's a cheap florist's bouquet . . .

Bound hands moving quickly now. Diving into the foul pile. Digging determinedly through rancid Chinese food and sticky duck sauce. Tossing aside empty coffee cups and more and more gooey flower carcasses. Plastic, she was seeking the feel of a thin plastic packet. Small, square, with a sharp edge . . .

Bang.

The noise came from directly behind her. The sound of a hand, a foot, connecting with a metal garage door. She couldn't help herself. She froze. Naked. Shivering. Elbow-deep in garbage. And listened to him once again announce his arrival.

Because he wanted her to know he was coming. He wanted her shaking, terrified, curled into a ball, already fearing the worst. That was the kind of man he was.

She smiled.

And this time, it was a happy expression on her face. Because now, in her right hand, she had it: the thin packet of flower food, generously included with most bouquets and exactly what she'd been looking for.

She hadn't lied to him before. He didn't know her. Which had been his first, and would now be his last, mistake.

Behind her, the garage door began its shaky ascent. Him dragging out the suspense as he slowly heaved it open.

No more time to wait. No more time to plan. She gripped the packet between her palms, then grabbed the nearly empty jug of antifreeze. Moving swiftly across the cracked concrete floor until she stood beneath the row of eyebrow windows. The weak light streaming above her, bathing the middle of the space in a dim glow while keeping her in shadow.

Garage door. Quarter of the way open. Now a third. A half.

She released her grip on the packet. Grabbed the anti-freeze jug first, pinning it between her feet, then used both hands to press down the child-safety lid and twist. The plastic cap clattered to the floor, but the rattle of the heaving metal door covered the sound.

Two-thirds of the way open. Now three-quarters. Enough for a grown man to walk through.

She placed the antifreeze to the side. Forced herself to take the time to shake the packet, settling the crystals to the bottom. Couldn't afford to waste any if this was to work.

He stepped into the space.

The bartender with the amazing pecs. Shirt already off. Muscles rippling in the moonlight. A beautiful physical specimen.

She should feel guilty for what she was going to do next.

But she didn't.

She stepped forward into the dim stream of light. Her nakedness clearly exposed. Her wrists clearly bound.

He smiled, right hand already moving to the waistband of his jeans.

'You don't know who I am,' she said clearly.

He paused, regarded her quizzically, as if she'd challenged him with complicated math.

Then . . . the bartender moved toward her.

She ripped open the plastic packet, took three quick steps forward, and tossed the contents into his face.

He reared back, coughing and blinking as the flower food hit his eyes, nose, mouth.

'What the . . .'

She grabbed the open jug of antifreeze, swirled it three times, and then . . .

A suspended heartbeat of time. He looked at her. Stared hard. And in that instant they finally saw each other. Not a ripped bartender. Not a stupid blonde. But dark heart to lost soul.

She sprayed the antifreeze straight into his face. Splashed it onto his exposed skin and the granules of potassium permanganate still clinging there.

One more heartbeat of time. Then . . .

The first tendrils of smoke. From his hair. His cheeks. His eyelashes. The man lifted his hands to his face.

Then basic chemistry took over, and the bartender's skin burst into flame.

He screamed. He ran. He beat at his own head as if it would make a difference. He did everything but stop, drop, and roll, panic having its way.

She stood there. Not moving a muscle. Not saying a word. She watched until at last he collapsed into a pile of smoking ruin. Other sounds penetrated then. Neighbors calling out into the dark, demanding to know what was going on. The distant sounds of sirens, as apparently one of the smarter ones had already called 911.

The woman finally stepped forward. She peered down at her attacker's remains, watched the smoky tendrils drift from his now blackened skin.

Friday night, she thought. She'd earned this.

3

'Who is she?'

'Don't know. Neighbor over there, Kyle Petrakis, claims he found her standing over the body. Stripped naked, hands tied, face bashed.'

'She did all this with her hands tied?' Sergeant Detective D.D. Warren knelt down, studied the charred remains of their . . . victim? Perpetrator? Body was curled in a near fetal position, hands clenched over the young male's face. A protective gesture, which, judging by the burn patterns across his head, shoulders, and face, had been too little, too late.

'Chemical fire,' the third detective spoke up. 'Combine potassium permanganate with antifreeze and poof.'

D.D. ignored the third detective, glancing up at Phil instead. 'So what do we know?'

'House belongs to Allen and Joyce Goulding,' her former squad mate rattled off. 'Older couple, currently waiting out the winter chill in Florida. They left behind, however, their youngest son, twenty-eight-year-old Devon Goulding, who trains as a bodybuilder by day, works as a bartender by night.'

'This is Devon?' D.D. asked, gesturing to the body.

'Umm, gonna have to wait on the fingerprints for that one.'

D.D. grimaced, made the mistake of breathing through her nose, grimaced harder. 'Where's our victim turned vixen now?'

'Back of a squad car. Refused medical attention. Waiting on the feds, whom she called directly.'

'The feds?' D.D. rose to standing, voice curt. 'What do you mean she personally invited the feds to our party? Who the hell *is* this girl?'

Detective number three did the honors: 'She called the Boston field office and requested Dr Samuel Keynes. Dialed the number off the top of her head, I might add. Would you still call it a party?' the newest member of Boston homicide asked conversationally. 'Or is it more like a barbecue?'

D.D. walked away. Turned on her heel, left the body, exited the garage. In her new and improved supervisory role she could get away with such things. Or maybe it was due to her current classification as restricted duty.

The fact that detective number three had taken D.D.'s former position with her former squad – an assignment D.D. could no longer hold, given her recent injury – was no reason to shun the thirty-five-year-old recruit. No, currently D.D. held the woman's name against her. Carol. As in Carol Manley. Sounded like an insurance agent. Or maybe a soccer mom. But definitely not a cop. No kind of serious detective went by Carol.

Of course, no kind of serious homicide unit sergeant obsessed about a new detective's name, or was petty enough to hold it against her. Maybe.

A year ago, D.D. hadn't worried about women named Carol. Or the future of her three-member squad. Or her own role with the BPD's homicide unit. She lived, ate, and breathed death investigations and was a happier person for it. Until the evening she returned for a late-night analysis of a crime scene and startled the killer still lurking there. One brief altercation later, she'd toppled down a flight of stairs and suffered an avulsion fracture to her left arm. No more lifting her gun. No more lifting her small child.

For the next six months, D.D. had gotten to sit at home. Nursing her wounds, worrying about her future, and, yeah, losing her mind. But slowly and surely, as her physical therapist, Russ, had promised her, the hard work had started to pay off. Until one day she could shrug her shoulder, and another day she could slowly but surely raise her arm.

Her strength wasn't there yet. Nor full range of motion. She couldn't execute such things as, say, the two-handed Weaver stance for shooting. But her pain was manageable, her injury improving, and her overall state of health excellent. Enough to convince the powers that be to allow her to return under restricted duty status. Meaning she now spent more time supervising as a sergeant than engaging in hands-on investigating as a detective. She told herself she could handle it. The work was the work, and either way she was solving crimes.

Of course, she continued to engage in thrice-weekly occupational therapy sessions where she used a hand weight in lieu of her handgun and practiced the motion of unsnapping her holster, then drawing and firing over and over again. She also spent some time on the shooting range. One-handed. Not as reliable. Not department SOP. But she had to start somewhere.

Otherwise, Phil and Neil, two of the finest detectives on the force, would forever be saddled with a rookie.

The Gouldings' garage was a detached, single-car unit set in the back of the property. Striding forward, D.D. vacated the structure, crossed the modest backyard, and headed for the street. Sun was just coming up. A gray, chilly dawn that seemed almost anticlimactic given the current level of activity. Patrol cars were stacked up along both sides of the busy neighborhood street, as well as the ME's vehicle and several larger, more impressive media vans.

The first responders had done an admirable job of roping off the property. From the gray-painted two-story colonial to the dilapidated rear garage, the officers had seized it all, establishing a strict perimeter of yellow crime scene tape that would make D.D.'s job that much easier. Nosy neighbors contained to the sidewalk across the street? Check. Rabid reporters confined to fifty yards away from the closest law enforcement officer? Check. And now for the trifecta . . .

D.D. discovered the woman sitting in the back of the third patrol car, shoulders shivering slightly beneath a blue BPD blanket, face staring straight ahead. A district detective sat beside her. The rear car door sat open, as if they were waiting for something or someone. Neither was saying a word.

'Margaret,' D.D. acknowledged the officer on the far side of the vehicle. This close, she realized why the vehicle door had been left ajar. Back at the crime scene, investigators had marked a bag of rotting food that had been pulled out of a trash can and torn open. The woman must've been at least elbow-deep in that mess, given the scent of rancid meat and sour milk wafting from her skin, let alone the streaks of slime marring her cheeks and mucking her hair.

'D.D.,' the district detective replied stoically. 'Heard you were back. Congrats.'

'Thanks.' D.D.'s gaze remained focused on the woman. The alleged killer. The alleged victim. The girl appeared young. Mid- to late twenties would be D.D.'s guess. With shoulder-length blond hair and delicate features that would probably be found attractive, if not for the assortment of bruises, smatters of blood, and smears of rot. The girl didn't look at her, but continued to focus on the back of the driver's seat.

Flat affect, D.D. noted. An expression most often found in homicide cops or victims of chronic abuse.

Standing outside the patrol car, D.D. leaned down until her face was even with the woman's. 'Sergeant Detective D.D. Warren,' she said by way of introduction. 'And you are?'

The girl finally turned her head. She stared at D.D. Seemed to study her as if looking for something. Then, she resumed her examination of the back of the driver's seat.

D.D. gave it some thought. 'Quite the scene in the garage. Chemical fire, I'm told. Basically, you burned a man alive with some kind of preservative mixed with antifreeze. You learn that as a Girl Scout?'

Nothing.

'Let me guess. Devon seemed nice enough when you first met. Good-looking guy, hardworking. You decided to give love a chance.'

'Devon?' The woman finally spoke, gaze still locked straight ahead. Her voice sounded husky. As if she'd smoked too much. Or screamed too loud.

'Victim's name. Devon Goulding. What, you never got around to asking?'

Cool blue eyes. Gray, D.D. thought as the girl glanced over.

'Didn't know him,' the girl said. 'We'd never met.'

'And yet here we are.'

'He's a bartender,' the girl offered, as if that should mean something to D.D. Then, it did.

'You went out tonight. To the bar where Devon worked. That's how you met.'

'We didn't meet,' the girl insisted. 'I was there with someone else. The bartender . . . he followed us out.' She stared at D.D. again. 'He's done this before,' she stated matter-of-factly. 'August. That girl who went missing, Stacey Summers. The way he grabbed me, tucked his head to hide his face from view as he pulled me down the back streets . . . He matches the man in the abduction video. I would search his property thoroughly.'

Stacey Summers was a Boston College student who'd disappeared in August. Young, beautiful, blond, she had the kind of beaming smile and gorgeous head shots guaranteed to grab nationwide headlines. Which the case had. Unfortunately, three months later, the police possessed only a single grainy video image of her being dragged away from a local bar by a large, shadowy brute. That was it. No witnesses. No suspects. No leads. The case had grown cold, even if the media attention had not.

'Do you know Stacey Summers?' D.D. asked.

The girl shook her head.

'Friend of the family? Fellow college student? Someone who once met her at a bar?'

'No.'

'Are you a cop?'

'No.'

'FBI?'

Another shake.

'So your interest in the Stacey Summers case . . .'

'I read the news.'

'Of course.' D.D. tilted her head sideways, contemplated her subject. 'You know federal agents,' she stated. 'Family friend? Neighbor? But you know someone well enough to dial direct.'

'He's not a friend.'

'Then who is he?'

A faint smile. 'I don't know. You'd have to ask him.'

'What's your name?' D.D. straightened up. Her left shoulder was starting to bother her now. Not to mention this conversation's strain on her patience.

'He didn't know my name,' the girl said. 'The bartender, this Devon? He didn't care who I was. I arrived at the bar alone. According to him, that's all it took to make me a victim.'

'You were at the bar alone? Drank alone?'

'Only the first drink. That's generally how it works.'

'How many drinks did you have?'

'Why? Because if I'm drunk, I deserved it?'

'No, because if you're drunk, you're not as reliable a witness.'

'I danced with one guy most of the night. Others saw us. Others can corroborate.'

D.D. frowned, still not liking the woman's answers, nor her use of the word *corroborate*, a term generally favored by law enforcement, not laypeople. 'Dancer's name?'

'Mr Haven't I Seen You Around Here Before?' the girl murmured.

On the other side of the girl, the district detective rolled her eyes. Apparently D.D. wasn't the first person to be asking these questions, or getting these answers.

'Can he *corroborate*?' D.D. stressed the legal term.

'Assuming he's regained consciousness.'

'Honey—'

'You should search the garage. There's blood in the far left corner. I could smell it when I was digging through the trash, trying to find a weapon.'

'Is that when you discovered the potassium permanganate?'

'He's the one who threw away the bouquet, probably

after using it to lure in some other victim. I'm not his first. I can tell you. He was much too confident, too well prepared. If this is his house, check his room. He'll have trophies. Predator like him enjoys the private thrill of revisiting past conquests.'

D.D. stared at the woman. In her years in homicide, she'd interviewed victims who were hysterical. She'd dealt with victims who were in shock. When it came to crime, there was no such thing as an emotional norm. And yet she'd never met a victim like this one. The woman's responses were well beyond the bell curve. Hell, outside the land of sanity.

'Did you know what Devon—'

'The bartender.'

'The bartender had done to these other women? Maybe a friend of yours told you something. Her own scary experience. Or rumors of something that may have happened to a friend of a friend?'

'No.'

'But you suspected something?' D.D. continued, voice hard. 'At the very least, you think he was involved with the disappearance of another girl, a case plastered all over the news. So what? You decided to take matters into your own hands, turn yourself into some kind of hero and make your own headlines?'

'I'd never met the bartender before tonight. I left with a different loser. He was the one I was trying to set up.' The girl shrugged, gaze once more locked on the back of the driver's seat. 'The evening's been filled with surprises. Even for someone like me, these things can happen.'

'Who *are* you?'

That smile again, the one that was not a smile but something far more troubling rippling across the girl's face.

'I didn't know the bartender. I've read about the Stacey Summers case, who hasn't? But I never thought . . . Let's just say, I didn't plan on some overpumped nightclub employee knocking me unconscious or carting me off as his personal plaything. Once it happened, though . . . I know survival skills. I know self-defense. I utilized the resources I found on hand—'

'You went through his trash.'

'Wouldn't you?'

The girl stared at her. For once, D.D. was the one who looked away.

'He started the war,' the girl stated clearly. 'I simply ended it.'

'Then called the FBI.'

'I didn't have any choice in that matter.'

D.D. suddenly had an inkling. It wasn't a good feeling. She studied her victim, a midtwenties female obviously experienced with law enforcement and personal defense. 'The special agent? Is he your father?'

The girl finally took her seriously.

She said: 'Worse.'

4

In the beginning, I cried. Which in time led to a sort of mindless humming, making noise for the sake of making noise, because it's hard to be alone in a dark wooden box. Sensory deprivation. The kind of torture used to break hardened assassins and radicalized terrorists. Because it works.

The pain was the worst. The relentless hard surface denting the soft spot on the back of my skull, straining my lower back, bruising my bony heels. I would feel the ache like a fire across my skin, until my entire nervous system roared its outrage. But there was nothing I could do. No new position I could adopt. Not a twist here or a bend there to relieve the pressure. To be trapped, pinned really, flat on your back on a hard pine plank, minute after minute after minute.

I think there were times, especially in the beginning, when I wasn't sane.

Humans are interesting, however. Our ability to adapt is truly impressive. Our rage against our own suffering. Our relentless need to find a way out, to do something, anything, to advance our lot in life.

I made the first improvement in my living conditions by accident. In a fit of fury against the pain in the back of my skull, I lifted my head and smacked my forehead against the wooden lid. Maybe I hoped to knock myself *unconscious. Wouldn't have surprised me.*

What I received was a sharp sting to my front right temple, which did, at least temporarily, alleviate the ache in the back of my head. Which led to more discoveries. Your back throbs? Smack a knee. Your knee hurts? Stub a toe. Your toe hurts? Jam a finger.

Pain is a symphony. A song of varying intensities and many, many notes. I learned to play them. No longer a helpless victim in a sea of suffering but a mad orchestral genius directing the music of my own life.

Alone, trapped inside a coffin-size box, I sought out each tiny register of discomfort and mastered it.

Which led in turn to leg lifts and shoulder shrugs and the world's most abbreviated biceps curls.

He came. He worked the padlock. He removed the lid. He lifted me out of the depths and reveled in his godlike powers. Afterward, a small offering of liquid, perhaps even a scrap of food as he tossed the dog the proverbial bone. He'd stay to watch, laughing as I cracked open the dried-up chicken wing and greedily sucked out the marrow.

Then, back to the box. He would leave. And I belonged to myself again.

Alone in the dark.

Master of my pain.

I cried. I railed against God. I begged for someone, anyone, to save me.

But only in the beginning.

Slowly but surely, dimly, then with greater clarity, I began to think, plot, scheme.

One way or another, I was getting out of this. I'd do whatever it took to survive.

And then . . .

I was going home.

5

D.D. discovered Neil in the upstairs rear bedroom of the two-story house. The youngest member of the three-man squad, Neil was famous for his shock of red hair and perpetually youthful face. Most suspects dismissed him as a new recruit, which D.D. and Phil had never stopped using to their advantage.

These days, Neil carried himself with more poise. In the past couple of years, D.D. and Phil had been pushing him to step up, take the lead. It had resulted in a few battles, given Neil remained most at home overseeing autopsies in the morgue. But D.D. liked to think she'd raised him right. Certainly, with her gone and Phil now serving as lead detective of the squad, Neil had better be lording over Carol, D.D. thought. It was the least he could do for her.

Neil glanced up as she walked in. He was kneeling on the floor beside a rumpled queen-size bed, holding a shoe box pulled from beneath the mattress. D.D. made it three feet into the cramped, dank space and wrinkled her nose. It smelled like unwashed sheets, cheap cologne, and gym socks. In other words, like the home of a bachelor male.

'Devon Goulding's room?' she asked.

'Looks like it.'

'Arrested development,' she muttered.

Neil arched a brow. 'We can't all be Alex,' he observed.

Alex was D.D.'s husband. Crime scene reconstruction specialist and instructor at the police academy. One of the more refined members of the species, D.D. liked to think, he had impeccable taste in clothing, food, and, of course, his wife. He also looked pretty good with mushy Cheerios glued to his cheek, which is how most breakfasts with their four-year-old son ended. Alex actually enjoyed doing laundry. Devon Goulding, on the other hand . . .

'Got anything?' D.D. gestured to the shoe box in Neil's hand. 'Say, a stash of trophies from previous victims? According to our femme fatale, who apparently had never met Mr Goulding before this evening, he's definitely done this before and might even be the perpetrator responsible for the Boston College student who went missing in August.'

Neil blinked. 'You mean the Stacey Summers case?'

'So I'm told.'

'By the woman who torched Devon in his own garage with her hands still tied?'

'The one and only.'

'Who is she again?'

'Interestingly enough, she was more forthcoming on Devon's alleged crimes than her own. But she's convinced he's a serial predator, and we should definitely check for trophies.'

'She looks familiar,' Neil said. 'I can't quite place her. But when I first arrived and spotted her . . . I thought I knew her from somewhere.'

'Quantico?' D.D. asked helpfully, as Neil had recently attended a training seminar there for detectives, and it would certainly explain the woman's knowledge of criminal behavior.

But Neil was shaking his head. 'I don't think so. Then again . . .'

'You ever hear about this chemical-fire thing?' she asked him now, Neil having the most extensive science background on her squad. Former squad.

'Yeah. One of those survival tricks for when lost in the wilderness, that sort of thing. Gotta admit, though, if I woke up trapped in a garage with my hands bound . . . Not sure that's the first thing that would pop into my head.'

'Seems to indicate higher-than-average self-defense skills.'

'Here's the thing, though,' Neil continued, rising to his feet. 'It shouldn't have killed Goulding. Incapacitated, maimed, traumatized, sure. But localized burning, relatively low heat . . . You'd be amazed at how much the human body can endure and keep on ticking. I've seen victims pulled from fiery wrecks with two-thirds of their skin toasted, and still, with enough time and treatment, they make it.'

D.D. shuddered. She didn't like burns. She'd once been sent to interview a survivor in a burn unit who was having the dead skin literally scraped from his back. Based on the guy's screams, she'd assumed he was dying, only to be told the whole treatment was designed to fix him. Not enough morphine in the world, the nurse had offered helpfully, scouring away.

'Now, it's possible Devon inhaled heat and smoke into his throat,' Neil was saying. 'Maybe seared his esophagus, which swelled up, closing his airway. But what the witness described sounded more instantaneous. Which made me think maybe he went into shock and his heart stopped beating.'

'Okay,' D.D. said. She still didn't know where they were going with this, but Neil had worked as an EMT before he became a cop. He often saw things she and Phil didn't.

'Of course, the deceased is a young, obviously fit male. Bodybuilder, by the looks of things.'

'You could see that?' D.D. asked incredulously, recalling the curled-up lump of charred remains.

'You couldn't?'

'Never mind.'

'Which leads to further considerations. Bodybuilders have been known to dabble in anabolic steroids, which in turn can lead to a whole host of symptoms, including high blood pressure and an enlarged heart.'

'And shrunken testicles,' D.D. offered up. 'High blood pressure is news to me, but the shrunken testicles, I'm pretty sure about.'

Neil rolled his eyes. 'We'll let the ME measure testicle size. Based on this, however, we're probably both right.' He jiggled the shoe box, and D.D. could hear the telltale noise of glass vials rattling together. 'Devon Goulding was definitely shooting up 'roids. For how long, I couldn't tell you. But even short-term use could have impacted his heart, and been a contributing factor in his death.'

'What about roid rage?' D.D. asked, considering the matter. 'I always thought that meant flying off the handle, but could it have led him to abduct a girl from a bar?'

'Beyond my pay grade,' Neil said with a shrug. 'In theory, long-term steroid abuse leads to diminished sex drive, which begs the question why would he *want* to kidnap a girl from a bar.'

'Giving in to his darker impulses was the only way he could get interested anymore? Violence his last remaining turn-on?'

Neil shrugged. 'Your guess is as good as mine. Based upon this box, I think we can safely assume Devon Goulding used steroids and it probably was a factor in his death. As for evidence of past crimes, additional victims, only one way to find out.' Neil set down the box, took one step toward the narrow dresser that was crammed up against the wall, and started pulling out drawers.

D.D. let him do it. She was on restricted duty after all. Neil could ransack the room. She crossed to the bed and inspected the contents of Goulding's shoe box. In addition to various colorfully labeled glass jars, there were numerous baggies of unmarked pills, supplements, hormones, God only knew. Could steroid abuse have led to Goulding's crime spree? Their lone survivor had implied she hadn't known him at all, had been at the bar with another man until Goulding had knocked out bachelor A and absconded with the girl. Certainly sounded primitive enough. It also sounded impulsive to D.D. Serial predators were more likely to stalk their victims, plan out the abduction. Whereas snatching a girl from outside a bar—

'Hey,' Neil interrupted her thoughts. He'd given up on the drawers and was once more on his hands and knees, feeling beneath the bureau with his gloved hand.

'Got something?'

'Maybe.'

It took him several tugs; then he retrieved a large, plain yellow manila envelope that had been taped to the bottom of the dresser. He shook it, and D.D. saw several small rectangular shapes move against the paper sheath.

Neil carried the envelope to the bed. The top flap wasn't glued down but fastened shut with metal tabs. He flipped them up, then did the honors of opening the envelope and pouring its contents onto the bed.

D.D. counted two credit-card-size objects. Except they weren't credit cards.

'Driver's licenses,' Neil said. 'Two females. Kristy Kilker. Natalie Draga.'

'But not Stacey Summers?'

'No Stacey Summers. Then again' – Neil held up one of the licenses to show a single bloody fingerprint – 'I think our world's most dangerous Girl Scout may have been on to something after all.'

They tore the rest of the room apart, D.D. starting with the bed, Neil continuing on to the dresser. They moved methodically and efficiently, teammates who'd done this kind of thing before. Later, the crime scene techs would return with fingerprint powder, luminol, and alternative light sources. They'd retrieve fingerprints, bodily fluids, and hopefully minuscule strands of hair and fiber.

For now, D.D. and Neil went for the obvious. Women's clothing, jewelry, anything that could tie back to other victims. Pay stubs and bar bills that might indicate other hunting grounds. And, what the hell, a killer's diary. You never knew when you might get lucky.

D.D. had to have Neil's help to lift the top mattress. Her shoulder already throbbed, her left arm too weak for the job. Neil didn't say anything. He came over. Together, they lifted; then he returned to his corner and she resumed her search of the bed.

She was grateful for her partner's . . . former partner's . . . silence. The fact that he didn't comment on the sheen of sweat already collecting on her brow, her clear shortness of breath. Supervisors were hardly expected to work crime scenes, D.D. reminded herself. Request paperwork on the subject, review all notes, sure. But this actual work thing . . . No, she was supposed to be safely ensconced back at HQ, where her lack of ability to carry a sidearm wouldn't be a liability to herself and others.

D.D. searched every square inch under the top mattress, then went to work on the box spring. Later she would have to ice down, while enduring Alex's knowing stare. But she was who she was. He knew it. Neil knew it. It was simply the Boston Police Department she was determined to fool.

'Got something.' She could feel it now. A hard lump near the top right corner of the box spring. Up close, she could see that the seam where the heavy-duty material from the sides of the box spring met with the flimsy top cover was frayed. She poked around with her gloved fingertips, and sure enough, wedged between a nest of coils . . . 'A box. Hang on. Slippery damn thing. And . . . got it!'

Gingerly, D.D. withdrew the metal box. Her entire left arm was trembling with fatigue. More weights, she thought vaguely. More weights, more PT, more anything in order not to feel this weak, in order not to *be* this weak in public.

But once again, Neil didn't comment. He simply took the small lockbox from her shaking hands and moved it to the corner desk, where they had more light.

The box appeared fairly standard issue. Gunmetal gray. Maybe six inches wide by two inches tall. Meant for a few precious or personal mementos, little else.

'Photos,' Neil said.

'What?' D.D. leaned closer, trying to make out the stack of pictures beneath the desk light.

'A black-haired woman. Again and again.' Neil flipped through the stack. Each photo revealed the same subject. Walking in a park, sitting with a cup of coffee, reading a book, laughing at someone off camera. The woman appeared to be in her early thirties, and beautiful, in a dark, sultry sort of way. 'Former girlfriend, maybe?'

'Stashed in a container inside his box spring?' D.D. was already shaking her head. 'I don't think so. Look like anyone you know? Stacey Summers? Wait, she's a petite blonde, whereas this girl . . .'

'Not Stacey Summers,' Neil agreed. 'What about our vic downstairs? Last I saw, she was covered in garbage. I don't remember hair color.'

'Also blond, with light gray eyes. Not this woman either.'

'D.D.' Neil spoke up quietly. He'd reached the last few photos. Both of them stilled. Same woman. Except she wasn't smiling or laughing anymore. Her dark eyes were huge, her pale face stricken. She stared straight into the camera and her expression . . .

Now, it was Neil's hand that shook slightly, and D.D. who didn't say a word.

Neil set down the photos, then returned with the two licenses they'd found beneath the bureau.

'Natalie Draga,' he said. He placed the ID next to the photo as both of them looked from photos to official ID, then slowly nodded. 'Thirty-one, address in Chelsea.'

'But no pictures of the second victim?'

'No. Just Natalie.'

'Personal connection,' D.D. murmured. 'She meant something to him. Hence all the images.'

'Worshipped her from afar,' Neil supposed.

'Or even a girlfriend. Except it ended badly. Maybe she rejected him. And then he turned on her.'

'And the second victim, Kristy? Plus, the woman downstairs?' Neil asked. They'd gone through the box; there were no more photos.

'Maybe he liked it,' D.D. theorized out loud. 'The first time was personal. The second and third were for fun.'

'There's no way of telling where these pictures were

taken,' Neil said. 'The framing is too close-up, there's not enough backdrop.'

'Our survivor claims there's blood in the garage.'

'I could smell something,' Neil concurred.

'Have the crime scene techs gather samples. And send more uniforms to the bar where Devon Goulding worked, with photos of all three known victims. Let's see just how close to home he was hunting. Grab a photo of Stacey Summers as well. See if she frequented that bar.'

'She was last seen at a different establishment, Birches over on Lex.'

'I know. But if she'd spent time in Goulding's bar as well . . . how many psychopaths can one poor girl run into?'

D.D. straightened, wincing as the motion jarred her shoulder, the growing ache in her back.

'You should go home,' Neil said. 'It's our job to handle all this, your job to tell us how we could've done it better.'

But D.D. wasn't listening to him. She was thinking. Of the garage, of Devon Goulding, of his latest victim, who'd beaten him at his own game and was now sitting in the back of a squad car. A blonde with FBI connections and knowledge of how to start a chemical fire. A woman Neil had thought he'd recognized.

She should know this, she thought. Could feel something stirring in the back of her mind.

A knock came from behind her; newbie detective Carol Manley stuck her head in the room.

'D.D., the agent our vic called at the FBI. He's here.'

6

Once upon a time, I could've told you all about myself.

I would've said with certainty that my name is Florence Dane. My mom, who dreamed big for her children, named me after Florence Nightingale and my older brother in honor of Charles Darwin.

I would've said that the happiest place on earth was my mother's farm in central Maine. Mounds of blueberries in the summer, acres and acres of potatoes in the fall. I grew up loving the smell of freshly turned earth. The feel of soil beneath my fingertips. My mother's contented sigh at the end of the day, when she gazed over all that she had accomplished and felt satisfied.

Our neighbors included several foxes, as well as bears and moose. My mother didn't mind our local wanderers, but was a firm believer in not feeding the wildlife. We were to coexist with nature, not corrupt it. My mother had grown up on a commune. She had many theories about life, not all of which made any sense to my brother and me.

Personally, I loved the foxes best. I would sit for hours outside their den, hoping for a view of the kits. Foxes are playful, like a kitten crossed with a puppy. They enjoy batting around golf balls or tossing small toys in the air. I learned this the way kids used to learn things, by hanging outside with the sun on my face, by trying a little bit of this or a little bit of that. I brought them an old rubber ball, a catnip-stuffed mouse, even a small rubber duckie. The adult foxes would sniff at the offerings hesitantly, while the kits would come bounding out of the den and pounce on the new toys without a moment's hesitation. Sometimes, I left a carrot or two behind. Or, if my mother was particularly busy and not paying attention, scraps of hot dog.

Just being neighborly, I tried to explain to my mother the first afternoon she caught me shredding cheese outside the den's opening. She didn't buy it: '*Every creature must learn to make it on its own. Encouraging dependence doesn't do anyone any favors, Flora.*'

But later, after a particularly bad snowstorm in early November, I caught her carrying scraps from dinner to the same den.

She didn't say anything, and neither did I. It became our shared secret, because back then, we couldn't think of anything more scandalous than domesticating wild foxes.

So once upon a time, here is something I could've told you about myself: I love foxes. Or at least I used to. That's not the kind of thing that's easy to take from someone. But I don't sit around and watch them anymore, or bring them toys, or smuggle them treats. Four hundred and seventy-two days later . . . I try to find peace in the woods. I definitely prefer the wide-open outdoors to small indoor spaces.

But some pieces of myself, some feelings . . . it's just not like that anymore. I can do the things I used to do, visit the same places, see the same people. But I don't feel the same anymore. Some days, I'm not sure I feel anything at all.

April is my favorite month. I'm fairly sure that's still true. The farm came with a rickety old greenhouse. How it survived each long, blustery winter we never knew. But by late April, as the snow finally thawed, we'd trudge through the mud and force open the warped door, the whole structure groaning in protest. Darwin would lead the charge inside, the lone male and self-appointed family protector.

My mother would come next with a wheelbarrow full of bags of loam and topsoil. I'd bring up the rear, carting plastic trays and, of course, packets of seed.

My brother, Darwin, went for speed. Tossing in handfuls of soil, jabbing in seeds. Even back then, he was impatient, wanting to be anywhere but there. My mother had named him well. He loved us, but from an early age we could both tell staying home wasn't his cup of tea. If the deep woods sang to us, then the entire world sang to him. So he worked beside us, fast, efficient, but his mind always elsewhere. My mother would watch him and sigh. He's a young soul, she would say, with a tender heart.

She worried for him. But never for me. I was the happy one. At least, that's how the story goes.

My brother returned from college the minute he heard about my disappearance. He stayed by my mother's side, first as her anchor. Then, when the first postcard arrived and it became clear I'd been kidnapped, my brother the adventurer became a warrior. Facebook, Twitter, these were the battlegrounds of choice. He created entire campaigns designed to rally complete strangers to help find me. And he brought me to life, personalized his little sister for the masses, photos of my first birthday, me on the farm, and, yes, me sitting on a knoll with fox kits. Except these photos weren't really for the masses. They were for my abductor, to make him see me as a little girl, a sister, a daughter. My brother made it his mission to humanize me in order to help save my life.

I think that's why he took it the hardest when I returned home and I was no longer the young woman from all those photos. I didn't smile. I didn't laugh. I didn't play in the dirt or go looking for foxes. See, my kidnapper had a mission of his own, to remove all shred of humanity from me. To hollow me out, break me down, to turn me into nothing at all.

You think you'll fight or at least endure. You promise yourself you'll be strong enough. But four hundred and seventy-two days later . . .

My brother had to leave the farm after my return. He had to get away from the sister I no longer was. I watched him go and was mostly grateful for his departure. One fewer set of eyes to follow me everywhere I went. One less person to be startled by the new, and definitely not improved, Flora Dane.

Once upon a time, I would've been saddened by my brother's departure. I would've told you I love him, miss him, look forward to seeing him soon.

Once upon a time, I would've told you that I love my mom. She's my best friend in the entire world, and while it was exciting to go off to college, I still look forward to weekends home.

Once upon a time, I was that kind of girl. Outdoorsy, fun-loving, happy.

Now, there are things I still can't tell you about myself.

There are things I'm still having to learn as I go along.

The sun is up now. Sitting in the back of the patrol car, blanket tight around my shoulders, garbage drying on my face, I feel the sky lightening around me. I don't look up. I don't look around. I don't have to see to know what's going on.

To my left, inside the house of my would-be attacker, the crime scene techs are now scouring every inch. A handful of detectives are also going through the structure room by room, cataloging each electronic device, glancing at piles of mail, combing carefully through the bartender's bedroom.

I hadn't been lying earlier. I'm not a cop or an FBI agent. I've never met the girl who disappeared three months ago, Stacey Summers. Like the rest of Boston, or the country, for that matter, I've simply followed her case on the news.

But then again . . . I know her. I recognize her beaming smile from her senior pictures, all big blond hair and round blue eyes. I recognize her exuberance in all the high school cheerleader photos, red pom-poms thrust into the air. Then there's the ominous videotape: security footage of a petite blonde being forcefully abducted by a hulking brute. Morning, noon, and night. There was never a bad time for news producers to roll the sensational image of a tipsy nineteen-year-old former cheerleader being dragged down a dark alley.

I read every account in the newspaper of her abduction. Sat mesmerized by her parents' appearance on a nationally televised morning show, though in theory, I've sworn off that kind of thing. I watched her father, the strong corporate type, struggle with his composure, while her mom, an older, still beautiful woman, hand tucked firmly in her husband's, begged for her daughter's safe return.

Beautiful, happy, bubbly Stacey Summers. Who, according to her parents, would never hurt a fly.

I wonder what things she didn't used to know. I wonder what lessons she's already been forced to learn.

The truth is, I know Stacey Summers. I don't want to. I don't mean to. But I know Stacey Summers. It doesn't take a PhD in psychology to understand that every time I look at her photo, or read another article, I'm really looking at me.

No one called my mother the first twenty-four hours after I went missing. No one knew I was gone. Instead, she received a confused message four days into spring break from my college roommate: Is Flora with you? Why didn't she tell us she was heading home early?

Of course, my mother had no idea what Stella was talking about. Apparently it took a good twenty minutes to sort out that I wasn't in Florida with Stella, nor was I magically back in Maine at my mother's farm, nor had I miraculously returned to my college dorm room. In fact, no one had seen me in days.

My mother is not the type to panic. She set down the phone and proceeded to cover the basics. Contacted my older brother. Checked her e-mail. Skimmed my Facebook page. Her heartbeat accelerated slightly. Her hands began to shake.

She drove to the police station. Later, she told me she felt it was important to talk to someone in person. But even reporting her concerns became confusing. My mother lives in Maine, but I went to school in Boston and in theory had disappeared while on spring break in Florida. The Maine officer was nice enough. He heard my mother out, seemed to agree that I wasn't the kind of girl to run away, though given the circumstances, they couldn't dismiss a drunken misadventure. He encouraged her to get the ball rolling by filing an official missing persons report, which was faxed down to the local PD in Florida.

And then . . . nothing.

The sun rose; the sun set. My college friends met with the police in Florida. They returned to campus in Boston.

They resumed taking classes. While my mother sat next to a phone that still didn't ring.

And then:

A single postcard delivered by mail. My handwriting, but another person's words. And suddenly, I wasn't a missing college student anymore. I was a suspected kidnapping victim who'd been dragged across state lines. Overnight, my case became red-hot news and my family's world exploded with it.

As a parent, my mother told me later, you'd like to think you'd have some control over your missing child's abduction case. But it doesn't work like that. The first thing law enforcement established was that she *wasn't* to call them; they would call her. In fact, my mother never even met many of the FBI agents working my case until the first press conference.

Instead, she got to meet her new best friends: the victim advocates. Which, given their title, you might make the mistake of thinking meant they worked on behalf of her, the victim. No. Victim advocates work for law enforcement or the attorney general's office. It depends on the jurisdiction. My mother dealt with six of them over the course of my abduction. Local, state, federal. They took turns. Because those first few weeks especially, family members are never left alone.

The advocates told her it was for her own sake. And when they first started answering her endlessly chiming cell phone, she thanked them. When they put up a sign in our front yard warning the media it was private property and they were not to trespass, she was grateful. And as they miraculously supplied yet another meal, while deftly shepherding her to a prepaid hotel room so she could snag at least one night's sleep, she wondered how she could survive this ordeal without them.

My mother, however, is not stupid.

It didn't take her long to realize that the victim advocates were always asking questions. About her children's lives, past love interests. About her life, past love interests. And hey, now that she'd had something to eat, why didn't she chat with the detectives for a bit? Which, in the beginning, she thought was so that the detectives could update her on what they were doing to help find me, but later she understood was so the detectives could grill her with even more questions. And oh yes, this morning her kind and compassionate victim advocate would take her around the house to collect possible pieces of information – cell phones, tablets, personal diaries. While the next morning, her victim advocate would chime out, hey, let's go take a poly, much in the same tone her friends once used to invite her for a mani pedi.

I disappeared in Florida. And my mother's life became a high-profile investigative drama, governed at all times by the nannies. Both of us, I guess, got lessons in survival. And both of us still know things that we wished we didn't know.

For example, I know a victim advocate will appear on Stacey Summers's doorstep this morning. Most likely someone close to her case. Maybe, like me, her parents actually value their advocate, having forged a bond. Or maybe, like my mother, they merely tolerate the relationship, one more intrusion in lives that certainly can't be their lives anymore.

The advocate will bear a photo of Devon Goulding, my now dead attacker and almost certainly a repeat offender. The advocate will ask if they recognize this man, is there any chance Stacey once knew him? The Summerses will immediately be bold enough, crazy enough, to have questions of their own: Is this the man? Is this the guy who took their daughter? What happened to Stacey? Where is she; when can they see her?

The advocate will say nothing. And eventually, the Summerses will succumb to bewildered silence, every crumb of information merely leading to more questions. They won't be able to ask Devon Goulding any questions. That fault is mine. But closure, the actual discovery of their daughter . . .

I glance back at the house. I hope these detectives can find the answers I didn't get a chance to hunt for. Such as whose blood is in the corner of the garage. And is Devon the one who took beautiful, happy Stacey Summers? And what did he do with her after that?

Because I know I've watched Stacey's abduction video more than I should. I know I sleep in a room wallpapered with stories of missing people who still haven't made it home. I know when I headed out last night, I was looking for things I probably shouldn't have been.

Once, I could've told you all about myself. Foxes. Springtime.

Family.

Now . . .

I hope Stacey Summers is stronger than me.

I would like to sleep. Lay down my head in the back of the patrol car and dream of the days before I ever thought of college or the lure of spring break, the promise of a sunny Florida beach.

Back in the days before I was always and forever alone.

A fresh clamor arises from across the street. I feel the shift and stir of the crowd accommodating a new and official arrival at the crime scene. I don't have to look up to know who it is. I called and so he came. Because that is how it is between us. My mother had her nannies, but for me, the relationship has always been something more.

A minute passes. Two. Three.

Then, he is here, standing outside the open car door, perfectly attired as usual, with his long, double-breasted coat buttoned up tight against the chill.

'Oh, Flora.' FBI victim specialist Samuel Keynes sighs heavily. 'What have you done?'

7

By the time D.D. made it down the stairs and out of the Goulding residence, her cell phone had rung three times and she'd been stopped twice. She had good news, she had bad news, and she had a growing headache from a fast-evolving case and a long sleepless night.

According to the deputy superintendent of homicide, a.k.a. her boss, she was under strict orders to wrap up the scene and get the hell out of Dodge before her exhausted detectives inevitably let something slip in front of the clamoring media and this whole thing blew up in their faces. D.D. didn't disagree. Short and sweet was never a bad plan when dealing with a homicide investigation. Unfortunately, she had a feeling they weren't going to get that lucky.

D.D. finally cleared the front step. A roar went up from the reporters gathered across the way. You would've thought the champion quarterback was taking the field, she thought dryly, and not just an overworked police sergeant emerging into public view. Reflexively she held up a hand. No need to block a gauntlet of flashes this bright and sunny November morning. She just didn't want to encourage any more shouted questions.

She headed right to where she'd last seen their victim turned avenger sitting tight in the rear of a patrol car, and sure enough . . . D.D. drew up short.

A tall, handsome black man stood beside the cruiser. No, a tall, beautiful black man. Perfectly sculpted cheekbones. Smoothly shaved head punctuated by an impeccably groomed goatee. Dark eyes fringed by impossibly long lashes. The man wore a double-breasted black wool coat, the kind favored by business executives and FBI agents. Except, up close, D.D. wasn't sure it was wool. Maybe more like cashmere, paired with a deep red silk scarf. Which, in the moment, made total sense to her. A man that handsome with a face that intelligent and a gaze that direct, of course he wore a thousand-dollar coat. And his non-bureau-issued car was probably a Bentley.

Belatedly, she realized she was staring, her mouth slightly agape. She snapped her jaw shut, squared her aching shoulders, and, what the hell, pretended like she was professional.

He held out a hand as she approached. 'Dr Samuel Keynes. Victim specialist. FBI.'

'Mmm-hmmm.' She returned the handshake. He had a firm grip. Naturally.

'And you are?' He awaited her reply patiently. Deep, deep dark eyes. Like melted chocolate. And clearly regarding her as if she were a lunatic.

'Sergeant Detective D. D. Warren,' she managed. 'Supervisor. Homicide. This homicide. Wait a second.' She frowned, regaining her composure. 'Victim specialist. Haven't we met before? Boston Marathon bombings . . .'

'I assisted with several of the families, yes.'

D.D. nodded. It was coming back to her now. The Boston PD had assisted with the FBI's investigation into the April 2013 Boston Marathon bombings. D.D. had personally handled several interviews, given the number of witnesses there'd been to question. In the task force briefings, she'd spotted Dr Keynes, as well as several other victim specialists, though at the time there'd been too much going on to make any introductions. They'd all been too busy grappling with the horror of the bombings, let alone an extremely complex, active case.

'You know our person of interest?' she asked now, gesturing to her victim/suspect, who still sat silently in the back of the patrol car.

'Flora?' he prodded quietly.

The girl finally glanced up. The bruise had started darkening around her eye, turning her skin dark purple, while the bridge of her nose was an angry red.

The adrenaline rush had left her system, D.D. observed, and now she was crashing hard.

'You might as well tell her,' the woman said. Sitting in the back of the patrol car, wrapped in the blue police blanket, she shrugged, still not making eye contact. 'Coming from you, she might believe. Whereas, anything I have to say . . .'

'Can be used against you in a court of law?' D.D. offered helpfully.

The girl skewered her with a look. 'Exactly.'

'Sergeant Detective Warren,' Dr Keynes began.

'D.D.'

'D.D., might we take a walk? Somewhere quieter?' He didn't have to specify the reporters. Already the noise had quieted down, all the better for the media to eavesdrop.

D.D. gave it a moment's consideration, then jerked her head toward the Goulding residence. It was bustling with crime scene techs but no journalists, which was as close to privacy as they were going to get.

She led the way, Dr Keynes falling in step beside her. 'Nice coat,' she said. 'Cashmere?'

'Yes.'

'Silk scarf?'

'Yes.'

'I gotta say, Boston PD isn't quite that generous. Then again, I don't have *Doctor* in front of my name.'

'My grandfather shined shoes for a living,' Dr Keynes offered lightly. 'My father, on the other hand, is a cardiothoracic surgeon. Graduated Harvard.'

'And you're continuing your family's upward mobility . . . in the FBI?' D.D. gave him a dubious look.

They'd reached the front door. Dr Keynes held it open, a touch of chivalry that was hardly necessary at a crime scene.

'I enjoy my work. And I'm fortunate to be at a place in my life where I can afford to do what I love.'

'I'm beginning to see what you and my person of interest have in common. Both of you do an excellent job of never actually answering my questions.' The front door of the Goulding house opened to a modest foyer, with the staircase straight ahead. Given that the room's wooden trim and staircase railing were currently being dusted for prints by a pair of crime scene techs, D.D. took a left turn away from the chaos. She and the good doctor arrived in a front sitting room that boasted a love seat, a coffee table piled with craft magazines, and a basket filled with balls of yarn. Someone, most likely Mrs Goulding, must be into knitting. There was something about that small detail that pained D.D. How did you go from being a woman known for your hand-knit scarves to being the mother of an alleged rapist?

D.D. came to a halt in front of the coffee table. It felt too intrusive to sit, so she remained standing, Dr Keynes doing the same. The small room was much warmer than outside, the air stuffy. Dr Keynes unbuttoned his coat, loosened his scarf. Underneath, he wore a dark suit. Standard government issue, she thought, except once again, the cut and fabric were much nicer than anything worn by the average agent.

'Dr Keynes,' she began, then paused a beat to see if he'd offer his first name. He didn't.

'I haven't worked with too many victim advocates,' D.D. continued at last. 'But my memory is that in the FBI, you're not the same as an agent. Your role is . . . ?'

'I'm a victim specialist. I report to the OVA: Office for Victim Assistance.'

'And you're a doctor.'

'Psychologist.'

'Specialty?'

'Trauma. I work mostly with victims of kidnapping cases, everything from child abductions to the oil executive kidnapped for ransom in Nigeria.'

D.D. studied him. 'I don't think . . . Flora? . . . is an oil executive.'

'Florence Dane,' he supplied, then gazed at her expectantly.

The name rang a bell. Judging from the look on his face, it should. Plus, Neil's comment from earlier, that he knew the woman's face from somewhere . . .

D.D. finally got it. 'Seven years ago. She was a college student. UMass. Went on spring break to Palm Beach and disappeared. The FBI handled the investigation . . .' She had to think. 'Because of postcards, right? The mom started receiving postcards, allegedly written by her daughter, but all from different states. The mom went on TV, held several press conferences trying to get the kidnapper to engage.'

'There were more than postcards. He sent e-mails, even a few videos. Reaching out to the mother, tormenting her, appeared to be as gratifying to him as the abduction itself.'

D.D. frowned. 'Florence Dane was gone a long time.'

'Four hundred and seventy-two days.'

'Jesus.' Despite herself, D.D. blinked. Very few victims were found alive after that length of time. And the ones who did . . . 'Long-haul trucker?' she asked now. 'The perpetrator traveled for his job, trucking, something like that?'

'Yes. Jacob Ness. He'd built a box in the back of his cab so he could keep his victim with him at all times. Most likely, Flora wasn't his first.'

'He's dead; that's my memory. You guys got some kind of tip. SWAT descended. Florence made it. Jacob Ness didn't.'

Dr Keynes didn't say anything. Very feebie of him, D.D. thought. She hadn't asked, so he hadn't answered.

'All right,' she stated more briskly. 'My suspect, Flora, is your victim, Florence. Once, she was abducted by a crazed psychopath, and now . . . what? She tracks them down at bars?'

'Only Flora can answer that question.'

'And yet she didn't. So far, all I can get out of her are theories on Devon Goulding's crimes, not her own.'

'That's the bartender? The one who allegedly attacked her?'

'That's the victim,' D.D. corrected. 'The once healthy male now reduced to crispy carnage in his own garage due to your girl's knowledge of chemical fire.'

Dr Keynes studied her, posture relaxed, hands in the pockets of his ridiculously expensive coat. 'I'm sure you've made some inquiries.'

'Couple of detectives reviewed the bar's security footage. They were able to *corroborate* that Devon Goulding worked last night. According to the video footage as well as eye-witness accounts, Flora was also present, though she spent most of the night dancing with another guy, Mark Zeilan. Interestingly enough, Mr Zeilan filed a police report shortly after three A.M., alleging that a bartender from Tonic physically assaulted him outside the establishment.'

'Also consistent with Flora's statement,' Dr Keynes observed.

'A video camera from an ATM machine a block away captures what appears to be Devon leading Flora away by the arm. As for how willing she is . . . I'm told that could go either way.'

'Fast-forward to the scene here . . .'

'By all means. Fast-forward to the Gouldings' garage.'

'First responders discovered Flora naked, with her hands bound before her.'

'You seem to be well-informed about the details.'

He dismissed that comment, saying instead, 'Bound wrists don't seem to indicate willingness.'

'Sorry. Given that it's a *Fifty Shades of Grey* world, I can't make that assumption. Tell me something, Dr Keynes. Are you Flora's victim specialist, or are you her shrink?'

'I am a victim specialist,' Dr Keynes stated clearly. 'Not a shrink.'

'But she called you. Not her mother. Not a lawyer. She called *you*. Why?'

'You would have to ask Flora that question.'

'You have a relationship,' D.D. asserted.

'No.'

'Uh, yeah. In the midst of a crisis, she called you. And I'm willing to bet, this isn't the first time.'

Dr Keynes thinned his lips. Such a handsome man, D.D. thought again. Beautiful, rich, successful. The crosses he had to bear. And yet there was something about him. A seriousness. A sadness? She couldn't put her finger on it. But there was a somber edge to his composure that just kept her from hating him.

'You should ask Flora more questions,' he said at last. 'She prefers honesty. A straightforward approach. I think you'll find . . . She feels alone, Sergeant. Her experiences, what she's been through. She's a very unique, very strong young woman. But she's also very isolated. There are few people who've survived what she's survived.'

'Meaning in a time of crisis,' D.D. murmured, 'she turns to the one person she thinks understands her. Which is not her family. It's you.'

'You should ask her more questions,' he repeated. 'And don't dismiss her answers. Since her return five years ago, Flora has made criminal behavior her specialty.'

'You don't say?'

'If she believes this bartender took other girls, I wouldn't be surprised to discover it's true.'

'Are you working with Stacey Summers's family?' D.D. asked abruptly.

Keynes shook his head; if he was surprised by this sudden change in topic, he didn't show it. 'A colleague of mine, Pam Mason, has been assigned that case.'

'Flora ever talk to you about Stacey's disappearance? Follow it in the news?'

'Contrary to what you seem to believe, Flora and I don't speak regularly.'

'Only when she's in police custody?' D.D. prodded.

'Judging by her bruises, she appears to be telling the truth about being kidnapped by Devon Goulding,' Dr Keynes stated neutrally. 'Meaning whatever steps she took to defend herself . . .'

'Why won't she accept medical assistance? If she's so

innocent, why not let a medical expert conduct an official exam, *corroborate* more of her story?'

'Victims of rape and other violent crimes often have an aversion to physical contact.'

'Really? Which explains why Flora Dane showed up at a bar, tossed back several martinis, and hit the dance floor with a complete stranger?'

'I'm not the enemy here, Sergeant Detective Warren. I'm merely endeavoring to offer some insights which might lead to a speedier resolution of this situation.'

'The situation being where your victim put herself in harm's way in order to do what? Trap a predator? Save the day? Exact vengeance for what once happened to her?'

Dr Keynes didn't say anything. Abruptly D.D. lost patience.

'You want speedy resolution? Do us both a favor and cut to the chase. How many times has Flora done this before? How many middle-of-the-night phone calls have you gotten to answer? Might as well tell me, because you know I can look it up.'

'Four.'

'Four?' Despite herself, D.D. was incredulous. 'Flora Dane has *killed* four times before? What the hell—'

'Not killed,' Dr Keynes interjected, voice firm. 'This level of self-defense is a first.'

'What? She merely scorched the other ones? Seared 'em with a lighter versus full-on chemical fire?'

'Flora has been assaulted prior to this occasion. If you read the reports, you'll discover that she responded with the appropriate level of force and didn't face any charges.'

'She's a vigilante. Your girl, your victim—'

'Flora Dane is a survivor.'

'Flora Dane is a nut. She's going to these bars looking for trouble. And she's finding it.'

Dr Keynes didn't speak right away. Smart of him, D.D. thought, because really, at this point, what was left to say?

'I'm going to pursue this,' she stated clearly. The room was small. Her voice carried and she let it. 'Maybe case by case you can dismiss Flora's behavior, but the overall pattern? With all due respect, Dr Keynes, Flora Dane's behavior is a threat to herself and others.'

'Let me be equally clear, Sergeant Detective Warren. According to Flora, she didn't know the bartender Devon Goulding prior to this evening. She did not set out to meet him, nor did she engage in any activity that warranted him abducting her from outside a bar and tying her up naked in his garage. As for what happened after that, be very careful about blaming the victim. Flora doesn't call me to bail her out; she's never needed to be bailed out. What she does need is a ride home.'

D.D. stared at him. 'Seriously. She called you, an FBI agent—'

'A victim specialist.'

'To give her a ride home.'

'There's more to it than that.'

'You mean, such as, as long as you're here, you can run interference with the police?'

'No, such as, as long as I'm taking her home, I can run interference with her mother.'

8

I dreamed of French fries. Hot, golden greasiness. Salt-encrusted decadence. Licking them, smashing them, stuffing them in my mouth. I wanted dozens. Bagfuls. Boxes full. Dipped in ketchup. Smothered in mayonnaise. Coated in ranch dressing.

And a burger dripping cheese on a pillow-soft white bun and piled high with fresh-sliced tomatoes, onions, and pickles. I'd take greedy, gulping bites, sinking in my teeth, feeling the fat and carbs explode against my tongue.

I dreamed of food. As my stomach growled and my muscles clenched and I whimpered in physical pain.

Then, I woke up.

And I could smell it. Here, in the room. Full fast-food glory. Cheeseburgers. French fries. Chicken McNuggets. I could hear it too, the rustle of food wrappings, the pop of a straw being thrust through a plastic lid.

I think I whimpered again. There's no pride in starvation. Only desperation.

Footsteps. Coming closer. For once, I prayed for him to step faster, advance more quickly. Insert the key in the padlock, twist it open. Please. Pretty please.

Whatever he wanted me to do. Whatever he needed.

French fries. The smell of French fries.

When he lifted the lid, I had to blink against the flood of light. From narrow beams through finger-size holes to a wash of bright white. My eyes welled. Maybe in response to the sudden onslaught of visual stimulation, but mostly due to the smell. The wonderful, intoxicating smell.

Memories. Hazy. Humanizing. Running through sprinklers on short chubby legs, laughing with little-kid glee as I tried to catch droplets of spray on my tongue. Then a voice, distant but familiar. 'Tired, love? Let's go get a milkshake . . .'

Fast-forward a couple of years. Fresh memory: hands age-spotted, shaking unsteadily as they set down the brown plastic tray. 'Ketchup? Nah. Best thing on fries is mayo. Now, looky here . . .'

For a moment, I am four, or six, or eight, or ten. I'm a child, a girl, a woman. I am me. With a past and a present. With family and friends. With people who love me.

Then he spoke, and I disappeared again.

There was only the food, and I'd do anything for it.

He had to help me out of the box. I did my best to exercise as much as I could in the narrow space, but time had grown long and I didn't always remember what I should do or if I'd already done it. I slept a lot. Slept and slept and slept.

Then I didn't have to hurt as much anymore.

When I finally rose to standing, my legs shook uncontrollably. I hunched reflexively, as if expecting a blow, but I couldn't blame my rounded posture on the box. I was always lying tall and straight in the box.

'Are you hungry?' he asked me.

I didn't answer; I wasn't sure if I was supposed to. Besides, my stomach growled loudly enough for words.

He laughed. He was in a good mood. Cheerful even. I found myself standing up straighter. He was cleaner tonight,

I noticed. Hair damp, as if he'd recently showered. And he was steady on his feet, gaze clear, which wasn't always the case. I found myself looking past him, to the battered gray card table. Food. Bags and bags. McDonald's. Kentucky Fried Chicken. Burger King. Subway sandwiches. A fast-food banquet.

He's bingeing, I realized. Food, not drugs this time. But why? And what about me?

'Are you hungry?' he asked again.

I still didn't know what to say. I whimpered instead.

He laughed magnanimously. This room was his kingdom. I got that. Here, I was his property and he got to revel in his power. Beyond these walls, no doubt he was a Loser, capital L. Men disrespected him. Women laughed at him. Hence, his need for this room, this box, this helpless victim.

And now, this exercise in terror.

I moved, tentatively. I'd learned by now that his permission was all-important. And everything he gave, he could also take away, so I had to proceed with caution. When he didn't object, didn't reach out a hand to stop me, I closed the gap with the food-covered table. Then I stood, head ducked, hands clasped meekly before me. I waited, though it was the most painful waiting I'd ever done. Each muscle trembling, my stomach clenched unbearably tight.

'What do you want?' he asked.

I frowned, his question confusing me. I didn't know what I wanted. I'd been trained these past few weeks to be no one, to want nothing. That was my job. Now, I was scared. Because the smell was intoxicating, overwhelming. I could feel my self-control slipping and I couldn't afford to mess up.

Worse than starving would be to stand surrounded by food and still go hungry.

'You should eat,' he stated at last. He jabbed my bony arm, pinched a protruding rib. 'Getting too thin. You look like crap, you know.'

He picked up the bag closest to him. Opened it up, waved it under my nose.

McDonald's French fries. Hot and golden and salty.

I could hear my grandfather again. 'Looky, kid, best thing on fries is mayo.'

I wondered if he was here to finally take me away. Except I didn't want to go away with my grandpa anymore. I wanted to be right here, in this crappy room with this terrible man and these wonderful, greasy fries. Please, please, please let me eat just one single fry . . .

I'd do anything, be anyone . . .

The man was unrolling the top of the bag. Now he reached in. Now he lifted out a red container marked with a single golden M. Fries jostled loose from the open top. They dropped to the floor, the grimy shag carpet. I watched them land, fingers clasping and unclasping, my whole body tense.

He was going to eat them. He was going to stand in front of me and eat each perfect, salty morsel. Laughing, gloating, gleeful.

And I'd have no choice but to kill him. I would lose control, I'd attack, and he would . . . He would . . .

He handed me the container. 'Here. Seriously. For fuck's sake, put some meat on your bones.'

I grabbed the fries. Both hands snatching up the red box. It wasn't hot anymore. The fries were lukewarm, grease starting to congeal. I didn't care. I tossed half the contents into my mouth, swallowing faster than I could chew. Food, food, food. Needed food, had to have food. God oh God oh God.

He started laughing. I didn't look at him, kept my attention focused on the bag. I needed to eat. I had to eat. My stomach, my body, every cell screamed for sustenance.

My mouth was too dry, the smooshed fries too thick. I tried to swallow, but only managed to gag until my eyes watered. I was going to be sick, I thought, except I couldn't be sick; I couldn't afford to waste that many calories. I tried to force the food down, a giant glob of congealed potatoes. My eyes watered, my throat constricting painfully. My stomach heaved in protest . . .

He placed his hand on my arm.

I stared at him, stricken. This was it: He was going to take the macerated fries right out of my mouth. Reach in a finger and scoop out the only food I'd had in days. And that would be that. He'd return me to the coffin-size box and I would die there.

'Slow down,' he ordered. 'Get some water. Take some time. Otherwise, you'll barf.'

He handed me a bottle of water. I took tiny sips, bit by bit, breaking up the glob of food, swallowing it down. When I finally reached for the next handful of fries, he took the box from me. This time, he separated out each fry on top of the grimy card table. One by one, I picked them up. One by one, under his watchful eye, I chewed, swallowed, chewed again.

When the fries were gone, he opened up the fried chicken and handed me a drumstick.

We ate together. Me kneeling on the floor, him sitting in a chair. But we sat together, eating our way through bag after bag of food. I became full faster than I wanted. I threw up, my stomach protesting the very food it couldn't wait to have. He didn't yell. Just ordered me to wash my face, then handed me a soda.

He fell asleep on the sofa while I was still resiliently picking my way through a turkey sandwich. When I couldn't take it anymore, when no amount of vomiting eased the pain of my overstretched stomach, I curled up on the floor next to his feet and dozed off myself.

When I woke up later, he was looking down at me.

'Girl,' he said, 'you smell like fast food and piss.'

After another moment, he folded his arms, closed his eyes. 'Tomorrow,' he grunted. 'Tomorrow, it's time for you to shower.'

And I was completely, utterly grateful to him.

9

The blond detective doesn't want to let me go. She threatens to get a warrant to compel me to submit to a physical exam. Why not, if I'm telling the truth? A medical exam would only further *corroborate* my version of being attacked by Devon Goulding.

I think she's a little hung up on the word *corroborate*.

No one is touching me. Not a doctor. Not a nurse. Not a vet.

When I make it that clear to her, that absolute, she seems to finally take the hint. She studies me long and hard, then agrees to my compromise: photos of the bruises on my face.

I understand what the detective wants. I understand what they all want. In this day and age, it's not enough to claim to be assaulted. A victim must prove it. For example, the size of this bruise on my face matches the approximate size of my attacker's fist. Or the one-inch laceration on my upper left cheekbone corresponds to the sharp edge on the perpetrator's oversize class ring.

As for other areas of inspection, I'm very clear: There's no need for a rape exam. Devon Goulding can blame the contents of his own garbage for helping me avoid that displeasure.

And I feared for my life. Waking up bruised, battered, stripped naked, wrists bound. I feared for my life. I feared for my life. I feared for my life.

Would you like my official statement?

I feared for my life.

Dr Keynes and I don't talk as he leads me to his car. Frankly, it's all just been said.

When I regained consciousness five years ago, Samuel was the first person I saw. He was asleep in the chair next to my hospital bed. He wore a charcoal-gray suit, jacket unbuttoned, red tie askew, left leg crossed over right.

His black dress shoes were shined to a high gloss. I studied them for a long time, mesmerized. Dress shoes. Men's patent leather dress shoes. I almost couldn't fathom the concept.

We discussed it later. One of our many conversations back in the day when I would talk to him and only to him. That something as simple as dress shoes could be so startling. As in, I was awake a good hour before I ever said a word, ever alerted anyone to my newfound entry into the land of the living. Instead, I simply lay there, staring at a man's shoes.

A symbol of civilization, we decided at last. A note of beauty and culture and care.

In other words, his shoes represented everything that I'd lost. Everything I thought I'd never see again.

The brain has a way of simplifying complex thoughts into a single, simple symbol. Coping, Samuel would tell me. In the beginning, it was too hard for me to put into words everything I'd lost, everything I feared, everything I'd gone through. So instead, I fixated on a highly polished pair of men's dress shoes.

'You called her,' I say now. Not a question. We've been through this drill too many times for that.

'You knew I would.'

Samuel drives with both hands. His hands are relaxed, fingers long and elegant on the wheel. He's a shockingly beautiful man. Unsettling even. In the beginning, I held that against him. How can you take anyone, but especially a doctor, seriously when he looks like he should be starring in a Calvin Klein ad?

In the years since, I've come to understand better. We all have our burdens to bear, even someone as pretty as Samuel.

He doesn't dress down, however. Or do anything else that might detract from his physical perfection. Far from it. I've never seen him in anything other than impeccably tailored clothes, hundred-dollar head shaves, and perfectly buffed nails. Even off duty, he looks like he stepped from the pages of *GQ*.

I think it's his own test. I dress myself up in cool-girl trashy, waiting for the next asshole to take the bait. While Samuel presents himself as just another pretty face. Then, he waits for you to underestimate him, because in that moment, he has you, and he knows it. His car matches the rest of him. Acura SUV, black on black. Immaculate leather seats, freshly vacuumed carpet. I'm surprised he didn't put down a towel before allowing me to take a seat. I might be immune to the scent of garbage, but he isn't.

Maybe he's planning on removing the cushion later and burning it. When it comes to Samuel, nothing would surprise me.

'If you've met one survivor,' he told me that first day in the hospital room, 'then you've met one survivor.'

That's what Samuel and I have in common: We are both survivors.

'Any chance she stayed in Maine?' I ask now, forcing my voice to sound light. I turn away from Samuel and look out the car window. Daylight is still shocking to me. All these years later, mornings remain a surprise.

'What do you think?'

I think he not only called my mother, but she's now waiting in my apartment. I think I'd rather go back to the crime scene, duke it out with the blond detective again.

'What are you doing?' Samuel asks presently.

I smile; I can't help myself. And I keep my face turned away. Samuel, of all people, knows me too well. Which is why I keep calling him. To remind myself that somewhere out there, someone knows who I am, even if I can't always remember.

When I woke up that day in the hospital in Atlanta, my mother and brother were still en route from Boston's Logan International Airport. Given that I had no friends or family in the area, Samuel had remained in the room as a source of support.

The minute the FBI agents started asking all their questions, however . . . I couldn't do it. I couldn't talk; I couldn't remember what they wanted me to remember; I absolutely, positively could not relive what they seemed to feel I should recall at a moment's notice. Instead, I curled up in a fetal position and shut down. They tried kindness, impatience, and then out-and-out badgering. It didn't matter. I didn't talk.

I couldn't.

Eventually, they left, under doctor's orders to let me rest.

Only Samuel remained. He took his seat. Crossed his left leg over his right. And that was that.

He never said a word. I closed my eyes. I fell asleep. Or tried to. The room would spin away. Other images replaced it. Light and dark. Screams and laughter. The feel of shampoo in my hair. The smell of ammonia. The way blood soaks into cheap carpet.

I saw things I didn't want to see. Knew too many things I didn't want to know. And I had my first real insight into victimization. There's no undoing. There's no rewind, or erasing, or unmaking. The things that happened, they are you, you are them.

You can escape, but you can't get away. Just the way it is.

I reached my decision then. I would tell my story once and only once. To Samuel. And then, that would be it. I would talk, he would listen, and then I would never speak of it again. For his part, Samuel wanted to ensure I understood that he was an agent of the police. Anything and everything I told him he'd be reporting back to the special agent in charge; he wasn't my shrink; we did not have doctor-client privilege. But as long as I understood that, he would listen to whatever I wanted, needed, to say.

So I talked. The words rushing out, pouring out. One long, horrible deluge.

I spoke for hours. Nurses came, checked vitals, adjusted monitors, then scurried away. Dark agents appeared in the doorway, only to be hastily dismissed. I don't know. I couldn't take it in, the room, the equipment, the endless interruption of bodies. I kept my body ramrod straight, hands at my side, gaze on the overhead lights, and I talked, and I talked, and I talked.

First a whisper. Then louder, steadier. Then . . . maybe I ended in a scream.

I don't really remember, to tell you the truth. It was like an out-of-body experience. All this horror I had to get out of me, and the only way to do that was to talk and talk and talk.

When I finally reached the end, midnight, small hours of the morning, Samuel staggered to his feet. His face was covered in a sheen of sweat. He didn't look so beautiful anymore.

His breath was ragged, as if he himself had just completed a long, hard race.

He made it to the bathroom. I listened to him vomit.

When he returned, however, his gleaming bald head was polished, his features once again composed.

He took my hand. He held it.

And I slept. Hours and hours, maybe even an entire day. I finally slept. When I woke up, my mother and brother were there and the real business of returning to the land of the living began.

I kept my word that day. I've never told my story again. Not to the detectives, not to the rabid prosecutor, not to my own mother. Samuel must've turned in a report; that was his job after all. I've never asked. I've never read it. I said all I had to say, all I could say, once, and then it was done.

The nice thing about my captor, Jacob Ness, being dead is that there's no one to rebut. My story is the story.

And both Samuel and I know it.

'Why did you go out last night?' Samuel asks me now. He eases up on the accelerator; we're nearing my Arlington apartment.

'I'm a young, single woman. People my age are supposed to go out at night.'

'Alone to a bar?'

'The band was excellent.'

He cast me a look.

'I didn't lie to the police,' I hear myself say. 'The bartender was as much a surprise to me as everyone else. If I hadn't been there . . .'

Samuel pauses a beat. Shrinks love a good waiting game.

'You killed a man.'

'Please. That Goulding guy would've attacked someone else, and that girl would now be dead. I saved a life last night.'

'And saving this abstract girl has value?'

'Absolutely!'

'What about your own life? Doesn't it have value?'

I roll my eyes. I totally set him up for that one and we both know it. 'You can't count that as a display of superior intellect,' I inform him. 'More like basic reflex.'

He ignores my sarcasm, continues more pointedly: 'I believe your mother would argue that, given a choice between worrying about you and worrying about a stranger, she'd prefer to know you're safe.'

I don't have anything to say to that. Or maybe I have too much. Such as, what does it matter? I could stay in every night for the rest of my life and my mother still wouldn't be happy. In fact, maybe she'd be better off if I finally did go out and meet a grand demise. Get the waiting game over with. Because, as my mother will tell you, there are worse things than having your daughter abducted.

There's getting her back and realizing you've lost her after all.

'You shouldn't have called her,' I say now.

'But you knew I would.'

'I can take care of myself.'

'Just ask Devon Goulding?'

'I did what I had to do!'

'No,' Samuel retaliates just as sharply. 'You set up what you wanted. There's a difference.'

I fall back into silence. We arrive at the three-story brownstone that houses my single-bedroom apartment. Samuel pulls into the driveway – temporary parking and a signal that he's not staying, just dropping me off.

'The local police are looking at you now,' he says quietly.

'Nah. That was just posturing. Blondie didn't have a real perpetrator to arrest, so naturally she toyed with me. But I'm telling you, by the time they're done shaking down that house, they'll find evidence of other victims. Then, they'll have real work to do and I'll fall by the wayside, just a curious footnote in the case file.'

Samuel looks at me. He has deep dark eyes fringed by heavy lashes. I imagine women must fall in love with him every day, gazing into those eyes, fantasizing about him staring back at them just as soulfully.

It's a bunch of effort wasted on a man who never does anything but work.

'You survived,' he tells me now, 'by doing what you had to do. By adapting. That's the nature of survival, Flora, and you know it.'

I don't say anything.

'You're strong and that helped you, but this doesn't have to define you. You are a young woman with your whole life ahead of you. Don't confuse what you had to do to survive with who you are.'

'A woman who takes on rapists?'

'Is that how you see yourself?'

He's waiting. He wants a better definition, a deeper look

into myself. Am I a vigilante? A self-destructive freak? How about a self-defense enthusiast?

Maybe I'm all of those things. Maybe I'm none of those things.

Maybe I'm a girl who once upon a time thought of the world as a shiny, happy place.

And now . . .

I'm a girl who went missing too many years ago. And remained away from home and from herself for way too long.

'My mother's waiting,' I say.

And he smiles, because Samuel, of all people, understands exactly what I mean.

'Sorry about your seat,' I say as I climb out of his car.

'Don't worry, I'm going to take it out and burn it.'

My turn to smile.

'Are you working with Stacey Summers's family?' I ask him abruptly.

He shakes his head. 'Are you?' he asks evenly.

'You know that's not my style.'

'But you're following her case.'

'Isn't everyone?'

Samuel flexes his hands on the wheel. 'Do you think he did it?' he asks abruptly. 'Do you think the man you just killed is the same person who kidnapped Stacey Summers in August?'

'I want to think that.'

'So you can feel better about what you did.'

'No. Opposite, in fact. If he's the one who attacked Stacey . . . He's dead now. Not exactly in a position to lead the police to her body. It'd be better, in fact, if it wasn't him. At least for her family.'

'So why are you asking about Stacey Summers?'

I open my mouth. I close my mouth. There are things I can't say, not even to Samuel.

I glance up, my gaze going to the top window of the brownstone and the outline of my mother waiting for me there.

'Thank you, Samuel,' I hear myself say.

I close the door. He backs out of the driveway.

Then, my real work begins.

10

Deputy Superintendent of Homicide Cal Horgan, a.k.a. D.D.'s boss, stood in her doorway.

'Heard you got a live one,' he said.

'We're still working the scene, but yeah, at first blush . . . The deceased, Devon Goulding, was most likely a serial predator. We recovered two driver's licenses, not to mention a cache of photos, which seems to indicate other victims.'

'Stacey Summers?' Horgan asked immediately, the missing college student being first and foremost on most law enforcement agents' minds.

Given the terrible abduction video and urgent nature, the Summers case had gone straight to 'red ball' status, detective-speak for all hands on deck. While D.D. wasn't the lead investigator, she'd spent the first week of the girl's disappearance conducting interviews and combing through reports with the rest of her colleagues. Her biggest contribution: spending several days interrogating the girl's boyfriend. All she got out of it was a young man's horror. Though Patrick Vaughn and Stacey had been dating only a matter of months, he was clearly smitten. Far from playing it cool, he'd broken down several times. Stacey was such a sweet girl. The real deal. Thoughtful, considerate, the kind of girl who'd never dream of running off or doing anything to hurt her family.

If she'd gone missing, then only the worst could've happened.

There were days it was good to be a cop. When you got to browbeat some lowlife schmuck into a righteous confession. Then, there were the days you made a clean-cut nineteen-year-old college boy cry.

D.D. hadn't loved that day on the job. Or, frankly, anything that had to do with the Stacey Summers case. They could place the girl at a local bar, where she'd gone to hang out with half a dozen female friends. Two beers under her belt, probably a little buzzed as she wasn't a big drinker, she'd excused herself to use the restroom.

Next thing anyone knew, a local business's security camera had captured video of the petite blonde being forcefully led away by a hulking male, face hidden from view. After that, nothing at all.

Not a single eyewitness, not another video frame. In a city heavily populated by nosy people and observant cameras, 105-pound Stacey Summers ceased to exist.

'I'm told this Devon Goulding was a big guy,' Horgan was saying now. 'Pumped-up. Steroid-sculpted. Sounds like our camera man.'

'Size is right,' D.D. agreed. 'MO . . . last night's victim he grabbed by the arm and dragged away. According to her, Goulding's posture, the way he looked away from the cameras, reminded her of the Summers abduction video.'

'So we got a lead?' Horgan pressed, half impatient, half hopeful. D.D. understood his pain. If Boston PD as an organization was under pressure to find cute, perky, never-hurt-a-fly Stacey Summers, then Horgan, as the deputy superintendent of homicide, was feeling personally responsible. Welcome to the chain of command.

'I'm not convinced.'

'Why not?'

'Assuming the two licenses we recovered tie to past victims, there's nothing linking back to Stacey Summers. We also found photographs consistent with one of the females from the licenses, Natalie Draga, but again, no evidence of Stacey Summers.'

'But you have at least two possible victims?'

'Natalie Draga and Kristy Kilker. According to Mrs Kilker, her daughter is currently studying abroad in Italy.'

Horgan arched a brow.

'We're working on corroborating that now,' she assured him. 'Same with Natalie Draga. Her driver's license is from Alabama. We're tracking down her family there.'

'So you don't know if these two women are missing or not.'

'No, sir.'

'But you know he attacked a third girl, the one who burned him.'

'You mean the one who killed him?'

Horgan shrugged. Apparently a dead alleged rapist didn't bother him much. D.D. knew many on the force who would agree.

'I have some concerns about this "new victim", Florence Dane.'

Horgan frowned. D.D. watched him mentally work his way back from the initial spark of name recognition, then: 'You're kidding. *Florence Dane?* The Boston girl who was kidnapped in Florida? Held for over a year? That Florence Dane?'

'Seems since her reentry into society, she's made criminal

behavior a bit of a hobby. Last night's attack marks her fourth instance of "self-defense" in the past three years.'

Horgan closed his eyes. 'That's not going to look good. Something like that . . . Goulding's family could argue she set him up. And suddenly, instead of us happily announcing there's one less predator in Boston, let alone possibly closing out two missing persons cases, we're going to have to investigate a rapist as a victim?'

'Exactly.'

'What do you have to corroborate Florence Dane's version of events?'

'Bruises on Flora's face. Eyewitness accounts from the neighbors that she was discovered naked and bound in Goulding's garage. Other testimonies from the bar where Devon worked that Flora didn't even talk to him last night, but was hanging out with some other loser, whom Devon punched in the face.'

'Okay. Sounds promising.'

D.D. shrugged. Winced at the corresponding stabbing pain in her shoulder, then quickly recovered. 'I don't like it,' she stated bluntly. 'The overall pattern of behavior . . . Flora Dane's good deeds are going to hurt us. Especially if it turns out nothing happened to those other girls, if it's just Flora's testimony on Devon Goulding's "true nature" and his actions last night . . . The Gouldings could make the case she baited their son. That, given her past trauma, she sees predators everywhere and took the law in her own hands.'

'Isn't that a Hitchcock movie?'

'*Twilight Zone* episode. Look, four instances of self-defense is more than bad luck; it's a pattern of bad behavior. And given the latest episode ended in a man's death, you can argue her behavior is escalating.'

'Meaning what?'

D.D. stared at her superior officer. 'Meaning we should charge her!'

'With what?'

'Reckless conduct. Why not? She set in motion the chain of events that led to Goulding's death. She should be held accountable.'

'I see restricted duty hasn't made you go soft.'

'Cal, it's not her job to police the world. It's ours. We know what we're doing. She, on the other hand, is a threat to herself and others. Not to mention, last night she potentially screwed up at least two other investigations.'

'How do you figure?'

'She killed Devon Goulding. Meaning if he did do something to Natalie Draga and/or Kristy Kilker, now what? Where are their bodies? What happened to them? I'd ask him, but oh yeah, he's dead. Meaning what the hell do we have to bring back to the families? Here's your daughter's driver's license – hope that's good enough? Frankly, of all people, Flora Dane should know better.'

'Tell her that?' Horgan asked evenly.

'Waiting to get more information on the two women. Then I'll bring it up.'

'You're definitely going to interview her again.'

'In my mind, this party is only starting.'

'D.D. . . .' Her boss hesitated. 'I know you pride yourself on being firm in your opinions. It's one of the things that ensures working with you is never boring. But Flora Dane . . . You might want to pull her case file. There's a good reason for her to see predators everywhere. Certainly, she spent more than a year getting a master class in criminal behavior.'

'Now you sound like her shrink. I'm sorry, her victim advocate. Seriously, the girl basically has her own FBI agent on a leash. Never seen anything like it.'

'All right. Plenty of questions ahead. But first, if you don't mind: Go home, D.D. Shower. What's that smell anyway?'

'Human barbecue. Or maybe rotten garbage?'

Her boss shook his head. 'Clean up. We'll have to do a press briefing in time for the evening news cycle. For now, keep it simple. Looking for information regarding Natalie Draga and Kristy Kilker, or anyone else who may have known Devon Goulding. No mention of Stacey Summers. No mention of Florence Dane.'

D.D. rolled her eyes at him. 'Now who wants the impossible?' Horgan flashed her a smile, then disappeared down the hall, leaving D.D. with mounds of paperwork and the smell of crime scene still lingering in her hair.

She went home. Given it was Saturday, Alex was home with four-year-old Jack. She discovered them sprawled on the living room floor, engaged in a fierce game of Candy Land. Jack was less interested in winning the game than he was in drawing the various character cards. Jolly was his favorite, and he'd been known to stash the card bearing the big blue gumdrop in his pocket or up his sleeve.

Alex glanced up from the game board. He gave her a welcoming smile, even as he sniffed the air.

Jack, on the other hand, came flying off the floor and flung himself around her legs. 'Mommy, mommy, mommy.'

No doubt about it, that never got old. D.D. ruffled his brown hair with her right hand, as her left arm had stiffened even further on the drive home. She was holding it protectively against her side, and sure enough . . .

'What'd you do?' Alex asked.

'Long night,' she offered. Jack was still hugging her. She hugged him back.

Alex was no dumb bunny. 'Paperwork doesn't require long nights. Paperwork can generally be reviewed in the morning.'

'Big case,' she mumbled. 'Perpetrator found . . . incapacitated . . . in his own garage. With ties to other victims.'

'Inca-what?' Jack asked.

'Incapacitated. Means he can't play Candy Land anymore.'

'I have Jolly,' Jack announced, and sure enough, he whipped the gumdrop card from beneath his sweater sleeve.

'Hey,' Alex complained. 'I've been looking for that.'

'Nuh-uh. You like Gramma Nutt. Everyone knows that.'

'Gramma Nutt advances you further on the board than big blue gumdrops,' Alex muttered. 'And saying I want Princess Frostine sounds funny.'

'I'm home just to clean up and eat,' D.D. announced, tone apologetic. Jack's shoulders sagged, but he didn't outwardly protest. At least not yet. Jack hadn't been thrilled when she returned to work after being home for so long with her injury. He was a kid, and kids liked their parents close. In the good-news department, she did get decent time off after working long stretches . . . but it felt like the past few weeks had seen more peaks on the job than lulls, and Jack was struggling with her long absences. Hell, she was still adjusting to the demands of full-time duty as well.

'Saw the news this morning,' Alex commented. 'Figured you might be busy. One of the reporters was already speculating you had a fresh lead in the Stacey Summers case.'

'What? How did they . . . how could they? Oh, never mind. Like the press has to be informed to state their opinions. But no, no connection to that case. At least, not at this time.'

Alex smiled. It creased the corners of his deep blue eyes. He was a good-looking guy, she thought, not for the first time. Salt-and-pepper hair, distinguished features. And hers. All hers. Who knew one workaholic detective could get so lucky?

She pried Jack away from her legs with a promise of future grilled cheese. That bought her enough time to shower, then throw on her favorite dark blue Ann Taylor pantsuit, which was her outfit of choice for press conferences.

In the kitchen, she poured two glasses of orange juice, then set to work slicing up a brick of cheddar. Her shoulder twinged again, and she couldn't completely suppress the wince.

'You overdid it,' Alex said, coming up behind her.

'Just need a little ice.'

'Or some rest, or a good night's sleep, or a little less stress.'

'Blah, blah, blah.'

'Phil's worried about you. Said you were on scene most of the night. That's hardly restricted duty.'

'Phil's secretly a woman. And worries about me more than my own mother.'

'Crime happens,' Alex said. He was already opening the freezer door, bringing out her favorite ice pack, perfectly molded to the shape of her shoulder. 'And it will continue to happen, whether you're working or not.'

'Especially if Flora Dane has her way,' D.D. muttered.

'Who?'

'Guy we found—' She glanced around the kitchen, searched for signs of Jack, who was probably in the family room, stacking Legos. Seeing that they were alone, D.D. continued: 'Guy we found dead started his evening abducting Flora Dane. Who turns out to be no stranger to kidnappings.

She turned the tables on him. Burned him to death with supplies she found in his trash.'

'No kidding?'

'I don't like it. Fourth time she's put herself in a dangerous situation since her return five years ago. What happens next? She takes on the entire Russian mob?'

'Better her than me,' Alex observed. 'You think she's a vigilante?'

'Don't you? Seeking out predators, time and time again?'

'So says the woman on restricted duty who's about to go back to work.'

'I'm a workaholic.' D.D. fired up the first grilled cheese sandwich. 'What's her excuse?'

Alex rolled his eyes. 'Sit, ice your shoulder. I can flip a sandwich.'

She sat. She iced her shoulder. She relaxed. At least as much as a woman like her could. Then in came Jack for a fresh round of sticky little-boy hugs and a fresh pat-down for hoarded Candy Land character cards.

Normal life. Real life. Her life.

Then, much as her husband predicted and respected, she headed back to work.

11

The first thing that hits me as I walk up the three flights of stairs to my tiny one-bedroom unit is the scent of freshly baked muffins. My mother. Under stress, she bakes. Cookies, brownies, breads, homemade granola, scones. I'm told during my abduction the entire community, not to mention the victim specialists, put on fifteen pounds.

She has a key to my unit. Three actually, as I'm partial to that many locks. Having opened my front door, however, she has left it unlocked behind her. Now, all I have to do is push it open. I know she doesn't do these things to consciously spite me, and yet already I can feel my shoulders tense. I'm not looking forward to the conversation to come. Most likely, she isn't either. Hence, muffins.

She's in the kitchen, bent over the oven, checking her project when I walk in. The police haven't given me back my real clothes after the night's misadventure. Did they even find them? I have no idea. If they did, the items would be kept as evidence. In the meantime, the district detective rustled up oversize gray sweatpants and a navy-blue Boston Police hoodie, most likely extra clothes stashed in the back of some officer's vehicle. Both items are huge. I have to hold up the elastic waistband of the sweatpants as I walk. My feet remain bare, meaning I don't make much noise as I pad across the hardwood.

I chose this unit for several reasons. One, being on the third story, it's harder for an intruder to access. Two, the old brownstones are famous for their high ceilings, bull's-eye molding, and bay windows. My unit is small but flooded with light from the old windows, and charming with its battered oak floors and beautiful wooden trim. Is there water damage on the ceiling? Sure. Peeling linoleum in the kitchen, not one of the owner's better renovation ideas? Yep. A shower that only yields hot water after three or four strategic whacks? Well, a girl like me can hardly afford the best.

Besides, I like my unit's flaws. It's scarred. Like me. We belong together, not to mention the elderly couple who are my landlords know my story and charge me only a fraction of the going rate for rent. Having turned down the requisite book deal and movie rights, reduced rent is as close to a post-abduction perk as I'm going to get. And given that I've never returned to college and still have no idea what I'm going to do with the rest of my life, money is an issue. For the past few months, I've been working down the street at a pizza parlor popular with college students and local families. My hourly wage is miserly, the tips only slightly better. But the work is mindless, and I appreciate that.

Is this the life I thought I'd be living at twenty-seven? No. But then, when I first left my mother's farm for college in the big city, what did I know? I enrolled to study French, for God's sake, mostly because I liked the idea of going to Paris. Maybe I would've become a teacher. Or returned to Maine and set up a small farm of my own, involving goats. I'd sell goat milk, goat cheese, maybe even goat-milk lotions and goat-milk soaps. All with labels in French. I was happy enough, naive enough back then, to have those kinds of dreams.

But everyone's dreams change, not just the dreams of girls who wind up kidnapped for four hundred and seventy-two days.

At least I'm not dealing with kids. Because that happens too. Held captive long enough, pregnancy, babies, can ensue. Jacob, however, was adamant on that subject. Once a month, he forced me to swallow some god-awful home-made brew he swore would prevent pregnancy. It tasted like turpentine and led to immediate, excruciating stomach cramps. The sexual assault nurse who performed my initial exam had been curious about the potion. Though, in her professional opinion, it was my extreme emaciation and total lack of body fat that probably truly did the job. Frankly, I didn't even have a period through most of my captivity; I was that thin.

Now, I watch my mother straighten in front of the stove, muffin tin clutched in an oven-mitten hand. She turns, spots me, and immediately stills. Her gaze takes in the oversize sweats that obviously aren't mine, then the garbage smeared across my cheek, my hair.

She doesn't speak. I watch her chest fill, a conscious inhale. Then the slow exhale as no doubt she counts to ten. Wondering yet again how to survive a daughter like me.

At her throat is a necklace with a single silver charm. A dainty but perfectly rendered fox.

She bought that after I went missing. When the FBI prepped her for the first press conference by dismissing her usual attire of wide-legged yoga pants and flowing hand-woven wraps such as the kind favored by Afghan tribal elders. No more bohemian, organic potato farmer from Maine. Her goal was to look like Mom, with a capital *M*.

An instantly recognizable and relatable maternal figure who would appeal to my captor's kinder sentiments, assuming he had any.

They stuck her in jeans and a button-up white shirt. Probably the plainest outfit she'd ever worn in her life, not to mention the real shoes versus her usual Birkenstocks.

I didn't see that first press conference. Or the second. I think I caught the third, when things were truly heating up. Even then, spying her, my mom, on the TV, standing in front of the microphone, flanked by suited FBI agents, wearing a light blue button-up shirt, more jeans . . .

My mom, but not my mom. A surreal moment in a life that had already taken a completely, horrifically surreal turn. I would've shut the TV off, wasted my rare privilege, rather than see this mom-but-not-my-mom. Except then I spotted the fox charm. Nestled in the hollow of her throat.

I never heard her words that day. But I knelt on the floor of that cheap hotel room and placed my finger against the charm around her neck, my finger so large, her form so diminutive on the small TV, that the tip of my index finger obliterated most of her head.

I might have cried. I don't really remember. I'd already been gone months by that point. I don't know if I had any tears left.

But I tried to touch her, this mom-but-not-my-mom. And for one moment, I was a child again, running wild on the farm, throwing golf balls for the fox kits and laughing as they batted them across the tall grass.

Now, she sets down the muffin tin on top of the stove. Her hands are shaking slightly.

'Are you hungry?' she asks, her voice almost normal. Her farm is three and a half hours north of Boston. Assuming Samuel called her the minute after I contacted him, she got into her truck immediately and has been driving since the crack of dawn.

'I should shower,' I hear myself say.

'Of course. Take your time.'

There doesn't seem to be anything else to say. I pad away, still holding the waistband of the sweats. Four whacks of the old plumbing later, the water turns steaming hot. I shed the baggy sweats. I step into the hard spray. And I let the water scald me.

For a moment, I can almost smell it again. Freshly roasted human skin. Like a pork barbecue.

Then the moment passes, and I close my eyes. The void fills me, and I welcome its emptiness.

To always be alone in a crowded room.

The only time I ever feel safe anymore.

After my abduction, when I returned to the land of the living, one of Samuel's first tasks was to develop my post-captivity support plan. Basically, he conducted an assessment of my coping skills, while also working with the victim specialists who'd assisted my family to understand the level of support network already in place.

While Samuel is an expert in post-traumatic stress, he informed me that he's not a fan of the term. In his opinion, it's often applied too readily and as a one-size-fits-all model. He's worked with dozens and dozens of survivors over the years, and while all of us experienced trauma, only a few genuinely qualify as suffering from PTSD. In fact, he warned my mother explicitly about making such an assumption, or even such excuses on my behalf.

Survivors make it because they learn to adapt. Adaptation is coping. Coping is strength.

My mother, my brother, myself should not expect me to

be weak now, nor actively foster dependency. Instead, we should all focus on reinforcing my natural resilience, which got me through the ordeal in the first place.

As for myself, the biggest mistake survivors can make, according to Samuel, is second-guessing their actions now that they're safe. So, no wondering why I went to the bar in the first place that night. Or why I didn't struggle harder. Or escape the first time Jacob left the cab of his truck unlocked. No matter that Jacob had pulled over his rig in the middle of nowhere and he was standing right there, taking a leak in a drainage ditch.

The past is the past. It doesn't matter what mistakes I might or might not have made. What matters is that I survived.

Samuel was right about the pitfalls of second-guessing. I don't suffer nightmares about Jacob as much as I suffer terrible anxiety over the might-have-beens, should-have-dones. My first enrollment in a self-defense course was an attempt to help mediate those nerves, make me feel more comfortable. Ironically enough, my mother supported that step, even took that first class with me. Samuel had approved as well. Reinforcing a feeling of personal strength, excellent.

It was right about the fourth or fifth class, and my growing interest in marksmanship, that my mother became concerned. I was living back home those days, and I overheard her discussing it with Samuel during one of his check-ins trying to assess how either of us, both of us, were doing.

Samuel is not a therapist, and certainly not my therapist. He had, however, recommended counseling for me, or therapeutic support, as he liked to call it. I'd resisted all attempts, though. Private sessions would by definition involve telling my story, and I was sticking to my guns: I'd told my story once, as promised. Never again.

Ironically enough, it was my mother who took Samuel's advice. I moved on to tactical driving classes, while she started meeting with the local pastor once a week.

Another one of those realizations that all survivors have to make: My abduction hadn't just victimized me but my entire family too. My mother, who, after the third postcard, pretty much gave up on the farm and turned her attention full-time to reaching out to a depraved kidnapper in the desperate hope of seeing her daughter again. My brother, who dropped out of college, first to answer endless police questions and later because, in his own words, how could he possibly concentrate knowing I was out there, somewhere, needing him?

Major crimes are like cancer. They take over, demanding an entire family's full resources. My brother became a social media expert, building a Facebook page, running Twitter feeds. And, frankly, trying to manage the press who camped out in the yard for weeks at a time, especially after Jacob mailed out a new postcard, offering fresh bait.

My mother spent her days with the victim advocates, as well as with fellow parents of missing kids. They offered support, mentorship, as she sought to come up to speed quickly on law enforcement, criminal behavior, media management. She got to learn how to craft messages for strategic press conferences, while also making the rounds on the morning news shows and nightly cable stations. She got to handwrite replies to hundreds, then thousands of letters from total strangers wishing for my safe return. And she got to endure other notes, Facebook posts, stating an obviously immoral teenage girl like me got exactly what I deserved.

In theory, there are some financial resources available to

victims of crime. The specialists diligently produced paper-work enabling my mother to possibly collect a couple of thousand here, or apply for a grant there. My mother will tell you she had neither the time nor mental focus. No, having your child abducted is a fairly impoverishing ordeal. My sin of heading out for a night of spring break drinking becoming my entire family's punishment.

In our case, the community rallied. Neighbors showed up and worked the farm in their free time. They got seeds started, crops planted, and then, as the ordeal continued to drag on, dealt with the fall harvest. The church held bake sales. Local businesses sent over checks. Local restaurants and delis provided food.

My mother will never leave her farm. Probably wouldn't have anyway. But the land, her place, her community, it's her solace, her anchor. It was there when she needed it most, and without it, I don't know what she would've done.

She has her place in the world.

It's my brother and I who remain adrift.

Darwin left. A year after my return, when I couldn't magically smile on command. When the pancakes I once loved were now a smell I couldn't stomach, he'd had enough. The family protector melted down, had a little episode involving driving way too fast with no headlights, and my mother realized all the love and attention I didn't want should be turned on him instead.

After many heartfelt discussions, she sent him to Europe. Got him a passport, a rail ticket, a backpack, and sent him off with a kiss and a hug. Go forth, young man, and find yourself, and all that.

Darwin doesn't send postcards. He knows better. But from time to time, we get a call. He's in London now. Likes it a lot. Is thinking of enrolling in the London School of

Economics. Certainly, he's bright enough, while having some pretty interesting topics to write about for his college entrance essay.

I think, more than anything else in the world, I would like my brother to have a happy ending. I wish he'd fall in love, land a great job, build a life. Then my mistake doesn't have to be his punishment anymore.

Which is funny, because I think he would say exactly the same about me.

I've showered long enough. Soaped. Shampooed. Conditioned. Done everything except feel clean.

The smell of burning human flesh.

Not pork. Maybe more like roast beef.

I saved a life, I remind myself as I whack the ancient faucet to off. Another girl is safe because of me. Another animal is off the streets.

The sun is out. My apartment smells like blueberry muffins. This is one of those moments when I should stop, give thanks for the day.

I think of Jacob. I don't want to. I just can't help myself.

I remember Jacob Ness, the man who took me, broke me down, and then rebuilt me for four hundred and seventy-two days.

And in the back of my mind, he's laughing at me.

My mother has cleaned the kitchen. If I hadn't emerged dressed and freshly showered when I did, I'm pretty sure she would've taken down and washed the French-printed valances she bought and installed last year. My mother is a farmer mostly because she needs to keep busy. She's one of those people who require a long list of chores, or her life lacks all meaning.

She's dressed like herself today. Black wide-legged yoga

pants with a funky print on the bottom hem, and a loose-fitting sea-foam-green, 100 percent organic cotton wrapped shirt. Over that, she's thrown on a man's unbuttoned gray flannel shirt. In Maine she'd blend right in. In Boston, not quite so much.

About six months after I returned home, she boxed up all the clothes the victim specialists had helped her buy for the press conferences. Together, we took the items to the thrift shop that operates out of the congregational church's basement. The ladies were pleased to receive such high-quality, hardly worn clothing items.

We called it Liberation. An ongoing campaign to get our lives back. My mother gave away clothes that were never really her. I painted my childhood bedroom butter yellow and resolved to be more appreciative of everyday beauty.

Let's just say my mother is doing better with the campaign than me.

When I reappear, she has heaped the muffins on a plate in the middle of the rolling butcher block piece that serves both as my kitchen-prep island and sole dining table. She has also poured two glasses of orange juice and cut up fresh fruit. Given my refrigerator held mostly bottles of water and cartons of stale takeout, she went to the corner store while I was showering.

Which, of course, compels me to turn around and check the front door locks. I snap the bolts home. When I return to her, I know my expression is disapproving, but I can't help myself.

'Muffin?' she says cheerfully, gesturing to the plate.

I take one. Suddenly, I'm famished. I eat two muffins, then devour half the bowl of fruit. My mother doesn't say anything, but picks at her own food. She probably ate hours ago. Waiting for me. Worrying about me.

Now, she's working on playing it cool.

'Samuel says you killed a man,' she says at last, waiting game obviously up.

I pick up my plate, carry it to the tiny sink. 'Self-defense. I won't face any charges.'

'You think that's what scares me?'

She's standing right beside me, and despite her best attempts at deep-breathing exercises, I can tell she's agitated.

It hurts me. It does. I don't know how to be her little girl anymore. I don't know how to turn back the clock and undo what was done. I can't feel what I can't feel. I can't be what I can't be.

But it pains me, this look on her face, this worry in her eyes. It kills me to know that the person I am now hurts the mother who's never done anything but love me.

'I didn't plan on what happened,' I hear myself say. 'But I was prepared. And I handled the situation. This guy, he's hurt other girls, Mom. But not anymore. He's done.'

'I don't care about other girls,' she says. 'I care about you.'

She hugs me then, hard and fierce. The way I know she's always hugged me. And I force myself to stand there. To not flinch, to not go rigid. To remind myself these arms are my mother's arms. Her hair smells like my memories of my mother's hair. This is the woman who tucked me in at night, and read me stories, and offered me warm milk when I couldn't sleep, and made me cinnamon toast when I was sick. A million tiny moments.

But it's all detached now. This is what I can't tell her, can never completely explain. The memories don't feel like mine. All of this, all of what was, feels like something that happened to someone else, home movies from somebody else's life.

Jacob Ness wanted a completely compliant companion. So he broke me down, physically, emotionally, spiritually. Then, when I was nothing, just a raw, helpless mound of human clay, he remolded me into being exactly who he wanted me to be. He became my world, my center, my guiding star.

And then . . . That last day. Those final few moments.

The story I told once and will never repeat.

He's gone now.

And I am lost. Forever untethered. Until my mother's hug feels like the comfort of a stranger.

My own brother ran away from the person I've become. But my mom is more stubborn.

'You can come back home,' she says now, an old argument. Fosters dependency. She knows it, and hastily adds, 'Just for a visit. A few days. We could make a girls' weekend out of it.'

'I'm fine.'

'Going out alone to a bar on a Friday night?'

'I can take care of myself. Isn't that the point?'

She draws back. She can't talk to me when I'm in this mood, and she knows it. Again, the worry on her face, which I feel as a fist in my chest.

'Flora.'

'I know you don't like my choices,' I hear myself say, 'but they're my choices to make.'

A winning argument in my mother's world, and she knows it. I watch her inhale deeply. Exhale slowly.

'If you won't come home this weekend,' she says presently, 'then tell me when.'

I accept her compromise. We pick a date, two weeks from now. I need to rest now, I tell her, but she's welcome to stay.

She shakes her head, though. A city apartment is no place for a Maine farmer. She prepares to leave, driving back another three and a half hours. A seven-hour round-trip to spend one hour with her daughter.

These are the things mothers do, she tells me as I watch her turn and walk downstairs.

When she's gone from sight, I close my front door. I work my locks. I turn back to my sunny, charming, battle-scarred apartment.

And I do exactly what I told my mother I would do. I head to bed.

I sleep. I don't always. Usually slumber comes fitfully for me. But now, fresh off my most recent kill . . .

I sleep like the dead.

When I wake up, the sun is gone, my room is dark, and I know immediately that I'm not alone. I can feel a draft against my cheek, the muted hush of an intruder's shuffling footstep.

Then, from just outside my open bedroom door. A shadow, dark and menacing. I open my mouth to say, who's there?

Except, of course, I already know.

The world is filled with monsters.

I need to move, leap out of bed, assume the defensive.

Instead, I make the mistake of inhaling.

Then, all I hear is the distant sound of laughter, right before the world goes dark again.

12

The hardest part about being held captive? You'd think it would be the starvation, punishment, degradation. The unbearable thirst for water, maybe. Or the relentless pain of a pine box pressing against your shoulder blades, flattening the back of your head.

Or perhaps the moment you realize you don't know how long you've been gone anymore. The minutes, hours, days have become a blur, and you can't remember now . . . Has it been a week, two, three? Is it still spring, or is it now summer? And what about Easter? Did Easter happen while you were gone? The annual brunch at your mother's house? Did your brother eat your chocolate bunny?

You try to hang on to these thoughts because they connect you to a larger world, some piece of reality where you're still a real person with a real life.

But the truth is, these moments are hard to remember, so inevitably you let them go. You think less and less of home and the person you used to be and the person you'll never be again. You just are.

You're bored.

Which becomes the toughest burden to bear. There's no friendly conversation or polite chitchat. No places to go. No people to see. There's no TV to entertain you with mindless blather, or a radio to engage you with a catchy song, or a smartphone to entice you with an exciting new text.

You exist in a sensory-deprived void, where you hum just for the sake of having something to hear. Where you take turns counting by twos and threes and fives just so your mind has something to do. Where you gnaw on your fingertips just to have something to feel. But even this can only kill an hour or two a day.

You sleep. Too much. You don't mean to. You understand you probably shouldn't; it would be better to remain alert. But you're tired, you're weak, and you're bored. Oh so bored! Sleeping becomes the only thing left for you.

I told myself stories. Children's books I remembered from school. Bible stories from church. In the beginning, I whispered them out loud. But my mouth was so dry and parched, the words got stuck in my throat. So after a while, I played the stories like movies in my mind. Not fantasies of my rescue, or images of my family and friends – that would hurt too much. Just fables, legends, fairy tales. Anything with a happy ending that would pass the time in my head.

But mostly, the stories put me back to sleep. So I would doze, on and off. Growing more and more disoriented, until at last, the sound of footsteps pounding down the stairs. A door squeaking open across the way. The rattle of the padlock, so wonderfully close to my ear. Then, at long last, the wooden lid would be lifted. He would appear.

And I would live again, saved from my boredom by the very man who'd put me there.

'Tell me about your father,' he demanded one day. He lounged on the sofa in dirty underwear, alternating smoking a cigarette with taking long pulls from his beer.

I sat naked on the floor, where I was allowed to remain longer and longer after our various sessions. Of course, the pine box remained in full view. I would sneak glances at it from time to time, as if contemplating a scary mask or coiled serpent. The object of my abject terror. And yet, from this vantage point, nothing more than a cheap wooden coffin.

I didn't answer right away. I was too engrossed in combing my fingers through the dirt-brown carpet, which turned out to be not one shade of shit brown but many.

He kicked my shoulder with his foot, demanding my attention. 'Tell me about your father.'

'Why?'

'What the fuck, why? I asked. You answer.' Another kick, this time to the side of my head. His thick yellow toenails were long and ragged; one sliced my cheek.

I didn't move away. By now, I knew it was pointless. Instead, I kept my gaze on the carpet. So many individual threads woven into one color pattern. Who would've thought? I wondered if it was difficult to make carpet. I wondered if I could pull out enough strands that it would be possible to choke myself with them.

'I don't remember him,' I said at last.

'When'd he die?'

'I was a baby.'

'What happened?'

'An accident. His truck rolled.'

'What was his name?'

I dug my torn fingernails deeper into the matted carpet. I could feel dust and dirt and small rocks. The fibers were so short, too short, really, to serve as much of a death weapon. Pity. And yet I still couldn't stop touching it. As far as entertainment went, dirt-brown carpet was as good as the room got.

I still didn't know where I was. A basement, I thought, because the only windows were set up high, and it always sounded as if someone was descending a staircase right before he barreled through the door.

I didn't think Florida had basements. Or not many. Did that mean I wasn't in Florida anymore? Maine had basements. Maybe he'd brought me all the way back to Maine. I was just down the street from my mother. If I could summon the strength, the energy, the good fortune to crawl up out one of those high windows, I could walk back to my mother's farm. And just like that, I'd be home again.

He kicked me again.

'Do you have a father?' I asked.

''Course.'

'Do you remember his name?'

'Nah. Too busy calling him Dickhead to learn the real thing. He was a trucker, though. Like me.'

'You're a trucker?' I couldn't help myself; I looked up in wonder, the discovery of personal information finally pulling my attention from the filthy floor.

He caught the look on my face and laughed. 'Well, shit, what'd you think I did in my spare time? Gotta work. Love nests don't come free.'

'Are we still in Florida?' I asked. 'Is it still spring break?'

He just laughed again, took another pull of beer. 'Gonna take off soon,' he offered conversationally. 'Big job this time. Could be gone as long as a week.'

The look he gave me was calculating. But I didn't consider that. I was too busy feeling the blood drain from my face. A week? Seven whole days? All alone in the box? My brain shut down. My bloody fingertips dug painfully into the carpet. A week?

'Molly,' he said. He wasn't smoking anymore. Instead,

the burning cigarette dangled from his fingers as he stared at me.

'What?'

'Your name is Molly. What's your name?'

I opened my mouth. I closed my mouth. I honestly didn't get it. Every muscle and bone in my body hurt. I wanted to escape the pain by going to sleep. Except I couldn't sleep. Because he was here, and I was out of the box, and the carpet contained half a dozen shades of shit brown, and this was as close to an experience as I was gonna get. Better than movies or video games or texting. The feel of grimy carpet beneath my fingertips. A real adventure park.

'What's your name?' *he commanded again.*

'Um. Molly?'

'Not like that. It's an answer, not a question. Come on now – what's your damn name?'

'Molly,' *I stated with more conviction, starting to catch on. So he wanted to call me Molly. Whatever. Molly, frankly, was hardly the worst thing that had happened to me.*

'Now. Your father's name?'

I paused. And for just one second . . .

It's Sunday afternoon. I'm all dressed up. I'm standing at my father's grave, holding my mother's hand while she cries silently, my brother standing stoically on her other side.

'He loved you kids,' my mother is saying, fingers tight around mine. 'He would be so proud . . .'

And just like that, I couldn't say the name. I could picture it engraved on the black granite marker, but I couldn't give it up. My daddy was nothing but a legend, a myth once told by my mother to me. But he was mine, and I had so little left.

The man kicked me again, back of the neck. I whispered:
'Edgar.'

In response he slammed his foot against me harder, this
time catching my ear. 'Liar.'

'I'm not—'

'Fucking idiot.' He waved his cigarette at me. I watched
the glowing end nervously. I knew what it could do. 'Your
father's name. I mean it!'

'Edgar,' I murmured again.

'Fucking liar!' he roared as he came off the sofa. 'Name,
name, name, give me the fucking name!'

'Molly, Molly, Molly,' I tried.

He whacked me on either side of the head as I cowered
with my face against the carpet. I thought, frantically,
crazily, I should pull out some of those brown threads.
Grab them between my fingers and twist. I could tuck them
behind my ears, take them with me back into the box. Oh,
the hours of entertainment ahead.

'Give me his fucking name!' the man was still screaming
at me. 'Last chance, girl! Or I walk out that door, and
you'll never see me again. Hell, you'll never see anyone
again. You're gone, don't you get it? You're just another
stupid drunk girl who disappeared on spring break. Think
anyone knows where you are? Think anyone cares?'

My mother, I thought. But I didn't say anything. I kept
her to myself. Just like my father's name, and my brother's
face.

'I'll stick you back in that box,' he was threatening now.
'I'll lock the lid and that'll be that. You'll die down here.
Rot away. Become just another stench in this room. And no
one will ever know. Your family will never see you again.
Never even identify your body.'

I was crying. He hit me harder. But it wasn't the beating

that had me undone. It was the thought of him locking me in the box and then taking off. Of me dying all alone in a coffin-size box.

Like my father rotting away beneath the earth.

When I was a little girl, I used to think my father could see everything. Like Santa Claus, or God, I suppose. My father wasn't a real dad at all but an all-knowing ghost, and I would look for him in the sunlight dappling through trees, in the shadows of the deep woods.

'Daddy,' I would whisper. And always, always, always, I knew he was there. Because, according to my mother, my father had always loved the forest.

Where I could not find him was in the stillness of a coffin-size box.

'Ernesto,' I whispered.

But the man was now too busy beating me furiously to hear.

I curled up tighter against the dirt-brown carpet. 'Edgar,' I shouted suddenly. 'Evan. Ernesto. Eli. Earl.' I made them up, quickly, frantically. Another game to pass the time. Names that begin with E.

Yelling the names again and again. Because the shit-brown carpet was composed of so many threads, and so was I, and I couldn't afford to give anything more away. There was too little of me left, and my father's name was part of that. A highly polished granite marker in the ground. A small but precious memory.

Eventually, the man wore himself out. He stopped beating and kicking, falling to the floor instead. He lay beside me, breath ragged from his exertions. We remained side by side in silence.

'Damn shame,' he said shortly.

I didn't respond.

'I mean, considerin' how nice I was planning on being and all. I mean, hell, taking you with me.'

I couldn't help myself. I stirred, shifting slightly against the grimy floor.

'A week in a big rig. Maybe it's not for everyone. I mean, I would definitely have to take the box, being your first outing and all. But still. You'd be on the road. Maybe I could let you out at night. You know, versus seven days shut up alone here. Maybe even eight, nine, ten days. A delivery takes as long as it takes. Man's gotta do his job.'

'Water?' I couldn't help myself. Seven days alone was terrifying enough, but a possible ten days without water? I'd never paid enough attention in science classes, but I was pretty sure no one could survive that long.

'All the more reason to join me on the road,' he informed me. 'All the more reason to give me a name.'

I lifted my head at last. I stared at him. His hard-lined face. His unshaved cheeks, his crooked tobacco-stained teeth. He was ugly and awful. He was powerful and divine, even more so than a ghost dad in the woods.

And I knew then, just as he no doubt knew all along, what I was going to say next.

'Everett. Everett Robert Dane.'

The man smiled at me.

'Now was that really so hard?' he asked me.

I didn't say a word.

He climbed off the floor, started rooting around on the coffee table.

'So. Time to write a note. I mean, as long as you're running off with me, don't you think you should at least tell your mother?'

13

D.D.'s Sunday morning began with a phone call. Walking into her office (no rest for the wicked, or for a homicide supervisor who'd just landed a major case), she was juggling coffee in one hand and her crossbody leather messenger bag in the other. She barely set down her travel mug in time to snag the receiver.

'Sergeant Detective D.D. Warren.'

'Is it true? Did that man take my daughter? Do you know what happened to her yet? For the love of God, why are we having to learn all this from the press? What kind of unfeeling monsters are you?'

D.D. slowed. She didn't recognize the voice, but could deduce from the level of anguish she was most likely talking to Stacey Summers's father. Given the beating Boston PD had taken in yesterday's news cycle – rumored suspect in college student's kidnapping found dead, Boston police refusing to discuss circumstances – she shouldn't be surprised. And yet still . . .

'Sir? With whom am I speaking?'

'Colin Summers. Who the hell do you think?'

'I'm sorry, but I have to ask the question. As I'm sure you've learned by now, the press isn't above resorting to tricks to get inside information.'

An angry sigh on the other end of the receiver, the sound of a man trying very hard to pull himself together. D.D. used the moment to set down her messenger bag, then pull out her chair and take a seat at her desk.

'Is it true?' Colin Summers whispered at last.

'At this time, we have no evidence linking Devon Goulding to your daughter's disappearance.'

'Stop. That's cop-speak for bullshit. This is my daughter we're talking about. Please just give me the truth.'

'Sir, I personally attended the crime scene. We've spent the better part of twenty-four hours tearing apart the Gouldings' house. I am telling you the truth: We've found nothing to link him to your daughter.'

'But in the news . . . They said he was a big guy. They said he matched the picture in the video . . .'

'That's true.'

'And he was a bartender. That could be the connection. Stacey was last seen at Birches downtown. He could've worked there.'

'We checked. Devon Goulding has no employment history with Birches.'

'But what if Stacey met him at the bar where he did work? Maybe he spotted her there. And he . . . liked her. That's how these things sometimes work, right? He took one look at her and she became his target.'

D.D. hesitated. Talking to grieving family members was her least favorite part of the job. It was tempting to answer all their questions. To soothe and to explain. But the truth was, her primary obligation wasn't to Colin Summers or his wife. It was to Stacey. And working a case was as much about safeguarding key details as it was about discovering new ones. She couldn't risk telling Mr Summers everything they knew about Devon Goulding. There'd been too many other occasions where the grieving father had shared valuable information with his wife or best friend, who inevitably shared it with another person, then another, until the next thing the police knew, everything they couldn't afford known about their ongoing investigation was now fodder for the evening news.

Most family members would tell you they'd do anything to help find their loved one. Unfortunately, for their sakes, what the investigating officer genuinely needed from them was restraint.

D.D. said: 'Did Stacey ever frequent Tonic bar?'

'I don't know. She wasn't a big drinker, or a big partier. But . . . she was social,' he conceded. 'If her friends wanted to go, she'd follow along.'

D.D. nodded. That was consistent with what they'd established up to this point. Yesterday afternoon, Phil had personally visited Devon Goulding's place of employment, Tonic, with a picture of Stacey Summers. Several bartenders recognized her from the news coverage of her case, but none could place her in the establishment. Of course, that didn't rule out Devon Goulding having crossed paths with her at a different time or at a different bar. Boston offered up a robust scene for the college crowd. The choices were endless.

Not to mention, given Goulding's abduction of Flora Dane, they couldn't argue that blondes weren't to his taste.

'Do you know Florence Dane?' she asked abruptly.

There was silence on the other end of the phone line. Silence that definitely went on several beats too long.

'Why do you ask?' Colin Summers spoke up at last.

'Has she been to your house? Has she met with you?'

'We met with her mother.'

'What?'

'When your child disappears . . . There's a program. Through the National Center for Missing and Exploited Children. Another parent, someone who's been there, calls to offer support. Rosa Dane was appointed as our mentor. Within the first twenty-four hours, she called, then stayed on the phone with my wife while she cried.'

'Have you personally met with her?'

'She's been to our house a couple of times. She's been very helpful, Sergeant. After what she went through . . . she understands. She listens and she helps. Which is more than we can say for the rest of you.'

D.D. winced at the man's bitterness, reminded herself again it was nothing personal. The family wanted answers. They wanted their daughter back. But to date the detectives could only provide more questions at best, and fresh suspicions at worst.

'And her daughter, Florence?' D.D. pressed again.

'I'm familiar with her case,' Colin Summers said, which was, in fact, no answer at all.

'She accompanied her mother on one of her visits,' D.D. stated.

'No.'

'Reached out via phone, e-mail, Facebook? You know her, don't you, Mr Summers? You've spoken to her personally about your daughter.'

'No.'

But D.D. didn't believe him anymore. There was something more here. Something he still wasn't willing to say. And then . . .

'Was she the one who killed him?' Colin Summers asked.

'Who?'

'Flora. Did she kill the bartender, the suspected kidnapper? Is that why you're asking all these questions?'

D.D. didn't say anything. So far, they'd managed to keep Florence Dane's name out of the news. Mostly by virtue of not having pressed any formal charges against her, meaning there wasn't any information for overeager reporters to discover.

'Why would you assume that, Mr Summers?'

'You investigators have your sources of information. The families of victims have ours. And given how likely you are to share with us . . .'

'We are all on the same side, Mr Summers. We're all doing everything in our power to get your daughter back.'

'Then why isn't she home?'

A click in her ear as Colin Summers hung up, clearly having gotten in the last word. D.D. held on to the phone receiver for a moment longer, feeling the weight of his rage. Indeed, three months later, why hadn't they found Stacey Summers?

And what the hell did Flora Dane know about the college girl's abduction that the rest of them apparently didn't?

Eight thirty A.M. D.D. had mounds of reports to sort through and approve, from the night-duty detectives on down. The joys of management, the burden of restricted duty. As a field detective, she'd always groused about the need to dot every i and cross every t. And yet reports mattered. Paperwork created the building blocks of a prosecutable case, and there was no point in identifying perpetrators and making arrests if you couldn't actually put the rat bastards away.

Paperwork mattered. Sitting here at this desk mattered.

Then again, so did asking the right questions.

What was it Dr Keynes had said yesterday? Flora preferred an honest, straightforward approach.

D.D. got up, retrieved her messenger bag, grabbed her travel mug, and headed out the door.

Florence Dane's registered address turned out to be a third-story walk-up in an older, slightly tired-looking row home. This time of morning on a Sunday, the house and street appeared quiet. D.D. walked through the unlocked outer door into the requisite inner vestibule lined with half a dozen metal mailboxes. Some were labeled with names; Flora's wasn't, instead providing only her initials, F.D. Another security-conscious decision from a woman who clearly took self-protection seriously.

The vestibule's inner door was locked but, as often happened in frequently trafficked areas, hadn't been pulled tightly shut. Flora definitely wouldn't have approved of D.D.'s ability to nudge open the door and walk straight in.

She could buzz up. It would be the polite thing to do, but where was the fun in that? Instead, D.D. spied the stairs straight ahead and made the executive decision to hike up three floors to Florence's apartment. Of course, she hadn't counted on her breath growing quite so labored – maybe it was time to cut back the hours in PT and work in some cardio instead – nor was she expecting to arrive at Flora's door and discover it cracked open.

D.D. hesitated, already feeling the hairs rise on the back of her neck. At first blush, there was no need for alarm. The door looked perfectly fine, no scratches on the locks as if they were jimmied, no shredded doorjamb. And yet . . .

She rapped hard. The door yawned wide.

'Flora Dane? Sergeant Detective D.D. Warren here to see you.'

No response.

D.D. took the first step forward, reaching instinctively

for her sidearm before remembering she still wasn't authorized to carry.

'Flora? You home? Florence Dane?'

Nothing. Not the sound of footsteps or rushing water or creaking inner doorways. D.D. took another step inside, encountering a kitchen dead ahead, tiny family room to the left, and another open doorway that provided a glimpse of a bedroom beyond it.

Lights were off. Granted, daylight streamed through the large bank of bay windows. But the sky was overcast, meaning corners of the apartment were still cast in gloom, giving the place a neglected feel. More than that, however, the apartment *felt* empty. For whatever reason, the front door had been left open, but Florence was no longer here.

Which made no sense at all. A woman who made studying criminal behavior her bread and butter leaving her apartment unsecured in downtown Boston? No way. Something was up. But what?

Slowly, keeping her back to the wall, D.D. made the rounds. Except, in the end, there wasn't much to see. The kitchen appeared immaculate, the modest seating area untouched. She used her toe to push in the bathroom door, taking in a pedestal sink, toilet, and standing-room-only shower. Nothing.

Finally, the single bedroom. Again, using her foot to open the door wider, careful not to touch anything. She spied a double bed, covers pulled back and obviously recently slept in. Next to it was a single nightstand table bearing a lamp and a charging iPhone. Which gave her pause. Because in this day and age, who stepped out for even the briefest errand without first grabbing her cell phone?

Next, D.D. eyed a rickety old desk, which bore a state-of-the-art Mac laptop. Finally, she let her gaze take in the room's main attraction: Newspaper articles. Photographs. Dozens of them plastered across all four walls. It took her only a moment to deduce the theme. Missing persons cases. Each and every one. Thirty, forty, fifty people, male and female, who'd stepped outside one day, never to be seen again. Including Stacey Summers, the *Boston Globe* article announcing her disappearance posted in a place of honor right above Flora's bed.

Definitely, Flora had been following the case. And now?

D.D. circled in place, taking in the full weight of one survivor's obsession. And she suddenly had a very bad feeling about things.

14

When I was little, I had a hard time falling asleep. I would spend my days running wild across the fields of my family's farm and through the dark Maine woods. And yet no matter how often my mom ordered me outside to 'burn it off', come nightfall I'd lie in bed with a spinning brain and twitchy legs.

My mother developed an elaborate bedtime ritual to help wind me down. First, she'd place both hands on the top of my head. She'd gently stroke my hair: 'This is Flora's head.'

Then she'd move her fingers down, trace the shape of my eyebrow, the curve of my ears, the line of my jaw. 'These are Flora's eyes, cheeks, ears, face. This is Flora's face.'

Next, she'd squeeze both my shoulders, not too hard, but firm. 'These are Flora's shoulders.'

More squeezing, of both elbows, my wrists, all five fingers of each hand. Compression, I later learned. My mother was practicing a basic therapy often used for hyperactive children. Basically, a joint-by-joint bear hug, as she squeezed my ribs, pressed against the sockets of my hips, then finished with my knees, ankles, feet.

'This is Flora's leg, Flora's knee, Flora's ankle. This is Flora's foot. And now, it's time for all of Flora to *GET SOME SLEEP*.'

When I was little, I would giggle at the end. And of course, I would beg her to do it again. Sometimes she would. But mostly, I got a peck on a cheek, maybe an affectionate tousle of my hair. Then my mother was up and out, a busy single mom with many worries to tend and chores to complete.

By the time I turned ten, eleven, twelve, the ritual died a natural death. Another stage from childhood passed through. Sometimes, when I was sick or feeling blue, my mother would return again. A quicker, abbreviated version, but just as comforting.

Once I hit high school, my mother teased it was now my turn to tuck her into bed. Being someone who regularly started her day at five, she certainly didn't stay up much past nine or ten. Sometimes, if I was feeling mischievous, or maybe just missed her, I would show up and make a big production of it. This is Mom's hair, this is Mom's eye. Oh my God, what happened to Mom's face?

If my brother was home, he might even join us. Holy crap, is that really Mom's hand?

Before long, the three of us would have collapsed with a fit of giggles, my mother at the bottom of the pile, shaking her head. Moments of a family. The kind of thing that somewhere in your heart you know is special, and yet you can't help but take for granted.

After I was found, my mother arrived at the Atlanta hospital. That first night, she touched my hair. Traced the line of my brow. Followed the curve of my ear. 'This is Flora's face,' she whispered to me.

I didn't look at her. I kept my eyes open, my gaze fixed on the ceiling. I didn't have the heart to tell her that her hands felt like sandpaper against my skin. And that, far from soothing me, I wished desperately, with every fiber in my being, that she'd just stop.

And yet in the weeks and months to come, on the very bad nights when I woke up screaming again and again, and my brother hovered uncomfortably in the doorway, my mother would take her place on the edge of my bed. She'd once again trace my cheekbones, squeeze my shoulders, compress the joint of my elbows, wrists, all five fingers of each hand.

Slowly but surely, my patient mother would help me find slumber again.

I am asleep now.

But it is wrong, bad.

I need to wake up. I have a sense of urgency, dread. A bad dream. I'm having a bad dream and I need to wake up now. Scream, yell, thrash. Then my eyes will pop open. I will find myself back in my own bed. My mother will be beside me, rubbing my temples even as I flinch. I'm moving. I shouldn't be moving.

Wake up, Flora. Wake up!

I try. I will my eyelids to roll up. I order my limbs to jerk to life.

Nothing happens. I can't move, I can't see. I can't find my way back to the safety of my locked apartment or my childhood bed.

A mist. I feel it, cool against my cheeks. I inhale instinctively, wrinkling my nose at the smell.

And then . . .

I am rushing away into the dark. My mother disappears from view, and even if her touch feels like sandpaper, even if I'm the one who constantly pushes her away, I still wish I could call her back.

I need to tell her something.

I need to say I'm sorry.

Wake up, Flora. Wake up!

But I can't.
I'm moving.
I shouldn't be moving.
I am in trouble.

15

Flora's cell phone was password protected. No surprises there. Instead, D.D. used her own phone to make the call. Boston FBI field office. Requesting one Dr Samuel Keynes. It took another three minutes for the operator to take her seriously enough to track down a federal employee on a Sunday. One more minute for Keynes to return her call. From there, however, the rest was a matter of seconds. Yes, he'd returned Flora to her apartment on Saturday. And no, she would never leave her apartment unlocked. He'd be right over.

Which didn't surprise D.D. at all. She didn't know much about victim specialists and their interactions with their charges, but it already had struck her that Keynes and Flora had an unusually close relationship.

D.D. had just finished conducting a visual tour of the outside of the apartment, as well as an inspection of the fire escape, when Keynes pulled up.

Keynes was wearing the same knee-length, double-breasted cashmere coat as the day before. How he'd gotten it dry-cleaned so fast, she'd never know, but it didn't contain the faintest whiff of human barbecue or rancid garbage. Maybe he'd simply willed the odor away. Walking up to the building now, shoulders set, gaze direct, he had that look about him: the kind of guy who could take over the world through sheer presence alone.

He also appeared grim.

'When did you arrive?' he asked.

'Thirty minutes ago. When you dropped Flora off yesterday, did you go inside?'

'No. Her mom was already here. I spotted her truck parked down the street. Flora headed upstairs to see her.'

'Has Flora contacted you since? Phone, text, Facebook post?'

He shook his head. 'Sign of forced entry?' He headed up the stairs, already on his way to the third-story unit.

'Negative. Fire escape also appears clear, but get this: That door is also unlocked. The bolt's been undone. Same with all the windows. Each and every one of them may still be closed, but they're unsecured.'

'Sounds like a message.' He was frowning.

'My thought exactly. But from her, or about her?'

Topping the stairs, Keynes strode straight inside the apartment, clearly familiar with the layout. He glanced around only briefly, then stated, 'Definitely, her mother was here.'

'What makes you say that?'

'Rosa cleans when under stress. The kitchen – that's her doing.'

'And Florence?'

'More relaxed in her housekeeping standards, prone to clutter.'

'So you dropped her off yesterday. She came upstairs to her mother. And then?'

Keynes produced his phone from his coat pocket. He hit a number while still walking around the gray-lit space.

'Rosa. Dr Keynes. How are you? I'm fine, thanks for

asking. You spent some time with Flora yesterday, didn't you? I thought I saw your truck parked down the street. Exactly. I understand. I know. Her behavior does appear to be escalating. Yes, thank heavens she was all right. Her staying at the farm is an old argument, Rosa. You know I can't intervene, not that it would make a difference with Florence anyway. Did you speak to Flora again last night? Maybe before bedtime? You called, but she didn't answer. Thank you. I'll do my best to follow up with her today. But of course. Pleasure to speak with you again. 'Bye.'

Keynes pocketed his phone, once again frowned. 'Florence's mother left her shortly after one yesterday. She hasn't heard from Flora since.'

'That unusual?'

'Not necessarily. But the unlocked apartment is.' He walked into the bedroom, glanced at the plastered walls but didn't seem surprised by the onslaught of articles. Instead, he headed for Flora's phone.

'Password protected,' he observed. 'So no way of checking the messages immediately. It's possible she headed out to meet someone.'

'And left her front door open behind her?'

'No sign of forced entrance. Or signs of a struggle. Given Flora's training, if someone had tried to grab her, she wouldn't have gone down without a fight.'

'Unless she was ambushed. Maybe while she was sleeping.' D.D. gestured to the bed, which bore the only signs of disturbance in the whole place.

'But how would the attacker gain entrance? Flora would've definitely checked the locks before heading to bed.'

D.D. sighed. That was the piece of the puzzle that kept stumping her as well. She'd only just met Florence Dane yesterday, but she already knew enough to know the girl was hardly foolish about these things.

'Let's check with the landlords,' Keynes decided. 'Maybe they heard something.'

The landlords turned out to be an elderly couple, Mary and James Reichter, who'd owned the residence for the past fifty-two years and lived in the first-floor unit. They recognized Keynes from other visits, and greeted D.D. with beaming smiles that made her feel like she should've come bearing some kind of housewarming gift.

She and Keynes politely declined their offer of coffee, but still found themselves ushered into the front parlor, which bore an antique love seat and enough original oak trim to make D.D. salivate.

She perched tentatively on the edge of the delicate sofa, letting Keynes take the lead with the questions as he seemed to know the couple.

It took some loud, if not downright shouted, inquiries to determine the Reichters had seen Flora return home yesterday, sometime around midmorning. Her mother had already arrived by then, showing up again after lunch with some blueberry muffins to share. Excellent, excellent muffins. Rosa was an exquisite baker.

Oh yes, Flora. No, they did not remember seeing her again. But then, they'd been watching their shows in the back of the unit. So she could've gone out. Possible. Was anything wrong? Something they should know?

Keynes trod carefully. He had a delicate touch with the couple, D.D. observed. More neighborly than official and yet at the same time keeping just enough reserve to have them striving to answer his questions.

Had they seen anyone else enter the building yesterday? Say, a stranger, someone they didn't recognize?

No.

What about sounds, or commotions? Maybe a disturbance in the middle of the night?

No, sir. And they would be woken up by such a thing. Didn't sleep so well these days.

What about new friends or acquaintances they'd recently seen with Flora? Or any inquiries about her apartment?

Well, except for the building inspector . . .

D.D. and Keynes both drew up, exchanged a glance.

'Building inspector?' D.D. spoke up.

'Day before. Or maybe the day before the day before. Time gets a little confusing,' James began, looking at his wife.

'Tuesday,' his wife provided. 'The building inspector came on Tuesday. Said our place was overdue for review. All private rental units have to be inspected by the city every five years, you know. Why, it's been ages since anyone's visited us. Guess we really do lose track of time!'

'You showed him around the entire building? All the units?' Keynes asked.

'James showed him around the outside, the fire escape. But inside the units, well, navigating the stairs at our age . . .' Mary smiled apologetically. 'We gave him keys to the units. Asked him to please knock first to alert the renters. He wasn't gone long at all. Did his thing, then came down to tell us all looked well. We'd get our updated certificate shortly.'

'Wait,' D.D. interjected. 'You have keys to all the units? Even Flora Dane's apartment?'

James seemed insulted by her tone. 'Of course. This is still our house. We are entitled to access. Plus, for the sake of maintenance or, heaven forbid, something like a fire. Our renters, they're very busy. It's easier if we can just go in, do what needs to be done when it needs to be done. We've never had any complaints or problems, not even from Flora. We respect her privacy, of course. We understand.'

The way he said the last word implied enough. That they knew Flora's history, and were familiar with why she felt a need for extra security.

'Was Flora home for the building inspection?' D.D. asked.

'I don't know, dear,' Mary answered.

'Did you tell her about the inspection? Mention it when you saw her again?'

'No, I don't believe we've run into her since it happened.'

'What did the building inspector look like?' Keynes asked.

'Oh, he was a nice-looking young man. Dressed a little casual for my tastes – tan slacks, a blue dress shirt, but then no one wears suits anymore. He had ID. I'm not naive, you know. I did make him show it.'

'What about his size?' D.D. spoke up more softly. 'Big guy? Small? Young, old?'

'Oh, he was very official-looking. Clean-shaven. Short dark hair. And big. Strong. Like a fireman. He looked like a very capable young man.' Mary smiled brightly.

A big man. A strong man. Who'd been handed over the keys to Flora's apartment by her well-intentioned landlords. D.D. looked over at Keynes. Could tell from the expression on his face he'd just connected the same dots she had. Such as, all the best locks in the world couldn't offer protection against a man with a key. Flora took pride in her preparations. And yet, if their suspicions were correct, her attacker had already been one step ahead.

Keynes rose to standing, offering his hand, finalizing their departure.

Out in the foyer, phone in hand, it only took D.D. a matter of minutes to confirm what both she and Keynes already knew: Boston's Inspectional Services Department hadn't sent anyone to this building in the past few days, let alone had anything scheduled for anytime soon. The building-inspector guise had been a ruse, a very effective means of gaining access to Flora's keys in order to make a master copy.

'I'll call the crime scene techs,' D.D. said quietly.

They headed back upstairs to wait in silence.

16

I'm awake.

My head jerks up, my eyes pop open, but I'm immediately disoriented by the fact I can't see. Black. Thick and impenetrable. I feel a sense of urgency. Fight or flight. I gotta fight. Except . . .

I can't see. Not at all. Up, down, left, right, I have no idea. I bulge my eyes as if that will make a difference.

Then it comes to me.

I'm in a room. I'm sprawled upon a bare mattress, wearing some kind of silky nightgown. My arms are bare, and cool metal bracelets encircle both my wrists. Handcuffs. I've been handcuffed, arms in front, hands at my waist. Furthermore, the manacles appear attached to a lead line of some sort, maybe rope, maybe chain. But I only have to give the slightest tug with my wrists to feel the corresponding resistance. I'm not just bound; I'm tethered to the ceiling, or a high spot on the wall.

As for the dark . . . I blink my eyes. Nothing. I try again. Still nothing. My eyes are open. There's no blindfold around my head. It's the room itself. Windowless and, most likely, painted pitch-black, until not a single ray of ambient light can penetrate the gloom.

I wonder if I'm underground, and despite my best

intentions, my heart rate accelerates, my breath growing ragged. Not underground. Not buried, please, please, please.

And for a moment, a split instant of time, other images come to me. Scenes from the past, another lifetime, another nightmare ago. I want to yell, scream, and beg. Bang my fists against wooden walls, kick my heels wildly.

Lying on the mattress, shivering uncontrollably, I dig my teeth into my lower lip, then ground myself with the pain. There will be no panic. There will be no pleading. So stuff it.

It takes a few deep breaths. The taste of my own blood against my tongue. But bit by bit, I feel my heart once again settle in my chest. Then, I close my eyes, because whether it's logical or not, it makes the dark easier to take.

Slowly, it comes to me. My last memory: waking up in my own bedroom, the sinister shadow in the doorway, then a mist in the air.

Chloroform, I'm guessing. Or some other aerosolized sedative. I was drugged and then . . .

A sense of movement. I wanted to wake up, but I couldn't.

I was brought here. Wherever here is.

Immediately, I'm dismayed. Not for myself. Instead, I see my mother's face. The mother who baked me muffins and hugged me hard and begged me to take better care of myself. She loves me so much. And now I've gone, and broken her heart yet again.

Because I'm already pretty certain that whoever broke through three locks to get into my security-tight apartment – let alone prepared this room, complete with chained manacles – is more than your average bear. This isn't me versus the arrogant loser I burned to death in his own garage, or even the amateur acts who preceded him. This is . . . something worse. Something more.

Someone to fear.

And I wish, for just one moment, I'd been brave enough to tell Dr Keynes everything that happened five years ago. But there are secrets all survivors keep. Most likely, I'm about to pay for mine.

Just like Stacey Summers did.

I fall asleep. I don't want to, but I can't seem to help myself. The residue of the drugs, maybe even habit forged years ago when I also spent hours, days, weeks at a time with nothing better to do. Fight or flight, except, being all trussed up on a bare mattress, I can't do either. So sleep becomes a flight of sorts, a temporary reprieve for my overworked limbic system, which can't figure out what else to do. So much adrenaline, stress, and fear with no place to go, nothing to do but wait.

Wait, wait, wait.

Wishing my eyes would grow accustomed to the dark. Wishing for any sort of ease in the relentless tar-black gloom. After a while, I give up on sight and focus on touch instead. Moving tentatively, I dance my fingers across the mattress. Identify its size, standard twin. Feel the welting of the edges, become aware of a faint odor of mildew. It's thin beneath me. Most likely old and tattered. Maybe even tossed on a street corner, then harvested by my host for just this purpose.

It's not particularly comfortable or soft or soothing. But I like the mattress. It's a source of thread and stuffing, maybe even wire coils. It's a tool, and I'll take it.

Next, I explore the garment now draped over my body. I'd gone to bed in an old T-shirt and men's flannel boxers.

Now I'm wearing some kind of short satin negligee. Lace trim around the neckline and bottom hem.

He changed my clothes. While I was unconscious, he'd stripped off my comfortable nightwear and replaced it with a more feminine – sexy? – counterpart. I'm tempted to feel insulted and violated by this act, but mostly I'm confused.

Most sexual sadist predators keep their victims naked – easy access, further degradation, take your pick. Or they might clad their unwilling prey in various S&M outfits/ gadgets that fit their masochistic fantasies. But this, a silk nightie, speaks to something else. It's – attentive in a way I already have a feeling I won't like.

Jacob rarely gifted me with pretty nightgowns or anything more than practical clothes. I was a possession, and who wastes extra effort on their coffee table?

This man, the newest predator, is a freak. I repeat the word in my head. Try to feel it forcefully. A freak, a mutant, an aberration. Something less than human. Nothing worth worrying about.

But I'm lying to myself. Because already I can feel the metal handcuffs cutting into my skin. And when I tug on my wrists to make my arms more comfortable, I'm terribly aware of the sound of a tethering chain unspooling from above.

Enough. I sit up. Swing my legs over the edge of the mattress on the floor. Remind myself this is already more freedom than I had with Jacob. Wow, a whole room at my disposal. I might just get giddy with the rush.

The dark is still endless, oppressive. I can barely make out the lighter shadow of my bare arms as I take the first tentative step forward. One step, two, three, four. The room is bigger than I expected; I still haven't come to a wall.

Then my foot connects with substance. A rattling sound as a plastic container tips over.

I reach down and explore with my fingers, but I already know what I've found. A plastic bucket. The latrine of choice for kidnappers and sadists everywhere. But of course.

Behind the bucket I discover a wall. Drywall. It surprises me. For some reason, I'd been expecting cinder block or maybe cheap wood paneling. But no. The wall is smooth and bare. Drywall, as in a real room of a real house. Which would also explain the thin carpet padding my bare feet.

If I really am in a house . . .

I halt, strain my ears. Trying to get a sense of traffic outside, or maybe the distant sound of footsteps echoing overhead. At first, I hear nothing at all. Soundproofing, to go with the blackout paint job. But then, faintly, steadily, it comes to me.

Breathing. In. Out. In. Out.

There is someone else in the room with me. I'm not alone.

I recoil. I can't help myself. Then, instinctively, I grab the empty plastic bucket and clutch it to my chest. As what? A hammer or a shield?

I'm not thinking anymore. I want to. But for all my experience, training, and bravado, my heart rate has once again climbed and I'm shaking uncontrollably on my feet.

While across the room, maybe five, six feet from me . . .

Breathing.

In. Out. In. Out.

He's here. Watching me. Waiting for me to panic, freak out, beg for mercy? Or just enjoying the show?

Just like that, I'm angry. I don't care what he does or what he thinks he can do to me. Compared to Jacob Ness,

Mr Silky Nightgown, Mr Breathing Heavy, is nothing but a carnival sideshow. A Freak.

Just because he broke into my triple-locked apartment, ambushed me with drugs, and spirited me away to some blacked-out dungeon . . . I refuse to be afraid of him.

Instead, I'm thinking of my first visit with Samuel, the day after I got out of the hospital:

'Do you remember what you did to survive, Flora? Every rebellion, every submission, every lie, every adaptation?'

My own slow nod.

'Good. Don't forget. Don't second-guess. Accept. It may not feel like it right now, but you're strong, Flora. You survived. Don't let anyone take that from you. And don't take it from yourself. You're a tough girl. Four hundred and seventy-two days later, you saved yourself. Based on that alone, you never need to feel frightened again.'

I set down the bucket. I focus on the sound of his even breathing. Slowly but surely, I match it to my own until I inhale as he inhales, then exhale as he exhales. In. Out. In. Out. We are breath for breath, perfectly pitched.

And I understand already, in this introductory battle of wills, the person who speaks first loses.

He'll move. I'm certain of it. No one goes to this much trouble just to watch. So I fix my gaze in the direction of his breathing, and I stare as hard and defiantly as I can. Come on, freak. Show me what you got.

In. Out. In. Out. I've never heard such even breathing. Without the slightest quickening from excitement, or a missed beat from shock. Just in, out, in, out. As if he really doesn't care that I'm upright and staring straight at him.

As if he really is that much in control.

With all the time in the world . . .

My own breathing hitches. I don't mean to. Hate to give

him the satisfaction. But the steady, even beat is getting to me. No one breathes that regularly. No one, in this situation, can possibly keep that calm.

Then, suddenly . . . a dawning realization. A slowly shuddering fear.

No, I don't want. Please not . . .

I can't help myself. Having had the thought, now I must know. Shuffling forward. One step, two, three, four.

My toe hits it first. I stop. Freeze in my tracks and focus my ears once again.

Breathing. Much closer now. But just as steady. In. Out. In. Out.

I extend my arms. Order myself to be strong. Remind myself I've already been through the worst; I can handle anything.

Still, as my fingers encounter the first wooden edge of the coffin-shaped box . . .

While from inside comes the continued sound of the occupant's steady breath. In. Out. In. Out. Sleeping, because what else is there to do when trapped in a dark wooden box?

I close my eyes. It doesn't help. I can still hear her breathing. My fellow abductee, his prior victim. In. Out. In. Out.

Oh no. Oh no, oh no, oh no.

'I am not afraid,' I hear myself whisper.

But in my mind, I can see Jacob, and he is laughing again.

17

Newbie detective Carol Manley was the first to arrive at Flora's apartment. But if she seemed surprised to discover her supervisor actually on site, she did a good job of disguising it. Phil and Neil followed shortly after, and then the party really got started.

District detectives were assigned to canvass the neighborhood and interview available residents for any possible witnesses to Flora Dane's recent comings and goings, while a sketch artist would be sent to visit the landlords. Carol volunteered to pull security video from the corner store, as well as peruse local traffic cams for any sighting of Flora. Given the volume of footage, however, they needed to narrow down the timeline of Flora's disappearance in order to be more efficient.

Phil did the honors of searching her computer, while Neil placed a call to the girl's cellular provider and credit card companies. Unfortunately, Flora's network browser didn't show any activity for the past thirty-six hours – since shortly before she headed out for her ill-fated adventure with the predatory bartender. Her cell registered only a single call from her mom the evening before, while her credit card hadn't been used in a week. Frugal of her, but not helpful for moments like this.

D.D. prowled the tiny apartment, feeling restless. Keynes was tucked in a corner, mobile phone pressed against his ear. He'd agreed to fill in the mom, not a job D.D. envied.

Like most major cities, Boston had electronic eyes everywhere. From business cams to traffic cams to ATM cams, every street, every corner, yielded possible surveillance opportunities. In theory, this should produce a bonanza of information for investigators. Except that was exactly the problem. There was too much footage, and much of it low-quality resolution. Meaning security footage worked best when used backward – first formulate what you think there is to see, at what time it most likely happened, and then go look for it.

So what exactly went down in this security-tight apartment? Yesterday, late morning, Dr Keynes dropped off Flora outside. Her mother was already upstairs, had made muffins. She fed them to her daughter; they caught up briefly. So, Mom, about last night . . . How did such a conversation go? And what did Rosa Dane think of her daughter's late-night escapades?

D.D. stood in the kitchen. She pictured herself as the mom, baking muffins. She pictured Flora walking through the door, clad in second-hand Boston PD sweats and covered in garbage. She remembered the smell that had coated her own skin from the crime scene, then, with a short nod, headed for the bathroom.

Sure enough, on the back of the door hung a bath towel, still damp. She removed the lid from the wicker clothes hamper tucked in the corner and immediately wrinkled her nose at the stench. Garbage-scented Boston PD sweats. Check.

So among Flora's first order of business upon returning home would've been to clean up. And then?

Girl had been up twenty-four hours at that point. She would've been tired, as well as hungry. According to witness statements, she'd been drinking at the bar, not eating.

D.D. was biased on the subject, but given a choice between eating and sleeping, she'd go with eating any day of the week. Especially given that Flora's mother would've been waiting for her in the kitchen, with the scent of home-made muffins wafting in the air.

Following that instinct, D.D. returned to the kitchen. This time, she discovered a gallon-size freezer bag tucked in the corner containing six blueberry muffins. The leftovers, she would guess. And they still looked delicious.

Next, she checked the refrigerator, where she discovered a brand-new jug of orange juice and bowl of recently cut-up fruit. Edges of the apples were just starting to brown, so she was willing to bet they came from yesterday's snack with the mom as well.

As for other contents . . . She pulled out some takeout containers, sniffed experimentally, recoiled. Best she could tell, Flora had one edible meal in her whole kitchen, and that was the food supplied by Mom. Which meant?

'She never ate dinner,' D.D. stated out loud.

'Pardon?' Dr Keynes had come up behind her. He still wore his coat, though it was now unbuttoned. How he didn't sweat, given the stuffy confines of the small space, she'd never know.

'Yesterday. Flora returned home, showered, ate with her mom a late breakfast, early lunch—'

'Brunch?'

'Sure. Muffins and fruit. Brunch. But that was it. I mean unless she went out. Which, given the lack of credit card activity, let alone her own state of mind . . .'

'She would've rested. Post-adrenaline crash.'

'Okay. But she ate with her mom, what, one or two in the afternoon?'

'Rosa confirmed she left shortly after one.'

'So most likely she would've lain down for a nap. Too early in the day to go to bed, bed.'

Keynes shrugged one shoulder. 'Given the large windows, the overall brightness of the space, I suspect she would retire to her room to rest.'

'You mean the shrine to kidnapping victims everywhere?'

Another elegant shrug. He turned and headed for Flora's bedroom. D.D. followed behind him.

Like the rest of the apartment, the room was small. The newspaper articles plastered all over the walls offered its main distinction. Otherwise just the modest desk and the rumpled bed, which definitely appeared to have been slept in.

D.D. pushed by Keynes's larger build, which nearly filled the narrow space, to cross to the bed. She leaned over the thin pillow, sniffed experimentally. When she looked up again, she spotted Keynes studying her.

'Searching for chloroform,' she provided. 'It has a distinct smell, which takes a bit to fade. Might be traces on the pillow. Or maybe that's just my imagination.'

'He would have to have subdued her quickly,' Keynes said. 'Otherwise, given Flora's training . . . Where are the signs of a struggle?'

He had a point there. The apartment appeared relatively untouched, one of the more unsettling things about the situation. And indeed, given what Flora was capable of . . .

'He had already made a key for the locks. It's possible he was already inside, waiting for her.'

'Not likely. Rosa was here for several hours before Flora

returned home. When Rosa is anxious, she doesn't just cook, she cleans.'

'And if she was puttering around, tidying up this small space,' D.D. filled in, 'where could an intruder hide that she wouldn't have seen?'

'Exactly.'

D.D. nodded, following the train of logic. 'All right. So first Rosa arrives at the apartment. Lets herself in, does her thing. Then you drop off Flora. Mom and daughter catch up, exchange words . . . ?'

She eyed Keynes expectantly. But he refused to take the bait. Apparently, he either didn't know what Rosa had said to her daughter – which D.D. didn't believe for a minute – or he didn't feel it was relevant to the investigation.

'Mom departs shortly after one. At which point, we know Flora *didn't* make any calls and *didn't* use her computer or credit cards. Which leaves us with?'

'She took a nap.'

D.D. liked it. Certainly, in her experience, unconsciousness was about the only thing that kept a younger person from his or her electronics.

'When she woke up,' she said, gazing at the rumpled bed, 'he was here. Already in the room. Already standing over her.'

'Because this is where he chloroformed her,' Keynes said.

'Yeah. And she never ate again. I mean, up all night, then returning to muffins and fruit . . . I gotta say, first thing upon waking, I would've been famished.'

'I'm told you're a woman who appreciates an all-you-can-eat buffet.'

'Checking up on me, Shrink Man? You've been told correctly.'

Keynes ignored her sarcasm, staying focused on the

matter at hand. 'He already had a key made. Meaning he could enter the apartment at any time.'

D.D. shook her head. 'He wouldn't go after her in daytime. Come on, the kind of guy who takes the time to copy a key is the kind of guy who does his homework. Given Flora's rap sheet—'

'Not a matter of public record.'

'He would've done some digging. That whole ruse, posing as a building inspector? This guy has patience. He would've taken proper precautions to abduct a target as high risk as Flora. Not to mention, this is a third-floor walk-up unit. She puts up a fight, the other occupants would come out to the stairwell to discover what's going on.'

D.D. paused, considered the matter. 'He needs it to be dark,' she reiterated. 'Otherwise, he's too exposed. Think about it. He can't use a rickety metal fire escape without calling attention to himself, meaning he had to have used the main stairs, just like the rest of us.'

'Does the building have a camera?'

'Former residential home? We're not that lucky. But consider his options. He knows he can get into the apartment. He's planning on ambushing Flora, rendering her unconscious, which means he then has to carry her out. Carrying an unconscious body down three flights of stairs is pretty noticeable. So he'd pick a time after dark. When most residents wouldn't be coming or going.'

'He watched the apartment. Got to know the routines.'

'Consistent with someone patient enough to scam himself a set of keys.'

'He'd also be watching Flora. Getting to know her routines,' Keynes provided.

D.D. nodded. She pushed her way back into the main living area, where she crossed to one of the front-facing windows. She drew back the filmy curtains Flora seemed to favour – the kind of gauzy affair that offered some privacy while also still permitting plenty of light – and peered out onto the street. 'We should investigate vantage points,' she murmured. 'Maybe even a new tenant in the surrounding area. If our theory is correct, our guy would've had to have been hanging out for a while in order to learn everything he needed to learn.'

'Permit parking,' Keynes commented.

D.D. nodded, having noticed the signs earlier. Meaning parking on these streets was restricted to locals, who had to prove residency in order to gain a parking pass. Those who parked without one risked being ticketed. Something else to have a local detective check out. Because their suspect definitely would've parked close in order to escape with an unconscious woman. Meaning if he didn't have the proper permits, they might find a trace of a parking ticket.

'Does Flora have a car?' she asked Keynes, as it was possible the kidnapper had stolen Flora's own vehicle for transport.

'No.'

'All right. So we're talking early nightfall. Not so late that Flora had woken up and eaten dinner, but not so early that it was still light out. Say, five thirty, six.'

'Seems like a high-traffic hour,' Keynes observed. 'Risks the other residents coming and going from work.'

'Unless that's how he does it.' D.D. paused, the idea grabbing hold. 'Social engineering. That's his thing, right? Pretend to be a building inspector in order to get a key. Maybe he dressed up for yesterday's event as well. Boyfriend? Taxi driver?'

'Escorting an unconscious woman from her apartment?' Keynes raised an eyebrow.

'EMT. Home health worker.' She glanced at him. 'Local cop? An occupation that could easily explain the situation, assuming he was noticed. Then, he'd simply brazen his way through. Walk straight down the stairs, with his drunk or sick or groggy female companion. In a neighborhood as high traffic as this one, simply acting as if you belong is half the battle.'

Keynes nodded. 'Officers should canvass for neighbors who were out and about yesterday around dusk. See if anyone noticed a particularly large guy who appeared to be assisting an impaired woman. Maybe an official worker of some kind who blatantly stood out.'

'A particularly large guy, just like Stacey Summers's kidnapper.' D.D. glanced at him. 'Did you know Flora's mom is a mentor for Stacey's parents?'

'Rosa mentioned it.'

'Flora seems to have taken an interest in the case as well.'

'As you can tell from the bedroom wall, Flora is interested in a good many cases.'

'But she's looking for Stacey Summers's abductor in particular. The way she spoke at the crime scene yesterday . . . That's who she was hoping to discover at the bar. And immediately, she drew a connection between that case and her own attacker.'

'Do you know why she does it?' Keynes asked softly. 'Why Flora continues to put herself in dangerous situations?'

D.D. shrugged. 'Adrenaline rush. Post-traumatic stress. Some God syndrome where she enjoys reveling in her own power after four hundred plus days of feeling powerless.'

'I don't know,' Keynes said, which surprised her. 'I doubt Flora knows why she's doing what she's doing either. Or, at least, can put her finger on one particular stressor. Who she reminds me of is a soldier who returns home from her tour of duty, only to re-up again and then again. At the end of the day, real life feels too alien, while knowing the war is still going on, that she has brothers out there still fighting . . .'

'Is that what those articles are?' D.D. asked. 'Her brothers-in-arms? The missing people she can't leave behind?'

'Maybe.'

'Do you think there's a connection between Flora's disappearance and Stacey Summers's kidnapping?'

Keynes didn't answer as much as he hesitated. D.D. did a little double take, letting the curtain drop and stepping away from the window.

'You do, don't you?'

'When Flora's landlady, Mrs Reichter, described the "building inspector", my first thought was the Stacey Summers abduction video. Not to mention, three months later, there are no leads, no additional witness statements, no new information in that case. You have to admit, it takes a particular kind of predator to pull that off.'

'You mean such as the kind of guy who would pose as a building inspector to copy a set of keys?'

'The idea crossed my mind. Plus, the front door of Flora's apartment being left open, all the windows unlocked. It feels to me, whoever did this – he's showing off. Bragging even. Which would make sense if this isn't the first time he's gotten away with something.'

D.D. arched a brow. She didn't know exactly what to make of Keynes's suspicions. Even if he was onto something, given how little they knew about Stacey Summers's disappearance, linking Flora's case to hers hardly helped them. What they needed was a detailed sketch provided by the elderly landlords downstairs. Then, they needed half a dozen witness statements tracking the perpetrator's trek through the neighborhood, plus a parking ticket issued to the evildoer's personal vehicle. Short of that . . .

D.D. turned toward the window again. 'Is it possible we have it all wrong? Flora wasn't kidnapped at all but simply broke under the stress of the past twenty-four hours and ran off?'

'No.'

'Because she wouldn't leave her cell phone behind, or her personal computer, yada yada yada.'

'No, because she wouldn't do that to her mother.'

D.D. sighed again. Everything about this case already hurt her, and she had a feeling it was only going to get worse. 'I need to talk to Rosa. Both about her daughter, but also her involvement with the Summers family.'

'If I might make a recommendation?'

D.D. shot Keynes a look. 'By all means.'

'I don't think you should question Rosa just yet. If anyone knows about the family dynamics and the latest developments, it's Pam Mason, the Summerses' victim advocate. You want insights, speak to her first.'

18

Would you like to know how to avoid abject terror?

How to fight nighttime chills, the fear of the bogeyman under the bed? How to sleep like an angel? Or walk down dark alleyways with a spring in your step?

Do you want to know how to be me?

First, you find the void. It's a place everyone has, deep, deep inside themselves. That spot no one can touch. I have it on expert testimony that some find it through meditation or Zen retreats or the diligent pursuit of mind-fulness. Let's just say I discovered the void under different circumstances.

But everyone has it. A place where you stand in silence. A place that permits you to be untouched even in a crowded room. A place where you are utterly, totally, simply, terrifyingly alone.

Once you are there, no one can hurt you. And once no one can hurt you, you never have to be afraid again.

It's the darkness that gets to me. I keep thinking that my eyes will adjust. That there will be a lessening of the gloom. But no. The pitch-black depths remain absolute. I hold out my bound hands time and time again to test; I still can't see them.

I'm left in a land of sound and feel. So I put both to good use.

I don't understand the purpose of the tethering chain connected to the handcuffs around my wrists. Best I can tell, I have full range of the room, so it's hardly limiting access. Is it to keep me from bounding through a suddenly opened door? Racing toward the light? I don't know, then force myself to put it from my mind. Motives aren't worth worrying about yet. Tangibles are.

I explore the room. Nine steps form the width, side to side. Twelve long strides provide the length. Contents appear to be three items: A twin-size mattress, flat on the floor, covered in a simple cotton blanket. A standard-issue plastic bucket sans handle. And a coffin-size box.

I still hear breathing. Slow and even. In and out. In and out. It becomes the background noise for my endeavors. Like the sound of ocean waves, the rhythm of my heartbeat. I already hate it.

Windows. Three of them. With my fingertips, I can make out the trim. Two upon one wall, both modest in size. Singles, I believe you'd call them. Classic New England architecture. The larger window is on the wall across from them. Twice as wide as it is tall, its dimensions remind me more of a mirror. When I run my fingers along it, I feel cool glass. In contrast, the smaller windows across from it are textured and rough, as if painted or otherwise obscured. I try to scratch at the coating with my fingernails but can't make a dent. So not residential paint, but maybe something more industrial such as powder coating or enamel. These windows must be outer windows, thickly covered. Hence my lack of light.

As for the larger, unpainted glass surface across from them . . .

I'm guessing that's an internal wall. Which doesn't make sense for such a large picture window. Unless, of course, it's not a window at all. A one-way mirror? That's what I'm thinking. I can't be certain, of course, but why construct such an elaborate setting for his playthings if not to watch the festivities inside?

I'm sure it's only a matter of time before the lights come on. Blinding, disorienting. And the UNSUB (ask Samuel; that's unidentified subject in FBI-speak) will take advantage of the chaos to check in on his charges.

Or maybe he's watching even now. Military-issued night-vision goggles, anything is possible.

You must understand: Whatever demented thing you're too scared to consider, that's exactly what they're already fantasizing about. The big bads out there . . . Denial won't help you. Suppression won't save you.

Best to meet it head-on. Understand the enemy. Accept their depravities. Then find the void and soldier on.

Breathing. Still so relentlessly even. In. Out. In. Out.

How can she remain asleep? How can she not hear me bumbling around in the dark, tripping over the mattress, stubbing my toe against a wall here, the box there?

I can't think about the coffin-size box. I can't consider its possibilities, its contents. If I do, I lose the void. Because I'm good alone. I understand alone. I intended, always, forever, to *be* alone.

So the box. The fucking Darth Vader wannabe, not part of the equation. A totally unwelcome addition to my plan.

Is she drugged? That's the only thing that makes sense to me. How else to explain unconsciousness lasting this long? Of course, I'm not sure how long this long has been. I fell asleep early afternoon. I woke up to an intruder in my apartment after dusk. And now?

I hate the damn dark. It's disorienting.

I center my thoughts. I comb the room. Using sight and sound, which can be more helpful than you think.

Above the larger window – the viewing window? – I identify a high wall-mounted object. Smaller, soft, and foamy to the touch, it's situated to the left of the smooth-glass mirror. A speaker, I'm guessing. He watches, and then, eventually, he'll talk. Orders, taunts, whatever.

But sooner or later he'll make himself known. And when he does, it'll be all about him asserting control.

Breathing. In. Out. In. Out.

I should use it. Roll it into the void, turn it into part of my separation. Like focusing on the wind in the trees, or utilizing the toll of a bell. I can't fight it. I can't change it. I can't block it. Hence, use it. Make it one with me.

I hate the damn breathing.

I find myself standing over the box. Tracing its shape, noting the roughness of the edges. A crude job. I'd like to say I recognize the craftsmanship. But cheap pine boxes are a dime a dozen. I never learned if Jacob crafted his own or purchased it elsewhere. I never asked the question before, and I certainly can't ask it now.

She's dying. I know that, kneeling over the box. Because that's what happens to girls trapped in coffin-size boxes. Physically, mentally, is there a difference?

This girl, whatever made her her, is ebbing away, leaking into the wood, the floor, the black-painted room. Bit by bit. Inch by inch. Soon, Evil Kidnapper will pop open this lid and she'll do whatever, say whatever he wants because it won't matter anymore. The person she was will be gone. Only the shell will remain.

Girl Bot. Ready for programming.

The type of automaton ready to give up her own beloved father's name.

I hate this girl in the box. As I discover myself slowly but surely shredding my own fingernails, a habit hard broken four years ago.

I fist my hands. Feel the pressure of my nails digging into my palm. And will myself into the void once again.

While she continues to breathe. In. Out. In. Out.

Padlock. Standard issue. That's what secures the lid.

I have a moment, tracing the metal latch, where once again I'm in a filthy, food-stained, sex-soaked basement, studying my own box from the outside in. The sense of déjà vu unsettles me, makes this whole thing feel way too personal. More like Evil Kidnapper went looking for me than I went looking for him.

Back into the void, back into the void, back into the void. Feel nothing. Analyze everything.

Her breathing. In. Out. In. Out.

Stacey Summers? Could it be possible? Have I found her at last?

Suddenly, the void is gone. I feel only panic instead. I hate her, this girl, Stacey Summers, whoever, I don't care! She shouldn't be here. I left behind this fucking box. I dealt with the devil; I bargained my soul; I did what, according to Samuel, survivors do in order to see another day.

So how dare some girl get herself trapped in a box again? How dare she ruin this for me?

In. Out. In. Out. Breathing. Breathing. Breathing.

And just like that, moving before I even know I'm going to move, I fist my bound hands together and smash them against the top of the box. Again. And again and again.

Wake up, wake up, wake up.

Wake the fuck up!

Breathing. In. Out. In. Out.

What the hell? Who can sleep through this? It must be drugs. The only answer.

I bang again. I can't help myself. I'm furious, at her, at me, at him? I don't know anymore. The box, I think. I'm furious at the fucking box. It must go. I need it to be gone.

I find myself shaking the whole thing. It's cheap enough, wobbly enough, to move beneath my angry ministrations.

While she breathes. In. Out. In. Out.

I pound the box. Its corresponding shudder gives me another idea. Under different circumstances, I would pick the lock. But having been abducted from the comfort of my own bed, I lack the tools I would normally have on me: two very tiny, innocuous-looking black plastic clips that are actually universal lockpicks. But maybe I don't need them. The box shudders and shakes every time I hit it. It's definitely cheap construction.

I batter against it with fresh determination. I shove it side to side, feeling the top loosen, the joints give. Until, with a horrific scream, I toss it onto its side, roll it all the way over, a full 360. When it rights itself again, rocking beneath my fingertips, I can feel the lid is ajar.

Breathing. In. Out. In. Out.

How can that even be possible? I grab the lid, wrench it further, until it dangles from its metal latch. Take that, Mr Amateur Hour.

Breathing. In. Out. In. Out.

I can't see. The darkness encroaches. The darkness obliterates. So I reach my hands in, fully prepared to grab the occupant from its depths and yank her to salvation.

Except . . .

Nothing. No body, no warmth, no solid mass. I find emptiness, emptiness, emptiness. And yet I can still hear it.

Breathing. In. Out. In. Out. Forever steady.

The rhythm of my heartbeat.

I search the entire coffin-size box. With my wrists bound together, my fingers fluttering like butterfly wings. Empty, empty, empty.

Until finally, at the base . . .

A tiny recorder. Taped to the bottom of the casket. Apparently playing over and over again: Breathing. In. Out. In. Out.

And in that instant, I'm sure the breathing is mine. Prerecorded while I was unconscious. Just as the box is mine.

There is no second victim.

There is only me.

Always me.

I look up at the glass window. I can't see it in the dark, but I can *feel* it before me. I know he's there. Watching. Waiting. Enjoying the show.

So I smile. I lift my wrists. I offer him one middle finger. Then I rise from the demolished coffin. I head to the single mattress.

And though my heart is thumping wildly, and my pulse racing uncontrollably, though I understand now that this isn't a matter of a simple kidnapping, that this man seems to know things he shouldn't know, that I am even less in control than I thought, not just another victim but perhaps *the* intended victim, I force myself to lie down and turn my back to him.

Find the void. Live in the void.

In the void, no one can hurt you. And if no one can hurt you, then you never have to be afraid again.

If I could go back in time, if I could do one thing, I would drive to my mother's farm. I would sit across from her. I would eat her homemade muffins, accept her sun-brewed tea. And I would let her love me.

Except, having spent so much time in an empty void, I no longer know how to feel again.

19

Once the decision was made to take me with him on his trucking route, 'Everett' swung into full preparation mode. He adopted my father's name, while I would be called Molly. He drilled me. My name, his name, made me sign another postcard for my mom. I wrote what he said, signed what he wanted. I thought my handwriting looked foreign and strange. Maybe this is what handwriting looked like for girls named Molly.

When I was done, fake Everett handed over stiff blue jeans and an oversize white T-shirt declaring Florida the Sunshine State. He'd included underwear and a bra as well, but the bra was several sizes too large and looked like something only a grandmother would wear. When I held it up questioningly, he just shrugged and knocked it to the floor.

He ordered me to shower – on account of the close quarters, he informed me. I noticed he had also recently bathed, hair actually combed, and was wearing one of his less-stained T-shirts.

He watched me in the bathroom as I quickly soaped up my dirt-encrusted skin, scrubbed my long, matted hair. He continued staring as I awkwardly sorted through the cheap, oversize clothes, doing my best to pull them up over my *still-damp skin. My hands shook. I kept my gaze on the dirt-brown carpet, certain at any moment he'd snatch the clothes away, toss me down, and . . .*

But he didn't. If anything, he seemed irritated by my clumsiness.

When I finally dragged the T-shirt over my dripping wet hair, he produced a comb from his back pocket and ruthlessly dragged it through my hair himself. Next up from his back pocket: scissors.

I flinched. In response, he chuckled.

'Hair's a fucking mess,' he said, his way of making conversation.

I wanted to tell him, of course it was a fucking mess. No hair, and certainly not my fine blond hair, was meant to be shampooed with a cracked bar of ancient hand soap. My locks were accustomed to a soothing regimen of tea-tree-oil-based shampoos and citrus-scented conditioners. Then there was the weekly deep-conditioning hair masque to add volume, and the monthly highlights for shine.

Once upon a time, I'd been a teenage girl. With standards. And gorgeous, glossy California-inspired long blond hair.

Now . . .

I kept my gaze lowered, feeling the stiffness of my new denim jeans, as he fisted the first clump of hair, then went to town.

Three snips. That's all it took. Three giant handfuls. Three decisive cuts. The wet strands rained down onto the carpet.

'Crap,' he said. 'I think I made it worse. Oh well. That's what hats are for.'

I didn't say a word. Just like that, I'd become Molly and we both knew it.

But we weren't done yet. He forced me to turn around,

covering my eyes with a black strip of cloth – smelled like a musty old T-shirt – then tied it behind my head, obscuring my vision.

I never got to watch myself leave the basement prison. Best I could do was track the tops of my bare feet as he pulled me across the dirty carpet to the far door. A creak as it opened and then, much as I'd suspected, stairs leading up.

He pushed me ahead of him. I stumbled once, twice, three times. He whacked me in the back of the head hard enough to make me wince, and I found my balance.

At the top, a brief pause as he reached around me to open another door. Then a change in flooring from cheap commercial-grade carpet to peeling gray linoleum. Was this his house? I wondered as he yanked me forward into what I assumed must be a kitchen. It smelled like the rest of him: disgusting.

I tripped over my own feet, again. Trying to slow things down, or honestly uncoordinated? I didn't know anymore. I'd agreed to my new identity. I'd given up my father's name rather than be left alone down in that horrible place. And yet . . .

Funny how you can fear change, even when already surrounded by the worst of the worst.

Fresh air. Suddenly, I could feel it. Stumbling through the kitchen, out another door, we'd exited the house. To the outside. Front yard? Backyard? Who knew, who cared? I was standing outside with the wind on my face. And for a second, I couldn't help myself. I dug in my bare heels. I lifted up my face.

Outside. Fresh air, the rustle of trees. After so, so long. (How long?) So, so long.

Fake Everett paused. He gave me one moment. I used it to peer straight up, over the top of my blindfold, and then

I could see them. Trees soaring high above me. Thick and dark against a dimly lit sky. Woods, forest, freedom. Maybe I really was only miles from my mother's farm.

'Georgia,' Everett said, as if reading my mind. 'Found this place years ago, my own little mountain hideaway. 'Course, old geezer who owned it died, and now his no-good kids want it back. So, we're outta here. Life on the road, that's more fun anyway.'

Trees, I was still thinking. Forest, woods, just like my mother's farm.

And then I couldn't see anymore because there were too many tears blinding my eyes.

With the blindfold on, I couldn't see my way around the house to his big rig. He had to help me step awkwardly onto the wide running board, then grab my arm as I tripped over the driver's seat. I'd never been in a semi before. Knew nothing about them. Long-haul trucks were merely vehicles I'd seen on the highway, carrying goods this way and that. Definitely, I'd spent more time and attention on my hair.

Now, fake Everett chattered proudly about his raised-roof sleeper cab, his home away from home. Came complete with a top bunk, coffeemaker, and of course a portable DVD player for entertainment. He dragged me around to the driver's captain chair as he was talking. I could feel carpet beneath my bare feet. Thicker and nicer than what had been in the basement. It smelled better in here too. Still tainted by the lingering odor of greasy food, but with an overlay of pine-fresh scent. As if at the least the truck had been cleaned recently. It deserved that much effort.

When I first heard the screech of a latch opening up, I didn't understand it. Then, fake Everett gave me a push, and I pitched forward, as if falling off a step or two. Before

I could recover, his hand was squeezing my shoulder, forcefully pressing me down.

Too late, I realized I was now standing on a hard wooden surface.

The smell of pine . . .

And just like that I was back in a coffin-size box, fully clothed this time, with a blindfold over my eyes.

'What's your name?' he demanded from above.

'Molly,' I whispered, too disheartened, too defeated for anything more.

'Mine?'

'Everett.'

'Who am I?'

'Whoever you want to be.'

'I'm your uncle. Uncle Everett. Where are you from?'

'Florida?' I guessed.

'With that accent? Hardly. We'll say your mama raised you up North, but now you're staying with me.'

I didn't say anything. He'd get his way; he always got his way. What did I care? Maybe I really was Molly now, because surely the girl I'd been . . .

'Loading up, dropping off, you're in the box,' he stated.

I didn't respond, feeling more confused than rebellious. Locked in a box with a blindfold on, what did it matter?

He tugged sharply on a ragged lock of my hair. I nodded belatedly, if only to show I was paying attention.

'Rest stops, sleepovers, you're in the box.'

I nodded again.

'Other times . . .' His voice drifted. He seemed to hesitate. 'Be good. Play your cards right and maybe you can come out for a bit. Keep me company.'

I frowned, not understanding. Was he saying I might

join him in the cab? As in sit in the passenger's seat? As in, like a real person?

'You'll sit on the floor,' he clarified now. 'No one can see you. Maybe, maybe not, I'll take the blindfold off. But you'll be out of the box. Assuming you're good, of course. Do exactly as I say.'

He paused, waiting expectantly. And, finally, I got it. I was leaving the basement, really truly leaving. And for my punishment/reward, I would now spend all my time, 24/7, with this man. This mean, filthy, awful man in his castle of a big rig, where he got to rule the highway, personal sex slave chained to his side.

And in that instant, I understood something else as well. That he was doing this versus killing me.

Which he'd promised to do so many times before, right before explaining how he'd then roll my body into the nearest canal and let the gators ensure my mother never saw me again.

Everett wasn't going to kill me. He was going to keep me instead.

I wondered, in the back of my mind, if that meant he'd grown to like me somehow.

And I wondered, in the back of my mind, if that meant I was supposed to like him too.

Everett planted the palm of his hand over my face and forced my head down into the box. I assumed the position, mind churning, as the lid came down. The padlock jangled. My moment of freedom ended. I became once again a girl in a coffin-size box.

Except now . . . Now I was a girl in motion.

He liked to talk while he drove the big rig. Complain, really. About the price of gas, the asshole in the Honda Civic who just flipped him off. The pricks at the understaffed loading dock who just cost him two damn hours, and now he couldn't even take a break for lunch.

In the good ol' days, he'd grouse, the smart trucker could fudge his driver's log and carry on. But no. Everything's now federally mandated electronic this and federally mandated electronic that. Big Brother. Always watching.

Welcome to the life of a long-haul trucker, he'd tell me. Working for assholes while driving through an entire country of assholes.

In the beginning, every time the rig's engine fired to life, I flinched. Every time the truck bounced down a rutted road, I went bug-eyed with nausea. After so much time alone in the basement, this – the smell of diesel, the roar of pistons, the violent hum of the beast – was almost too much to take.

And yet, much like my experience with the overwhelming boredom of the basement, I learned to adapt. I relaxed my shoulders into the jerk and sway. I absorbed the relentless growl and hum. And bit by bit, I started to discern the nuances of different road surfaces, the cruising speed of highway, the deep grind of slow climbs.

Life on the road. Where, according to fake Everett's incessant grumblings, he was permitted to drive eleven out of fourteen hours, before taking a mandated ten-hour rest. Then, regardless of actual time on the clock – say, 11:00 P.M., or 2:00 A.M., or 4:00 A.M. – he'd start driving again.

And true to his word, away from loading docks, rest stops, and the hustle and bustle of civilization, he'd pull over and let me out. I got to pee squatted behind bushes versus trapped in my own filth. I got to eat Egg McMuffins for breakfast, Subway sandwiches for lunch, and fried chicken for dinner.

'Downside of the job,' Everett would say, handing over yet another bag of fast food while self-consciously patting the grotesque swell of his belly.

Dinner was inevitably followed by other demands. He'd driven all day. 'Course he needed to blow off some steam. And he had his love nest all ready to go.

Was it better being out of the basement? Was it worth it being out on the road? Where, from time to time, the blindfold came off, and I watched the world whiz by in a blur of greens and blues and grays.

So many other vehicles racing side by side. So many other drivers. An entire country filled with assholes, as Everett liked to say.

And yet not a single one who ever saw me.

Everett talked a lot. Complained mostly. And sometimes, once in a while, he even cried in his sleep.

Which is how I finally learned about Lindy.

20

D.D. liked to be prepared. Hence, before she and Keynes met up with victim specialist Pam Mason at the FBI's Boston field office, D.D. did the practical thing and Googled her. According to the woman's professional bio, Pam Mason had a master's in forensic psych from John Jay. She'd worked crisis management at a major women's shelter in Detroit – talk about baptism by fire, D.D. thought – before joining the FBI. She'd moved around the bureau for the past fifteen years, including a stint in Miami specializing in human trafficking, then a position with the squad specializing in crimes against Americans overseas. The victim specialist was known for her work on a major kidnapping case in Mexico where the oil executive was returned alive, and for a situation in Guatemala where three young American missionaries weren't.

In other words, the woman's work history was as impressive as the number of frequent-flier miles she'd accumulated. D.D. wondered what she thought of life in Boston, let alone her current assignment with the Summers family.

Keynes had arranged for them to meet in his office at the FBI's downtown Boston headquarters. The meeting place didn't surprise D.D.; federal agents were big on home-court

advantage. Though why anyone would consider the enorm-
ous concrete structure – one of Boston's ugliest buildings, in
D.D.'s humble opinion – an advantage, D.D. would never
know. Then again, compared to the Hoover building in
DC . . .

Never let it be said the federal government was known
for good taste.

D.D. debated bringing Phil along. Sure, he had his
own work to do with his own squad and his own co-
detective, *Carol*, but the FBI valued appearances. Given she
was meeting with two federal employees, it felt logical,
even balanced, for there to be two representatives from the
BPD.

But the moment she thought it, D.D. knew she wouldn't
do it. Precisely because it smacked of politics and she hated
that crap. She'd called Keynes from Florence Dane's apartment not because he was a big-time federal guy but because
he was a known associate of the victim. She planned on
keeping that tack here. Flora's disappearance was a BPD
case all the way, hence D.D.'s involvement as a supervisory
officer. Interviewing Dr Keynes and victim specialist Pam
Mason was her call, and she would handle it.

She was pleasantly surprised to find Keynes waiting for
her in the lobby of FBI headquarters. Given it was Sunday,
and federal agents prided themselves on working bankers'
hours, versus an urban detective's relentless 24/7 drill, the
building was quiet. D.D. still had to present her credentials
and sign her life away – but, sadly, no registering of the
sidearm she was no longer qualified to carry. Once she'd
secured her visitor's pass, Keynes escorted her to the
elevators and away they went.

He wasn't one for small talk. No 'How was the parking,
did you find the offices okay, what do you think of the

weather' chatter. Instead, Keynes stood quietly, hands clasped before him as the floors flew by.

He'd discarded his heavy black coat, first time D.D. had seen him without it. For his Sunday attire, Keynes had gone with an impeccably tailored charcoal-gray suit, with just a hint of texture to the fabric. D.D. wondered if he had a whole closet full of suits, each one looking more elegant than the last. And just how much time and money did he spend on wardrobe anyway?

She had on her caramel-colored leather jacket. It was her favorite; she wore it right up to the coldest, darkest days of winter. Now, she noticed how shiny and worn the leather appeared at the cuffs. Oh yeah, and the apple juice stain lower right side. Awesome.

Elevator stopped. Doors opened. Keynes gestured for her to step out first so she did the honors. According to D.D.'s research, the FBI had more than 120 victim specialists and four managers. Dr Keynes, as one of the head muckety-mucks, was entitled to his own office, complete with an imposing cherrywood desk, a long bank of bookshelves, and a smaller seating area to one side.

His desk bore a state-of-the-art-looking computer, a leather cup of requisite pencils and pens, and, of all things, a Rubik's Cube – colors mixed. D.D. couldn't help herself. Her gaze went immediately to the '80s phenomenon, and she was already itching to solve it.

'You can, you know,' Keynes said, following her gaze.

She kept her hands fisted at her side. 'Who messed it up?'

'I did.'

'To solve later? Or as a test for this little meeting?'

'Sergeant, you read entirely too much into a common toy.'

She eyed him warily. 'You're a behavioral expert. Of course I'm suspicious.'

He smiled. It was a good look on him, easing the severity of his smoothly shaved scalp, high-sculpted cheekbones. For a moment, he almost appeared human.

'I like to shuffle the cube. It helps me think. Given what we discovered at Flora's apartment . . . I've had much to think about.'

'I like mobiles,' D.D. found herself saying. 'Studying intricate patterns where at first glance it appears as one graceful, multileveled whole, and yet is in fact many separate levels moving in precise rhythm.'

A rap on the door behind them. D.D. and Keynes turned to find a woman standing in the doorway. Pam Mason, D.D. assumed.

At first glance, the woman was older than D.D. would've thought. Ash-blond hair worn in a close mass of curls that was last popular right around the same time as the Rubik's Cube. Even though it was Sunday, she'd followed Keynes's professional wardrobe example, though with less elegant results, having selected a block-cut, 1990s tan suit with padded shoulders and a cream-colored silk blouse that buttoned all the way to the throat and was finished with some kind of silk ruffle.

The victim specialist appeared about D.D.'s height but, with the cut of her jacket, appeared significantly wider. She was also a woman on a mission. She entered the office, simultaneously tucking a file folder under one arm while sticking out her other hand.

'Sergeant Detective D.D. Warren? Pam Mason, victim specialist. I understand you have some questions about the Summers family.'

The woman grabbed D.D.'s hand in a firm grip, shook it

twice, turned to Keynes with another brisk handshake, then moved straight to the seating area, ready for business. D.D. had to admit, she didn't care for the woman's suit, but she had to like the woman's style.

A considerate host, Keynes did the honors of offering up coffee. Both women immediately agreed, and he disappeared in search of every investigator's favorite beverage.

'Dr Keynes has apprised me of the situation,' Pam stated briskly.

'Okay.' D.D. shrugged out of her leather jacket, her motions awkward given the stiffness in her left shoulder. She took a seat. 'I'm sure you can understand we're operating on the QT for the moment regarding Florence Dane's disappearance. Press gets a hold of this . . .'

'You mean the same media that raked the BPD over the coals on the evening news?'

'Thank heavens it was a Saturday,' D.D. commented, as the weekend news had notoriously lower viewer numbers than the weeknight editions.

Pam Mason arched a brow but kept the rest of her thoughts to herself. She folded her hands, placed them on the small table. 'How can I help?'

Keynes reappeared. He bore two mugs of steaming coffee for them, nothing for himself. Man was so superhuman he didn't even require caffeine? Figured.

'I understand that Rosa Dane is acting as a mentor for the Summers family.'

Pam Mason nodded.

'I'm wondering . . .' D.D. had to collect her thoughts, not sure how much she wanted to say. Not sure how much she had to say. 'I'd like to understand more about the Stacey Summers case. From the family's perspective. The father, Colin, called me this morning. At the first mention of Flora's name, he already assumed she was involved in taking down Devon Goulding. Given we never released that detail to the press . . .'

'He knows things.'

'Exactly. Combine that with the fact Flora has taken a personal interest in Stacey Summers's disappearance and now appears to have gone missing herself . . .'

Another arched brow, then it was Pam's turn to collect her thoughts. She took a sip of coffee.

'I'm assuming you're familiar with the details of Stacey's abduction,' she said at last, 'given that the BPD is handling the case.'

'I know we have the world's most-watched kidnapping video, and yet no real leads.'

'Do you think she's alive?' Pam asked abruptly, which was not the question D.D. had been expecting.

She found herself staring at Keynes, of all people, who sat with his long, elegant fingers steepled in front of him.

'What's that expression?' D.D. replied finally. 'Hope for the best, but plan for the worst? I hope Stacey is still alive. But given the statistics on missing persons cases . . .'

Pam nodded. No doubt she was as familiar with the primacy of the first twenty-four hours as the rest of them.

'I guess the question is,' D.D. found herself saying, 'does the family believe? Or maybe' – she thought about it – 'does Rosa Dane, as their mentor, believe?'

'The family wants to believe,' Pam supplied. 'Most families do. But as the days stretch longer with no sign of their daughter . . . They are under a tremendous amount of stress, both feeling the pain of their daughter's disappearance and the agony of their own helplessness.'

'How are they coping?'

'Interestingly enough, it's the mother, Pauline, who is probably doing the best, though I'm sure Colin would disagree. By all accounts, the marriage is a solid one. Traditional New England roles. He's a workaholic investment banker; she raised their daughter, tends the home, and is involved in the community. Church, local high school, various charities, the like. Stacey is their only child; Pauline suffered several miscarriages before her birth, which makes Stacey a miracle child.'

D.D. winced. She couldn't imagine that kind of salt on the wound; to have already lost multiple babies, then, nineteen years later, having the lone survivor, no doubt the apple of her parents' eyes . . .

'Stacey is described as kind, vibrant, happy, athletic,' D.D. said. 'Mother or father?'

'Definitely takes after the mom. They're very close, the kind of mother-daughter that are often mistaken for sisters. Pauline took the news of Stacey's disappearance very hard. I'd never describe her as weak, but she's one of those women who wears her heart on her sleeve, which makes her transparent in her pain.'

'Support network?' D.D. asked.

'Good. In addition to church ties, they have a close network of friends in the neighborhood, other families from Stacey's school, that sort of thing. In the beginning, they were deluged with food, offers of assistance, et cetera, et cetera. One of my first jobs, in fact, was turning everyone away, given Pauline's delicate mental state.'

'Delicate mental state?'

'The initial shock definitely overwhelmed Pauline. She fell apart. But, to be fair, she then let her support network help put her back together.

'The tight network of ladies from church, fellow moms,

her own sisters, they give her strength. Colin, on the other hand, concerns me more. He's the consummate alpha male. For most of his life, there's been no problem he couldn't solve. Now this. The very foundations of his world have been rocked. Pauline externalizes her pain, which allows others to help bear the load. Colin purely internalizes.'

'He was quite . . . angry . . . when he spoke to me by phone.'

The victim specialist merely nodded.

'And Rosa Dane's role in all this?'

'She's the equalizer between the two. She's empathetic enough and optimistic enough for Pauline – Rosa's daughter's safe recovery one year later being an example of success. But Rosa is also tactical, which is what Colin wants. She's well versed on media appearances, as well as the need in this day and age to work social media.'

'Bet the lead investigator loves that,' D.D. muttered.

Pam Mason shrugged. All detectives wanted to control their own investigations. And all families wanted to be involved.

'Was Stacey close to her family?' D.D. asked.

'Very.'

'Any reason to harbor any suspicions on the home front?'

'No. I've spent three months with the Summerses. They really were the postcard for family closeness. And frankly, I don't say that lightly. In my line of work, I spend more time pulling skeletons out of closets than framing happy family photos.'

'So Pauline is leaning on family and friends to get her through, while Colin nurses his rage and rides the local investigators. Is he back to work?'

'Yes. Limited hours, but I recommended his return. Staying home isn't good for him. Work is how he copes.'

D.D. couldn't argue with that, given her own predilections. 'Is the wife angry about that?'

'No. Like a lot of stay-at-home wives, she's accustomed to the house being her domain. Her husband's sudden appearance twenty-four/seven strained the patterns of their marriage more than it helped. Part of my job is to help a family understand that the more it deviates from its established rhythms during the time of crisis, the more everyone's stress escalates. Normalcy is also an excellent coping strategy.'

'Does Rosa Dane agree with that?'

The victim advocate hesitated. 'Rosa is a rare mentor. She listens to Pauline. She talks to Colin. I've . . . been impressed. Generally speaking, the National Center for Missing and Exploited Children's program . . .' Pam Mason made a noise in her throat.

'I've never worked with a family mentor,' D.D. confessed.

'The program has the best of intentions: Let parents who've already been through the worst offer support to families who've just entered the crisis. I'm sure the volunteer mentors receive some training for the role, but at the end of the day . . . they're laypeople, not experts. They've had one experience. Whereas someone like me' – Pam's gaze flickered to Keynes – 'like us . . . there is no such thing as one response to crisis. Our job is to appraise the family and identify the approach that is right for this one particular situation. Whereas the volunteer mentors . . . inevitably, they are operating from a place of their own trauma. Whatever advice they offer, suggestions they have, has more to do with who they are and what they went through than the family they are supposedly aiding. To me, they're more inclined to try and fix whatever they perceive as having gone wrong in their case than help the new family through

their own experiences. Now Rosa, on the other hand . . .'
Pam frowned. 'She's the rare mentor who seems to be able
to distinguish between her daughter's disappearance and
what the Summerses are now going through.'

'How often does she meet with them?'

'In person? Not often. Rosa lives three, four hours north,
and given in the first four weeks, the media circus camped
out on the Summerses' sidewalk . . .'

'She speaks to them by phone.'

'Mostly. How often is hard for me to say. The Summers
phone rings a lot.'

'But you've seen her, obviously.'

'Twice. First time she spent the day with mostly Pauline,
quietly holding her hand.' Pam paused, regarded D.D.
intently for a second. 'That's rare, you know. Just *being*
with someone. I'm the supposed expert, and I'm not even
that good at it.'

'You have a job to do,' D.D. countered. 'That's different.'

The victim advocate shrugged. 'Second visit was at the
five-week mark. Pauline was coming out of the worst of her
funk. Rosa had more of a strategy meeting with both
Summerses. Questions they should ask, rights they have,
resources that are available to them. In particular, Colin
wanted to know media strategies, how to make a personal
appeal for his daughter's safe return, that sort of thing.'

'I've seen a couple of those on the news,' D.D. agreed.

'Rosa's advice was solid enough. Most of it was things
we'd already told them, but I can understand it sounding
better coming from someone who's been there, done that.
The biggest thing she repeated – which I appreciated – is
that this is a marathon, not a sprint. If they really want to
be there for their daughter, they need to come up with a
way to stop living from minute to minute waiting for the

phone to ring and settle in for the long haul. Come up with a system for family and friends to visit where it's helpful but not overwhelming. Return to work, the everyday patterns of life. Ignore the press, unless it's on their terms.'

'And her advice on managing the case detectives?' D.D. asked, because there had to be advice on investigator relations. Any family had issues with investigator relations.

'The detectives are not their friends or allies. They work for the state. If the Summerses really want to know what's going on, they should hire their own private detective.'

D.D.'s eyes widened. 'Did they?'

'Colin talked about interviewing candidates.'

'Lovely. More cooks in the kitchen. Bet the case agent will love that.'

Pam merely shrugged. 'Do I think a private eye is magically going to make a difference in finding Stacey? No. Do I think it helps Colin feel more in control of the situation, and therefore ease some of his stress in the short term? Sure. Problem is, Rosa Dane had it right: This is a marathon, not a sprint, meaning eventually a PI's lack of progress will be just as hard to take.'

'So when did they meet with Flora?' D.D. gambled.

'Rosa's daughter? They haven't, to my knowledge.'

'Did Rosa discuss her daughter's experience?'

'Yes.'

'So they're familiar with her case. Makes sense they might want to personally meet her, don't you think? The walking proof that a young girl can disappear from a bar and still one day be found safe?'

'Maybe. But I've never seen Flora at the house.'

D.D. frowned. 'She was following the Summers case. Closely.' She shot Keynes a look. He didn't deny it.

Again, Pam shrugged.

'Could she have talked to them by phone?' D.D. asked.

'Possible. They never mentioned it, but Colin, especially, isn't one to share. Why are you so sure she had contact with them?'

'Colin, when he called this morning. He asked directly if Flora had been the one to kill Devon Goulding, which was a pretty big conversational leap. Furthermore, when I pressed him about Flora, he immediately became evasive. I would swear he must know her, if only from what he wasn't willing to say.'

'I never saw her at the house,' Pam considered out loud. 'And Pauline never mentioned anything to me, but it's possible Flora met with Colin at his office.'

'Why meet with him and not Pauline? Talk to the father but not the mother?' D.D. asked.

'I might know the answer to that,' Keynes spoke up abruptly. He was relaxed back in his own chair, fingers now clasped on the table.

'By all means,' D.D. indicated.

He turned his gaze to his fellow victim advocate. 'According to your assessment of the family dynamics, Pauline, the mother, functions as the heart of the family – the emotional epicenter.'

'True.'

'While the father, Colin, he's the brains and the brawn. He's focused on tactics, strategies, anything to ensure his daughter's safe return.'

'Alpha male,' Pam agreed.

'Flora isn't interested in emotions. She's not comfortable with them. Tactics, on the other hand, getting things done . . .'

At that moment, D.D. got it, knew exactly where Keynes was leading.

'Colin Summers didn't hire a private investigator to find his daughter,' she said.

Keynes shook his head. 'No. Chances are, he hired Flora instead.'

21

Are you in pain right now? Do your joints ache, your fingers burn? Does your skull throb? No? Then you're fine.

Are you thirsty right now? Doubled over with hunger pangs, licking at your own skin just to have something to taste? No? Then you're okay.

Are you freezing right now? Or maybe overheated, with sweat streaming down your face? Feeling either stifling hot or bone-cracking cold? Not yet? Then you've got nothing to complain about.

Are you lonely right now? Terrified or frightened or overwhelmed by the dark? Are you thinking that if he left right now, never came back, there would be nothing you could do? You would be stuck here. You would die here, all alone. And your mother would never know, never even get to bury your body. Just as he has threatened, promised, time and time again.

No?

Then you're fine.

Listen to me. Believe me. Trust in me. I know what I'm talking about.

I'm comfortable. I'm not in pain or hungry or cold or hot or frightened. I need nothing. I want nothing.

I am fine.

Locked alone in the dark, I'm perfectly all right.

When I wake up again, I'm immediately aware of a change to the room. Food. The smell of roasted chicken wafts toward me through the dense black. And the scent of something hot and savory. Gravy, dressing, mashed potatoes? Maybe all three? My stomach growls immediately, and despite my best intentions, I start to salivate.

I still can't see. I remain alone in a sea of night. Not even a sliver of light to illuminate the frame of a doorway. But the smell is strong and fresh. Definitely, there's food somewhere in the room.

I sit up gingerly, feeling around with my fingertips. The last thing I want to do is knock over a plate of sustenance and waste this unexpected offering. I still have no sense of time or rhythm in this sensory-deprivation chamber. Does a chicken platter mean it's dinnertime? Of the day I was taken or later?

And does this mean I'm entitled to food, three hots and a cot, as the saying goes? Or is this yet one more experiment being conducted by Evil Kidnapper? First, to explore my reaction to a cheap pine coffin. Now, to witness the animal in the zoo at feeding time.

Had he read my case file? Maybe he's one of the crime junkies who followed my case in the news? A fan of sorts who heard about a girl who was kidnapped and held in a pine box. Except, instead of being horrified that such a thing could happen . . . it struck a nerve. Unlocked a deep dark fantasy he never even knew he had.

Such guys exist. After I returned home, I received letters from several of them, turned on by all the lurid details of my captivity. I even received a marriage proposal.

Because Jacob Ness isn't the only monster out there, and yes, they take an interest in one another's work.

I remind myself I'm not interested in motives yet. Just tangibles. And the scent of chicken could promise more than just food. What about a ceramic plate? Or, better yet, a cutting knife?

I move slowly off the mattress, dropping to my knees, as my tethering chain rattles behind me. It irks me to crawl on the floor. I'm nearly positive he must watch through the one-way glass, wearing night-vision goggles to penetrate the gloom. Because, again, why go to all this trouble if not to enjoy the spectacle? Most likely he waited till I'd dozed off, then opened the door I haven't found yet, delivered the food, then exited in time to take in the show. I hate the idea of some person, some faceless, nameless freak, watching me crawl. But tripping over the dinner offering would be worse, so forward I go, bound hands in front of me, chain rattling behind me as I inchworm forth.

The smell is coming from the opposite side of the room, where the pine box was. I make my way carefully through the dark, feeling my way with my fluttering fingers. Sure enough, I hit the edge of the pine box with my left shoulder. I pause, back up, feel around the edges.

He's rebuilt it. Son of a bitch. I'd smashed the thing apart, left it in half a dozen distinct pieces. Why not? But now, it's once again intact.

I curse, am tempted to halt my pursuit of roasted chicken in order to destroy the box out of pure spite. But I force myself to stop and think.

Why rebuild the box? Head games? Because even now, somewhere outside the viewing window, he's grinning to himself, watching me explore a cheap pine coffin with my fingertips. He wants a response, is probably leaning forward in anticipation of my look of terror. Fuck him. No way I'm giving him that satisfaction.

Okay, so when did he rebuild the box? Surely if he'd come into the room, even while I was sleeping, and worked on it, I would've heard him. And given I'd yanked apart all the various wooden panels . . .

He must've removed it. Snatched up the pieces and carted them out. Then, after rebuilding it – or buying a second one? – redelivered it.

This makes me frown. I keep my back to the one-way mirror, feeling suddenly uneasy. I'm not sure which thought disturbs me more. That my captor can enter and exit the room multiple times without rousing me, or that he might have an unlimited supply of cheap pine coffins.

I finger the lacy edge of my satin nightgown. Again, the level of preparedness indicated by his actions. A predator who is more than your average bear. A man who's done his homework.

He knows me. I'm almost certain of it. One of the men who wrote me a letter in the past five years? One of the very many predators, who read every salacious detail of my captivity and thought, wow, if only I could get a girl like that for myself?

My hands are shaking. With my wrists bound, I can feel my fingers tremble against one another and I hate the weakness. Worse, my instinctive desire to start picking at my own thumb. Find a ragged edge. Tear off the nail. Use the pain to ground me.

As I did, so many minutes, hours, days ago, when I was trapped in the box.

Food. I can smell it, so close it tantalizes. I need to focus. I'm hungry, definitely, and given I don't know when I might be able to eat again . . .

Evil Kidnapper might have read all about me. Evil Kidnapper might even feel he knows me.

But that was the old Flora. Not the one who's spent the past five years studying, training, preparing. I am now Flora 2.0.

I'm a woman with promises left to keep.

Dinner. The promise of sustenance. I will not waste it just because of a stupid pine box, some twisted blast from the past, or the unnerving realization someone is most likely watching me.

Time to eat.

I scoot around the box, inching forward with my bound wrists rocking against the floor. I explore between the box and the wall for the prospect of roasted chicken. But . . . nothing.

I move all around the box, continue through the rest of the room.

Nothing.

Finally, I sit back on my heels next to the bare mattress, my back once again to the watcher's window, and contemplate things.

Smell is hard to trace. It could be coming from another room, I suppose. Or, worse, he's piping it in somehow. Maybe from the grate next to the one-way glass. Meaning there's no food at all. This whole thing is just like some bad science experiment, where I'm playing the role of mouse in the maze.

But the smell is so strong, so close.

Heat. It comes to me. I'm not just smelling chicken, but I swear I can feel it. Steam wafting through the air. And I felt it strongest, smelled it sharpest, over by the pine box.

My shoulders come down. Immediately, I know what he's done. Son of a bitch!

I cross back to the rebuilt – second? – box. Sure enough, crude holes are drilled in the lid. (Should I rub my fingertips against the jagged edges? Tear my own flesh, jam a sliver into the softness of my skin, then suck out the blood? Good times from the good old days. Is that what he wants from me?)

I keep my fingers fisted tight as I lean closer and sniff at the first hole. Chicken, no doubt about it. And yes, I don't just smell it; I can feel it. A trace of heat and steam wafting up from the inside of the box.

Son of a bitch.

I find the padlock easily enough. Of course it's locked, because why not? As long as you're torturing someone with the olfactory promise of dinner, of course you're going to lock the actual food away. I mean, leaving the lid open, where would be the fun in that?

Am I hungry right now? Yes. Am I thirsty right now? Yes.

But am I in pain? Am I terrified, depressed, beaten, too hot, too cold, too overwhelmed? No. Then I'm all right. I can think this through.

Option one, walk away. Or, being me, more likely turn around, once more flip him the finger, then resume my position on the mattress. Disadvantages include going hungry, but also . . . food might not just be food. What about utensils, plates, hell, a plastic cup? Resources, potential tools. The box is a care package of sorts. And being all alone in the dark, I can't afford to give up on the contents.

Which means I'm going to have to open the box. I did it once before by hammering it apart with my bound wrists. I was pretty pissed off at the time and, frankly, trying to shake up the occupant. An approach I'm not so sure will yield great results for my prospective dinner.

I could pick the lock. Mattress has coils, coils mean metal springs . . . It would take some effort, but I have no doubt of my ability to make it happen.

At which point, he would also have no doubt of my abilities.

Do I want that? To give away so much so soon? To someone whose motives I don't yet understand and who apparently can enter and exit this room without waking me?

My right thumb, slowly but surely seeking out my left thumb nail . . .

Who is this guy? What the hell does he want from me? Why this terrible, awful satin nightie?

And the box, the box, the box?

I hang my head. For one moment, I'm not all right. I hate it here, I hate this man, and I hate myself because I did this to myself. Five years ago, I escaped, and yet I've never gotten away. Jacob might as well be standing in the dark, laughing his fool head off.

My own brother running away from the person I'd become. And my mom . . . my poor, resigned mother, who gave up so much, only to one day realize the daughter she loved so much will never come home again.

She just gets the shell.

The smell is starting to fade. The chicken, once piping hot, now starting to cool. And that, as much as anything, gets me moving again.

Do you know who I am? I'm a girl who once loved to frolic with wild foxes.

I'm the girl who survived four hundred and seventy-two days in and out of a cheap pine coffin.

I'm the girl who's going to get out of this alive.

I fist my fingers. I raise my bound hands, and I swing them like a boom against the side panel of the box. It shudders beneath the force of my blow. So I do it again and again. Bashing against the sides, turning my own body into a sledgehammer and wielding it forcefully.

My knuckles bruise. My skin splits, as rough edges of the box catch and abrade. It doesn't stop me.

Long ago I learned to separate my mind from my body, my emotions from my pain. And these lessons serve me well.

As I batter the box into submission.

When the side finally caves in, there's a cracking noise. I like it. I can't see what I'm doing, so it's nice to hear a satisfying wooden groan. Now I slow, picking my way through shards of wood, till I can wrap my fingers around the edge of the collapsed lid and jerk it up and over. The metal padlock rattles, still intact but now completely useless given the entire other half of the lid has been wrenched from the body of the coffin.

Good luck rebuilding this one, I think, and despite myself, I'm curious what its fate will be.

But first, to the victor goes the spoils.

It takes a minute; then I find it. Styrofoam plate, my first disappointment. Plastic bottle, however, so maybe water. No utensils. I search and search and search. Nada. But the plate . . . In the dark, I poke the contents with my finger. Roasted half chicken, cubes of potatoes, and what feels like some sort of rubbery vegetable.

Finger food. Don't mind if I do.

I turn toward the one-way mirror. I stare right at it, do my best to peer through it as I pick up the roasted leg and go to work. My fingers are greasy. The chain rattles down from the metal bracelets circling my wrists, rubs against my bare thigh. My satin nightie has ridden up, but I make no move to adjust it.

Does he want me to be refined? Hence the new nightwear? Well, that's not what he's going to get. This is me, practical, methodical, efficient as I work my way through the contents on the plate.

The chicken isn't half bad. Nor the potatoes or what turns out to be green beans. Not that I'm seeking flavor. I chew for sustenance, because now I'm not hungry. And after several cautious sips of the water, nor am I thirsty.

I am fine.

I'm okay.

I am alone in the dark and I'm perfectly all right.

Later, my back to the watcher's window, squatted down to shield my body from view, I fold the Styrofoam plate around my fists and use it as a makeshift shield as I hammer my hands against the shattered side of the coffin. My efforts are rewarded as I break off two, three, four shards of pine. Now I just need a place to hide them. In the dark, dark room, where I can see nothing, but he can see all.

I cup the thin splinters in my palms, then wrap my hands around the two-thirds-full water bottle. Let him think I'm trying to hide that as I shuffle back to my mattress, plastic bottle clutched to my chest.

I lie down with my back to the one-way mirror. Then, moving slowly, I use the longer, sharper wooden shard to work the welted edge of the mattress. I only need a small slit, one inch across does it. Then I can slide in the first wooden splinter, the second, the third.

Pine is a soft wood. I doubt the fragments will be terribly effective as weapons. But then again, jab a sliver in the eye . . .

Resources. What I have that he doesn't even know he should take away.

I curl my knees up and around the water bottle.

I think, as I start to drift off again, that I'm not hungry, I'm not thirsty. I'm not cold, I'm not hot. I'm not in pain, nor exhausted, nor terrified.

I am a girl ready to fight.

22

In a detective's world there was one true blight on society, and it wasn't the master criminal; after all, superpredators were few and far between. It was the media.

Sunday afternoon, D.D. definitely needed to question Colin Summers. In the comfort of his own home would be ideal, as the less he felt threatened, the more likely he would be to talk. However, given the various media-fueled rumors that Devon Goulding was the same man who'd kidnapped Stacey Summers . . . D.D. didn't have to drive out to the Summers residence to know it would be a war zone of illegally parked news vans, feisty photographers, and rabid reporters.

The arrival of a Boston sergeant detective known for her past work on several major cases would only fan the flames. Even sending out Pam Mason, the family's victim specialist, would stir the pot.

So, Sunday afternoon, D.D., Keynes, and Pam Mason sat in Keynes's office and, instead of actively searching for Florence Dane, brainstormed ways of outsmarting the media in order to get Colin Summers alone for questioning. It took another round of coffee to get the job done, with Keynes sticking to water.

D.D. didn't trust him. Anyone who could appear that alert and engaged without at least one cup of joe?

Pam came up with the winning plan. She would call Colin. Request that he come to his office for a meeting with her. He would understand immediately she had something to say outside the prying eyes of media. And while the news vans could follow him to his downtown office building, they were shut out of the high-rise itself, given it was private property. Colin could ride the elevator up to his eleventh-floor suite, which should be relatively quiet on a Sunday afternoon.

D.D. and Pam would meet him there. Keynes would remain behind, as three against one would appear too threatening for the kinds of questions they needed to ask.

Keynes didn't argue, merely nodded. D.D. wondered what it would take to ruffle the senior victim specialist. Or maybe that was the point. In his line of work, at this stage of his career, he really had seen it all.

Pam made the call. D.D. could only hear her side of it, but it was clear Colin was already champing at the bit, demanding to know who what why when and how. But Pam, an experienced handler, kept her voice calm and her request simple. Meet me at your office. Meet me at your office. Meet me at your office.

Eventually, Colin must have given up on beating his head against the iron wall of her answers, and agreed to meet her at his office. Three o'clock.

The hour wait gave D.D. time to check in with her team. Keynes showed her an unoccupied office she could use, and she quickly dialed Phil, filling him in on the game plan.

'So you want me to meet with Colin Summers at three?' he asked.

'No.' She frowned over the phone. 'I got it.'

Pause. 'Can I ask a question?'

'Maybe.'

'What part of duty are you restricting, I mean, given that you *are* on restricted duty?'

'I'm not carrying my sidearm,' she informed him curtly. 'Why? Think I need one to interview an investment banker?'

'No. I think you need to trust your squad. Let us work while you boss us around. Come on, what's not to love?'

'I don't have time for this conversation,' she informed him.

'You mean the one where I'm right and you know it?'

She growled. Her former squad mate didn't laugh. 'D.D., we care about you. You're just coming back from a major injury suffered on the job when you went off all alone, without notifying Neil or me, to review a crime scene. Can you not see the pattern? And do you not understand how much that hurts us? No, no. I'm wrong. How much that *pisses* us off? We were your partners, and you didn't even give us a chance to have your back.'

That brought D.D. up short. One, because Phil, father of four, never swore. And two, because calm, good-natured, always-understanding Phil definitely sounded angry.

'I didn't mean it that way.'

'You never mean it that way. That's the point. You think of yourself—'

'I think of my case!'

'Which has a whole team working it! Exactly my point.'

D.D. didn't know what to say. Phil was chastising her. Phil never chastised her. That was her job.

'So . . . you want to question Colin Summers?' she asked quietly. Though she didn't want Phil to interview Stacey Summers's father. She wanted to do it. Meet the man, pass judgment on how he responded to each line of inquiry. It was her nature to want to do and see for herself. Not because she didn't trust her squad, but simply because she was who she was.

Just ask Alex.

'I can't,' Phil said.

'You can't?'

'I got a bead on Kristy Kilker, whose driver's license we found in Devon Goulding's bedroom.'

'The one who's supposedly studying abroad in Italy?'

'Yeah, did some digging. According to her university, Kristy never signed up for a study-abroad program. So either she lied to her mother or her mother's lying to us. I got uniform patrol officers picking up the mom now and bringing her down for questioning.'

'Keep me posted. Any word on Natalie Draga?'

'Yeah, heard back from her grandmother in Mobile. Natalie headed to Boston last year. Called home a few times, but Grandma Draga hasn't heard from her in a bit. Best she recalls, Natalie had gotten a job as a waitress in a bar. But it doesn't sound like she and her granddaughter are exactly close, so as for such details as where Natalie lived, possible roommates, friends, Grandma Draga doesn't know, doesn't care.'

'Which bar?'

'Grandma didn't know. But per your savvy restricted duty sergeant commands' – Phil uttered the words dryly – 'couple of district detectives paid a visit to Devon Goulding's employer yesterday afternoon—'

'Tonic.'

'Yep. They flashed photos of Natalie Draga and Kristy Kilker. Bar manager ID'd Natalie Draga as a former employee, but claims she hasn't seen her in months. Draga walked out one day, never came back.'

'Kristy Kilker?' D.D. asked, wondering if they could be

so lucky as to have both women connected so quickly to Devon Goulding.

'No such luck, but Carol is headed over to Tonic now to copy Natalie's pay stubs,' Phil said. 'More and more . . .'

'Looks like Devon Goulding has direct ties to at least Natalie Draga. Working at the same bar and all.'

'Carol will figure out the details,' Phil assured her.

D.D. tried to stop her automatic snort. She was only half successful.

'Come on now,' Phil said immediately. 'Why are you so hard on her? Carol Manley is a perfectly good detective with an excellent track record. Not to mention she has a golden retriever named Harley. How can you not like a woman with a dog named Harley?'

D.D. didn't answer. Her feelings regarding the new detective were irrational, and she knew it.

'I thought Carol was reviewing video feeds from all the cameras surrounding Florence Dane's apartment?' she asked.

'Officers are executing those warrants now. When they have the videos, she'll start reviewing. But in the meantime . . .'

D.D. couldn't argue with that. It did take longer to amass security footage than one might think.

'We need to find Flora,' she muttered.

'Then given that you're the boss, how 'bout requesting more manpower? Because between working Devon Goulding from yesterday and now this from this morning . . . we're stretched thin. You know, so thin, even the restricted duty boss lady feels a need to work in the field.'

'Touché.'

'Not that it's my place to tell you what to do.'

Phil sounded cranky again. D.D. hesitated. Wondered if

there were things here she was still missing. God knows she'd never considered that Phil and Neil might be taking her injury so personally. Left alone, she had a natural bossy streak even before she, the younger detective, was appointed a supervisor over Phil, who had more years on the job. Though she'd always been the lead detective on their three-man squad . . .

'Phil . . .' she started.

'Hold on. Okay. Mrs Kilker has just arrived. Time for me to earn my paycheck. Good luck with Colin Summers.'

'Same.'

'Then come home?'

Cop-speak for returning to HQ. 'Sure. Then I'll be home.'

'See you here.'

Phil hung up. D.D. stood there a while longer, wondering again what she was missing and, if she was such an excellent detective, why the men in her life remained such mysteries to her.

Colin Summers worked for a major investment bank in the financial sector of Boston, adjacent to Faneuil Hall. From the FBI's downtown office, it was easier for Pam and D.D. to walk to the stately pink-granite building than battle out-of-state tourists driving hopelessly lost on increasingly narrow side streets.

D.D.'s favorite leather coat wasn't completely up to the job of battling the late fall chill, but she hunched her shoulders and soldiered through. Pam, she noticed, had exchanged her suit jacket and silk blouse for a cable-knit sweater and gold-toned scarf. Still dressy, but more approachable than the earlier buttoned-up affair. Not a bad strategy, in other words, when about to ambush an angry father about just how far he might have gone to get his missing daughter back.

Like many corporate offices in Boston, the banking building had a manned lobby even on Sundays. Pam did the honors for both of them, flashing her ID and stating they had a three o'clock meeting with Colin Summers. The young rent-a-cop stifled a yawn – no doubt they'd interrupted quality time watching YouTube videos on his cell phone – then dialed up. Colin must've already been there to vouch for them, as they were immediately waved through.

'I'll take the lead,' Pam said briskly as they rode the elevator up.

D.D. didn't argue. Pam had an established relationship with the subject, and despite what Phil might think, D.D. wasn't that big a control freak. Maybe.

They arrived on the eleventh-floor lobby. One set of glass doors to the left, a second set to the right. Both appeared dark and secured. Pam turned to the left, and sure enough, a man appeared on the other side of the door, gaunt face already set in a grim mask as he buzzed them through.

D.D. had never met Colin Summers before. Just spoken to him by phone, plus seen him on TV, pleading for his daughter's safe return. He must've recognized her from various press conferences as well, because immediately:

'I knew it! I knew it! If *she's* here' – he stuck a finger out at D.D. – 'then that Goulding bastard's death did have something to do with my daughter. Did you find her? Do you have news? Where is she? Where's Stacey!'

'Colin,' Pam said. Not soothing, which surprised D.D., but firm. 'We haven't found Stacey. Trust me, I'd be sitting with both you and your wife right now if we had.'

Colin scowled but nodded. Apparently, that made sense to him.

'We do, however, have a new line of inquiry that might help us find her. So please, may we?'

Pam gestured to the glass doors, which Colin had buzzed open but was still blocking with his body. Grudgingly, the man fell back. Pam shot D.D. a look, then both of them entered.

They walked into a tight receptionist area, punctuated by a striking wall of gray slate. Modern and sophisticated, as befitting a major i-bank. Colin headed to the right, swiping his employee ID as they passed through another set of secured doors. Then they entered the heart of the matter, a vast open space dotted with cubicles in the middle and a row of rooms with a view to the right.

Most of the cubicles were empty, as they'd hoped, the space only half lit. But D.D. could hear the clickety-clack sound of typing in the distance, as well as the low murmur of a voice on the phone. Young up-and-comers she figured, still fighting to get ahead by logging Sunday hours.

A vice president with the firm, Colin had already paid his dues. He led them to the proverbial corner office, and D.D. couldn't help but be impressed. A massive cherry desk. Mammoth black leather executive chair. Even more startling, a city view. Sure, he was peering down a narrow street running between two other high-rise buildings, but still . . . the cobblestones of Faneuil Hall beckoned in the distance, bustling with tiny wide-eyed tourists and hungry locals enjoying the weekend.

D.D. tore her gaze from the windows and took in the gold-framed diplomas punctuating the adjacent wall. Pam Mason hadn't been lying; there appeared to be no problem Colin's advanced intellect and financial success couldn't solve.

Except, of course, for the matter of his missing daughter.

Colin had already taken a seat behind his mammoth desk. Under normal circumstances, D.D. thought, he would've been considered good-looking. Close-cropped sandy-blond hair, intense blue eyes, trim, athletic figure. Work-hard, play-hard kind of guy.

His mouth, however, was set too hard and thin. Not cruel, but grim. And his face, upon closer inspection, was hollowed out. A workaholic under more than his usual load of stress. A man watching helplessly as his family fell apart.

He didn't offer water or coffee. He just sat, the desk an obvious shield before him, as he stared at D.D. and waited for her to speak.

Pam took one of the wingback chairs from the seating area and dragged it over. Perfectly calm and unruffled, she gestured for D.D. to take a seat. Then she dragged over a second chair for herself.

True to her word, D.D. waited for Pam to take the lead. Which, given how hard Colin was staring at her – as if already he considered D.D. the enemy – was definitely the right approach.

'How is Pauline?' Pam asked after a moment. She took her time getting settled into her seat, making herself comfortable. In contrast to Colin's grim features, she appeared relaxed, engaged; she could've been meeting old friends for brunch.

'How do you think?' Colin bit out, eyes blazing. 'Especially given . . . yesterday.'

'Did you know Devon Goulding, Colin? Ever frequent Tonic bar, recognize his picture on the news—'

'You mean other than he's a perfect match for the guy who abducted my daughter?'

'Sergeant Detective D.D. Warren' – Pam turned abruptly – 'can you please tell Mr Summers what you found in Devon Goulding's house?'

D.D. startled. She had no intention of giving up any such information. But Colin was already leaning forward, face nearly feverish. He wasn't going to back off, she realized. He believed they knew something and were intentionally keeping him in the dark. As long as that was the case, they would get nothing from him and go nowhere in this interview. She'd agreed to let the victim advocate take the lead, so Pam Mason had made the executive decision: Sometimes you gotta pay to play. They would pay Colin Summers with this information. And hope he returned the favor.

'We found photos,' D.D. offered, 'belonging to a young woman he was clearly stalking. We also found driver's licenses hidden away in his bedroom. We have yet to locate either woman from the licenses.'

Colin hissed in a breath. As much as he'd clearly been anticipating such news, it had still caught him off guard.

'We believe Devon Goulding was a predator. We believe it's possible that both of those young women fell victim to him, that their licenses are trophies of a sort.'

'He killed them,' Colin said.

'We don't know. We have detectives working on locating each woman. But as of now . . .'

'You can't find them.'

'We haven't found them.'

'He killed them,' Colin repeated.

'Give us another forty-eight hours,' D.D. said, thinking of the progress being made by her very excellent team, 'and we can probably answer that.'

'Now, tell him what you didn't find,' Pam interjected firmly.

D.D. kept her gaze on Colin Summers, who was still leaning forward, shoulders rigid.

'We didn't find any sign of Stacey. No photos. No

driver's license. Not a strand of hair, nor trace of fiber.'

Colin didn't sit back. He didn't relax. He just continued to stare at her as if he couldn't absorb such news.

'Mr Summers, I told you the truth this morning. We believe Devon Goulding was a rapist, maybe even a murderer. But we don't, as of this time, have any reason to believe he was the man who took your daughter. In fact, given his custom of keeping trophies – the driver's licenses, photos – chances are, he's not.'

'But you're here.'

'Colin,' Pam interjected, 'it's time for you to tell us what you know about Goulding. Why you suspect him for your daughter's case.'

'What? How would I know him? I just heard about him on the news, like everyone else.' He shot D.D. another angry glance.

'Really? And what did Flora have to say about him?'

Colin flinched. His gaze dropped. Abruptly, he sat back. All the better to put distance between him and them, D.D. thought.

'Colin, I know you want answers.' Pam again. 'I know you love your daughter. I know you would do anything to get her back.'

'Did you hire a private investigator?' D.D. spoke up. 'To help find Stacey?'

Colin didn't speak. He no longer appeared angry to D.D., but stark. A father who was trying to keep his heart from breaking.

'Mr Summers, I can get a warrant for your phone records,' D.D. continued, 'as well as for the security cameras in this building. Such actions will take away resources the Boston police could otherwise spend continuing the search for your daughter, but if I have to . . .'

'I know Rosa Dane,' he conceded abruptly. 'She's our mentor. I told you that.'

'She shared her story with you, correct? That's part of her role. Letting you know what she went through and, even more importantly, that even after being kidnapped for over a year, a daughter can come home again.'

Colin nodded.

'Rosa's honest. She told you about Flora's struggles, didn't she? About how you can get a happy ending, but still not live happily ever after. How her own daughter has spent the past five years obsessed with criminal behavior and self-defense in order to try to feel safe again.'

Colin didn't say anything.

'And that got you to thinking. The police haven't been able to help you. Apparently, you weren't satisfied with any of the private investigators you interviewed—'

He scowled at Pam, clearly irritated that the victim specialist had revealed so much.

'So what about Flora Dane? What about a girl who's truly been there and done that? Who's become something of an expert on kidnapping and abduction. Why not talk to her?'

He chewed his lower lip.

'You met her here,' Pam spoke up. 'In this office. It's the only place you have any privacy. And you wouldn't want Pauline to know – it would upset her. And you wouldn't want me to know because I wouldn't approve. So you contacted Flora and arranged to meet her here. Remember, Colin, we can pull security footage.'

'Fine. I met with Flora. In this office. We just talked, though. After everything Rosa had said, I was curious to meet Flora in person. A survivor, you know. Someone who did make it. As for Flora, she'd clearly been following Stacey's case. She had questions of her own.'

'When did you meet with her?' D.D. asked.

'I don't know. Three weeks ago?'

'I want the day. Monday, Tuesday, third Saturday of October? Be specific.'

Colin scowled, but after a moment, he pulled out his cell phone, consulted his calendar. 'Tuesday, second week of October, three P.M. Better?'

'How long did you talk?'

'Hour. Maybe ninety minutes.'

'Did she have theories on Stacey's abduction?' Pam interjected.

Colin shrugged. 'Nothing new, just the usual. What did we know of her online activities? Who were her friends she went out with that night, how big a drinker, could she handle herself? She wanted to know about Stacey's . . . resources. I mean, my daughter's athletic. People don't always take it seriously, but cheerleading is an intense sport. Flora said that would be a mark in my daughter's favor. Then she wanted to know if Stacey had taken any self-defense, karate, carried Mace, anything like that. She hadn't. What about mental resilience. How my daughter functioned under pressure. I . . . I couldn't really answer. Maybe Pauline could. But my job, my whole life, has been to keep my daughter from being under that kind of stress. To take care of her. To keep her safe.'

Colin Summers's voice broke. He looked away. Neither Pam nor D.D. spoke. After another moment, he composed himself. 'I said Stacey's smart. If she could figure a way out, she would. But also . . . Stacey's sweet. And I don't just mean that as her father. From a very early age, she has always been so . . . likeable. Total strangers gravitate to her. And she gravitates to them. She's one of those people, she sees the best in everyone. Flora said . . . Flora said that might help her. She said the guy who kidnapped her used to talk about killing her all the time. She listened. Agreed with everything he said, did whatever he wanted. And eventually, the guy didn't talk about killing her anymore. Eventually, he decided to keep her instead.'

'Did Flora think Stacey was still alive?' D.D. asked curiously. Too late, she caught Pam's warning glance.

'Of course my daughter is still alive!'

'And Flora agreed with this assessment.'

'She thought it was highly possible!'

'Colin,' Pam interjected quietly, 'did you hire Flora to find your daughter?'

'No. Of course not. I mean, she's just a kid herself. A past victim. I'd never do such a thing.'

'Remember, we can subpoena your financials.'

Colin glared at the victim specialist. 'At what point are you on my side on any of this?'

'Why don't you consider me on Pauline's side?' Pam Mason smiled sweetly. Colin blanched.

'I didn't hire Flora. Not . . . exactly.'

'She offered to help,' D.D. filled in.

'She was already well versed on the case! Had been following it on her own. And her mother hadn't exaggerated. The things she knew, talked about. Flora Dane was more impressive than any of the private investigators I interviewed. And definitely more vested in finding my daughter than any of you detectives have been!'

D.D.'s turn to arch a brow, but never argue with a grieving father.

'How much did you pay her?' she asked in clipped tones.

'Nothing.'

But D.D. caught the edge. 'Nothing . . . yet?' She sat

back. 'Reward. You offered her a reward if she helped find your daughter.'

'We're already offering a public reward. Nothing wrong with that.'

'I disagree. Flora Dane may talk the talk, but at the end of the day, she is just a young woman. A past victim. You took advantage of her obsessions.'

'She offered. Given how little progress *the professionals* have made, I didn't feel inclined to argue. But no money has changed hands and you can't prove anything.'

'Did she bring you word of your daughter?'

'No. Actually, I hadn't heard anything more from her. But I figured it would take time for her to work her channels, as she called it. Then, Saturday, when I turned on the news and heard about that bartender . . . I knew. I knew it had to be Flora, searching for my daughter.'

'Except Devon Goulding didn't kidnap your daughter.'

'Shouldn't you be asking Flora about that?'

'We can't. Flora's gone missing. In fact, we have reason to believe she was abducted from her apartment sometime late yesterday. Perhaps by the same man who took Stacey. I guess you can say we do have a new lead in your daughter's case, Mr Summers. We're no longer looking for one missing girl, we're now looking for at least two.'

23

No one wants to be a monster.

Fake Everett told me this time and again. It wasn't his fault he was the way he was. He didn't ask to have sex fantasies every minute of every waking hour. To be turned on by pictures of big-boobed girls bound and gagged. To be aroused by the sound of metal chains snaking across the floor.

He once read a news story about a peeping tom discovered in the honey bucket of some state park's composting toilet.

The peeping tom made up some tale of having lost his wedding ring, had to go in after it. But the police discovered the guy had a whole history of being caught in port-a-johns, outhouses, all that crap – fake Everett would laugh as he said the word crap, pleased with himself.

Anyway, some expert claimed the guy had a potty fetish. He was aroused by standing in poo, spying on strange women doing doody.

Not making this up, fake Everett would say, taking his hands off the steering wheel of his big rig, as if to prove his point.

Now, who in his right mind would choose to be turned on by crap? Everett would continue. It was a sickness, clearly, an obsession he probably wished he didn't have.

*Imagine a life sneaking around looking for public potties?
Covered in stench?*

*Well, kidnapping me, raping me, assaulting me, that
wasn't his fault either – fake Everett was very earnest on
this subject.*

*For as long as he'd had memory, he'd been filled with
thoughts of sex. Even as a little boy, before he knew what
sex was, he'd stare at boobs and wish he could touch 'em.
His mom's, his grandma's, total strangers'. It didn't matter.
He knew there was something out there he wanted, had to
have. Just took him a bit to understand what it all meant,
and then . . .*

*He'd tried to be normal, he'd whine. Have a girlfriend,
stick to missionary, tell himself he could be satisfied with
three times a night. He'd even gotten himself a wife. Surely
that would work.*

*Except he didn't want plain-Jane sex. He didn't want
some dutiful wife lying like a cold fish beneath him. He was
a man; he had needs. And obsessions. Deep hardwired
fantasies and thoughts he couldn't let go, even if no one
understood but him.*

*He'd beat up his first wife. Pounded her to a bloody pulp
so bad he'd had to call an ambulance. The docs in the ER
had ratted him out, and the police had arrested him while
his wife was still unconscious and couldn't explain it was all
her fault – a good wife should never say no.*

*He'd had to serve time, which had been a lesson in and
of itself. Plenty of sex behind bars – don't get him started
– but none of it was his kind of deal. Definitely no place for
a man with his needs.*

*In prison, he'd had to attend group sessions. For rage
management. Impulse control. Even learned about sex
addiction. First time he'd ever heard there was something*

abnormal about wanting so much sex all the time. Something unhealthy.

He decided when he got out he'd try to quit. Like an alcoholic, he'd go cold turkey. No sex, no terrible hungers, no fits of rage, no more time in jail. Good deal.

Except people can live without alcohol. But no man can live without sex.

Which is how he ended up attacking a fourteen-year-old girl.

Not his fault. He didn't ask to be born this way.

No one wants to be a monster.

His mama wasn't bad. His father, well, yeah, he was a real asshole. But he was never around. Nah, fake Everett was raised by his mama, who worked two jobs, chain-smoking in between. When he was real little, he'd shuttled between her and his grandma's house. When he was older, six or seven, he stayed home alone. He'd watch TV shows where the women were super skinny with massive chests and clingy tops. Then he found his father's stash of skin mags. After that, he couldn't wait for his mother's work shifts. He spent hour after hour flipping through pages, staring at the pictures.

When he was thirteen, he explained as we drove across the state of Alabama, he wanted to be a porn star. Thought it would be the best job in the whole world. 'Course, when he turned sixteen and his chest was still a scrawny, hairless wasteland, and his face was covered in acne, and his hair was an oil slick . . .

Even a total fuckup like him could realize porn stars looked one way . . . and he didn't.

He still loved porn. And now, thanks to the wonders of the Internet, he could take it with him everywhere.

None of this surprised me. I already knew the second

fake Everett was done driving for the day, he'd load up his favorite sex videos into the DVD player, pop open my prison, and we'd be off and running. It didn't matter if I was tired or hungry or sore. It didn't even matter if he was tired or hungry or sore. A man had needs. This was his biggest need.

No one wants to be a monster.

You can teach yourself not to feel anything. To fly away. Sometimes, I pictured myself in the meadow, playing with the foxes. But I didn't like that. It felt too tainted. So I pictured bright blue sky. A bluebird sky, we called it in New England, when the winter sky turned a rich, true blue, versus the overbright, summer-bleached alternative.

During the day, I was the perfect listener. An audience of one for a man who could really talk and talk and talk. Then, by night, I became an inanimate object, to be moved and positioned and posed this way and that by the same narcissistic asshole. What did it matter to me?

Eventually, when he was done, he'd offer me food. Or a drag of his cigarette. Or a swig from his beer.

We would sit in silence, the big rig filled with the scents of sweat and sex. And for a minute, or two or three, he'd almost seem happy.

'You're pretty,' he told me once. 'That's why I had to take you. I saw you. Dancing. All that hair jiggling right above your ass. Made a man look, all right. Except, of course, a girl like you . . . you'd never even give someone like me the time of day.' He stated it matter-of-factly. I didn't argue. 'So I did it my way. And here we are. Touring the country like two crazy fools. Now what d'you think? Burgers or pizza for dinner tonight?'

He fed me. Then there would be more sex. Then, back

to the box for me. Except as days became weeks . . . Sometimes, he fell asleep. Sometimes, I got to stay there, lying on the softness of the sleeping bag, my wrists still bound, one ankle shackled to a large metal ring on the floor, but still . . .

I didn't sleep those nights. I forced my eyes to stay open. I drank in the slippery feel of the nylon sleeping bag versus my usual bed of hard pine. I took in the softness of night, just beyond the sleeper cab's narrow windows. I listened to him snore, and I thought, if I could just get my bound wrists around his neck. Or find the strength to press a pillow against his face or shove a pencil into his eye.

But I never made any such moves, never acted on my own fantasies. Sometimes, when he was sleeping, he almost looked human. Just another guy grateful to have survived another day.

I wondered if his mother or grandmother were still alive. I wondered if they missed him, or if they knew by now who he truly was and regretted their mistakes.

I didn't think of my mom anymore. Or my brother or the beauty of foxes. I lived flying against a bluebird sky. And there were good days, where I got to sit on the passenger's seat of the cab, my bound hands out of sight, and watch the countryside rush by. And there were bad days, where something pissed him off and he drank more and hit more and punished me more.

But there were lots of days that were merely days. When fake Everett would talk. I would listen. The road would roll by. And maybe a song would come on the radio, and I would surprise myself by humming along, and he would surprise me by joining in. And we'd sing along to Taylor Swift.

I learned he liked The Carol Burnett Show *and* I Love Lucy *episodes and* Bonanza, *which he used to watch with*

*his grandma. While I talked about SNL and my addiction
to Grey's Anatomy.*

*'McDreamy,' he said, surprising me. Later he showed up
with a box set of Grey's Anatomy's first few seasons and
loaded a disc into the DVD player for me.*

*That night, as he pounded away like a jackhammer, I
thought of Seattle hospitals and ridiculously good-looking
doctors and maybe one day, someday, a hunky intern
holding my hand as they rushed in my bruised-and-battered
form. I'd been rescued. I'd escaped. I'd finally killed fake
Everett, and now for my reward.*

*A McDreamy of my own to heal my wounds and keep
me safe forever.*

*But I didn't dream that much. I didn't think ahead or
wonder about that future or what would one day become
of me. Mostly, I flew against a bluebird sky, my body bound
but my mind long gone.*

*'Lindy,' he woke me up, crying out in his sleep one night.
'Lindy, Lindy, Lindy.'*

*He sounded like he was sobbing piteously, fingers
scrabbling against the sleeping bag beside me.*

'No, no, no,' he cried. 'Oh, Lindy!'

Do monsters have nightmares? Do they even dream?

*He sounded like he was dying. As if his world had ended.
As if fake Everett must've once had a heart because now it
was being ripped out of his chest.*

*I found myself running fingers down his back. I could
feel the tension in his muscles, the raggedness of his breath.
A man in pain. I stroked his back again, gently, until
eventually, he sighed heavily. His shoulders came down. He
slept.*

*Later, when he woke up, and declared once again that a
man had needs, I didn't shy away. I kept my eyes open,*

staring at him, wondering who Lindy was and what she'd done that gave her such power over him.

And what I could learn from her.

More days. More nights.

Till one afternoon, he pulled into a truck stop. Went inside to grab coffee and, without thinking about it, left me sitting there. Hands bound, left ankle shackled to yet another metal ring on the floor, but still, sitting in plain sight.

A state police cruiser pulled in, parked beside me. Door swung open. A tall man in uniform stepped out. He spotted me, nodded once, fingers on the brim of his cap, and I . . .

I sat with my hands fisted on my lap. I said nothing. I did nothing.

While my heart accelerated madly in my chest and for a moment . . .

I had a memory. Like a tickle in the back of my throat. My mom. I could picture her perfectly. Her arms outstretched, waiting for me. She was saying a name. Molly. Except that wasn't quite right. Was it?

I wanted to raise my bound hands. I wanted to bang on the window, show my tied wrists. I wanted to yell, my name is . . . My name is . . .

I wanted to beg, please just take me home.

The state trooper staring right at me. Myself, hands on my lap, staring right back.

And then, in the next instant, I could see what he saw. A skinny, white trash girl with cheap clothes, lifeless eyes, and hacked-off blond hair. I saw Molly. Sitting in a big rig. Waiting for her wife-beating man to return to her.

And I didn't feel like a bird about to burst out of its cage. I didn't feel like a girl about to go home.

I felt ashamed. Like the shit-brown carpet, so many shades of nasty.

I wiped my mother's image from my mind. I replaced her face with a bluebird sky. And I focused my gaze dead ahead.

The state trooper walked away.

Fake Everett returned. He spotted the cruiser. Jerked open the cab door, already appearing panicked. Then he saw me, just sitting there, eyes locked forward.

He got in, buckled up, drove away.

Neither of us said a word.

That night, when he was done, he didn't put me back in the box. He let me stay out. Night after night. Day after day. No more coffin-size box.

Because Flora didn't exist anymore, and we both knew it.

I wrote another postcard to my mom.

Dear Mom, *I wrote.* Having the best time, touring the country with the man of my dreams.

24

Upon waking, I reach immediately for the water bottle, discovering it still tucked in the curve of my body. Good.

Lights remain out, the room its usual soul-sucking black. It doesn't frighten me as much as it makes me impatient. Sooner or later, he's going to flash on the lights. Not even monsters want to spend all their time in the dark.

For now, I orient myself, concentrating on the thin plastic of the water bottle, the lacy edge of my ridiculous nightie, and the welted edge of my mattress. And moisture, I realize belatedly. On my cheeks. Along with the taste of salt.

I've been crying in my sleep.

I dreamed of Jacob.

I lift my bound hands and quickly wipe the tears from my face. I don't think about it; I don't dwell on it. Survivors should never second-guess. If I hadn't done what I did, I'd never be here today.

Once again kidnapped, dealing with cheap pine coffins.

I make a barking noise that might be laughter. Hard to tell. My throat's dry. I decide to risk a small sip of water. It's an important resource. A person can survive weeks without food, but only days without water. I know these things now. I deliberately researched them.

Which makes me angry at the impenetrable dark again.

I didn't study and train all these years just to be locked away like a pair of old shoes. Where the hell is my captor anyway? Doesn't he want to gloat? Punish me? Assert his sexual superiority? What kind of freak goes to all this trouble, then never shows his face?

I sit up, swing my legs over the edge of the thin mattress.

An old pro by now, I sniff the air first, trying to detect any new scents that might indicate another meal delivery, even the smell of soap, shampoo, body odor, to signal someone else's presence in the room.

I get nothing.

Next up, as long as I'm playing blindman's bluff: sound. More carefully modulated breathing? Or the distant hum of traffic beyond the blacked-out windows, muffled thumps or thuds from other rooms in the house?

Once again, nothing.

I start crawling. Bump against the plastic bucket, veer right. I continue through the room to where there should be the remnants of the pine coffin. Except this time, when I find nothing, it actually means something.

He's removed the shards. Realized they could be utilized as weapons and quickly carted them away? Which, of course, makes me immediately wonder about the ones I stashed inside the seam of my mattress. But I don't dare double back to check, not when he could be watching.

Instead, I sit back on my heels, considering.

How is he doing this? Entering and exiting the room so quietly? It's one thing for him to observe through the viewing window, then make his move once he thinks I'm asleep. Except I'm an extremely light sleeper. The odds of him dragging entire coffin-shaped boxes in and out without me ever stirring . . .

He must be drugging me. Sneaking in and placing more

chloroform over my mouth? Except, contrary to popular belief, it's not that easy to instantly knock someone out with a chloroform-soaked rag. Meaning I should've woken up fighting or, even now, detected remnants of the odor in the air.

On the other hand, addicts, sniffers, and the like have perfected mixing chloroform with other drugs to produce a much more powerful cocktail. If my abductor has access to the Internet or spends any amount of time in a nightclub, God only knows what he could've learned.

Which leads me to an even more basic question: How is he getting in? So far, I've found evidence of two single windows on what I believe is the exterior wall, plus the larger pane of glass, the one-way mirror, on the opposite wall.

But there has to be a door, of course. Every room has a door.

I focus my eyes in the gloom. Trying to identify a thin seam of lighter dark framing a doorway.

But no matter how much I squint and strain, I see nothing. Evil Kidnapper's blackout capabilities are very good.

Fine, the Helen Keller method it is.

I crawl toward the wall with the viewing window first. If the two single windows are on an exterior wall, then basic architecture makes this the longest interior wall, which, in my mind, makes it the most likely to have a door. In fact, the more I think about it, the more I'm convinced this wall must abut a hallway, hence the viewing window. He stands in the hall, staring in.

I stand up gingerly once I hit drywall. It feels strange to stand, and it occurs to me I've spent most of my time on my hands and knees, crawling around in the dark. Falling back into bad behaviors, I realize, making myself small. But there's no reason in this space I can't stand and walk. For that matter, some yoga and light calisthenics would be a good idea. I'm fed. I'm hydrated. I should also work on remaining strong.

I find the black-painted trim of the viewing window easily enough. It's nearly as long as the full stretch of my open arms. But, upon further inspection, it's not mounted in the middle of the wall, as you might expect. No, it's off to one side, leaving plenty of wall space to the left for a door.

I shuffle sideways, fingers skimming over the drywall. I wonder if he's standing on the other side of the viewing window right now. Intrigued by my efforts? Nervous?

There are so many kinds of predators in the world. Those who require submissive victims.

And those who like it when you fight back.

The obvious sign of a door would be a doorknob. Definitely no such luck. So I sway side to side, slipping my fingers across the wall in broad horizontal strokes, determined to feel the slight hiccup that would indicate the edge of a door. But nothing, nothing, nothing.

I pause, consider the room design again. I'd pictured the two single windows as being part of an external wall. Say, the front of a house. Which would mean this room is positioned as a long rectangle in the home.

But what if the two single windows are actually on the side of the house? Meaning the room isn't a horizontal dash, but a tall I. That would put the viewing window on a wall most likely adjacent to another room – a viewing room to go with the viewing window? – while one of the narrower walls would be most likely to open to a corridor.

I shift counterclockwise, moving from the long wall to

the skinnier one. Again, my fingers span from side to side, looking for a protruding doorknob, a narrow ridge. And then . . .

I find it. No doorknob, but definitely a seam in the wall. Which I can trace up to the top of my fingertips, then down to the floor. And across. Yes, a door. Fit flush into the black-painted walls with no protruding knob or metal locking mechanism to make it stand out.

How does he open it then? A knob on his side? But surely he'd want it secured as well? Maybe he has bolts mounted on the outside of the door that he can manually work, then pull the door open and walk through.

I know in the next moment what I'm going to do.

I return to my mattress. Turn it so it faces not the viewing room but the door. I take a seat, and with my body as a shield to block my motions, I feel gingerly for the ripped edge of the mattress, my stash of wooden shards. I pull out two, feeling instant relief, which I refuse to show on my face. He's not the only one who can keep someone in the dark.

I position my makeshift weapons along the length of my thigh. Then I reach down for the hem of my ridiculously stupid satin nightie and begin to tear. One long strip. Not easy to do, as the satin is happy to rip up but not across. Through sheer stubbornness I eventually win.

Then I have it. Two soft pine wooden stakes as weapons.

A strip of cloth tied around my mouth and nose to block (maybe, doubtfully) any kind of nefarious sleeping gas.

And a plan.

I take a seat, butt on mattress, shards tucked beneath my leg, out of sight, and water bottle on my lap.

I stare directly in the direction of where I know the door has to be.

And, fingers wrapped around my weapon, I wait.

* * *

I think I dozed off again. The effect of total darkness? Disorientation from the kidnapping? Drugs in my water?

But this time, I catch the telltale rasp of a metal bolt sliding back. I told my subconscious what to listen for, setting it like an alarm, and it didn't let me down. I force myself to remain still, not lifting my head, not giving any sign of consciousness. It's possible there's more than one predator. I've read several cases of kidnappers who work in pairs. Now is not the time to be stupid.

My bound hands press the two long, skinny pine shards into one larger, heavier unit. While my homemade satin mask wicks the moisture from my mouth and delivers the scent of musty cloth.

Slowly, the door eases open. Shades of black, I realize. No brightly lit corridor to suddenly flood my room with slashing rays of light and rouse me from slumber. No, this is a stealth job, all the way. As the shadowy figure moves from the darkened hallway to the even more impenetrable gloom of my space.

My fingers tighten on the pieces of wood.

Not terribly tall. Or maybe he is hunched?

Moving carefully, very carefully, as if not to wake me.

I remind myself not to move. I remind myself to stay very still. Wait till the figure steps all the way into the room.

Except, halfway through the door, the figure stops. A hand comes up . . .

To spray a drug? To render me unconscious?

I can't take it anymore.

I spring. With the sound of rattling chains, I leap to my feet and dart forward, pulling heavily on my tether.

No thinking. Just moving. Bound hands clasped tightly around the pine shards.

The man realizes too late what's about to happen. He turns defensively, raises an arm to block.

But I have trained harder. I have trained better. I drop beneath his forearm and drive my pine stakes into his ribs.

He screams. High, shrill, distinctly feminine.

He drops to the ground, while behind him, the door slams shut.

Myself, standing wide-eyed in the dark. Clutching my bloody weapon. Wanting to wave it triumphantly over my fallen target.

Except . . .

Something is not right here. The scream. Distinctly feminine. The fallen figure whimpering and cowering at my feet.

Slowly, I sink to my knees. Slowly, I set my wooden shards on the floor. And slowly, ever so slowly, I reach for the huddled form beside me.

I encounter fistfuls of thick, shoulder-length hair. It tells me everything I don't want to know.

'Stacey Summers?' I whisper.

She cries harder, and I find myself nodding in the dark.

I've finally found who I've spent weeks looking for.

And I just stabbed her.

25

After the interview with Colin Summers, D.D. returned to HQ as promised. No doubt her in-box was already over-flowing with reports to edit, warrants to review, and interrogations to read. She felt antsy, keyed up in a way she didn't like. Nervous about seeing Phil? Or simply over-adrenalized by a series of crimes that didn't make sense?

First the Devon Goulding scene, where the victim had turned out to be the perpetrator, and his attacker also their prime suspect. Florence Dane had annoyed D.D. then, and not just with her unwillingness to answer routine questions, but because Flora didn't fit.

Plain and simple, policing was about playing the odds. Find a wife murdered in her home, arrest the husband. Beaten child, handcuff the parents. Poisoned executive, haul in his hot business partner and former lover. Knowing who did it was rarely rocket science. Proving it was where D.D. and her squad mates earned their keep.

Then, you got cases such as Florence Dane. Where you were looking at an animal with hooves and stripes, and yet it definitely wasn't a zebra.

D.D. still didn't know what Flora was. Who she was.

Having finally made it safely home, why would the woman keep seeking out danger time and again? Because

D.D. had no doubts: Flora had met with Colin Summers. And she'd made finding Stacey Summers her own personal mission. The question was, did Flora really want to save a young college student? Or did she simply want a fresh target to kill?

In D.D.'s mind, that was a fifty-fifty proposition. Which didn't make her less keen to locate Flora, but rather gave her a certain urgency on the subject. One way or another, whatever had happened to Flora and Stacey, *whoever* had happened, it was going to end badly.

Because that's how Flora needed it to end, D.D. thought. Something had happened five years ago, between her and her first kidnapper. After four hundred and seventy-two days of captivity, something had gone down that left Jacob Ness dead and Flora very much alive. Except Flora had never gotten over it. And, even now, seemed to be seeking out the same sequence of events over and over again.

Entering HQ, D.D. spotted Phil walking across the cavernous glass-and-chrome lobby with a steaming cup of coffee. Never one to shy away from conflict, D.D. headed straight to him.

'Any chance that's for me?'

Phil clutched his coffee close. 'Back off. I've spent the past two hours with a crier. Trust me when I say I need this more than you.'

D.D. had to think about it. 'Kristy Kilker's mom?' she asked while sniffing at the wafting scent of dark-roasted bliss.

'Doesn't know a thing. Honestly thought her daughter was studying abroad in Italy. Totally fell apart when I informed her Kristy had never signed up for any such program. Oh hell, take it. I'll grab another.'

Phil thrust out his coffee. D.D. didn't argue. Peace

offering, she decided, then gamely followed Phil into the lobby cafeteria where he could grab a second cup.

'She hasn't heard from her daughter in months. Was less than thrilled, but figured Kristy was busy with her studies. Not to mention the two of them had a bit of a brouhaha right before Kristy supposedly left town. So maybe Kristy's nursing her wounds. Needless to say, to discover her daughter had been lying all along and was never in Italy—'

'She close to her daughter?' D.D. asked, though the 'brouhaha' combined with the fact Kristy had deceived her mother about her trip seemed to say enough.

'Used to be. According to the mom, Kristy changed when she went off to college. Became less communicative, more secretive. Nancy – Kristy's mom – worried her daughter had fallen in with the wrong crowd, that sort of thing. It was her idea for Kristy to sign up for the international program. Figured it would be good for her to have a change of pace. She funded it too, which wasn't easy on her secretary's salary. So to find out Kristy lied about the program as well as pocketed the funds . . . Nancy's not having a good day.'

'She able to give you the names of some of Kristy's college friends?'

'Yeah, and I sent some uniforms over to start on-campus interviews, with the dean of admissions, current professors, that sort of thing. But I don't think that's where the magic is.'

Phil paid for his second coffee. They walked together to the desk sergeant, flashing ID, getting waved through. D.D. headed for the stairwell, if only to torture her one-time squad mate further.

'Okay, so where's the magic?' she prodded as Phil began to climb the stairs wheezily beside her.

'Kristy had a job to help with her living expenses. Part-time cocktail waitress.'

D.D. paused midstep. 'Someplace near Tonic?' Devon Goulding's bar.

'Yes. At Hashtag. Just up the street. How much do you want to bet, after hours, Goulding was known to hang out there as well?'

'Oh, you're not getting money out of me that easily. You got detectives visiting the place and flashing photos?'

'As we speak.'

'Which would connect Devon Goulding with Kristy Kilker, who hasn't been seen or heard from in . . .'

'Mom hasn't gotten a call since June.'

D.D. resumed climbing. 'That's like five months ago. She really thought her daughter was still hanging out in Italy?'

'Kristy had planned to travel around on her own, after the program ended in September. The whole "me, my backpack, and various youth hostels" experience. Which, by definition, would mean she wouldn't have much money left for international calls and apparently the mom herself doesn't care for e-mail.'

'So we have Natalie Draga, who left home a year ago, and Kristy Kilker, who's been MIA for at least five months. Now, we know Natalie Draga actually worked at Tonic. Carol have any luck talking to the manager?'

'Yeah.' They'd rounded two flights, kept on trucking. 'Manager confirmed that Natalie used to be an employee. Nine months ago, however, she stopped coming in. Never called, never showed up to collect her last paycheck. Manager still has it sitting in her personnel file.'

'That doesn't sound good. Was Devon working there nine months ago?'

'Devon Goulding has been an employee in good standing

for the past three years. Excellent bartender. Does have a tendency to flirt with customers, fellow employees, et cetera, but what are you gonna do? His looks helped draw in the crowds while deterring overly aggressive riffraff. That he could be a rapist, no way. Manager doesn't believe it for a second.'

D.D. arched a brow.

Phil nodded. 'Exactly, especially once Carol started asking about temper tantrums, rage management. Manager's story changed. As a matter of fact, in the past year or so, Goulding's behavior has taken a turn for the worse. In fact, he got in a fistfight with another customer several months ago. Manager had to clean it up, Goulding promised it would never happen again.'

'So Goulding's roid rage was making itself known,' D.D. guessed. 'And he now has ties with at least two missing women.'

'Yep.'

They'd finally arrived on their floor. D.D. felt energized. Phil looked like he was about to keel over.

'So what happened to them?' she asked out loud. 'Kristy Kilker, Natalie Draga? Where are they now?'

Phil shrugged, his look saying what they both already knew. Most likely, they were searching for bodies, and the number of dumping options in Boston . . . Just ask Whitey Bulger. Boston was a criminal's playground.

'Techs have seized his vehicle,' Phil said.

Which made sense. If Devon had been hauling around bodies, he'd need a private means of transport. 'And if it has a navigation system . . .' D.D. prodded.

'We should be able to download frequently driven routes. Whatever he did, wherever he took them, chances are he'd want to visit.'

'Absolutely,' D.D. agreed. 'To relive the glory, revel in his own power, all of the above. Maybe . . .' She thought of the pictures of Natalie Draga, so many photos, clearly from a man either in love or worshipping from afar. 'Maybe,' she decided, 'even to mourn. If Natalie was his first . . . he might not have intended to kill her. Maybe he really did just want to talk, or win her back, assuming they'd once been together. But when that didn't work . . .'

Phil shrugged. The motives for murder were many and varied. At this point, it mattered less to the team why Devon had killed the girls and more what he'd done with them afterward. Sometimes detectives worked to put away the bad guy. And sometimes detectives worked to find closure for the families.

Speaking of which . . .

D.D. and Phil walked down the corridor to the homicide unit.

Where D.D. found Rosa Dane waiting for her, Samuel Keynes by her side.

Rosa was definitely dressed for comfort – yoga pants, an interesting assortment of tops that seemed to end in an oversize blue flannel shirt. Her son's shirt? Maybe even her late husband's, given the frayed cuffs and hem. It definitely contrasted with Keynes's classically tailored suit.

Rosa's face, however, was pure Flora. Or vice versa. The grim set of her lips, the hard line of her jaw. Clear gray eyes that peered straight at D.D. and didn't flinch. Rosa's hair was lighter, blond streaked with gray. But otherwise, she could be her daughter's older sister.

D.D. thought of what the victim advocate Pam Mason had said about how close Stacey Summers was with her mom. She wondered if Rosa saw the parallels with the relationship she used to have with her own daughter, and whether that helped her or hurt her when it came to mentoring the Summerses.

'She's missing.' The woman stated the phrase. Again, eyes clear, jaw set. 'When Samuel called' – she nodded her head in his direction – 'he didn't say as much, but the questions he asked. I've been asked those questions before.'

'I suggested she meet with you directly,' Keynes spoke up. 'And I assured her you were doing everything in your power to help locate Flora.'

D.D. resisted the urge for sarcasm. Now was not the time. With one last parting glance at Phil, whose expression was completely sympathetic, she motioned for Rosa and Keynes to follow her to her office.

'After talking to Samuel,' Rosa continued, falling in step behind D.D., 'I tried calling Flora again. Four, five times. She never called back. It's not like her to go so long without making contact; she knows better.'

'Would you like some coffee?' D.D. asked.

'So I drove down. Hoping for the best, because that's what mothers do. But I knew. The entire way. Driving, driving, driving. I knew she was gone. Then, arriving at her apartment, seeing the police cars . . . I spoke to the Reichters. They told me what happened.'

D.D. had finally reached her office. Not the largest or grandest in the unit, but perfect for private conversations. She ushered Rosa and Keynes inside, once again offered coffee, water, any kind of refreshment. Keynes shook his head. Rosa simply stared at her. D.D. took the hint.

'We are actively searching for your daughter,' D.D. stated, making herself at home behind her desk. 'We have concerns for her safety.'

Rosa smiled. It was not a happy expression, and

immediately, D.D. recalled Flora sitting in the back of the patrol car just yesterday morning. Survivors, D.D. realized. She was dealing with not one survivor of a traumatic kidnapping seven years ago but two of them. Mother and daughter. And the scars the ordeal had left on both of them.

And Keynes, standing patiently beside the door as Rosa took a seat. What was his role in all this? Just what kind of victim specialist remained on such familiar terms with a mother and her daughter five years later?

'I'm here to file a missing persons report. That will help, yes?' Rosa's tone was even.

D.D. nodded. She kept her gaze on Samuel, who hadn't spoken since entering the office and yet he seemed to assume he was part of this meeting. Why?

'I last saw her around one fifteen yesterday, Saturday,' Rosa said. 'You need to know that too.'

D.D. picked up a pad of paper, made a note. The woman was clearly a pro.

'She was dressed in her pajamas: blue plaid cotton boxers and a white T-shirt. Last I knew, she was planning on taking a nap, after being . . . out all night. I can go through her clothes and tell you if anything else is missing.'

'That won't be necessary.'

'You think she was taken from her bed, then. Kidnapped straight from her apartment.'

'There were no signs of a struggle,' D.D. said.

'He ambushed her. Drugged her?'

'We're still looking into that.'

Rosa nodded. Her face remained set. Not calm, nor simmering with the barely suppressed rage that animated Colin Summers's entire body. Instead, she was preternaturally composed. Like a fellow cop, D.D. thought. A woman who'd been there and done that before.

The woman gazed up at Keynes. He gave a faint nod, and she reached down for her oversize cloth shoulder bag, digging around until she produced a manila folder. 'Recent photo,' she said, placing it on D.D.'s desk. 'Written description. Her fingerprints are already on file.'

D.D. took the file.

'What about Flora's cell phone password?' D.D. asked. 'Because we're subpoenaing records of her texts and messages now, but that will take a few days, versus if we could access the phone directly.'

Rosa rattled off four digits. D.D. wrote them down, then glanced up. 'That's not a birthdate,' she said.

'No. It's a random code. More secure. Flora was big on security.' A slight fissure in the woman's composure. Rosa squared her shoulders, soldiered on. 'She shared the code with me, however. More security . . . in case something happened to her.'

'Were you worried about Flora, Mrs Dane?'

'Yes.' No hesitation. No shirking.

'Do you know what she'd been doing? Even before Devon Goulding?'

'Yes.'

D.D. leaned forward, resting her elbows on her desk. 'Mrs Dane, do you think Flora was truly trying to save the world, or do you think it's possible that Flora has a death wish? That she wasn't looking to continue her good work, she was looking to end things?'

Rosa Dane's facade cracked. A wide, gaping schism that revealed a world of pain and sorrow and resignation. A mother's aching, powerful, powerless love for her daughter.

Keynes reached out and gently squeezed her shoulder.

'She was my happy child,' the woman whispered. 'Darwin . . . he was old enough to feel the loss of his father.

To know, at an early age, that a phone can ring and nothing will ever be right again. But Flora was just a baby. She didn't bear those kinds of scars. She loved the farm. Chasing the hens, planting spring seeds, running through the woods, sneaking food to the foxes. She loved everything, everyone. All I ever had to do was open the front door, and she was happy.

'He put her in a box, you know. He shut her away in a pine coffin, day after day after day. And when he finally let her out, it was under the condition that she call him by her late father's name.'

D.D. got up. She had a box of tissues on the filing cabinet behind her. Now, she placed it on her desk in front of Rosa Dane. But the woman remained dry-eyed, stoic. The kind of grief too deep for tears. Keynes's hand was still on her shoulder. He seemed in no rush to pull it away.

'Do you have a child?' Rosa asked.

'A son, Jack. He's four, currently obsessed with Candy Land.'

'And if something happened to him?'

'I'd do whatever it took to get him back,' D.D. agreed.

'I did. I completed paperwork and designed fliers and personally worked the phones. Then, after that first post-card . . . I wore what the victim advocates told me to wear. I said what the FBI experts told me to say. I went on national television and begged for my daughter's life.

'Then I waited, and waited, and waited. Morning shows, nightly cable news. Watched my son return from college and lose himself to Facebook drives, Twitter appeals. Neither one of us had any idea. We'd been a family, just a family of farmers from Maine. Except then my daughter disappeared and for four hundred and seventy-two days . . .'

'I'm sure the police appreciated your cooperation.'

'They didn't.' Her voice was blunt. 'The investigators were hopeless. No leads, no clues. First it was all don't call us, we'll call you. Then, later, why hadn't I done this, why didn't I do that, as if suddenly it was my fault they couldn't find her. You know who helped us find Flora?'

D.D. shook her head.

'Jacob Ness. Him and his damn messages. At a certain point, postcards weren't enough. He started sending e-mails, even posting on her Facebook page. Escalation, they called it. But he e-mailed one too many times and an FBI agent in Georgia was able to trace the IP address to some Internet café that was part of a truck stop. But if not for that message, Flora would still be lost. We found her not because the police were that smart but because Jacob was that stupid.'

'Is that what you told Mr and Mrs Summers?' D.D. asked.

'Yes.'

'Did you know that Colin met with Flora? Did you know that she had agreed to help find Stacey?'

For the first time, Rosa fell silent. She sat back. Not saying yes, not saying no, but processing.

'Do you think the same person who took Stacey has now kidnapped Flora?' she asked at last.

'We don't know what to think. But it's certainly a possibility.'

'I love Flora,' Rosa whispered.

D.D. didn't say anything.

'I will always love her. That's what mothers do. But I . . . I miss her.'

D.D. remained silent. Rosa looked up, eyes so much like her daughter's, searching D.D.'s own.

'My daughter disappeared March eighteenth. My

beautiful, happy child. The girl who loved to climb trees and eat blueberries straight from the bush. I can remember how she looked, the full brilliance of her smile. I can remember how she felt, hugging me as if her whole body depended upon it. The lilt of her voice – 'bye, Mom – as she was halfway out the door, always cheerful, never worrying because of course we'd see each other again. My daughter disappeared March eighteenth. Seven years ago. Jacob Ness destroyed her, as surely as if he'd fired a bullet into her brain. And now . . . I love her. I will always love her. But this new Flora, she scares me. And she knows it.'

'Did Flora ever talk to you about the Stacey Summers case?'

'Never.'

'But you can believe she'd take an interest, go looking for Stacey herself.'

'I've seen her bedroom wall, Detective.'

'Was she getting counseling, therapeutic support?'

Rosa glanced up at Keynes. He'd finally taken his hand off her shoulder. Now, his arm hung by his side. Was it just D.D., or did he seem smaller somehow? Lonelier?

'Samuel designed a plan for her reentry,' Rosa said, gaze on the victim specialist. 'In the beginning, it included sessions with an expert in trauma. But Flora didn't care for those meetings. She claimed they didn't help. Ironically enough, it was her first self-defense class that made the most difference. After having spent so long feeling powerless, she delighted in discovering her own strength. Samuel approved. The best antidote for anxiety is confidence.'

'But she didn't stop with a few self-defense classes,' D.D. filled in.

'She became . . . obsessed. With both safety and security

and then other missing persons cases. All the other children out there who still haven't made it home again.'

'Do you think she could find Stacey Summers?' D.D. asked.

'I'm afraid that she could.'

'Afraid . . .' D.D. didn't have to consider it too long. 'You think there's more to it than saving others. You think it's also about punishing the perpetrator.'

Rosa didn't look at Keynes this time when she spoke. She stared straight at D.D.

'After everything Jacob Ness did to her, he died too quick.'

'What happened when they rescued Flora?'

'I don't know. You'd have to contact FBI agent Kimberly Quincy out of Atlanta. She's the one who located Jacob and led the raid to rescue my daughter.'

D.D. glanced at Samuel, who nodded.

'Were you there?' she asked him.

'No.'

'But you know what happened.'

'Only from hearsay. And as for anything Flora might have told me . . . We struck a deal that first day. She told me her story once. I repeated it for the official record. And now, we both keep her focused on the future.'

She turned her attention to Rosa. 'You've mentioned a brother—'

'Darwin.'

'Are he and Flora close? Would she have spoken to him about what she was up to?'

'Darwin is in London,' Rosa said.

D.D. shrugged. 'Which is why there's texting, e-mail, Skype?'

She kept her gaze on Rosa, who was clearly hesitating.

Interestingly enough, it was Keynes who spoke next, except not to D.D., but to Rosa. 'Have you told him?'

'No.'

'Wait,' D.D. spoke up. 'You mean you haven't told Darwin his sister is missing?'

Keynes continued as if she hadn't spoken. 'Are you going to tell him?'

Again, that hesitation. 'He's just getting his life back. If you could've seen him, what this did to him the first time she disappeared. The helplessness, the hopelessness. He gave up college, halted his entire life. And then she came back. Our own happily-ever-after. Except . . . she wasn't happy. The mood swings, the night terrors. The feeling that some imposter had taken her body. This wasn't my daughter, his sister. This couldn't be our Flora.'

Rosa looked up. 'He's just now getting himself together. How do I call and spring this on him? Again. So, what, he can drop everything? Again. Feel helpless and hopeless. Again. Even if he did come back, to do what? No postcards this time. At least not yet. In fact, best I can tell, you have no leads at all.'

'So are you going to tell him?' D.D. repeated Keynes's question, because she thought it was a good one.

'He can't help you,' Rosa said. 'Darwin has been away for years. He's doing his own thing, being his own person. Whatever Flora was up to, she wouldn't have told him. She's hurt him enough already, and she knows it. Now if you don't mind, it's getting late. I'm tired. I need a place to stay, and I'd like to use my daughter's apartment, if that's possible.'

'You're not heading back to Maine?' Keynes asked.

'No.'

D.D. had to glance at her watch, get her bearings.

Sunday, 7:00 P.M. Where had the day gone? Just this morning she was working a dead rapist case, and now . . . She had to think about it.

D.D. said, 'Apartment is off-limits for tonight; we're still processing. How long do you plan to stay?'

'How long will it take you to find my daughter?'

D.D. didn't have an answer for that one.

'I'll do my best to stay out of your way, Detective.' Rosa Dane gathered up her things. 'But don't expect me to remain on the sidelines. My daughter isn't the only one who learned some hard lessons seven years ago. You have your job. And now, I'm going to do mine.'

Rosa swept out the door, Samuel Keynes following close behind.

'Hang on,' D.D. tried to say.

But neither one of them turned around.

26

The girl is crying.

I can't see her, only hear her in the pitch black. I should do something. Move, talk, assist. I can't. I just . . . can't. Somehow, I've retreated to the far wall, sitting on the mattress with as much distance from the girl as I can get, knees curled to my chest, bound arms looped around my knees. I'm too stunned to react. I know how to take care of myself. Are you in pain? Are you hungry? Are you thirsty? Are you uncomfortable? No? Then you're all right.

I'm uncomfortable, I think wildly. I have training and preparation and experience. But I never saw this coming. I'm supposed to take care of myself, fight to save myself. Not . . . this.

Her cries are quiet. More whimpers than sobs. The kind of crying done when you're exhausted and dehydrated. When you've already used up your supply of real tears and this is all you have left.

I recognize this kind of crying. I've done it myself.

Water. Somewhere along the way, I dropped the water bottle. I should crawl forward and find it. I should crawl forward and . . . help.

It's not easy to do. In fact, it's excruciatingly difficult. Why? I'm the one who collects images of lost people. I'm the one who assigned myself as personal savior of Stacey Summers. So now, faced with the opportunity to really, truly lend a hand . . .

I don't want her to be her.

I don't want her thinking I can actually save her.

I don't want her, I don't want anyone, depending on me.

She's a resource. Is that a cold thought, a callous thought? But it comes to me. She's a resource. Her clothing, items she might have in her pocket, clips from her hair. Who knows? And if she's been allowed more freedom and privileges, say, a belt buckle – oh, the possibilities.

Now I must move forward. I have to engage. She's a resource, and a victim must use all resources available to her.

I pitch forward onto my hands and knees. Using my inchworm crawl, weight on my elbows, I wiggle forward in the dark.

She's fallen where I attacked her, sprawled in front of the suddenly appearing, disappearing door. Pulled shut, locked tight. I can't make out any sign it was ever there. The wall has gone back to being just a wall, the crying girl the only evidence anything happened at all.

'Stacey?' I whisper as I crawl forward.

She doesn't answer. Just whimpers.

My bound hands connect with the water bottle, knock it sideways. I pause, feel around more gently, until I can clasp it between my fingers. I wriggle forward, then bump against the girl's body.

Leg. Clad in denim. Blue jeans. She's in real clothes, versus my silly nightgown. The realization gives me hope. If she has pants, then maybe she also has a belt. With a metal buckle. That would be perfect. Oh, the locks you can pick, the things you can do, with the tongue of a belt buckle.

'Stacey,' I whisper again.

Still no response.

It doesn't feel right to simply pat her down, as if she were a suspect at a crime scene. But she won't talk to me either. I try to think of what I should do.

That last day, when the police found me, pouring through the hotel door and windows like a swarm of black armored ants, what had I been like, what had I wanted?

I'd been crying. I can remember that, but it feels far away and distant, something that happened to another person another lifetime ago. There was a female agent there. She kept saying 'Florence Dane' over and over again. The name confused me. Tickled the back of my throat, as if I should know it.

'Flora,' she tried again.

I think I spoke then. I think I said, 'My name is Molly.'

They exchanged looks, whispered responses. She placed her hand on my shoulder. 'My name is Special Agent in Charge Kimberly Quincy. I'm with the FBI. You're safe now. Okay? You're safe.'

I flinched when she touched me. Then felt myself go incredibly still. I wasn't shocked, I wasn't elated, I wasn't relieved.

I was suspicious. I was steeling myself for the blow to come.

She let go of my shoulder. She offered me water. Introduced me to a couple of EMTs who wanted to check me out.

'Would you like me to call your mom?' she asked.

But all I could think of was Jacob. Poor, poor Jacob.

And the blood all over my hands.

I couldn't respond to the Kimberly agent. I never talked. Or screamed. Or cried. I simply held myself very still. That day, and the next, and the next.

A girl who'd been born and raised in a coffin-shaped box.

I'm not that girl, I remind myself now. If I'm not that girl, then I must be the FBI agent, the Kimberly person. So what did she do? Spoke briskly and moved with authority. She ushered me through a flurry of medical exams and necessary questions, while keeping up a steady flow of conversation, whether I chose to answer or not.

She was normal, I decide. Sounded normal, acted normal. That's what she was trying to give me. After four hundred and seventy-two days, she offered normalcy.

I take a deep breath. Begin.

'My name is Flora.' Is it just me, or did my voice falter at the sound of my own name? I repeat myself, this time for my own sake. 'My name is Flora.' Not Molly.

'I'm sorry I attacked you.' Am I? Maybe. I don't know who she is yet, or her role in all this. Only a fool rushes to judgment.

'I'm going to try to help you. I'm sorry if it hurts, but I have to feel out the wound. I have some water. Would you like water?'

Her crying has puttered out. She appears to be listening to me. Her breath is still shaky and fluttery. Shock? Fear? Anything is possible.

She doesn't say yes or no to water, but whimpers again.

'I'm going to touch you,' I say now. 'I'm sorry. You probably don't want to be touched anymore.' I hadn't wanted to be. 'But I can't see you. This is' – I shrug, feeling a helplessness I already hate – 'the only way I can figure out what's wrong.'

I don't know what else to do. She's not talking, but at least is holding still. Is that an implicit yes or a mental hell no? I wonder if this is how the FBI agent felt five years ago.

Less like she was saving a terrified girl and more like she was dealing with a feral cat.

Bare feet. That's my first discovery. The girl is clad in jeans, but no socks and shoes. Evidence she's not allowed to leave the house? I allow myself a small moment of mourning for the opportunities shoelaces might have presented. Resources, resources, resources. But no sense in mourning what you never had to lose.

Next, I move my bound hands up her leg, fluttering my fingers across the line of soft worn denim. Old jeans. Her personal favorites? I tug experimentally, not sure if that's appropriate or not. But it's as I expected. The jeans are loose on her. If these were her original pants, she's recently lost a lot of weight.

She must be lying on her side because next I come to the faint curve of her hip. She hisses in a breath, and I suspect I'm close to the wound. When the door first opened and I lunged forward, I was aiming for the stomach, a gut job. I'm hoping, for both our sakes, I hit her ribs instead.

I feel weird, my cheeks flaming in the dark, as I come to the waistband of her jeans. Low-riders, frayed to the touch. I can't help myself. I'm not trying to stroke a sliver of bare skin at her waist, but of course I do. She shivers, flinches in response, and I blush even harder in the dark. I have to force myself to continue. I need to determine if she has a belt. Leather belt, corded belt, anything with a buckle . . .

No such luck.

Okay, this is it. The stab wound. I have to be close. And I'm no longer embarrassed. I'm petrified. I can't see. Not an inch, not a bit. What if I hit a piece of wood and drive it deeper? What if I hurt her worse?

I'm not cut out for this. I didn't train for this. I'm supposed to be alone. I'm all right alone.

Because now I'm uncomfortable. And uncomfortable is not the same as okay.

My hands are shaking uncontrollably. I hold them right above her, but I just can't do it. I will hurt her. I will make things worse. I'll learn, once and for all, just how much damage I've done.

Fingers. Suddenly closing around mine in the dark. She doesn't speak. Just the sound of her breathing, not calm and even but fluttery and frightened, as she takes my bound hands. And lowers them to the pool of blood at her side.

I've made a mess of things. I don't need light to know that. I recognize the streaks of moisture, distinct in sticky feel and rusty scent. Blood combined with shards of wood. Slivers really. Pine is too soft to make a great weapon. As I'd hoped – feared – I'd missed her belly, gouging against her ribs instead. Unfortunately, upon contact with hard bone, the pine had given up the fight, shattering into countless slivers. The girl's injury feels less like a stab wound and more like an encounter with a porcupine.

She is crying again, hiccupping in the shaky, shuddering pattern of someone in great pain.

I feel myself freeze up. I can't do this. The Kimberly agent never had to do this.

All that blood. So much blood five years ago. My hands, my face, my clothes. But none of it was mine.

I'm rocking back and forth. No, now is not that time. There are tears on my cheek. No, there will be no crying.

I'm a survivor, I'm a survivor, I'm a survivor, and Samuel himself said survivors must never doubt what they had to do.

'I'm going to pull them out,' I hear myself say.

She has released my hand. Her body is quivering,

definitely distressed. I try to move as gently as possible, but given that I have to find each wooden shard by feel, there's no way not to jar the wound. She hisses and moans, but remains passive beneath my clumsy touch.

To the best of my knowledge, I'm not making any sound, but I can taste salt, so apparently there are tears on my cheeks as I gingerly pinch and pull each piece. Some of them are very small, definitely more like slivers. Two pieces are thick and bulky. Shards. Do they hurt worse? Does it matter at this point?

I stabbed up with two pieces of pine clutched together. The end result is a bloody, pulpy mess, somewhere between road rash and a pin cushion.

It's not going to work, I think again and again. In the dark, I'll never get them all, only the obvious ones. And as anyone who's ever gotten a sliver knows, even the tiniest piece of foreign object embedded under the skin will eventually fester and inflame.

But I don't know what else to do. So I keep at it, arms shaking from the strain of moving so carefully, salt coating my cheeks. Five minutes, ten, twenty. But eventually I reach a point that when I wave my hand right above the wound, I can't feel any obvious protrusions. Surely she has wood still stuck in her side. How can she not? But under these conditions, with not even a flashlight to work by, there's nothing else I can do.

We need light. And bandages. And hydrogen peroxide and, oh yes, a real doctor, not just me.

I press my fingers gently against the wound. It feels about two inches wide, four or five inches tall. But maybe shallow? Or is that just wishful thinking?

She hisses again. Shudders.

'Does . . . does anything else hurt?' I don't know what

else to look for. What else to do. My fingers are sticky. Covered in blood. Her blood.

She doesn't answer. I continue speaking out loud, making the decisions for both of us: 'I think . . . I think we should leave it unbandaged for now.' Versus shredding more of my satin nightie for the cause. 'I don't think it's deep, but it's . . . messy. It needs to dry out. Scab over.' Plus I'm worried that trying to bind the wound will drive remaining splinters deeper beneath her skin.

She still isn't talking.

'I have some water. I'm, um, going to pour some over the area. Rinse it out.'

Waste of a resource? I don't know. I launched an attack. Sure, I hit the girl, not my abductor, but my show of defiance most likely caught him off guard, maybe even pissed him off. He could pull resources. No more dinner deliveries or other presents wrapped in cheap pine coffins.

Which brings me to another question. The girl's hands. Is she bound, like me? And why was she sent into the room?

I finish what I started. Uncapping the water bottle and releasing a slow trickle over the girl's side. I am sparing. I can't help myself. Some lessons cost too much to learn.

I rub a little on my hands, then wipe my hands as best I can against the thin carpet. I replace the cap on the water, then sit back on my heels.

There's no polite way to do this, so I just do it. Finish feeling up the girl in the dark. Cotton shirt, maybe a T-shirt. Chest, neck, face, thick shoulder-length hair. Her arms, which I trace all the way down to her handcuffed wrists. Then, because I know something about these things, I skim around the line of the metal bracelets, where I can feel the roughness of new scabs, interlaced with the smooth ridge lines of old scars.

'You were kidnapped too. A while ago. Long enough for your first wounds to have had time to heal.'

The girl doesn't move. Nor does she speak.

'Are you Stacey Summers?' I ask.

Nothing.

'I know your parents. I met with your father. They haven't given up hope. They're still looking for you.'

A slight hiccup. Surprise? Shock? A twist of hope?

'My name is Flora.'

I wait. My fingers still on her wrists.

And then, just as I'm beginning to give up hope, I feel her hands curl against mine.

'M-m-molly,' she whispers in the dark. 'My name is M-m-molly.'

Seven years later, that's all it takes.

My blood turns to ice.

My hands flinch, recoil protectively to my chest.

And I know . . . and I remember . . . and I feel . . . and I . . . and I . . . and I . . .

'No,' I whisper.

But this poor girl, my pain, my punishment, has finally found her voice.

'My name is Molly. Molly. Molly. Molly. My name is Molly.'

I don't look at the viewing window. I don't look to the sealed-up wall where I now know there is a door.

I look down at the carpet. I look deep into myself. And I think, all these years later: Oh my God, what have I done, what have I done, what have I done?

27

'Go over to him. Go on. Do it. Walk right over and tell that drunkass cowboy you're a kidnapped girl. Let's see if he'll rescue you. No? Don't think he'll believe you? Or afraid that he will?'

Standing beside me at the bar, Everett's voice held an edge. He'd already tossed back several shots, not that it mattered. He'd been on a streak lately. Angry, surly, demanding. Nothing I did was right, and nothing I gave him made him happy.

I didn't know what had changed, but . . . something had.

Three days off before the next transport. He'd found us a cheap strip motel. In the beginning, I'd liked the time away from the rig. A floor that didn't constantly rumble beneath my feet. A view of green trees that didn't blur as they flew past on the interstate.

But Everett . . . Less driving meant more drinking. More sex. And none of it was ever enough. He just got angrier and angrier and angrier.

Tonight, he'd returned to the room with a bag in his hand. Thrown it at me.

'Clean yourself up. You look like a fucking loser and smell even worse. What's with the hair anyway?'

Most of the time I wasn't allowed to shower. Let alone shave my legs. But tonight, I'd cleaned up. Then looked in the bag to discover a dress. Kind of. Not a pink-flowered or yellow flowy sundress, like the kind I might have worn a lifetime ago, heading out on a summer afternoon in Maine or enjoying a spring afternoon in Boston.

No. This dress was red and slinky and very, very tiny.

I'd trembled when I held it in my hand. And for a moment, my gaze drifting up to the reflection of a girl in the steamy mirror . . . pale skin, gaunt cheeks, gray eyes so huge and shadowed in her face.

Ghost girl, I thought. Then my entire body shook.

Everett was waiting for me when I came out of the bathroom, tugging self-consciously on the hem plastered to the top of my thighs. No bra or underwear. Everett didn't believe in such things.

He didn't say anything as he eyed me up and down. Just grunted, drained the rest of his beer, then shouldered by me to scrub his face, slick back his hair.

I tried to practice sitting while he was gone. Fiddling with the halter top to cover more of my chest, plucking at the clingy fabric. In the bag, I found a pair of platform sandals, strappy black. Not right for the dress, I thought, before I could help myself. But in another life, with another outfit, I would've liked these shoes.

Again, that strange sense of déjà vu.

Ghost girl.

It came to me: the new dress, new shoes, combined with Everett's fresh rage. This was it. He'd always warned me, the day he grew bored, that would be that.

He'd shoot me. Strangle me. Stab me. I couldn't even remember anymore. So many methods he'd discussed. But it all ended the same. My body dumped in Gator Alley.

My mother never knowing what happened to me.

Bathroom door opened. Everett stalked out, hands fisted at his sides.

'We're going out,' he announced.

I trailed out the door behind him.

Ghost girls didn't argue.

Ghost girls never stood a chance.

Bar was a small honky-tonk. Peanut shells on the floor. Alan Jackson on the jukebox. Crowded. Was it a Friday night? Saturday? Days of the week challenged me. As well as cities, states, basic geography.

I saw men in jeans and T-shirts, women in tighter-fitting jeans and T-shirts. Definitely, no one in a clingy red dress.

Patrons stared at me when we first walked in, gazes flickering to Everett. But no flashes of recognition, no twinges of suspicion. After all this time, I didn't expect anyone to look at us twice. Even now, one by one, they shrugged off the sight of a too-pale, too-skinny girl in a hooker's dress and resumed their drinking.

Everett, after all these days, weeks, months of instructing me to keep my head down and my mouth shut, actually beamed at my side. Which only heightened my tension.

Ghost girl drifting through the bar. Ghost girl ordering a beer.

Did my head nod along in time with the music? Did I tap my fingers against the shiny wood top? Old habits from a former life, when bars were fun and life was meant to be lived and you never knew what good time waited just around the corner?

Beside me, Everett chugged his beer, tossed back a shot, then demanded a second round. He could drink. Hard.

Often. But rarely at bars. Too expensive, he'd complain. Why pay some assholes four times more for something he could buy cheaper on his own?

But tonight, he was running up the bill. Drumming his fingers relentlessly against the scarred bar top. Gaze roaming the room.

'You're the prettiest girl here,' he said.

I paused, gaze fixed forward, hands wrapped tight around my sweaty bottle of Bud. I took a sip.

'You heard me.' He tossed back his whiskey. 'Prettiest girl here. You should keep your hair red. I like it.'

He set down the shot glass, placed his fingers on the bare skin of my neck. I didn't flinch. All this time later, I just stared at him and wondered what he was going to do next.

He laughed. He ordered another round. And he kept his left hand curled around the nape of my neck, that hard, glittering look in his eyes.

I sipped my beer. Ghost girl just trying to get through.

Then, I made a mistake. Glanced up. Happened to spot a guy at the end of the bar who was staring hard at me.

Everett, who missed nothing: 'Go on. Walk right over to him. Tell him you're a kidnapped girl. See if he'll save you.'

I shook my head slightly, reverted my attention back to my beer. My second, my third? The night was moving too fast. And Everett was scaring me.

'What's your name?' Everett leaned down, his drunken breath whispering across my cheek.

I didn't answer.

'Seriously. I mean it. What's your name?'

'Molly,' I murmured, gaze fixed on my bottle of Bud.

'Nah. Fuck that. Your name, your name, your name. Your real name?'

I looked up. I couldn't help myself. I stared at him a very long time. His flushed face, his overbright eyes.

He's using, I realized. Something other than just alcohol. The mood swings, tension, all-night sex marathons. He was on something. Everett on a drinking binge was scary enough. This, I couldn't imagine.

'Please,' I whispered. Pleaded. Though what did it matter? When had my begging ever made a difference?

'Do you know what today is?' he asked abruptly.

'No.'

'It's our anniversary, sweetheart. One year. One full year. Just you and me. Now how about that.'

He clinked his shot glass against my beer bottle, tossed back the whiskey, and twirled his finger for a fresh round.

I couldn't breathe. I found myself staring at him, his red-flushed cheeks, bloated face, greasy hair. But in my mind, I was somewhere else. Far and distant, where the wind in the trees blew clean and crisp, and there, just for an instant . . . a fox darting behind a bush.

'You're dead.'

He spoke the words matter-of-factly, jarring me out of my reverie.

Bartender was back. Shot and a beer for Everett. Fresh Bud for me. I wish I had water. I really could use a glass of water.

'Know how they look for missing girls? Always search the hardest the first forty-eight hours. Then, of course, make a show of it for a week, or two or three, feed headlines to the local news. I know you saw your mom on TV one afternoon. 'Course, she made a big show of it. 'Cause that's what happens for a bit. But fifty-two weeks later? You're

not front-page news anymore, little girl. Not even yesterday's leftovers. Hell, six, eight, a dozen other pretty young things have disappeared between then and now. They get the headlines now. You . . . You're already filed away. Even now, some detective's sitting around, trying to work up the courage to call your mom and explain about how gators get the job done.

'Think she'll do a service? I mean, even without the body. Maybe just a little gathering, family and friends. Put your memory to rest.'

I couldn't breathe.

'You want that, don't you?' His voice dropped low, sounded nearly concerned. 'You want your mama to move on with her life, right? Not suffer forever.'

'Is that what happened to Lindy?' I heard myself say. 'You fed her to the gators too?'

He recoiled slightly, fisting his shot glass. 'Shut up, girl.'

'Are you sorry? Do you wish you'd kept her longer? Is that why you still cry for her at night?'

'Shut. Your. Fucking. Mouth.'

But I was on a roll. Powered by three beers, a too-tight, too-red dress, and the knowledge we were in a public place. Later he would make me pay, but for now, this moment on our one-year anniversary . . .

'Did you love her?'

In a flash, his left hand was on my neck. Fingers digging in, slowly tightening. But I kept my eyes open, my gaze on his face, and in that second, I saw it. Pain. Sharp and brittle. Followed by hurt. Long and deep.

I still didn't know how or why. But Lindy held power over him. Lindy, mythical, unknown Lindy, was everything I was not.

'Jealous?' he drawled.

'Are you going to kill me?'

'Yeah.'

'Tonight?'

'Maybe.'

'Tomorrow?'

'Probably then too.'

'You'll be all alone.'

'Nah, just gotta head back to Florida. One-year anniversary. Don't you know, it's spring break.'

I stared at him. On and on and on, and just for an instant . . . I could almost see us. After all this time of living minute to minute, of keeping my head down, of hoping, praying, begging just to survive.

Here we were. One full year later. Beauty and the beast. A monster and his plaything.

A young girl who was never going home again.

'Do it,' I told him, and now my eyes were the ones that were overbright. 'Now. Just squeeze your fingers. No one's looking. It'll be all over before they notice. Come on. I know you want to. Just kill me. Right. Now.'

His face darkened. He did want to. The idea intoxicated him, excited him. I could feel the roughness of his fingertips digging into my skin, itching to get it done.

I'd die in a hooker's dress. But at least here, in a public place, he'd have to flee, leave my body behind.

Funny, the things you can come to view as a victory.

'You're gonna fuck that cowboy,' he said.

'What?' The change in topic confused me.

'End of the bar. Asshole who won't stop looking at you. Come on now. Walk on down. Make his day.'

'No.'

'Why, too good for him?'

I didn't speak.

'Tell him the truth. I don't care. Tell him your name. What's your name again?'

I shook my head, clutched my beer. Why did he keep asking me that? My name, my name, my name. My real name. He was giving me a headache.

'You're done,' he whispered. 'One year later, I bet your mama's already cleaned out your room. Packed up all your little pom-poms and teddy bears. Put it all away. What do you think? She'll turn the room into a home office? Maybe a craft center. But face it, if you showed up on her doorstop tomorrow, there'd be no place for you to stay. I'm all you have left. You and me, girl, till the end of time. Or tomorrow morning, when I wake up sick to death of you. Now. Cowboy. End of bar. Go fuck him.'

'No.'

His fingers moved. No longer squeezing. Stroking the back of my neck as the hair prickled on my skin.

'You didn't want me. Pretty girl like you. If I hadn't grabbed you drunk and sloppy off that beach, you'd never have looked at me twice. But now you got me. I've fed you, clothed you. Hell, I've taken you out and showed you the country.'

I didn't speak.

'I'm your first real man. First guy who told it to you straight, showed you the real world. Never lied, never prettied it up. Rest of your short life, wherever you go, whatever you do, you ain't never gonna know another man like me.'

I risked a glance up into his feverish eyes.

'I'm your world, Molly. Your whole entire world. I am your everything. Except to me . . . you ain't nothing but a

piece of garbage. Here today, gone tomorrow. Replaced next time I head to Palm Beach. No one the wiser. Now. Cowboy. End of the bar. Do it.'

'No.'

'What the—'

'Not on our anniversary.'

He paused, scowled. Studied me.

And I got it then. Ghost girl. The feeling of déjà vu that had been haunting me all night. Everett was mean. Everett was cruel. And one day, he would kill me, dump my body in a swamp.

But now, tonight, he was also right.

One year later, I was never going home.

The girl I had once been, she was dead.

And now, there was only me and my strange, twisted relationship with this man. I could keep going along, struggling through day to day. Or . . .

I reached out and, for the first time of my own volition, placed my open palm on Everett's chest. He startled. Couldn't help himself. And for just an instant, I caught it in his eyes. Uncertainty. Longing. Fear.

Emotions I associated with Lindy, now slowly but surely being transferred to me.

No one likes being alone. Not even the monster under the bed.

I rose off my stool. I took the shot glass from his hand. Then I leaned forward, and with my entire body pressed against his, I whispered, 'I want a present.'

'Wh-what?'

'A gift. For our anniversary.'

'Now, girl—'

'Your name. Your real name. Isn't that what you've been asking me all night? I think you're right. We are special.

Meant to be. I want to know your real name. One year later, what can it hurt?'

He eyed me, my lips so close to his own. I could see him thinking. I could see him considering. Then I felt his hands on my hips.

'Jacob,' he said roughly. 'My name is Jacob.'

'Pleased to meet you, Jacob. Now, take me home and I'll show you how much I appreciate a real man like you.'

28

D.D. arrived home just in time to put Jack to bed. His little round face lit up at first sight of her, stubby arms reaching out. And she felt the customary pang in her chest. A love a suspected killer had once warned her about, the kind of deep powerful emotion that would move mountains. And yes, if the occasion warranted it, justify pulling the trigger.

But for now, she didn't have to worry about such dark things. For now she got to nestle beside her little man, tucked in tight in his wooden red race car bed, and open up *The Runaway Bunny*.

Alex watched from the doorway, a smile on his face. From time to time, she glanced over at him, sticking out her tongue, crossing her eyes. Family fun with both her favorite guys. There had been a time in D.D.'s life she never would've thought she could have all this. Now, it amazed her that she'd ever gone without. Especially after a day like today, she needed this. Alex, Jack, her family, these moments, they grounded her.

And not for the first time, she wondered what she would do if something ever happened to her son. Twelve years from now, a phone ringing in the middle of the night, announcing her teenage son had disappeared. D.D. honestly didn't know where mothers like Rosa Dane, fathers like Colin Summers, found the strength to carry on.

Of course, family life wasn't all fairy tales. D.D.'s job was demanding, and Jack had officially reached the age where he had his opinions on the subject. She'd been gone most of the weekend. Home just in time for a story.

So of course, the moment she closed the book, climbed – cumbersomely – off the low-slung toddler bed, the theatrics began.

Sticking out his bottom lip. Staring at her with liquid-blue eyes so much like her own. Alex had given him a bath before bedtime, and now Jack's light brown hair stood up on the top of his head, world's cutest mohawk.

'Good night,' D.D. repeated firmly.

Quivering. The bottom lip. The whole chin. And then . . .

Full-frontal assault. Launching his little body across the toddler bed and slapping arms and legs around D.D.'s body. She staggered back, hands dropping down belatedly to strong little arms that had already attached themselves with the strength of octopus tentacles. Serial killers she could handle. But God save her from the strength of a little boy who didn't want to go to bed.

She could hear laughter behind her. Alex, enjoying the show. And, of course, making no moves to intervene. He'd already spent the weekend battling the kid. This was all on her.

Toddlers, D.D. had learned, were a lot like criminals. You basically had two options for management: promise a reward or threaten with punishment.

She couldn't punish her son for missing her as much as she missed him, so she went with the promise of a second story if he'd get back into bed. Which led to a third, then a fourth, before his heavy-lidded eyes finally sagged closed, and she staggered out of the race car bed, feeling Jack had probably won that war but officially too tired to care.

Alex was waiting for her in the family room. He had poured two glasses of red wine, and had an ice pack at the ready.

'I'm not sure which of these I'm looking forward to more,' she said, gaze bouncing between the wine, the ice, the wine again. 'How sad is that?'

He smiled, helped her shrug out of her leather jacket. Ice pack on the shoulder, wineglass in hand, life was good again. She sat back on the sofa, put her feet up on the coffee table, and sighed.

'How is your vigilante?' he asked.

'Missing.'

'Fled from the new sheriff in town?'

'No.' She turned her head against the sofa cushion to regard him seriously. 'We think she might've been kidnapped. Maybe even by the same person who abducted Stacey Summers.'

He made her start at the beginning. Which, given how many hours she'd logged in the past forty-eight, should've been draining. But the crazy part of marriage, D.D. had discovered, was that no matter what her day had been like, it didn't feel completely true or real or meaningful until she'd come home and shared it with Alex. Of course, him being a crime scene specialist – blood spatter, more specifically – didn't hurt. He often saw or thought of things she'd overlooked.

'Any video?' he asked now, referring to footage collected from local security and traffic cams.

'When I left, the first batch of videos was just arriving. The new detective, Carol, promised to stay to sort through them.'

'Just the way you say her name makes it sound like you're biting into a pickle.'

'Nuh-uh.'

'Uh-huh.'

She glared at him. 'In the morning, we'll see how she did.'

'But you're not releasing anything to the press?'

She sighed, took a sip of wine. 'Tougher call. It's going to be a media sensation, no doubt about it. Semifamous former kidnapping victim abducted again? We want to get our ducks in a row. Confirm she absolutely, positively has been abducted before we lead with a story that's going to bring all the crazies out of the woodwork.'

'What kind of confirmation?'

'A clip from the video feeds? Say, an actual shot of Flora being dragged from her apartment? Or, now that we have the pass code to her phone, maybe some kind of proof she was definitely investigating Stacey's disappearance or, even better, had a solid lead that may have gotten her in trouble? Let's face it, second we announce this kind of news it's going to be a media circus. Which, unfortunately, will take time, energy, and manpower away from the actual search for Flora and Stacey. The mom doesn't mind keeping quiet for now. My impression is that she has no love for the press.'

'But if Flora really is missing . . .' Alex countered.

'Then we need to find more witnesses and engage the public in the hunt, which calls for a press conference.'

'Gotta love the job,' Alex said.

She made a face at him.

'Anything found at the apartment?' he asked.

'No. Except for her unmade bed, it's pristine. Mom apparently is a neat freak, and had tidied up hours before.

Given Flora's training, we suspect it had to be an ambush. Maybe he even drugged her. Otherwise there should be signs of a struggle.'

'I could take a look at it,' Alex offered. 'I have some time before I have to head to the academy tomorrow, if you want a second set of eyes.'

'Given how much we don't know at this time, I'd welcome a second set of eyes, or a third, or a fourth.' She shifted restlessly, adjusting the ice on her shoulder. 'Strangest aspect of the scene: The front door as well as all the windows were unlocked. I mean, I get the front door. Guy thoughtfully prepared himself a master key ahead of time, then used it to access Flora's apartment. But why unlock all the windows? Why even take the time for such a subtle piece of theatrics?'

'To prove he could? To emphasize no one is safe?'

'Arrogant,' D.D. muttered.

Alex shrugged, topped off his wine. 'Not the first time. But sounds like your missing girl, Flora, has some skills as well. She might have been abducted, but she's hardly a helpless victim.'

'True. I think I'm gonna make a call in the morning. Talk to an FBI agent out of Atlanta, Kimberly Quincy.'

'Name sounds familiar.'

'I spoke with her once before, couple of years ago for the Charlene Grant case. Quincy was apparently the agent who finally located Jacob Ness. She led the raid to rescue Flora.'

Alex gave her a look. 'And you want to talk to Quincy why?'

'I don't know,' D.D. said honestly. 'But somehow . . . Whatever happened five years ago, Flora's never gotten over it.'

'How could she?'

'Sure. But most victims of these long-term kidnappings, they retreat. They work on their recovery, focus on appreciating everyday life, write a book, sell movie rights, whatever. According to Flora's mother, however, Flora never talks about her time with Jacob Ness. And yet . . . the self-defense classes. The bedroom wall lined with missing persons cases. Her obsession with Stacey Summers. Flora's absolutely, positively still driven by what happened to her. My guess: If I'm going to anticipate what she did leading up to Saturday afternoon and what she's capable of doing next, I need to learn about her own experience. She survived the unthinkable once before. So what compels her back to that same set of circumstances? Is there some wound she's trying to heal? Or a lesson she still hasn't learned?'

'Survivor's guilt.'

'Maybe.' D.D. adjusted the ice pack on her shoulder. 'I'll tell you what she should feel guilty about, though. Her mom. Her poor mother. Having to go through this all over again.'

D.D. didn't sleep well. Not unusual when working a major case. Her mind swirled with investigative details, leading to dreams of faceless girls running down endless black corridors. Then D.D. was racing breathlessly through a shadowed house . . . basement . . . house again . . . heart thundering against her chest.

She rounded a corner and there she was: Flora Dane. Or Stacey Summers? No, definitely Flora Dane, holding a gun leveled at D.D.'s head.

'Bang,' dream Flora said. 'You're dead.'

D.D. woke up. D.D. got out of bed.

She crept into her son's room. Soothed herself with the sight of him sleeping peacefully. Then, she headed to the kitchen and got serious about her day.

* * *

FBI agents had a tendency to work civilian hours. Sure, they bragged about their 'go bags', ready to fly out the door at a moment's notice. But compared to the demands of urban policing, say, a Boston detective's job, fed hours were pretty sedate.

D.D. decided to play an educated guess. If memory served, SAC Kimberly Quincy had two daughters, meaning, like most parents, she was up early. Combine that with the horrendous traffic in Atlanta – what with that Spaghetti Junction, whatever – any commuter had an incentive to head to the office sooner versus later. Meaning D.D.'s best bet for contacting the federal agent would be first thing in the morning.

Five thirty A.M. seemed a tad early, so D.D. worked on her shoulder and arm PT. She showered, changed, then heard Jack calling. Scooping him out of his race car bed with her good arm, she remembered the mandatory *vroom, vroom* noises; then they were zigzagging down the hall, careening downstairs, before a pedal-to-the-metal sprint for dinosaur-shaped pancakes in the kitchen. The dino shapes were courtesy of molds purchased by Alex, an impulse buy that had caused D.D. to roll her eyes, but God knows Jack adored them. Pancakes were definitely twice as good when shaped as a brontosaurus.

Jack took breakfast in his footy pajamas, as pancakes were a messy, mapley affair guaranteed to wreck any hope of clean clothes, let alone the amount of syrup he managed to get in his fine hair. The pajamas would go in the wash. As for the maple syrup do . . . D.D. thought he could carry the spiky-haired look. Syrup, hair gel. In the world of toddlers, what did it matter?

Having missed so much time with her son, she did the honors of dressing him for preschool. Then she produced

Candy Land, and with a stack of color-coded cards, not to mention Jolly the gumdrop, to keep Jack entertained in the family room, D.D. retreated to the kitchen to dial Atlanta.

She got lucky on her first try.

'Quincy,' the FBI agent answered.

'Morning. Sergeant Detective D.D. Warren from Boston PD. We spoke once before. Couple of years ago. Charlene Grant. You handled her friend's murder in Atlanta.'

'Oh yeah. Hey, good job on that one. Honestly didn't think Charlie would survive the twenty-first.'

'Well, every now and then this job is actually gratifying. So, I'm working a new case and your name has come up.' D.D. filled in the agent on Flora Dane's recent activities leading up to her disappearance. 'I understand you're the agent who finally located Jacob Ness.'

'True.' The agent's voice had grown quieter, somber. Some cases left a mark. D.D. already suspected Flora's case, the raid to rescue her, was one of them. 'What do you know of Flora's kidnapping seven years ago?'

'Not much. Boston wasn't involved, as she disappeared down in Florida.'

'Yes. Pretty typical setup. College girl on spring break out drinking with friends. She needed to use the restrooms, they let her go alone, and just like that, she was gone.'

'I'm working something similar right now,' D.D. said, wondering already if that's why Flora had responded so strongly to Stacey Summers's abduction.

'Unfortunately, the case was a slow starter. Drunk friends don't make the best reporters. Not to mention they got it in their heads that Flora had headed home – and I don't mean their hotel room. I mean sometime in the middle of the rum-soaked club scene, she'd decided to return up North, so they didn't exactly comb the beaches looking for her.'

'Oh jeez.'

'Eventually one of the girls thought to call Flora's mom up in Maine. Now, the mom's a smart, tough woman. Ruth? Rachel?'

'Rosa.'

'Rosa. That's it. She filed the missing persons report and got the ball rolling, but at that point the trail was already forty-eight, fifty-six hours old. Local PD did a little digging, came up with nothing.'

D.D. nodded her head, not surprised. Missing persons was always a race against the clock. In this case, Flora had never stood a chance.

'How'd the FBI get involved?' D.D. asked.

'Postcard. I can't remember all the particulars, but a matter of weeks, maybe a month later, Rosa received a postcard from her daughter. It was postmarked Jacksonville. Looked like her daughter's handwriting. But the content raised some red flags.'

'How so?'

'I can e-mail you a copy, but . . . the tone was almost manic. *Having the best time, Mom! Met the cutest guy! You should see where I'm staying. Perfect room! Couldn't be happier. And the sex is fantastic. Give Chili my love.*'

'What?' D.D. asked, genuinely startled.

'Yeah. Not exactly the kind of note most girls send home to their moms. Rosa Dane got a little upset, to say the least. Now, the reference to Chili – that was Flora's first dog, long deceased. The BAU profiler who assisted with the case believed Jacob made her include that detail to authenticate the note – it couldn't have been sent by a random stranger who read about her disappearance in the paper. The UNSUB wanted Rosa, all of us, to know this was the real deal.'

'I'm sure you also analyzed the handwriting?'

'Yes. But that analysis was actually less than a slam dunk. Certain letters were deemed a match. But the letters were smaller, crunched, and shaky, which muddled the findings.'

D.D. had to think about it. 'Because Flora was writing it under duress? Or because she herself had changed? Terrified? Abused? Starving?'

'All possibilities considered at the time. The most important takeaway was the overall message. Flora was having the best time ever. With some cute guy, having fantastic sex. No hey, Mom, sorry I took off while on spring break, but you don't need to worry, I'm with some friends. In other words, the UNSUB wasn't interested in covering up Flora's disappearance. He solely wanted to taunt the mom with the obvious message that Flora had been kidnapped.'

'Is this the part where the profiler claims the evil UNSUB was potty trained at gunpoint?'

'Oh, our profiler had even more opinions than that. But we were still assembling information back then. We had a first message and a postmark. The Jacksonville police traced the postcard to a single post office located off a busy interstate. No video cameras on the outside boxes, however, so that became a dead end.'

'But there was more.'

'Yes. Three months later a second card arrived. The first had been of a beach sunset. This one was a Georgia peach, and postmarked Atlanta.'

'Ah, and now you join the hunt,' D.D. filled in.

'And now I join the hunt,' Kimberly agreed. 'Contents of this postcard were similar. Amazing time. Best guy ever. The sex is even more incredible, and good news, I've finally lost those last ten pounds.'

'She'd lost weight?' D.D. had to think about it. 'Did Flora Dane need to lose ten pounds?'

'No. She was an active outdoorsy girl. According to her mom, she didn't have ten pounds to spare.'

'Oh my God.' For the first time, D.D. got the pattern behind the messages. It left her feeling queasy. 'He was starving her. That's the taunt. Everything he says . . . The cute guy, that's her ugly-ass kidnapper. The amazing sex, that's the endless nights of sexual assault. And losing ten pounds . . . What a . . .' D.D. didn't have a strong enough word for Jacob Ness. It was a good thing he was already dead, or she would've felt a need to track him down and kill him all over again.

'At this stage, Flora had been missing approximately four months. With evidence that she's still alive and has crossed state lines, now it's full-on federal mobilization. Except . . . we couldn't gain any traction. There was no video, no witnesses to her abduction. Did she walk out with a guy? Was she ambushed? We couldn't find anyone who saw anything.'

'I have video of an abduction,' D.D. offered, 'and we still can't find anyone who knows anything. What about the postcards?'

'We traced the second note to the originating post office, but again, no video, no witnesses. All we got was that both post offices were near major interstates. Easy on and off for someone who's traveling.'

'Does the second postcard include anything personal?'

'*Please feed the foxes*. Apparently, when Flora was growing up, she liked to tame the wild foxes on her mother's farm.'

'Rosa's necklace,' D.D. said. 'It has a fox charm.'

'Exactly. Handwriting on the second postcard shows further deterioration. It's spidery, shaky, lacks strength. If you're into graphology – predicting personality based on, say, the slant of your handwriting – Flora's breaking down.'

'I'm familiar with graphology,' D.D. supplied. 'Not sure what I think, but in a case where you don't have much else to go on . . .'

'You take whatever you can get,' Kimberly agreed. 'Given our lack of leads, and the UNSUB's clear interest in Flora's mom, the profiler advised a press conference with Rosa front and center. The UNSUB was communicating with her. Now it would be her turn to communicate directly with him. And, frankly, see if we could elicit some kind of response.'

'Did it work?'

'Not that we could figure out at the time. The profiler drafted a media message designed to humanize Flora, focus on her loving family, unique upbringing in the wilds of Maine, her kindness to others, et cetera. Rosa was dressed up to appear as all-American mom as possible. Basically, the kidnapper was crafting one storyline – an overly sexualized college girl obsessed with guys. We went to the other extreme, a nature-loving good girl adored by everyone who knew her.'

D.D. couldn't help but arch a brow. That didn't quite jibe with the dark, edgy Flora she knew. Which made her wonder: Maybe Flora's mom had been right after all. D.D. had never met and would never know the real Flora Dane. She had only encountered Jacob Ness's twisted creation, four hundred and seventy-two days in the making.

'Rosa did her part,' Kimberly was saying now. 'She stood up there, looked right in the cameras, and delivered a message that was empathetic, genuine, and moving. The news teams ate her up. We got full national coverage for a solid week, boosted by her appearances on several major morning shows. Which is not something easy or automatic for a woman who up until then had been happiest driving a tractor.'

D.D. understood. What the media expected of victims in this day and age wasn't for the faint at heart. Let alone when the lead investigator was standing at a grieving parent's shoulder saying this must be done – you want your kid back, then this is what it takes, exposing your heart and soul on the national stage.

'What happened next?' D.D. asked.

'Nothing.'

'Nothing?'

'Nothing. Week after week. Month after month. Trail went cold. Rosa talked and talked and talked. Received no postcards or messages in reply. We blasted Flora's picture all across the world. We got no credible leads. Which, at a certain point, starts to tell you something. Such as Flora's either locked away so tightly there are no witnesses, or he's done a bang-up job altering her appearance. And he either doesn't care about the press conferences – or he didn't see them.'

'Didn't see them?'

'Our profiler, Ken McCarthy, didn't believe it would be possible for the UNSUB, who'd started the conversation, to simply walk away. So if our attempts at communication weren't eliciting a response, maybe he wasn't getting the messages. Which brought us to the next phase of our investigation, where we chased down every southern recluse and off-the-grid survivalist with a history of sexual assaults. Now that was a list.'

'Not a bad strategy,' D.D. granted. 'Certainly someone like that would fit your profile. Taunting the mother as a proxy for an authority figure, right?'

'Hey, we're the FBI. We can make anything look good on paper. Unfortunately, we were wrong.'

'So what happened?'

'Jacob. Eventually, he reached out again. Except this time, it wasn't a postcard. It was an e-mail sent from a dummy account to Rosa's personal e-mail. It contained an audio of Flora talking.'

D.D. winced. She couldn't imagine what that must have been like for Rosa. To, after all this time, hear her daughter's voice and yet the things, the terrible, twisted words that must've come from her daughter's mouth . . .

'Escalation of communication is not atypical,' Kimberly said quietly. 'We assured Rosa this was a good thing. It meant Flora was still alive. It meant, as strange as it sounded, that he still cared. Now, him moving to e-mail helped us. We could trace the IP address back to an Internet café, this time in Alabama. And, like the post offices, located near a major interstate. This led us to our next investigative leap, from looking at survivalists hunkered down in backwoods to looking at someone who was mobile. Say, salespeople, truck drivers. Given the long hours on the road, these people might not catch the morning news shows or the five o'clock wrap-up, hence the UNSUB's lack of reaction to our TV blitz. We adjusted our communication strategy accordingly, targeting mediums that would be more accessible to someone with a transient lifestyle. We emphasized social media, such as daily Facebook posts that the UNSUB might access during his downtime on a laptop or mobile device. We also targeted local radio stations and independent newspapers, the kind of daily pubs that are easily accessible at diners, gas stations, motels.

'Flora's brother created a whole Facebook page for this phase, plastered with personal photos of Flora as well as snapshots from her daily life, the farm, the woods around it, a fox playing in the backyard. He also sat with his mom and generated lists of Facebook posts, one for each day, covering everything from Flora's favorite book to local events, family anniversaries she was now missing. We invited friends and neighbors to contribute as well. Anything to remind the UNSUB over and over again of who Flora truly was, a young woman deeply missed by family and friends.'

'He issued communications to break her down. You built her back up.'

'We needed him to make contact. If countering his message drove him to send more and more postcards, e-mails, videos, all the better for us.'

'He sent videos?'

'Provoking him into further outreach remained our best strategy for catching him.'

'Did you design this strategy?' D.D. asked.

'Yes.'

'According to Rosa, Jacob's stupidity is what got him caught – he sent one too many messages and you nailed him. But, talking to you, that was the plan. You weren't waiting for him to randomly e-mail. You were baiting him into further communications.'

'This kind of strategy . . . It's hard on the family.' Kimberly sighed. 'The investigative team might have been the general, sitting in a back room, strategizing away, but Rosa, Darwin, they were our foot soldiers. They had to sit down every day and beg for Flora's life. They had to suffer through degrading postcards, audio recordings, and then that video . . . We advised both of them not to watch. But of course, they were so desperate for some sign, some connection to their loved one. The brother vomited. Twice. And Rosa . . . She went blank. We ended up calling for medical. I thought she'd broken, and we'd never get her back.

'I understand the family has a different perspective on things. Of course they do. At the end of the day, they were the best tool we had to get Flora back. We used them shamelessly. And it worked.'

'So how did you find him?'

'As we hoped, Jacob started communicating more. Especially via e-mail. Which allowed us to start tracking his progress across the southern states. By fourteen months in, we were sure he had to be a truck driver, delivery man, something of that nature. The bulk of the e-mails were from Internet cafés, some truck stops, all located near major interstates. So we shored up state police patrols of those areas, faxed Flora's photo to all the major truck stops. We wanted to apply pressure, but not too much.'

'You didn't want him to panic, dispose of her.'

'Exactly. But mostly we focused on the Internet cafés. Four hundred and seventy-one days later, he sent an e-mail we could trace back to a cybercafé at a truck stop he'd used once before. I personally drove out to the truck stop to interview the staff. All those postcards, e-mails, outreaches later, Jacob had revealed more of himself than he realized. Sure enough, the moment I started to describe the kind of man we were looking for, the manager ID'd him. Jacob was a regular. Stopped by at least once a month, if not more, on his route. The manager didn't know Jacob's last name, but he could describe his rig; we connected the remaining dots from there.

'Jacob Ness. A registered sex offender who'd already served time for molesting a fourteen-year-old girl. Suspected of several more sex assaults. Currently working as an independent contractor for several major delivery firms, driving a big rig.

'In a matter of hours, a state trooper discovered Jacob's transport parked outside a motel just off the interstate. I mobilized SWAT and we got serious.'

D.D. didn't need the FBI agent to say anything more. She could already picture it perfectly in her head. The adrenaline rush of such moments. At the cusp of breaking a major case. Do everything right, you get to save the girl, catch the bad guy. But one wrong move . . . girl winds up killed, bad guy escapes, and a life, a family, your career is over.

Yeah, she could picture it.

'What'd you do?' she asked.

'We confirmed with hotel management which room Jacob was in, and that he'd entered with a female companion. The room was an end unit with no rear door. That was the good news. Now, for the bad news: We had reason to believe Jacob was in possession of at least one firearm, if not more. Also, our profiler, McCarthy, believed that if cornered, Jacob would be most likely to shoot Flora, then himself, rather than surrender.'

'Suicide by cop?'

'Possible, but only after killing Flora. McCarthy felt at this stage of their relationship, Jacob felt a strong attachment to Flora. The nature of his taunts, his need to torment the family. She was his, and he wouldn't give her up without a fight.'

'Relationship.' D.D. had to think about this. She was familiar with Stockholm syndrome, though more from movie plots than real-life experience. That syndrome, made famous by the Patty Hearst case, described how a victim bonded with her attacker over time, feeling empathy, even loyalty, for the very person who had caused her harm. But D.D. had never considered such a process in reverse. That by virtue of time and total dominance, a kidnapper might develop a certain affection for his captive. Jacob Ness had been a long-haul trucker. Meaning for years he'd been traveling alone, living in isolation, until the day he'd snatched Flora Dane and brought her along with him.

Four hundred and seventy-two days of companion-ship later . . . D.D. could see why he'd be loath to give her up.

'Did you worry about Stockholm syndrome?' she asked Kimberly now. 'That Flora might not welcome your rescue efforts?'

On the other end of the phone, D.D. could hear the agent's hesitation. 'We were prepared for anything,' Kimberly said at last, which D.D. took to be a yes.

'So you have an armed subject holed up in a hotel room with a victim who's suffered severe long-term trauma. What did you do?'

'Let SWAT lead the charge,' Kimberly said bluntly. 'They fired in half a dozen canisters of tear gas through the room's front window. Then they took down the door.'

The federal agent paused. 'They found Jacob sprawled on the ground, clearly incapacitated by the gas. Next to him was a damp hand towel. Apparently, he'd noticed the officers mobilizing outside, had made some effort to prepare for their charge. But he hadn't been fast enough.'

'And Flora?'

'She sat on the floor beside him. She had a wet towel tied around her mouth and nose. She also had a gun.'

D.D.'s eyes widened. Of all the things . . . 'She had Jacob's gun.'

'Yeah.'

'Did she point it at the SWAT team?'

'No. She had the gun on her lap. She was . . . stroking Jacob's face. She was wiping the tears from his eyes.'

'Oh.' D.D. didn't know why, but somehow that image was worse.

'Jacob was conscious when I entered the room. Whispering to Flora. The gas was already starting to dissipate, we needed to move quickly, but no one wanted to rush Flora as long as she had the gun. We were afraid if we spooked her . . .'

'She might open fire.'

'It was a strange sight. He was begging her. Jacob Ness was sprawled on the floor, begging Flora to kill him.'

D.D. didn't have words for that.

'I tried to get her attention. I called her name, tried to get her to look at me. But she wouldn't respond. Not to me, not to any of the officers. Her attention was solely for Jacob, stroking his hair, rubbing the tears from his cheeks. She seemed not just attentive to him but . . . tender.'

D.D. knew tear gas. It didn't just inflame the eyes. It turned the subject's nose, everything, to a giant, streaming mucusy mess. Jacob Ness would've been in a great deal of discomfort. Desperate for water to flush his eyes, tissue to blow his nose. But he hadn't surrendered. Instead, the man who'd been taunting his victim's family and investigators for more than a year had pulled himself together for one last move.

'What did he do?'

'He kept talking to Flora. Talking, talking, talking. And then, just when we thought we'd have to make our move one way or another, Flora suddenly leaned over and whispered something in his ear.'

'What?'

'I don't know. Flora's never said. But she told him something. And the expression on his face . . . Jacob Ness looked scared out of his mind. Then Flora grabbed the gun off her lap and pulled the trigger. Forty-five Magnum to the top of the skull. It got the job done.

'Flora dropped the gun. SWAT took her down. And that was that.'

D.D. couldn't speak.

'You know about trauma bonding, right?' the agent asked abruptly. 'Forget kidnapping victims, you see it all the time with battered women. They're isolated, at the mercy of their dominating spouse, going through intense spells of abject terror followed by even more emotionally draining periods of soul-wrenching apologies. The trauma itself creates a powerful bonding element. The things these two have gone through together, how could anyone else ever understand? It becomes one more thing that makes a woman stay, even after her husband has beat the crap out of her again.'

'I know trauma bonding.'

'I expected to see it with Flora Dane. How could you not? Four hundred and seventy-two days later, I couldn't even get her to respond to her own name. Instead, she identified herself as Molly, the name Jacob had given to her.'

'Okay.'

'Trauma bonding is most likely to occur in situations where the victim is isolated and the perpetrator appears all-powerful. We found in the rear of Jacob's cab a wooden coffin bearing a padlock. It bore traces of Flora's hair as well as DNA.'

D.D. closed her eyes. 'That's isolating,' she agreed.

'Jacob put her in the box. But Jacob was also the one who took her out. Jacob starved her for long periods of time. But he was also the one who gave her food.'

'Which would make him all-powerful.'

'So here's the issue: Flora absolutely, positively shows signs of trauma bonding. Which, we know from other cases, makes victims stay even when they could run.'

'Flora had opportunities to escape but didn't take them.'

'We learned that, by the end, Flora accompanied Jacob everywhere of her own free will. He could leave her sitting alone in restaurants or waiting for him in hotel rooms. She stayed, which to outsiders makes her appear complacent, a willing victim. Anyone who has experienced trauma bonding, however, will tell you that in those moments, she was just as physically restrained as if he'd wrapped her in chains. Such is the power of the bond.'

'Okay.' D.D. was familiar with trauma bonding, though it was hard for her to associate the Flora she had met forty-eight hours ago, the woman who'd burned Devon Goulding alive, with that level of submission.

'Trauma bonding can also lead to someone committing acts they wouldn't normally have done otherwise.'

'Patty Hearst, wielding the M1 carbine.'

'Exactly. There are many well-documented cases of victims that, over time and torture, have become accomplices to their own attackers. In this case . . . we found more than Flora's DNA in that pine box. In fact, we found DNA from several different unidentified girls.'

'Oh.' D.D. didn't know what else to say. The FBI agent was right: Especially in cases where the victim was held for a long period of time, many reached a point where they assisted in ambushing others. It was tempting to lay blame, though psychologists would frown upon such things. Kimberly had been right: The trauma bond coerced the victim into compliance as powerfully as physical force. 'You think Jacob Ness might have grabbed additional girls.'

'I think I would've liked to ask him that question. In

fact, the more we dug into his life, the more suspicions we had. Unfortunately, we'll never know exactly what he did. How many women he might have raped and even murdered.'

'What does Flora say?'

'She doesn't. She's never talked about what happened to her. In the beginning, we gave her time and space, based, frankly, on the advice of Dr Keynes. But later . . . We know that box held girls other than Flora. We can't, however, say when the evidence got there. For example, maybe the DNA from other victims occurred *before* he kidnapped Flora versus during the same time period. Given that, we don't have grounds to subpoena her. If she doesn't want to talk, she doesn't have to.'

'You think she's covering for herself? For what she might have done, under duress or not?'

'I think there are questions I'd like to ask that Flora's gone out of her way not to answer. Not to mention . . .' Kimberly paused again. 'Between agent and investigator? Because in this day and age, when we're never supposed to blame the victim . . .'

'By all means.'

'As I was leading Flora out of the hotel room, she paused for one moment, looked back at Jacob's body. She'd lost the towel by then. I could see her face. And just for a second, her eyes sparked. It was like watching a machine come to life. She appeared . . . triumphant.'

'Having just shot her own kidnapper?' D.D. guessed.

'Or, maybe, having just killed the only other person who knew exactly what she'd been up to over the past year. I can tell you one thing: Dozens, if not hundreds, of law enforcement officers were involved in the search for Flora Dane. And yet, for all of us, four hundred and seventy-two days of that woman's life remain a complete mystery.'

29

I'm not okay.

I want to be. I want to be strong, in control, resolved. Not hungry, not thirsty, not hot, not cold, not in pain, not terrified. I am the new and improved Flora Dane, the kind of woman who will never be a victim again.

I'm shaking uncontrollably.

The name. Why does this girl call herself Molly? She's not Molly. I know she's not Molly because I knew a Molly once. I *was* a Molly once. That can't be a coincidence, right? And the pine coffins. The endless procession of cheap pine coffins . . .

What the hell is going on here?

He's dead. Jacob's dead. I have to tell myself this. I'm huddled in a corner, bound arms looped tight around my knees. Jacob's dead and I know Jacob's dead because I pulled the trigger. I felt his blood, bits of his skull, blow back into my face. I left that room, finally free after four hundred and seventy-two days, with Jacob's brain matter stuck in my hair.

He's dead. He's dead. He's dead.

I have tears streaming down my cheeks. I hate myself for the weakness.

And I hate even more that small, miserable, pathetic part of me that still misses him.

I am not okay.

The girl is on the mattress. I think. She crawled there on her own. She's sleeping now. Or has fallen unconscious. Or is dying. Probably, I should check on her. But she said her name is Molly, and now I can't stand her.

That FBI agent, staring straight at me: '*Flora, Flora, Flora.*' Myself, no idea who she's talking about: '*My name is Molly.*'

Victims and captors form a bond. You don't have to like it. You don't have to understand it. That's just the way it is. Dr Keynes explained this to me many times. I couldn't help forming a relationship with Jacob any more than I couldn't help being hungry, thirsty, and tired. Human beings are social creatures. We aren't meant to live in a vacuum. Or, more specifically, locked away in a coffin-size box.

Jacob might have been evil, but he was also very smart. He knew what he was doing every time he stuck me in that box and denied me light, food, water, companionship. And he knew exactly what he was doing each time he took me back out. Becoming my hero. Becoming the all-powerful father figure I never had. Of course, I listened and obeyed. You don't piss off the all-powerful father figure. And you don't leave him either, not even when you might suddenly, unexpectedly have the chance. Because he is all-powerful. And if he says he knows where your mother lives, and your brother, and your den of favorite foxes, and he can track them down and kill them anytime he wants, you believe him.

When he says you're his favorite, and he never meant to keep you alive this long, but somehow you've grown on him. You're special. Worthy. Maybe even the one woman who could finally make him happy . . .

You believe that too.

And this girl? Huddled away across the room from me in the dark. Has she also been shut up in a box? Has she also endured hours, if not days, on end of her own pathetic company? Until she too would've sold her very soul just to get out.

I can't trust her. That's the problem with girls who were once trapped in coffin-size boxes.

Just ask Jacob. You can't trust any of us.

I scrub at my face with my bound hands. I can't keep doing this, I think, rocking back and forth. I was stupid for trying to find Stacey Summers, for arrogantly thinking I could take on the big bads of the world. I was misguided. I was . . . I don't know. Everything my mom and Samuel accused me of. And now, I see the light. I repent. I just want out of this godforsaken pitch-black room. I just want to return to my apartment and resume normal life again.

Except, of course, I've never figured out how to do normal. How to settle for everyday routine.

I'm not okay. I'm not okay, I'm not okay, I'm not okay.

'Why?'

The girl speaks. The sound of her voice, so unexpected in the dark, shocks me into paying attention. I wait, ears attuned.

'Why?' she whispers again. 'Why, why, why?'

I wonder if what she means to ask is, why me?

I unloop my arms from my knees. One last scrub of my cheeks. One last sniff.

I pull myself together.

I have a headache. That's real enough. My head feels fuzzy and my body lethargic. I wonder once again about drugs. Misted into the air, injected into the water bottle? I can't smell or taste anything, but I definitely don't feel like myself. Of course, trauma can do that to you.

But I'm functional. I can sit, I can stand, I can move. Time to do something.

'We need to get out of here,' I say out loud. I sound hoarse. Raw. And determined. Almost like a woman who knows what she's doing.

The girl doesn't reply.

I rise to my feet, shuffle forward to the wall where I know the door is. This time, feeling around with my fingertips, I can easily determine its edges. The door opens out – that's my memory. The door opening out, the silhouetted form stepping in, then myself lunging forward with my wooden dagger.

I push against it now and feel it give slightly.

I stop, stunned by this development. Surely my mind is playing tricks on me. And yet, another experimental push. The door jiggles. It's closed, I realize, but maybe not locked tight. Ordinarily, you'd simply turn the handle, retracting the latch from the hole in the strike plate, and voilà, open sesame. Except in this case . . . I blink my eyes several times, contemplating options. On this side of the door, there's no knob to turn. But if I could find a way to suppress the latch, say, shimmy in a sliver of wood? I might get lucky.

Of course, I need a piece of wood. I think there might be one more tucked in the mattress. I can't remember. My thoughts are muddled. Stress. Fatigue.

The presence of a girl named Molly.

No choice. I have to do this.

I retreat from the secret door, crawling toward the mattress.

I don't know what to say. Everything will be okay? So sorry to have stabbed you? Who the hell are you anyway?

What I manage is: 'Hey.'

She whimpers.

I don't want to know her name, I decide. I'm not having that conversation. Instead, it's time to get practical.

'Do you know where we are?' Fresh whimper.

'Is this room part of a house? Are we on the first floor, second floor?'

More whimpering.

I can't take it anymore. I sit back on my heels, inches from the mattress, and make my voice as hard as possible. 'Hey! We need to get out of here. *You* need medical attention. Now start talking. Where the hell are we?'

She doesn't whimper this time. More like a shaky inhale. Then, just when I'm wondering if I'm going to have to slap her or something, she whispers: 'Why-why-why are you making me do this?'

I keep my voice firm. 'Which floor are we on? Which level of the building?'

'I don't know. Why—'

'Were you kept in a room?' I interrupt. 'Something like this one?' Or maybe exactly this one, as the previous occupant.

I can hear a shuddering exhale.

'How long have you been here?' I don't mean to ask that question. It's not relevant. But I can't help myself.

She doesn't answer, and a second later, I realize she probably can't. Certainly, I'm already confused on timeline, disoriented by the lack of light.

'What's the last thing you remember?' I ask instead.

'Dancing.'

'You were at a bar, a nightclub? In Boston?'

It takes her a bit, but finally, 'Y-y-yes.'

'Did you drink too much?'

A small hiccup I take to be yes. Kids, I think. We're all so young and fearless once. Nightclubs are nothing but a source of adventure. And a fourth, fifth, sixth rum runner the best idea in the world.

I hated myself for my own stupidity, waking up in a coffin-size box. Minute after minute, day after day, so much time to do nothing but repent.

And yet, if there's one thing I miss . . . One reason I ended up taking so many self-defense classes.

I would give anything to feel that young and fearless again.

'It's okay,' I hear myself say, and there's a gentleness to my voice that catches me off guard. 'What happened next?'

'Why, why, why,' she mutters, and I can tell she's on the verge of tears again.

'Do you live in Boston?' I ask, trying to regain her focus. 'Your family, yourself, you're from around here?'

'Y-y-yes.'

I consider my next step. Asking her name directly hasn't worked, God knows it didn't for me in the days right after my 'rescue'. I can't explain it. It seems strange, surreal, thinking about it now. Twenty years later, how can you lose your own name, that reflexive, immediate sense of self? All I can tell you is that pine coffins work an awful lot like cocoons. At a certain point, it's easier to let go, shed the layers, emerge anew.

Become the person he wants you to be, because to hold on to the past, the last sight of your mother's face, hurts too much. So you let yourself go, assuming one day, when you get out of here, you'll find yourself again.

Not understanding it doesn't work that way.

A sense of self is such a fragile, powerful thing. And once you lose it . . .

I wonder again if this girl is Stacey Summers. If we had some light, if I could just see her . . . But now, the two of us are alone in the dark.

It shouldn't matter. A victim is a victim is a victim, and there are a lot of them out there. Just look at the articles plastering the wall of my bedroom. But something about Stacey . . . The photograph of her smile. The way her father talked about her, so much raw pain in his voice. I wanted to find her. I wanted to be the one to bring her a happy ending.

Maybe her happiness, by association, would rub off on me. I would save her, but she would help me find the light.

At least that's what I thought three months ago.

Am I crying again? I don't know. I am not okay.

I reach out. I find her cuffed hands on the edge of the mattress. She flinches but doesn't recoil as I finger the marks on each of her wrists. Fresh lacerations, old scars. Could wrists accumulate so much damage in just three months? Or am I dealing with someone gone far longer? How long did it take me before I gave up my name?

I don't know. All these years later, so much I don't know.

'Why, why, why?' she whispers in the dark.

It comes to me. The work-around. The kidnapper might have forced her to take a new name, but the identities of other people in her life . . .

'Tell me about your parents,' I say.

She whimpers.

'Your father. What's his name?'

I can hear her head tossing against the mattress, agitated.

'Is it Colin?' I ask.

'Why, why, why,' she says.

'Can you give me a cheer?' I ask the possible former

cheerleader. 'Give me an *E*. Give me an *S*. Give me a *C*. Give me an *A*, a *P*, an *E*. What does that spell? *ESCAPE!*'

I might be losing it. The edge of my voice contains a hint of hysteria. But she's stopped moving, is listening to me intently. Have I finally hit upon the remnant of a memory? Some inner trigger that will help snap her out of this?

'Why?' she whispers in the dark. Then: 'Why are you doing this to me?'

'Because we need to get out of here. Because I'm working for Colin Summers. Because I promised him, I promised myself, I'd bring you home safe.'

She doesn't speak. Is it just me, or do I detect a sense of wonder?

'I can do this,' I inform her, forcing myself to sound confident. 'The door, I think I can jimmy it open. I can get us out of here, but I need your help.'

She doesn't move.

'You don't need to be afraid of him,' I add belatedly. 'First time, he caught me off guard. But now, I'm ready.'

'Who?'

'The big guy. The one who took you from the bar, grabbed me from my apartment. I think he might be drugging me.' I'm babbling now. 'I mean, how else can he keep getting in and out of the room without waking me? So we'll have to think of something. Maybe tear apart the mattress, jury-rig something with stuff, strips of cloth? We have resources, we just have to use them wisely.'

I'm getting ahead of myself. What I really need is the last sliver of wood I'm pretty sure is still stashed inside the mattress. Except she's still not moving off it.

'Why?' she whispers.

'Why what? Why am I helping you? I already told you that.'

'Why are you doing this?'

'Because we need to get out! Because I promised your father—'

She whimpers, recoils. In the dark, I can feel her snatch her hands back.

'Hey,' I try to reassure her. 'It's okay. Whatever he promised, whatever he threatened . . . He can't hurt your family. That's just something these guys say to control you. Trust me. It'll be okay.'

'I'll do what you want! Please. I already told you that.'

'What do you mean, you already told me that?'

'I've been good. I've been so good. I've done everything you said.' In the dark, she moves suddenly, seizes my hand. 'Please. I did exactly as you said. Ever since you brought me here. I've done everything you told me to. Now, please, let me go home. I won't tell anyone if you'll just let me go home again.'

30

Ten thirty Monday morning, D.D. finally arrived at HQ. She felt slightly breathless, mind still whirling from her conversation with the Atlanta FBI agent and the circumstances surrounding Flora Dane's rescue from Jacob Ness. D.D. was also acutely aware of how behind she was in her supervisor duties. Actually working the case, check. Processing paperwork and managing leads, on the other hand . . .

She would be good today, she promised herself as she hammered up the stairs, coffee in one hand, leather messenger bag in the other. She would sit. She would focus. She would behave like an actual supervisor of homicide, butt glued to her chair, eyes on the stack of files on her desk. She would skim reports, dot i's, cross t's, and, you never know, make a groundbreaking discovery that would blow the case wide-open. Who said desk jobs didn't matter?

Her resolution lasted as long as it took to round the corner to her office, where she found BPD's newest detective, Carol Manley, waiting for her. The petite blonde was wearing yesterday's clothes and was nearly bouncing in place, hair standing on end.

'Have you been here all night?' D.D. asked with a frown.

Then: 'Wait a second. You were going through the videotapes. Did you find footage of Flora's abduction?'

'No. I found the building inspector.'

'You mean the kidnapper disguised as a building inspector?'

'No, the actual building inspector. Turns out, he's for real!'

Detective Carol Manley had definitely not slept the night before, and apparently she'd compensated with many, if not dozens of, cups of coffee. D.D., who prided herself on speaking caffeine, had to ask her to slow down several times to get the story out.

Carol had reviewed the footage pulled from various cameras in the vicinity of Flora's apartment. But she hadn't made any significant discoveries.

'There's too many images,' she explained in a rush. 'Too many locals, too many cars, too much foot traffic. Each frame, each camera, there are dozens and dozens of people. And since I don't know who I'm looking for, how do I sort that out?'

'You start by looking for Flora,' D.D. interrupted.

'Sure. Flora. Except what Flora? She was gone Friday night, Saturday morning. I think I found a traffic cam clip of Dr Keynes's car turning down her street, but that's it. No Flora walking the streets after that, and it's not like I have direct video of her building. Best I can do is check traffic cam footage of cars passing through the intersection near her apartment to see if she's in any of them. But again, so much traffic, so many cars, and so many windows.'

D.D. rubbed her forehead, conceding the point. Pulling local video always seemed like an excellent idea until, of course, you were the detective wading through it.

'So I got to thinking,' Carol continued in a rush. 'What I needed was more information, another visual clue. Then it occurred to me, the landlords, Mary and James Reichter, had said the building inspector had visited on Tuesday.'

'Except the Housing Inspection Division has no record of that.'

'Exactly! But why not start with traffic cams from Tuesday, right? Generally speaking, there's less traffic midmorning on a Tuesday than, say, a Saturday night. Plus, we know the suspect is a big guy, which would make him easier to see on camera. I figure maybe I can get us a video shot of the actual kidnapper or, if I'm really lucky, his vehicle and license plate.'

D.D. couldn't help herself: She was impressed. Searching for images of the suspect from his visit to the apartment on Tuesday did make more sense as a starting point. And, yeah, a license plate . . .

'But you didn't find him?' she asked Manley now.

'Oh, I found him. Riley Hayes. Except he's not some guy pretending to be a building inspector. He's an actual subcontractor who inspects buildings.'

'What? But the department—'

'Hasn't seen his report yet. Hayes is still writing it up, that's why there's no record. But the traffic cam captured a vehicle passing through the intersection on Tuesday with a logo on the side: Hayes Inspections. I copied down the plate, made some calls, and voilà. Inspector Riley Hayes, who did visit the Reichters' building on Tuesday.'

'But . . .' D.D. frowned, took a slug of coffee, frowned again. 'I want to speak to him.'

Manley beamed, bounced up and down on her toes again. 'I know. Which is why I have him waiting for you in room six.'

* * *

D.D. had to take a minute. She stashed her messenger bag beneath her desk, shrugged out of her jacket, took a few more hits of caffeine. Her mind was whirling again, and not in a good way. The building inspector couldn't be an actual inspector. Because that wouldn't make any sense. A suspect checking out the building as a ruse to access keys would explain how the same person was able to enter Flora's locked-tight apartment. But a real building inspector actually doing his job . . .

What were the odds?

Carol was waiting for her outside the meeting room. The detective was armed with a fresh cup of coffee, apparently oblivious to the twitch developing in her right eye. An experienced overcaffeinator, D.D. recognized the symptoms of a dark-roasted high, soon to be followed by an excruciating ice pick to the temple low. Good luck with that, she thought, then opened the door to the interview room.

The BPD's headquarters was a modern glass monstrosity that you either loved or hated. Either way, it wasn't the dilapidated, leaky-pipe, stained, dropped-ceiling affair featured on so many cop shows. The homicide unit's offices could've passed for an insurance company's digs, with an expansive bank of windows, tasteful gray cubicles, and a blue sweep of commercial-grade carpet. Keeping with that theme, the department included several smaller rooms for private chats with families, quieter conversations between detectives.

Room six was really just that. A small room featuring a modest table, a couple of chairs. A viewing window that could be accessed from the hall. It was neither intimidating nor welcoming, which made it perfect for conversations like this: where D.D. was interviewing either a possible suspect or a fellow civil servant.

The inspector glanced up as D.D. opened the door. At first look, he was younger than D.D. would've thought. Close-cropped dark hair. Square jaw. Block shoulders. Big guy, the kind who would leave an impression on elderly landlords such as Mary and James Reichter. In his dark blue dress shirt, name embroidered in white thread on the left side, he also struck the right chord of confidence. Strong, competent professional.

No wonder Mary and James had handed him the keys to their building. D.D. imagined many female tenants and home owners would've gladly done the same.

'Riley Hayes?' she asked now, entering the room.

He nodded, not quite meeting her eye. Nervous, she thought. On the sketchy side of honest.

Then again, so were many people when summoned to HQ for official police questioning.

Carol Manley followed D.D. into the room, closing the door behind them. The room wasn't that big; D.D. and Carol took a seat at the table, across from their person of interest, and there was just enough space left over to breathe.

Carol set down her mug of coffee. D.D. saw the man's gaze flicker toward it, a reflexive inhale of wafting steam, but he didn't say a word.

'You inspected a building last week.' D.D. rattled off the address while opening the file Manley had prepared on Hayes. D.D. skimmed the background report, noting a couple of traffic tickets, nothing of real interest.

Across from her, Hayes nodded. 'That's right.'

'How long have you been an inspector?'

'Six months.'

'Kind of young.' D.D. looked up. 'Says here you originally trained as a fireman.'

'I was a fireman. Till I injured my back. On the job. Doctor's orders transferred me to this.'

'Like the work?'

He shrugged, gaze on the table. 'It's a job.'

'Hayes Inspections. You own the firm?'

'My father. George Hayes. His company.'

She found that interesting. 'How many buildings do you inspect a week?'

'Depends on the week. Some buildings, such as the Reichters' place, aren't that big, don't take too long. Other properties . . . you can spend days.'

'Why the Reichters' building?'

'Came up in the computer as overdue. City has a backlog right now, has hired firms such as my father's to clear it.'

'So you were there because of the computer?'

He finally looked up, meeting her gaze for the first time. 'You can call the Housing Inspection Division. What's this about again?'

D.D. ignored his question. 'According to the landlords, they couldn't take you around the building. Too many stairs.'

'That's right.'

'Instead, they gave you keys to the various apartments.'

Across from her, Hayes paused, seemed to be considering. 'Did someone say they're missing something? Is that what this is about?'

'I'm not interested in robbery,' D.D. informed him. 'Not my department.'

Hayes frowned, appeared even more confused, which was right where she wanted him. 'Anyone home in any of the units?' she asked.

'Yeah. As a matter of fact.'

'Who?'

'Woman. Third floor. I was going to put that in my report: She wouldn't let me in.'

'Do you know her name, Mr Hayes?'

'No. Wouldn't say she was the kind of person inclined to chat. Didn't seem to care much for city ordinances either.'

'She didn't believe you were a building inspector?'

'I had to show her my ID. Twice.' First flicker of emotion on his face: annoyance. 'Even then, she said she'd have to call in to confirm before I could enter.' He shook his head. 'Some people.'

'Did she let you in?'

'No. When she called the department, no one picked up. Plus . . .' He hesitated.

'What?' D.D. prodded him. 'Plus, what?'

'Her locks. She has multiple key-in, key-out bolts. I informed her those weren't to code. In an emergency situation, they would impede the fire department's ability to access her apartment.'

D.D. was intrigued in spite of herself. 'And how'd she take that?'

'She informed me that fire was the least of her concerns,' he said dryly. 'Then she ordered me to go away; she didn't need any bureaucrats to teach her about safety.'

'What did you do next?'

He shrugged. 'Asked if I could at least check her unit for fire alarms, emergency egress.'

'She agree?'

'Please. She pointed out one alarm in the hall ceiling, which could be viewed from the doorway. Informed me I should be able to see from where I was standing that it worked just fine – the green LED light indicated it had power, while the red flashing light indicated battery backup.

As for her unit's emergency egress, I was welcome to check out the fire escape – from the outside.'

'She sounds charming,' D.D. assured him. 'Can you describe her, please?'

Hayes startled, seemed surprised by this request. 'I don't know. Small. I mean . . .' He blushed. 'Most girls seem tiny to me. Blond hair, kind of messy. She was dressed casual. Baggy sweats, bare feet. I don't know. She wasn't very friendly, that's what I remember most.'

'And girls are generally friendly? Young, good-looking guy like you?'

He hesitated, his expression once again wary. 'What do you want? Did she say something about me?'

'Why? You do something wrong? Maybe lose your temper, grow frustrated? Clearly, she wasn't treating you with the respect you deserve.'

Hayes shook his head. 'Look, I don't know what's going on here. Yeah, I inspected the Reichters' apartment building. Yeah, I talked to some woman on the third floor. But that was it. She didn't let me in, I didn't push it. I made a note of the one working smoke alarm I could see, and then, yes, I walked around the building and checked out the fire escape.'

'Climb up it?'

'Of course.'

'Peer in her window?'

'What? Hey, listen to me.' Hands up now, flat on the table, his broad face flushing. 'I did my job, nothing more. I don't know what she said, but whatever it was . . . I walked the building, inspected the fire escape, that was it. Ask the Reichters. I returned all the keys to them, couldn't have been more than fifteen, twenty minutes tops. And I can show you the draft of my report – the diagrams, everything

I have to do. Fifteen, twenty minutes is about right. So whatever she said happened, it didn't.'

'Care to take a polygraph?'

'Seriously? I mean . . . Do I need a lawyer? What happened?'

'Name Flora Dane ring a bell?'

'No. Should it?'

'That was the woman, the third-floor apartment.'

'I don't know. Like I said, she wasn't a talker.'

'She's missing.'

'What?'

'She's gone missing. Was possibly kidnapped. Saturday night. Most likely by someone who had a key to all those locks on her door.'

Hayes shut up, face going pale. He looked at D.D., then Carol Manley, then D.D. again. D.D. couldn't tell what was going on in his mind anymore. Guilt? Innocence? Denial? Rationalization? He was sketchy, she decided. Just enough to be worth provoking.

'I gave the keys back to the landlord,' he stated now. 'Whatever happened, it's got nothing to do with me.'

'Easy enough to take an impression of the keys – or make an actual copy.'

'No. I wouldn't.'

'Where were you Saturday night?'

'What?'

'Saturday night. Where were you?'

'I had a date.' Hayes sat up straighter, voice picking up. 'Boston Beer Garden. I was out with a group of friends. I can get you their names.'

'What time?'

'Seven.'

'Before that?'

'Getting ready. I have a roommate. He can tell you.' Hayes nodded now. He saw his way out and he was taking it. 'Look, ask my dad, ask whomever. I'm a good guy. I show up, do my job, end of story. Tuesday at the Reichters' building . . . I don't know what happened to that woman, but I promise you: It had nothing to do with me. Saturday night, I was out with friends and I can prove it.'

Ten minutes later, back in D.D.'s office.

Carol Manley: 'I don't think that guy copied a set of keys or kidnapped Flora Danes.'

'No.'

'But if not him, who could gain that kind of access? Open a triple-locked door, grab a highly trained semiprofessional in her sleep?'

'I have no idea,' D.D. said.

'So we start back at the beginning. We look at the victim, Flora Dane.'

'Sure.'

'Well, and Stacey Summers, because maybe it's the same guy, right? Except then there's Devon Goulding, whom Flora killed, and the pictures of the missing women, whom maybe he killed.'

'Couldn't be Devon Goulding,' D.D. said. 'He was already dead when Flora went missing.'

Carol sighed, dragged a hand through her rumpled hair. 'I'm confused,' the new detective said.

'Me too,' D.D. agreed. 'Me too.'

31

The woman who looked like my mom was talking on TV.
Sitting alone on the bed in the cheap motel room, I stared
at her image. Sound was off. I watched her lips move and
felt a sense of déjà vu. For a moment, I could almost hear
her say, 'This is all of Flora, getting some sleep!'

I climbed off the bed, approached the TV.

A silver fox charm nestled in the hollow of her throat. I
touched it, my finger so big against the small screen it
obliterated all of the woman's head. And I felt it again, that
sense of déjà vu. Because I'd done this before, seen the
woman who looked like my mom talking on TV. But that
was months and months ago, eons ago. Way back when I
was still a girl who thought I might one day go home.

Now, her picture back on TV caught me off guard. She
shouldn't still be talking about me. She shouldn't still be
missing me.

Jacob said nobody missed me anymore. Jacob said I was
already dead. Jacob said my family was better off without
me.

Jacob, Jacob, Jacob.

Jacob, who'd left me once again.

He'd screwed up a job. Not that he would admit to such
a thing. But last month's bender had led to last week's

delivery arriving late. Guy hadn't been happy. Yelling on the loading dock. I don't know what all was said. I sat inside the cab, the way good girls do, waiting for my man to return to me.

When Jacob finally climbed into the driver's seat, he was furious, hands fisted on the steering wheel, lips set into a grim line. We'd gone straight from shipping and delivery to a truck stop. He'd parked the rig, ordered me out. Inside the convenience store, he'd loaded up on beer, a carton of smokes, and, on second thought, some chips. Then we'd hoofed it three miles, to a strip motel he'd spotted from the highway.

Once inside, it'd been beer, cigarettes, sex, except not always in that order. Eventually, I got to eat some potato chips, but that was days ago, and now I was hungry.

He'd left first thing this morning. Like he had yesterday, the day before. Where he went, he didn't talk about. Beer, cigarettes, sex. That was all this room was about.

Did he lose his job? He didn't seem to be in a hurry to hit the road again. Was he broke? If he didn't work, how would he cover the cost of the motel rooms, food, cases of beer?

What would become of me?

My mother who didn't look like my mother. She had tears on her cheeks. She was crying on TV. More than a year later, still pleading for my safe return.

'This is all of Flora, getting some sleep!'

Footsteps outside the window. Quickly, I snapped off the TV, retreated to the bed.

Jacob walked through the door two seconds later. Wearing his usual grease-stained jeans, yellowing T-shirt, open flannel shirt. Beneath one arm, he carried a case of beer. In the other, a brown paper bag. Most likely Four

Roses whiskey, which he'd down straight from the bottle.

'What are you looking at?' he asked as he caught me staring. 'What? You still in your pajamas? Like it would fucking kill you to clean yourself up while I'm gone.'

I fingered the edge of my black satin nightgown, edged with cream-colored lace at the top and bottom. He'd bought it for me a couple of months ago. I thought he liked it.

He slammed down the beer. The whiskey. I eyed him up and down, desperate for some sign of food.

'What?' he demanded again, shoving a cigarette between his crooked teeth.

'We're out of chips,' I whispered.

'Chips? That all you care about? Stuffing your face? Jesus, no wonder you've gotten fat.'

I didn't say anything. My hip bones jutted out beneath the shimmer of black satin. I was many things, but probably not fat.

'Bad day?' I asked at last, not sure what to say.

'Are there any others?'

'You, um, you've been gone awhile.'

He didn't say anything.

'Yesterday too. The day before.' I couldn't look at him while I spoke. I picked at the fabric balls on the worn blue comforter.

'Jealous?' he asked. He ripped open the case of beer. Picked out the first can. 'Figuring out the thrill is gone? I'm a man, you know. Ain't no girl, 'specially not some cheap piece of trash like you, that's gonna hold my attention for long. Maybe' – he turned, hefted up the can – 'maybe I went sightseeing.'

I stilled, feeling my heart accelerate in my chest. He could be lying. He liked to torment me. But the sneer on his face, the hard look in his eyes . . .

I swallowed, pretended my hands weren't now shaking on the comforter.

'This is all of Flora, getting some sleep.'

But who is Flora? And how could she ever go home again?

There was just me. This room. This man. My life now.

'Take me,' *I heard myself say.*

'What, wanna meet your replacement?'

'Sure.' *I kept my voice level, forced myself to meet his gaze. 'I want to see if she's pretty enough for you.'*

I'd caught him off guard. My secret weapon, my one redeeming trait. No matter how much he sought to control me, from time to time I still surprised him. And he liked it. Even now, I could see the spark of interest in his eyes. He set down the beer, gaze lingering on my thin satin slip.

'All right,' *he said.* 'But you don't get to change.'

I followed him out of the room barefoot, arms crossed self-consciously over my chest. For the first time, I noticed his rig now parked in front of the motel. No attached container, of course, just the sleeper cab, which was noticeable enough. He climbed aboard. Midafternoon. Sun was blazing. Where I had grown up, sun brought people outside to enjoy the weather. But down here, the heat had the opposite effect, driving everyone indoors to the comfort of air-conditioning.

No one noticed as I walked half dressed around the cab, then clambered on board. Jacob fired it to life, and off we went.

He drove in silence. I figured we'd head toward the beach, the strip of bars we'd visited the first night, where the serving girls wore short shorts and midriff-baring white Ts, a look that would've been better if most of the women had been younger than forty and not bloated with layers of this-is-what-half-a-dozen-thankless-kids-do-to-your-figure fat.

But he headed away from the strip, turning off the highway, down small side roads. He headed toward a neighborhood.

At the last second, he stopped, pulled over beside a strip of marshland, long-fingered grass blowing in the wind.

'We walk,' he said, looking at my bare feet, challenging me to complain.

I didn't. I got out. Kept to the sandy side of the smoking-hot blacktop and trudged forward. Movement in the brush beside me. Could be birds. Snakes. Critters. I didn't think about it. Just kept walking.

Jacob strolled in the middle of the road, smoking a fresh cigarette, not saying a word.

Road was broken up. Potholed in the center, crumbling at the edge. Not the best road, not the best neighborhood. Houses were small and flat, pastel colors as faded as the laundry hanging from drying lines.

I could hear dogs barking in the back, babies crying on the inside. Here and there, tired kids stood in the dusty front yards, staring at the smoking man and half-dressed girl. Jacob kept moving and so did I.

A turn here, a turn there, and then we were behind a row of houses, partially sheltered by a ridge of overgrown shrubs. Jacob slowed, his footsteps faltering.

Just for a moment, I saw something pass across his face. Yearning.

The look of a man who cared.

He stopped.

I faltered, almost ran into his back. This time, something slithered out, over my foot, and it was definitely a snake. I smothered the scream just as Jacob's hand slapped over my mouth.

'Not one word,' he instructed hoarsely. I could see the fanatic gleam in his eyes. Whatever I was about to see, whatever we were about to do, it was very, very important to him.

I am not myself, I thought as I turned with him toward the last house on the block. Sagging black shutters, peeling pink paint, dilapidated roof. This is not me, I thought as we moved closer and closer, Jacob's cigarette long cast aside, and now . . .

A knife at his side.

This is not Flora, I thought, a girl who once played with foxes, now standing outside a chain-link fence, peering in.

I spotted my rival immediately. Back slider of the house was open. She sat inside, in the relatively cool comfort, watching TV. She had long dark hair gathered in a loose ponytail. A faded green tank top paired with cutoff jeans. She stared at the old TV, chain-smoking, her long arms shockingly pale for these parts. But it worked for her, the dark hair, cream-colored skin. Like Snow White, all she needed now was blood-red lips.

I knew, before she ever turned around, that she was prettier than some bony New England blonde like me. No, she was dark fringed lashes, razor-sharp cheekbones, and long sultry nights.

My replacement. Jacob's new toy.

And I realized, in the next instant, he hadn't brought the knife for her. He'd brought the knife for me. One quick thrust and I'd be all done, rolled into the swamps for the gators to feed on. Just as he'd always promised.

'This is all of Flora, getting some sleep.'

Is that what death would feel like? Finally getting some sleep?

Inside the house, the girl turned her head. Alerted by a

noise, our presence? I found myself holding my breath, while Jacob inhaled sharply beside me.

She looked older than I'd expected. Not a sweet young thing. Maybe closer to midtwenties. Which surprised me. Jacob always favored teenagers. Easier to train, he'd told me.

I glanced at him now, trying to understand.

And . . .

The look on his face. Adoration. Fixation. A man fully, hopelessly in love. A man looking at this new girl in a way he'd never, ever looked at me.

My turn to inhale sharply, and in the next moment, I understood. This was no random girl, no spur-of-the-moment replacement.

'That's Lindy,' I said.

'Shhh. She'll hear you!'

'She's still alive?'

"Course she's still alive!'

'You didn't grow tired of her? Kill her and feed her to the gators?'

'What the fuck are you talking about?' he whispered hoarsely. 'I'd never hurt her.'

'You love her.'

'Shut the fuck up.'

'You do. You actually . . . you love her.'

The girl in the house turned, alerted by our conversation. She rose to standing, looking in our direction.

Beside me, Jacob once more sucked in his breath. He watched her walk toward us, completely transfixed.

I knew then that I hated this girl. She was the true enemy. If Jacob had never loved her, never lost her, he wouldn't be snatching the rest of us off of Florida beaches. Somehow, she'd inspired him; then she'd twisted him.

And now, after everything I'd survived, everything I'd done, she'd be the one who'd take Jacob from me. Because of her, Jacob would finally use that knife, then feed my body to the local wildlife. My mother would never learn what happened to me. She'd spend years talking in front of all those cameras, wearing her little fox charm and pleading for a daughter who was already dead.

I hated Jacob then. Hated him as much as I had that very first day, regaining consciousness in a coffin-shaped box.

But I hated this girl even more.

Lindy. The girl who'd started it all. The girl who'd ultimately destroy me.

Unless, of course . . .

I killed her first.

32

'We found a body.'

'Don't you mean bodies?' D.D. glanced up from her desk to find Phil standing in her doorway. He was shaking his head.

'No. Body. At one of the destinations listed on Goulding's vehicle's GPS.'

'Kristy Kilker or Natalie Draga?'

'That's what we're going to find out.'

D.D. automatically pushed back her chair, then caught herself. 'Wait. Is this a test? Because I heard you, you know. I get that I'm headstrong and controlling, and I should trust my partners and have more faith in your abilities to get things done. Meaning, you get to go see the body. And I get to await your report like a good restricted duty supervisor? And then—' She caught herself, as surprised as anyone by the sudden thickening in her throat. 'Then you won't be mad at me anymore.'

'I'm not mad at you.'

'I do trust you,' she got out while she could. Because now she was remembering yesterday's conversation with Phil and it stung. She'd never say it out loud, but Phil was the closest thing to a surrogate father figure that she had, especially given that her own father didn't approve of her job. She didn't miss her parents, who lived in Florida. She didn't even mind anymore that they didn't understand her job. But Phil, his clear disappointment in her . . . that hurt.

'I trust you, Phil. I trust Neil. And I miss you guys. Every day. I miss our squad, our partnership. I don't like feeling like I let you down. Because you're my team. You've always been my team, and let's face it, not just anyone wants a team member as headstrong and controlling as I am. I know that. I definitely know that.'

'Are you done?'

'Maybe.'

'Because this isn't a test. Though, for the record, you are headstrong and controlling.'

'I know.'

'And you should have more faith in us.'

'I know.'

'But you're also you, and I know you, D.D. Most of the time, when I'm not completely exasperated or frustrated or scared out of my mind, I even like you. So now that we both agree that I'm right and you're wrong, are you going to come along or not?'

'Come along?'

'To the crime scene. With the body. But I get to drive.'

D.D. didn't need to be asked twice. 'Okay!'

'You really are a lousy restricted duty supervisor.'

'Yeah. Been thinking that a lot myself.' Which still didn't stop her from grabbing her leather jacket and walking away from her desk.

'So where are we headed?' she asked as she followed Phil out the door, world order officially restored.

'Mattapan.'

'Again? Why are the bodies always hidden in Mattapan?'

'Because some neighborhoods are just like that.'

* * *

Mattapan had a nature park run by the Mass Audubon society on acres of land that used to belong to an abandoned state mental hospital. Which Phil and D.D. were both very conscious of as they skirted the perimeter of the property, sticking close to the elaborate wrought iron fence that separated the unexpected expanse of leafy trees from the dense urban jungle that surrounded it.

They'd been to this park before. They'd walked these grounds when the skeletal remains of the abandoned mental facility had still winked shattered glass eyes from atop the hill. They knew all about the ghosts of this area's past, and the mummified remains of six girls they'd excavated from an underground pit last time they'd been here.

Following Phil toward the first wooded trail, D.D. had a chill, and it wasn't from the weather.

In theory, the Boston State Hospital was long gone. Half of the green space had become the Boston Nature Center, home to 150 species of birds and 350 species of plants in the midst of a densely packed neighborhood where the triple-deckers were jammed shoulder to shoulder and most looked worse for the wear.

Bostonians came from all over to walk through these trees, listen to the birds, admire the butterflies. That the park came up as a frequent destination in Devon Goulding's GPS could just mean he was someone who enjoyed communing with nature.

Except, of course, the park also represented a decent chunk of tucked-away green space, which is exactly what a killer would need to bury a body.

According to Phil, they'd brought out dogs first thing this morning. It had taken them less than twenty minutes to make the find: a low mound of earth resting next to an equally long depression in the ground, both just starting to be reclaimed by the undergrowth.

Laypeople generally gravitated toward the mound when digging for a body. Experienced pros like Boston's ME department, however, knew better. The mound was formed from all the displaced dirt the killer had excavated from the grave – digging down, dumping shovelfuls of soil to the side. The depression, that was the grave. Where the subject had interred the body, then covered it with enough soil to make it relatively level. Never once considering the effects of putrefaction. That flesh and muscle would eventually decay, slide off the bones, melt into the very ground. That if blowflies had found a way to lay eggs on the body before it was interred, this process would happen even faster – let alone critter activity as a new food source was introduced into the local area.

Shallow graves took on a life of their own. And eventually, all bodies did what they were meant to do. Decay. Ashes to ashes, dust to dust. Disappearing back into the earth, until months later, a uniquely shaped depression was formed. The kind of hollow that any experienced homicide detective could look at and say, hey, betcha a body is buried there.

The ME's full team was out. This kind of retrieval was conducted like an archeological dig, with the leaf-strewn area beneath the trees already marked into a series of grids. Each shovelful of earth that was removed went into a marked container, to be sifted through later for signs of additional evidence. It would take all day for the ME to remove the body, D.D. knew, and weeks, if not months, before Ben would issue his full report.

D.D. and Phil approached, making sure they didn't get too close. Ben Whitely was very good at his job, which was to say he was territorial and had little patience for stupid cop tricks.

He'd also once been romantically involved with their squad mate Neil. After the breakup . . . everyone was professional. Nothing was quite the same.

'Morning, Ben,' Phil called out. An opening salvo.

He received a grunt from a burly figure hunched over the shallow grave, seemingly brushing at the dirt. D.D. recognized his actions from past retrievals: They had exhumed all the way down to the body, and Ben was now dusting the final layer of fine soil from the mummified skin, bones, whatever was left.

This close, D.D. could catch a whiff of decomp mixing with the peaty smell of soil, fall leaves. So the remains weren't fully skeletal yet, which would make sense given the timeline of the missing women's disappearances.

'Male or female?' D.D. asked. Unlike Phil, she didn't waste time on pleasantries. Which, she happened to know, made her one of Ben's favorites. He didn't care for pleasantries either.

'Female.'

'Time of death?'

'Bite me.'

D.D. and Phil exchanged glances. Apparently, that was a question to be answered back at the morgue. Made sense. The rate of decay in shallow graves varied wildly, depending on depth of grave, insect activity, that sort of thing. Ben would have to analyze soil samples taken from beneath the body to pinpoint time of death, and even then he'd grumble about the accuracy. Which made today a better day to be a homicide detective than an ME.

'Clothing, jewelry, any unique indicators we can use for identification?' D.D. asked. Personally, she was hoping for replacement parts – anything from breast implants to artificial knees, all of which came with serial numbers that could be traced back to the recipient.

'Got an earring,' Ben supplied, not looking up. 'Gold hoop. Some clothing. Blue jeans maybe. Cotton top. Can't tell if there's anything in the pockets. Not there yet.'

D.D. looked at Phil. 'Neil and I came across a stash of photos of Natalie Draga in Goulding's room. I don't remember her wearing hoop earrings.'

'I'll call Neil, ask him to double-check,' Phil said. 'Kristy Kilker?'

'We didn't find any pictures of her. Just her driver's license.'

'He can check that too. Just in case she's wearing earrings in that photo.'

D.D. nodded, though it was a long shot. Some women wore the same earrings day in and day out, but a twenty-something girl out on the town? Chances were Kristy had different accessories for each outfit, that sort of thing.

'Hair appears to be brown,' Ben offered from the grave.

Which would be consistent with either Natalie or Kristy.

'Got something on the fingernails. Polish. Maybe dark pink, red? Either of your missing girls partial to manicures?'

Phil made a note. One more detail to track down.

'Are you sure there's only one body?' D.D. called out.

Ben finally glanced up, skewered her with a glance.

'Never mind.' Even D.D. knew when to beat a hasty retreat. 'So . . .' She tried to pick her next question carefully. 'We have two missing girls. One last seen nine months ago.' Natalie Draga, who'd never collected her last check at work. 'One vanished more like five months ago.' Kristy Kilker, who'd called her mother once or twice since the alleged Italy trip.

'If I had to pick between the two . . .' Ben went back to brushing.

'Sure.'

'Body's on the fresher side. Been here like a two-to-three-month window.'

D.D. glanced at Phil.

'Only tells us how long ago the body was buried,' Phil warned. 'Natalie Draga might have gone missing nine months ago, but that doesn't mean she was killed then.'

D.D. nodded, understanding his point. They didn't know enough of Goulding and his MO. Had he kept the girls alive for a bit? The haunting photos of Natalie Draga seemed to imply as much. Then again, they had nothing on Kristy except for a bloody license. Questions D.D. would've liked to ask Goulding. Except, thanks to Flora Dane, he was no longer available to answer.

'Call Kristy's mom,' she instructed Phil at last. 'Ask her about favorite earrings, nail polish. Maybe she can give us a starting point.'

Phil nodded, moving off to a separate bank of trees to work his phone.

D.D. stood alone, watching the ME carefully brush dirt from the remains of at least one missing girl who would finally go home again.

'Pretty in Pink,' Phil reported fifteen minutes later. 'Kristy's go-to nail polish. Wore it all the time. Was also partial to a pair of gold hoops, which were a sixteenth birthday present from her mom.'

'Kristy Kilker,' D.D. said.

'Not enough for an official ID.'

'No. We'll have to wait for Ben to work his full magic at the lab. But chances are . . .'

'Kristy Kilker,' Phil agreed.

'So where is Natalie Draga? A second dump site? Are there other frequent destinations recorded in Goulding's GPS?'

'Not that would work for stashing bodies. This is it.'

'And the dogs have covered the entire park?'

'Yep.'

'So where is Natalie Draga?' D.D. asked again.

Phil had no answer.

D.D. looked around, at the trees, the gawkers, the milling crew of blue-clad crime scene technicians. 'Phil, what are we missing?'

She called Samuel Keynes. She didn't know why. He wasn't an investigating officer but a professional headshrink. He didn't catch bad guys; he assisted with victims. And yet . . .

Everything about this case came back to Flora Dane. And given her disappearance, the closest link they had to her was Dr Keynes. Which was interesting in its own right because most of the time, D.D. would peg the mother in a situation like this. But for all of Rosa's fierce protection of her daughter, their relationship was strained. Flora herself hadn't called her mother after Friday night's incident. She'd called her former victim specialist instead.

Keynes picked up after one ring. Almost as if he was expecting her call.

'Do you know someone named Natalie Draga?' she asked him.

'No.'

'What about Kristy Kilker?'

'No.'

'Flora never mentioned these names? Never talked about trying to locate either woman?'

'No. Sergeant Detective—'

'But she did talk to you about Stacey Summers? Come on. Now is the time to be open and honest, Doctor. Because I have one dead body and I'm pretty sure there's about to be more. Flora talks to you. Flora tells you things she doesn't tell anyone else. Not even her mother. So what did she tell you about Stacey Summers?'

'Saturday morning's phone call was the first contact I'd had with Flora in months. At least six months. We are not that close, Sergeant Detective. Not nearly as close as you think.'

'But she tells you things. Things she tells no one else. This morning, I spoke to the FBI agent who rescued Flora. According to her, she has lots of questions about what Flora did during her time with Jacob Ness. But Flora won't answer those questions. She'll only talk to you.'

'I provided a full report of Flora's statement. Contrary to what you're implying, everything I heard has been made available to investigators. That Flora didn't want to share her experience again and again . . . that's hardly unusual for someone who's been through her level of trauma.'

'Did she do it? Help kidnap other victims?'

'Not that she ever revealed.'

'Is that what this is? All this vigilante business? Survivor's guilt to cleanse her conscience of what she did during her captivity?'

'Your guess is as good as mine.'

'No. Not true. One, you're the expert. Two, she trusts you. And she keeps calling you. When she's in trouble, when she needs help, your number is the one she dials. Five years later, Doc. How many families are still calling you five years later?'

Keynes didn't say anything.

'Then there's the mom,' D.D. continued, thinking out loud. 'Rosa Dane. She seems pretty comfortable with you as well. Does she also keep you on speed dial, or do you call her? Because Flora doesn't and you know that bothers her.'

Then, it came to D.D. The way Keynes had touched Rosa's shoulder yesterday in her office. The way he'd stood so solidly beside her when, frankly, there was no reason for him to be there at all. But he'd come. At Rosa's request. And he'd stayed. The good doctor and Rosa.

'Does Flora know?' D.D. blurted out. 'About you and her mom. Have you ever told her?'

'Sergeant Detective, do you have any new leads on Flora's disappearance?'

'Answer my question first.'

'I will not.'

'It's relevant—'

'It is not. Now, do you have any new information—'

'Rosa's standing there,' D.D. filled in abruptly. 'She's standing right beside you, and she's asking about her daughter.'

Keynes didn't answer, which D.D. took to be a yes.

'Rosa doesn't know, does she?' D.D. said more softly. 'Your feelings for her, you've never said.'

'I assure you—'

'I am mistaken. Got it. Your relationship with the family is purely professional. Proper feebie like you—'

'Sergeant Detective—'

'I have a body. One of the women we believe Devon Goulding abducted, we've found her remains based on evidence we recovered from his house.'

'You believe you've just discovered one of Goulding's victims? In other words, Flora was right in her actions on

Friday. If she hadn't killed him, it might be her body you were discovering now.'

'Flora's gone. And whatever happened to her has to have something to do with Devon Goulding, Stacey Summers, and at least two other missing women. It would be too coincidental for it to be otherwise. So I'm asking you one more time, did Flora ever mention the names Kristy Kilker or Natalie Draga?'

'And I'm telling you, I hadn't spoken to Flora in months before Saturday morning.'

'Which only tells me when you spoke to her, but doesn't answer the question of what she said. Come on, Keynes. I might not have the initials PhD after my name, but that doesn't mean I'm stupid.'

'Do you have any new leads on Flora's disappearance, Sergeant Detective?'

'No.'

'Please call me when you do.'

Keynes disconnected the call. D.D. stood there, gnashing her teeth for a while longer. Wondering once again at the relationship between the victim specialist and the Dane family. And why, once again, she had a feeling he wasn't telling her everything.

D.D. convened the task force meeting at one. Ordered in sandwiches and cookies because it was always good to keep the troops motivated. She also added salad, because most of them were at the stage in life where they had a deeper appreciation for dark leafy greens.

Alex walked in as they were just getting started. He was dressed in his official academy shirt and slacks. She remembered his offer to tour Flora's apartment this morning and figured by the intent look on his face he'd made it there. She waved for him to take a seat, and he helped himself to a turkey sub.

'This is what we know,' D.D. stated, standing in front of the whiteboard at the head of the conference room. She liked running these meetings. Frankly, she needed an opportunity to organize her thoughts on this case.

Now she tapped a list of bullet points, sadly a much shorter list than the second column, which included all the questions they couldn't answer.

'Flora Dane headed out Friday night, most likely in search of Stacey Summers's kidnapper. In her own words, she'd targeted some loser at the bar when a second suspect, Devon Goulding, entered the picture. He punched out Flora's original partner, then dragged her off. When she regained consciousness, she was tied up naked in his garage. When he reentered the space, presumably to rape her, she retaliated by setting him on fire using items she'd found in his garbage.

'Devon Goulding died on scene. Upon further investigation, we found the driver's licenses for two other women, Natalie Draga and Kristy Kilker. As of Saturday morning, we began investigating the whereabouts of these two women. At the same time, Flora Dane returned to her apartment, where she spent some time with her mother. Shortly after one P.M. on Saturday, Rosa Dane departed her daughter's space. And Flora has not been seen since.'

D.D. had added a timeline to the bottom of the whiteboard. She now tapped Saturday afternoon on the bar.

'We believed initially that Flora was abducted by a large man who'd posed as a building inspector days before in order to gain access to her apartment keys. However, we have tracked down the inspector, who it turns out is real enough and has no criminal record. He also has an alibi for the time in question. Which leaves us with . . .'

D.D. moved on to her second, longer column.

'Four missing persons cases: Stacey Summers, Natalie Draga, Kristy Kilker, and Flora Dane, all of which may or may not be related. One possible but now deceased perpetrator, Devon Goulding, who is connected to at least three out of the four missing women. And one body, discovered just this morning based on information from Goulding's vehicle's GPS. We do not have definitive ID, but believe the remains belong to Kristy Kilker. Meaning we may have found one of the women. But where are the others? And if Goulding is the one behind it all, how could Flora Dane disappear *after* his death?'

'Do we know she was kidnapped?' Phil spoke up, leaning back from the table with a chocolate chip cookie halfway to his mouth. 'I mean, wasn't half our suspicion based on this inspector the city housing department swore it never sent? Now that you've determined the visit was legit, what are we left with? Unlocked front door. Undisturbed apartment. What if Flora simply took off? Got a hot lead on Stacey Summers, freaked out we'd figure out what she was up to after she burned Goulding to death. So she disappeared on her own accord.'

D.D. shrugged – hard to argue with that line of reasoning. Still: 'Call me sentimental, but if Flora planned to take off for a few days, I think she'd let her mother know, even if she simply made up some excuse. But she'd call her mom, tell her not to worry. Except, of course, she didn't.'

'We'd never call you sentimental,' Neil assured her from the back of the room.

Phil nodded grudgingly. 'Saw the mom leaving yesterday. Tough cookie, but definitely shaken up.'

'She was at Flora's apartment,' Alex spoke up. All heads turned toward him. 'At D.D.'s request, I swung by. Rosa

Dane was already there. She'd brought a tin of muffins for the landlords and was waiting for me on the third-floor landing to break the crime scene tape. She's, uh, she's something else.'

'She baked homemade muffins in a hotel room?' D.D. was still trying to work that out.

'If you let her stay in her daughter's apartment, she's promised us cake.'

'You let her in?'

'Judging by the look on her face, it was going to happen. At least this way she had supervision.'

'Was an FBI officer, Dr Keynes, with her?'

'No. Just her.'

D.D. nodded but remained frowning. Her conversation with Keynes still bugged her.

'Did Rosa notice anything?' D.D. asked at last.

'Nothing appears missing, all Flora's clothes are intact, that sort of thing. The bed was unmade, but according to Rosa that's not atypical. Flora isn't a stickler for neatness. That's more the mom's department.'

'What did she do in the apartment?' D.D. asked.

Alex shrugged. 'Walked around. Seemed to be absorbing the space. She spent a fair amount of time in her daughter's room, reading the articles on the wall.'

'Are any of those cases Natalie Draga or Kristy Kilker?' a new detective spoke up.

'No,' D.D. answered. 'Neither girl was ever reported missing. Natalie was in Boston on her own. Kristy Kilker's mother thought her daughter was in Italy. So, in theory, Flora was focused on Stacey Summers.' She returned her attention to Phil. 'Any leads from Flora's cell phone or computer?'

'Working through both of them now. Flora was definitely

fixated on the bar scene in Boston. She'd been reading up on Tonic in the days before she headed there.'

D.D. frowned. 'But Stacey Summers disappeared from Birches, meaning something else had to have put Tonic on Flora's radar screen. What?'

Around the table, no one had any answers.

'Natalie Draga used to work at Tonic,' Carol Manley piped up. 'Maybe Flora did know something we didn't know. I mean, just because Natalie wasn't formally declared missing doesn't mean a friend hadn't started asking around, hey, any of you seen Natalie lately, that kind of thing. Given Flora's obsession, maybe such rumors caught her attention.'

D.D. nodded. Which was exactly why she'd grilled Keynes on the subject. Because Flora did have an obsession when it came to missing persons, and seemed to be better informed than even the police.

'All right,' D.D. said. 'For now, let's focus on the case we know Flora was definitely working, Stacey Summers. I want some suits paying visits to Stacey's family and friends. Except, this time, show them Flora's picture. Let's see how far she got with her own investigation. Because if Flora was looking at other bars in the area, then I'm guessing one of Stacey's friends must have mentioned something. Maybe Tonic was a nightclub they'd visited often in the past, or Stacey knew someone who worked there. Maybe Flora even figured out that another pretty girl who used to work at Tonic hasn't been seen for months. Honestly, I have no idea. But whatever the connections are here' – D.D. drew lines between Natalie, Kristy, Goulding, and Stacey Summers – 'we need to figure them out.'

'I might have one clue,' Alex offered. He'd finished his sandwich, was now wiping his hands. 'On the fire escape outside Flora's apartment, I found traces of glitter.'

'Glitter?' D.D. didn't mean to sound so dubious; it just wasn't the type of clue she'd expected.

'Hey, for us crime scene geeks, glitter is the new duct tape.'

'I don't even understand that statement,' D.D. assured her husband. Around the table, her fellow detectives were nodding.

Alex leaned forward. 'Glitter is nearly perfect trace evidence. It's very easy to transfer while also being highly unique. Better yet, like duct tape, there are extensive databases available to help determine the particular source of the glitter in question. For example, glitter is present in everything from women's makeup to greeting cards to various clothing items. Needless to say, the size, color, cut of each of these sources is different. Better yet, on a microscopic level, you can tie an individual piece of glitter to a specific cutting machine from a specific manufacturer, proving once and for all the glitter found on the victim's bed definitely came from the same source as the glitter on the killer's fancy shirt. Good stuff, glitter.'

'So what did you find on the fire escape?'

'I found traces of gold on the handrail, I'm guessing transferred from contact with a subject's hand. With Rosa's help, I examined Flora's clothing. No sources of glitter there. No glitter in the bed either, which would have occurred if Flora had gotten some on her skin, say, when she was out and about, then transferred it to her sheets when she tucked in at night. She did have glitter in some of her cosmetic products, but those particles are too fine to match with the fire escape sample.'

'What does that mean?' D.D. asked him.

'It means someone was out on the fire escape with traces of glitter on his hands, clothes, et cetera.'

'And that helps us how?'

'Find a suspect, we can use glitter to place him or her on Flora's fire escape. Or—' Alex's gaze grew more thoughtful. He pointed at the circle of names D.D. had joined with lines on the whiteboard. 'We believe these cases are all interconnected, yes?'

D.D. nodded.

'Then let's search Devon Goulding's house for signs of glitter. Kristy Kilker's body as well. If we find traces matching Flora's fire escape on either of these other sources, then there's your proof. These cases are related.' Alex nodded solemnly. 'The glitter tells us so.'

33

The girl is insane. Molly, Stacey, whoever she is, has definitely been shut up too long, suffered too much trauma. I don't know. But she's crazy to think *I'm* the one who has something to do with this. I save people. Which sometimes does involve hurting others.

Devon Goulding, his skin smoking, then catching on fire.

But I only attack bad people.

And this girl here.

That doesn't count.

I make the girl move. Actually, I advance closer and she drags herself off the mattress, away from me in the dark. Whatever. It allows me to retrieve the last shard of pine coffin from inside the mattress lining. It's thinner than I'd like. Decent length, though.

I bring it to the door and get to work. My first challenge, trying to figure out in the dark the approximate location of the latch in the switch plate. I have to think back to other doors. It works best to stand and simply reach automatically for a doorknob.

Once I have that height, I attempt to slide in the wooden shard, only to discover that, as flimsy as it is, it's still too thick. I sit in the dark and shred it down. Not hard really. The wood pulls away in long strips.

There's something rhythmic to the work. Therapeutic.

Why would the girl think I had something to do with this?

A shadow looming in my doorway, voice thick with menace. An intruder who got through all my locks without ever waking me. An attacker who removed me from my apartment before I struck a single counterblow and delivered me here.

Sitting in the dark, shredding a piece of pine coffin, I feel the memory become thinner and thinner. Less a memory and more a bad dream. The man's face . . . I can't picture it. What did he do next? Lunge forward, I would guess, but I can't recall. And I . . . I lay in my bed and waited for him to ambush me?

My head hurts again. I instinctively raise a hand to rub my temples, and hit myself with the tethering chain.

Which presents my next challenge. Even if I get the door open, how do I get out of the room? I doubt my tether is long enough. My handcuffs will have to go. Mine and hers, I decide. So we can work together.

Or she'll run away. From me.

I feel bad. I don't know why. I'm not sure how I ended up here. I don't know what's going on. A girl brainwashed into calling herself Molly. The delivery of pine coffins, a regular blast from the past.

Someone coming in and out of this room, and again, I never wake up, never respond to the disturbance. Because I'm drugged. Or because I'm expecting them?

I shake my head. Hard. No.

I have nothing to do with this. I don't hurt people.

Only Devon Goulding, screaming as he clutched at his burning skull.

Only a beautiful girl who threatened to take Jacob from me.

That memory comes from nowhere. Hastily I push it away.

'Survivors do what survivors have to do,' I mutter in the dark. 'Don't second-guess your choices.'

I wish Samuel were here. I could use his calming presence in the dark.

Stacey Summers, I think in the next instance. The video of her abduction. Big guy leading her away. Proof positive someone else is involved.

Second rational thought: I've spent the past few weeks going all around town, various bars, restaurants, college hangouts, asking questions about Stacey Summers. Maybe I came closer than I realized to discovering the perpetrator involved. And maybe that person became suspicious, looked me up.

My story is hardly private. Please, four hundred and seventy-two days locked in a coffin? The press loved it. No aspect of my degradation, no salacious detail of my captivity, was spared front-page glory.

Not a single person understands what I went through. And yet everyone knows my story.

The nightgown, my stupid flimsy nightgown . . . I try thinking about that. Had Jacob bought me a lacy, satiny nightgown? He bought me some clothes, a summer dress. What do I recall, what did I ever mention out loud . . .

I start to shiver. Goose bumps up and down my arms. I'm going to vomit. I'm going to be ill . . .

I drop the pine shard, my breathing ragged, my hands shaking uncontrollably.

I find myself on my knees, head hanging low, trembling even more violently now and fighting the urge to be sick.

I know something I don't want to know.

The past does matter. The past has everything to do with this.

Except I can't afford to stop and think about it. Because the past is the past, and the only way out of this room is to move forward. Deep breath. Forget coffins, and nightgowns, and Jacob Ness. Forget everything.

I'm Flora 2.0. I have training, I have skills, and I'm going to get the fuck out of here. Save myself. Save Stacey Summers.

So, wooden sliver in the door frame. Proceed.

I want to go home.

I want to see my mother with her ugly flannel shirts, the silver fox charm nestled at the base of her throat. I want to throw my arms around her, and even if it won't be a hug the way we used to hug, or feel the way it used to feel, I want it to be good enough. I want her to know I miss her. And I love her. And I'm sorry.

She worked so hard to get back a daughter neither of us understands at all.

She still works so hard to love me.

I wedge the pine shard into the seam around the door. Slowly but surely, I shimmy it up until I encounter resistance.

The door latch. Okay, this is where the magic needs to happen.

I pause, consider the next steps.

Best-case scenario is that I somehow succeed in suppressing the latch and pushing open the door. At which point . . .

Wounded girl can walk out. Me, I'll only make it as far as my leash.

And we'll be encountering . . . how many people? What kind of threat?

Not me, I insist. I am not the bogeyman in the dark. I didn't kidnap Stacey Summers, no matter what she thinks. I certainly didn't kidnap myself. I mean, just because I don't remember anything after my mother left, don't know anything about how I got into this room . . . No psychotic breaks here.

I'm not the monster.

Of course, once, a long time ago . . . My heart is beating faster again. I find myself sitting on my heels. Suddenly, all I can think of is Jacob.

Nobody wants to be a monster.

It's true. Nobody does want to be a monster. Not even me.

And yet . . . and yet . . . and yet . . .

Now is not the time, I remind myself again. I'm getting out of this room. That's the deal; that's the mission.

But first there's the matter of handcuffs.

Finally, something I'm good at. I leave the door, wooden piece still jammed into the frame. I wiggle backward to the mattress, where I give up on subtlety and, using both hands, tear at the fragile cover. I rip down long strips of thin covering. The material, old and frayed, hardly puts up a fight.

Inside, I find stuffing. It smells musty, maybe even faintly herbal. I have a sense of déjà vu, as if I should know what I'm smelling. Italian cooking? But that's not right. I move on, registering the crumbly feel. Foam padding, I deduce, that's disintegrated with age. I keep digging.

The mattress is thin. The kind meant to top a cot, or be used for one of those Ikea chairs that folds out into a bed, that kind of thing. It's possible it's just a giant slab of foam. But it didn't feel that way, lying on it. It had sections and lumps and nooks and crannies.

Even cot mattresses can have coils and springs for durability. Especially in a college town like Boston, where half the apartments are furnished by Ikea, it's possible this mattress started out in someone's dorm before being repurposed here.

I keep digging, and sure enough . . .

Metal. Wire. Coiled inside the foam. Everything is a resource. This mattress is my resource. And I'm going to use it to get us out of here.

I'm weak, shaky, stupid with stress. It takes me much longer than it should to find the end of one of the bound coils and slowly but surely straighten it. I don't know if I can pull it out. I don't think I'm that strong in my current state. So I go with reworking one end of the coil.

I have these gadgets at home, see. Fashioned from plastic, they look like tiny little black clips. Except they're not. They're universal handcuff keys. Available from most major Internet retailers. Usually, before I go out, I tuck them in my hair, the world's shortest bobby pins, where they're accessible for emergency situations. Silly me, however, I never thought to sleep with them behind my ears, meaning they aren't with me now.

But I can remake them. I've used them enough. I know them that well. And the thinness of the metal mattress coil is just about right.

My fingers slip in the dark. I gouge the side of my hand with the wire, hiss with the pain. But I keep going, even as I stab another finger, jab my palm, slice open the back of my hand. Both of my hands are slippery with blood by the time I deem my homemade gadget about right.

I take a break. Wipe my hands on the carpet. Steady my breathing.

'What are you doing?' the girl asks in the dark.

'Why? Still scared of me?'

'The door isn't locked. I didn't lock it.'

'But you unlocked it.'

'Had to. Open the door. Check on you. Those were my orders.'

'From whom? Who told you?'

'You know,' she whispers. 'You know you know.'

'I'm not the one calling the shots here,' I insist, though I don't know why I bother.

'Door is closed,' she whimpers. 'No getting out from the inside. I tried, I tried, I tried. There is only the dark. And bad things happen in the dark.'

'You ever spend time in a pine coffin?'

The girl doesn't answer.

'We can all survive more than we think,' I inform her. 'And I don't plan on being a victim ever again.'

Not when I can be the monster.

I position my cuffs over the hooked mattress spring and get down to business.

It takes me several tries. In this case, it doesn't matter that I can't see because I've practiced enough times with my hands behind my back; I'm used to going by feel, not by sight. I'm accustomed to the key being smaller, however, not fixed in place, and that takes some getting used to.

But handcuffs aren't the most sophisticated locks in the world. And I am a girl who's really, really practiced.

With a click, the first bracelet releases. Faster this time, I undo the second. And then, for the first time in I don't know how long, my hands are my own. I lift them up, massage my wrists. It feels wonderfully strange to separate my arms, move them independently.

I can feel the girl watching me in the dark. I know she

can't see my movements, but must surely hear something. Or maybe simply sense the wonder of this small improvement in our circumstance.

'Would you like your hands free?' I ask.

'Wh-wh-what?'

'Would you like your cuffs removed? I can take them off.'

'What do I have to do?'

'Crawl over here.'

'That's . . . that's . . . it?'

'Just move toward the sound of my voice. I'll help you.'

She hesitates. She fears me. With good reason? I don't know. I can't make sense out of all this. There are things I don't get. How did I go from my apartment to here? Was there really an intruder in my doorway? And how did I end up trussed up like a Thanksgiving turkey, putting up no resistance, no fight, not even awareness, as someone opened the door to this room and delivered not one but two pine coffins?

How did someone as smart as me become that stupid?

The girl moves toward me in the dark. I can hear her, slow and shuffling. I catch her sharp hiss of breath as she moves wrong, aggravating her injury. The one I gave to her.

Then she arrives, so close to me I can feel her breath. I reach out, take her hands, feel the line of her metal cuffs with my thumbs.

'Just hold still,' I tell her. I adjust her wrists over the hooked coil and, closing my eyes for concentration, work on guiding my makeshift lock pick into the tiny holes on each metal cuff.

It's not smooth or simple or brilliant. But eventually, I get the job done.

The handcuffs fall away. I can feel her lifting her hands, twisting her arms this way and that.

It's true, what I'd suspected. You don't need eyes to experience wonder. You can feel it, even in the dark.

'Why?' she asks, her favorite question of the day.

I tell her the truth. 'Because we're getting out of here.'

34

'I'm going to visit Tonic this afternoon. Samuel said I should tell you.'

'Excuse me?' Sitting at her desk, D.D. adjusted the phone against her ear, certain she'd heard wrong.

Rosa Dane continued: 'That's the last place my daughter went. I would like to see it.'

'Did you find something in her apartment? Some lead we missed involving her search for Stacey Summers?'

'No. But I spoke to Colin this morning. He admitted Flora had taken a personal interest in his daughter's case. Given that . . . There has to be a reason Flora went to Tonic on Friday night. My daughter wouldn't have just gone out to a bar.'

D.D. took a deep breath, forced herself to process. She didn't disagree with Rosa Dane; Tonic was definitely a place of interest, as just discussed by the task force. Having said that, cops didn't like civilians meddling in their investigations. Especially not a case as red-hot as this one, and with so many moving parts. D.D. had returned from the lunch meeting to find a report from the lab on her desk. The stain in Devon Goulding's garage had tested positive for human blood. Furthermore, it matched Kristy Kilker's blood type.

Conclusive, no. That would take DNA testing. But getting more and more interesting. Goulding almost certainly had something to do with at least one woman's, if not two women's, disappearance. Given that Flora was actively looking for Stacey Summers, how coincidental could it be that she'd ended up in his garage herself?

Which brought D.D. back to why civilians shouldn't be involved in police investigations: Flora's actions Friday night had led to Goulding's death, eliminating the police's best source of answers. Detectives knew better than to burn a person of interest alive. Apparently, vigilantes didn't.

'Tonic is a nightclub, I doubt it's even open this afternoon,' D.D. hedged, while she tried to decide if Rosa's proposed visit was the best or worst idea she'd ever heard.

'I spoke to the manager. She's agreed to meet me there at four.'

Rosa had called the bar's manager. But of course. 'And you reviewed this plan with Dr Keynes?'

'I asked him to come with me. He has insight into my daughter that I value.'

Sure, insight into the daughter, D.D. thought cynically. Except the moment she thought that, she found herself uncomfortable again. Keynes had feelings for Rosa, D.D. was positive. Spoken, unspoken, returned, unreturned, who knew. But did that alone explain his level of involvement?

'Samuel recommended that I contact you as well,' Rosa was saying over the phone. 'Something about how territorial local detectives can be. How you might not view my actions as helpful but threatening. He advised me to be respectful. I'm going with honest.'

'Apparently.'

D.D. frowned, glanced again at the lab report on her desk. 'Fine,' she said abruptly. Rosa wanted to visit Tonic.

Well, so did D.D. So why not kill two birds with one stone? Visit the nightclub Flora had been investigating while also spending more time with the girl's mother.

'I'll meet you there at four. Bring Dr Keynes as well. He can offer more of his professional insights.'

Rosa didn't say good-bye or thank you. She simply hung up. As she'd said, not ready for respectful but at least being honest.

D.D. grabbed her jacket, headed out.

D.D. had never been a nightclub sort of girl. A good Irish bar she appreciated. But blackout surfaces, strobe lights, loud music, not really her style even when she'd been young and, supposedly, hip.

It was always interesting, she thought, to visit such places by the bright light of day. Sort of like catching a movie star without her makeup on. At night, with the lighting just so and the floor crammed with writhing bodies and the stage dominated by the next up-and-coming band, the place probably felt electric.

Four P.M. on a Monday, it reminded her more of a college student with a hangover. The floor was sticky and covered in shredded cocktail napkins. The dark-painted walls were scratched and dinged, the bar area tired. The place looked like it could use a refurbishment, or at least a break from its high-risk lifestyle.

Rosa and Keynes had arrived first, and were already talking to a woman near the back. They made quite a trio. Rosa in her usual yoga grunge, Keynes in his classic gray suit, and the manager in nightclub black-on-black.

Currently, the dark-haired manager had her eyes locked on Keynes. He wasn't even talking, and she still stared at him, entranced. Apparently, Keynes's cheekbones worked even on a woman surrounded by pretty and even prettier staff.

D.D. walked up. She flashed her credentials, purely to establish dominance. Because, yes, she was that petty.

No dice. The manager kept her attention fixed on Keynes. On the other hand, Keynes smiled slightly, as if he knew exactly what D.D. was doing and appreciated the effort.

'Sergeant Detective D.D. Warren,' D.D. spoke up crisply, never one to back down from a fight.

The manager finally dragged her attention away. 'Jocelyne. Jocelyne Ethier.'

'You're the manager?'

'Yes. I've worked here five years.'

'Were you here Friday night?'

'Yes. I split my time between the back office and, of course, making frequent tours of the floor, just to make sure things are going smoothly. I, um, I recognize the picture of her daughter.' She flickered a sad, nervous glance at Rosa. 'I noticed her at the end of the night, when things were winding down. She was out on the floor, still dancing.'

'Did you happen to see who she was with?' D.D. asked.

The manager shrugged. 'There was some guy holding a beer, watching her. I assumed they were together. She was out of his league, I can tell you that, but . . .' She shrugged again.

'What did the guy look like?'

'Average. Khakis, long-sleeve, light blue button-up. Like a wannabe finance guy or something. Not really much to look at.'

D.D. nodded. That was consistent with what they knew thus far. 'I understand Devon had worked here for the past three years.'

'Yes.' The manager's face shuttered. 'Um. Devon.

Excellent bartender. Reliable, which is tough enough around here. But also . . . he had the look. We're a nightclub. Appearances matter.'

'He worked out,' D.D. supplied neutrally.

'He did. His chest . . . Women and men lined up for at least one more drink.' The manager still didn't look up. Uncomfortable about talking about a recently deceased employee? Or something else?

'He mind the male attention?' D.D. asked.

'Not that I could tell. My impression was that he worked pretty hard to look the way he looked and he enjoyed showing it off.'

'He have a girlfriend?'

'Not that I knew of.'

'And you and he . . .' D.D. let her voice do the asking.

'No,' the manager said flatly. 'I run the asylum; I don't frequent with the inmates.'

There was an edge to her voice, however, that spoke of a lesson learned the hard way. A woman scorned.

'What about Natalie Draga?' D.D. switched gears.

'Natalie . . . She worked here. Briefly. I think I showed her file to one of your other detectives.'

'Did she know Devon?'

'Would've been hard not to. He was one of our regular bartenders, she was around for at least a couple months. As for fraternizing . . . Back-room staff hookups are about as common as front-room players. Anything's possible.'

'What about Kristy Kilker?'

'Who?'

D.D. flashed a photo. The manager shook her head. 'I don't recognize her. The volume of people who pass through here on any given night, however . . . I'm only familiar with the regulars.'

'You didn't know Stacey Summers,' Rosa spoke up.

'No.'

'But that doesn't mean she didn't come here on occasion,' Rosa supplied.

'It's possible. Like I said, the volume of people in a night . . .' The manager shifted uncomfortably again. 'Of course, what happened to her, that video of her abduction on the news. It's every manager's nightmare. We made some changes to our procedures immediately.'

'Really?' D.D. interjected sharply. 'Because given what your own bartender did on Friday night . . .'

Ethier stiffened, her expression turning wary. 'I didn't know, okay? Is that what this is about? Because I've already told all this to the first detective you sent over. No, I didn't suspect my own bartender was a rapist. No, I didn't realize Devon had ambushed some girl on Friday. He left abruptly. Didn't come back. Was I pissed? Yes. But did I think, did I imagine . . .' She thinned her lips. 'This is a hard job. The amount of turnover in staff, vendors, customers. I don't know everything that goes on. No matter how hard I try, I *can't* know everything that goes on.'

'Do you know the staff at other nightclubs such as Birches?' Keynes spoke up. In contrast to the manager's heated voice, his tone was perfectly neutral. The woman's shoulders relaxed marginally. She conceded to meet his gaze.

'Sure. The industry isn't as big as you think. The bartender fired from Birches today will most likely be asking me for a job tomorrow, so it's good to be able to compare notes. Nigel is the head manager at Birches. He's been quite distraught by the Summers case.' Ethier's voice grew defensive again. 'We try to keep an eye on our customers, you know. Bartenders, staff, the door attendees. Everyone is trained to be aware of who's had too much to drink, who might need a ride home. Something like the Summers case – it's bad for all of us.'

'You noticed Flora on Friday night.' Keynes again, voice still calm. 'You saw her on the dance floor. You paid attention. As you say, that's your job.'

Ethier didn't speak.

'And yet, when your bartender exited the door after her—'

'I didn't see that!'

'Why not?'

'It was two A.M. Closing. There were a million things going on. I wasn't even out front anymore. I was in the back, working on receipts.'

'What about cameras?' D.D. spoke up. 'From your back office, surely you can watch live video streams from the dance floor, bar area, entrances and exits. Standard operating procedure for most clubs.'

The manager flushed, said nothing.

'You do have cameras?' D.D. pressed.

'Of course! But I checked for the first detective who stopped by. The, uh, the cameras weren't working that night.'

'What do you mean, weren't working?'

'They were turned off. Shortly before closing.'

'And who did that?'

'I don't know.'

'What do you mean—'

'Ms Ethier.' Keynes again, working his Zen voice. 'Is this the first time the cameras had been turned off?'

The woman shook her head. She looked either guilty or distraught, D.D. couldn't decide which.

Keynes continued on: 'How many times before? And who would have access?'

'I started noticing it around a year ago. A night here, a night there. Except the past few months . . .' Ethier took a deep breath. She glanced at Keynes, as if pleading for understanding. 'I was beginning to have suspicions.'

'Suspicions of what?'

'It was too often. Too regularly. I should've reported it to HQ, maybe installed a lock on the closet containing the security system. I had my suspicions, maybe drug deals or theft. But not kidnapping. You have to believe me. Not . . . assault, not that. But yes, someone was tampering with our system, I . . . I did know that.'

'You're a good manager, aren't you, Ms Ethier? You can't see everything, as you said. But you try. So you noticed, you have been noticing, something with your staff was off.'

'Ever since Natalie . . .'

'What about Natalie?'

D.D. let Keynes take over the questioning. Because he'd roped the manager in now. She was making direct eye contact, staring right at him. And D.D. could already tell, what the manager had fed them the first time around regarding Natalie Draga had been the party line. Now, finally, they were honing in on the truth.

'Employees come and go. That's true. And they don't always leave forwarding information. But to not pick up a check . . . Who doesn't pick up a paycheck? And I suspected that she and Devon had a thing. Not my business. But again, if she was with him, all the more reason to stay, you know.'

Keynes nodded.

'But she didn't come in. Left work one day, never showed up again. And Devon . . . he wasn't sad. Wasn't distraught. If they had a thing and she suddenly split town, shouldn't he have been upset?'

Keynes nodded again.

'But he wasn't. If anything . . . he seemed cheerful.'

'You wondered about Devon Goulding,' Keynes said.

'There was nothing I could do,' the manager expelled in a rush. 'I never saw anything wrong, heard him say anything inappropriate. But just . . . his moods, these flashes of rage. I don't know. Devon . . . Devon didn't seem like Devon anymore. He seemed darker.'

And that hurt her, D.D. filled in the blanks. Because at one time, Ethier had felt as if she knew him well, intimately. She'd been involved with him, whether she was willing to admit it or not.

'Did Devon have access to the security system?' Keynes asked gently.

'Yes.'

'You believe he was the one who turned it off Friday night.'

Ethier looked at D.D. She exhaled, a confession of sorts. 'Yes.'

'You noticed my daughter Friday night,' Rosa spoke up abruptly. 'You said you saw her dancing. But you've also said you can't track everything. So why did you watch my daughter?'

Ethier flushed. 'The way she was dancing, she was calling attention to herself. But also . . . she seemed alone.'

'You worried about her,' Rosa provided.

Again, that faint hesitation. 'I checked in on her. I wanted to make sure she was all right.'

D.D. got it. 'You wanted to make sure she hadn't caught Devon's eye.'

'She was dancing with another guy. I swear. She was dancing with Mr Normal. So then, I stopped watching. I counted receipts instead.'

D.D. leaned forward. 'Stacey Summers,' she prodded. 'Think. Now is the time. When you saw the video of Stacey Summers, did you recognize her as one of your customers? Is there any chance she also knew Devon Goulding?'

'God's honest truth, Detective: I have no idea. I am so sorry. But I have no idea.'

D.D. nodded, stepped back. Rosa and Keynes did the same. While the manager, Ethier, remained standing there, looking like a woman who'd just taken a beating, and her work shift had yet to begin.

'One last question,' D.D. said. 'Does this place use any glitter?'

Restrooms. Tonic offered up a basket of toiletries for its patrons, male and female alike. D.D. and Rosa did the honors in the ladies' room, while Keynes took the men's room. D.D. found what she was looking for almost immediately, a hair gel product laced with gold glitter. She gave Keynes a quick call to learn he'd discovered the same. Nothing like a bit of sparkle for the discerning clubber with a big night ahead.

She held the gel under the overhead lights, watching the way the various gold particles shimmered. As Alex had said, the pieces appeared individual, distinct. And sticky. Chances were, even after hand washing, showering, minute pieces of the gluey sparkle lingered for days.

Just waiting to be transferred from a kidnapper's hands to a victim's apartment, or even her body?

D.D. dialed Ben Whitely, who most likely was still exhuming the body at the nature park.

He picked up the call, as charming as ever. 'Whatever it is you want, I don't know. I didn't know five hours ago. I don't know now. And if you don't leave me alone long enough to finish wrapping up the scene and transport the body to the lab, I may never know anything ever again.'

'I need you to check something for me.'

'D.D.—'

'It will just take a second. Can you shine the flashlight on the body's hair? Look for gold. As in glitter.'

'The hair is brown and completely saturated in dirt. How do you expect me to— Wait. There do appear to be some reflective particles. It's possible I'm looking at glitter.'

'Can you remove a small sample? I'm going to send a uniformed officer to you immediately for pickup. Thank you, Ben.'

D.D. clicked off the phone, stood there thoughtfully.

Rosa came up behind her. The woman appeared tired, but was in control as always. 'The glitter is important?'

'Yes.'

'What does it mean?'

'It means . . .' D.D. shrugged, still fumbling her way through a case with more questions than answers. 'It means my husband was right. Natalie Draga, Kristy Kilker, Stacey Summers, your daughter. All of their disappearances are connected.'

She looked at Rosa. 'The glitter tells us so.'

35

Laughing. Jacob had a joint. They passed it back and forth between the two of them, heads bowed close together, giggling like schoolgirls. I sat alone at the tiny kitchen table, rubbing my bare arms for warmth, watching them in the family room.

Turned out, the new girl wasn't new at all. She'd recognized Jacob. Threw open her long, creamy arms in greeting. He'd wrapped her in a tight embrace. A hug. Jacob hugged her.

I hadn't been hugged . . . in a very long time.

Not since the days of the woman who looked like my mother and wore a silver fox charm around her neck.

At first, Jacob had been reluctant to enter the yard. 'Nah,' he'd said. 'She told me, last time she caught me, that she'd call the police. That'd be it. Back to the slammer, and we both know I ain't ever going back there.'

'Then it's a good thing she's not around,' the new girl had said, hands still on Jacob's shoulders.

'Come on now. You don't need this kind of headache. I was just . . . in the area. Wanted to say hey.'

'Hey,' she said, and I swore his eyes glittered with tears.

'I don't mean to bother you,' he whispered. 'You were right last time; I'm an ass. I should just stay away.'

But he wasn't moving, and neither was she.

'I was mad,' she said suddenly. 'Last time I saw you. The things you said. I wasn't ready to hear. Maybe I didn't want to know. But I've been doing some thinking since then. Sometimes, I even hoped you'd stop by again, so we could talk. 'Cause I think . . . maybe there's some truth in what you said.'

'What d'you mean?'

'You know what I mean.'

'Lindy . . .'

'Come inside. Come on. Just have a visit. We'll catch up. This time, I'll listen. I promise.'

'But if she—'

'She's not coming back. I'm telling you the truth. She's gone, and she's never coming back again.'

That seemed to do the trick. Jacob stopped resisting. He followed the beautiful girl across the burned-out yard. I trailed behind the two of them, already forgotten.

I hated this new girl who wasn't new. I hated her long dark hair. I hated her gleaming brown eyes. I hated the way she smiled at me, as if she already knew things I didn't. Such as I was the one just passing through. She would always be the real deal.

The house was shabby. Dirty stucco-colored linoleum in the kitchen. Tired cabinets with sagging doors. Furniture patched with silver splashes of duct tape. It made me feel better. Some basic female instinct: At least my house is nicer than yours.

Except, of course, I didn't have a house. I had a coffin-shaped box in the back of Jacob's sleeper cab.

I couldn't breathe. I didn't know why. My throat was closing up, my heart rate too high.

Jacob, holding the knife down at his side. Now drinking

and smoking with this girl, the legendary Lindy whom he talked about in his sleep. They were together. Before. Now. Forever. She would always be his.

Which made me completely expendable. Gator food. Literal white trash.

I was going to be sick. Except I hadn't eaten enough lately to vomit. My hands trembled, my left knee jogged uncontrollably. Stress, fear, fatigue, hunger. Take your pick. I suffered, suffered, suffered.

While Jacob sat on the sofa, and laughed and smoked dope with the most beautiful girl I'd ever seen.

I don't know when I first moved. I just did. Stood up at the table. Not like they were paying attention to me. Walked toward the jumbled collection of broken-down drawers, sagging cabinets.

A ratty kitchen. A shabby kitchen. But still a kitchen. And every kitchen stocks similar items. Such as knives.

The paring blade, short and easy to conceal? Or maybe the butcher knife. Go full psycho.

In the end, I selected a model in between. Without ever truly thinking about it. If the new girl wasn't really new, then I could make a decision without really deciding.

Giggles. High-pitched. Happy. And just for one moment . . .

I am home. I am rolling on a bed, all tangled up with my mother, my brother. We are laughing, laughing, laughing. This is Mom. This is Mom, all cracked up!

The softness of the down covers, the smell of spring rain and loamy earth right outside the window. The sound of my mom, my brother, laughing hysterically.

Home. Home, home, home.

Snapping back, I looked down at my pale skinny arm. I studied my hand holding the kitchen knife. And I realized then, truly got it, that I wasn't going home again. I would never roll on that bed. I would never laugh with my family.

I would never go to that place. I would never be that person.

That girl was dead.

All that was left was this moment, this place, this knife in my hand.

I held out my left wrist, studied the maze of red scars, blue veins. It would be so easy. One swipe here, one swipe there. Leave Jacob to clean up the mess.

Gator food. Literal white trash.

My mother never knowing what happened to me. Denied even the comfort of burying my body.

She deserved better.

So for her sake, as much as my own, I took my knife and drifted into the family room.

They didn't see me coming. Too busy whispering and giggling, reminiscing about the good old days, whatever. Their heads were bowed, Jacob's hair gray-streaked and greasy, hers dark and silky.

It made it easy to launch the first strike. My arm raising all the way up, just like every slasher film I'd ever seen, except this time, I was the crazy-eyed stalker instead of the doe-eyed college student.

Nobody wants to be a monster.

Or do they?

Arm coming down, down, down.

A scream, sharp and shrill. Mine? Nope. Definitely hers. The beautiful new girl came shooting off the sofa, blood blossoming down her back where I had raked the knife across her shoulder blade.

'Shit!' *Jacob exploded, fear just beginning to penetrate his doper's glaze. 'What the fuck, what the f—'*

I turned to him next. Arm up, up, up.

Arm coming down, down, d—

She launched herself at me. The new girl who wasn't new fought like a hellcat. She tackled me down to the ground. Fingernails slashing down my face, going for my eyes. Screaming words at me in a language I didn't know. Not Spanish. Something far more exotic.

As I heaved against her reflexively, forgetting all about the kitchen blade, which had scattered from my grip.

But she didn't. Her gaze flashed to the knife, resting several feet away. Her face sharpening with a look of cunning.

I realized what she was going to do the second before she made her move. A fresh launch, this time from my chest, toward the blade. I turned with her, grabbing at her left arm, as if to hold her back.

She kicked at me without ever losing focus, stretching long, and just like that, she had the knife, turning back, looming over me. The smile on her face. Feral. Happy.

So Jacob wouldn't be the one to kill me after all.

Interesting.

Knife. Not going up, up, up. What would be the fun in that? But instead twirling lazily in front of my eyes.

She spoke again, whispers of death in her exotic tongue. No translation required to understand she was going to slice me up. And she was going to enjoy doing it.

'Stop!' *Jacob's hand, snapping around her wrist.* 'Gimme that. Stupid bitches.'

She yelled at him. In English this time. Demanded the right to finish what I'd started. I didn't speak. I didn't move. My heart was beating too fast. I lay on the floor, the fallen gazelle trapped between two lions.

'She has her uses,' Jacob was arguing, the first time I'd heard him give me any credit. 'Not for you to decide anyway. She's mine. Get your own plaything.'

Then, after a long exchange that went over my fuzzy, blacking-out head – she was still sitting on my chest – a sudden change.

The girl stood, removing her weight and allowing oxygen to come flooding back. She tucked away the knife but still peered at me in triumph.

'You,' Jacob addressed me. 'You got work to do.'

It took me a bit to sit up, climb shakily to my feet.

'You attacked my daughter,' he said.

Daughter?

'Violated her hospitality. Now you gotta pay. She demands a tribute. Since she can't kill you, you gotta go out, find her a replacement toy.'

I couldn't do it. I begged, pleaded. Jacob had tried before. Talk to that girl in that bar. Go chat up that woman in the corner. Bring her over to me.

Before, I'd always been able to distract him. Have another beer. Let's go back to the rig. Let's put a new song on the jukebox.

But now, he was adamant. I would go out with him and his daughter. I would befriend a girl of their choosing. And I would introduce the woman to them.

Or Jacob would leave me alone with his daughter and an entire collection of kitchen knives.

For emphasis, she produced the knife, then slid the blade down my forearm, both of us staring in fascination as the blood welled to the surface.

In the end, I caved. You tell yourself you will be strong. You tell yourself this is impossible, it can't get any worse. You even tell yourself you'd rather die.

But the truth is, it's hard to give up on life. I don't know why. Surely giving up would've made more sense. I should've gone with my first instinct and slashed my wrists in the kitchen.

But I hadn't. I didn't.

I wanted to survive.

And now . . . this.

I bandaged Lindy's shoulder. I'd hit all bone, leaving a long but shallow groove across her shoulder blade. By morning, she wouldn't feel a thing.

Only my terror would go on and on and on.

She dressed in a deep purple, a shade so dark it was nearly black. I was given some of Lindy's clothes, a worn pair of jeans, already falling off my bony hips, and a T-shirt tied beneath my breasts. Lindy had a car. A clunker to match her home.

Jacob drove. Lindy sat with me in the back, gloating over what was to come.

'How long have you lived here?' I tried to ask. 'How often do you get to see your father?' I nearly tripped over the word father*. But Lindy wouldn't talk. She had her eye on the prize, a fun night out on the town.*

The bar Jacob finally chose was a dive, a barely standing shack at the edge of a barely there beach advertising cheap beer. The kind of place that would make discerning patrons shudder and dedicated drunks cheer. The kind of place Jacob himself fit right in.

Lindy stood out. Too young, too beautiful in her purple-black dress and long, loose hair. Men stared at her in instant lust, women in instant hatred. She smirked at all of them, following her father through a maze of closely packed tables.

In contrast to her, I went unnoticed. Too pale, too

skinny, too all-washed-up. Not even a drunk, more like a heroin addict.

I didn't know what else to do, so I followed them to the worn driftwood bar, earning points by association.

Jacob ordered up shots of tequila. A round for all three of us, and an instant bloom of fire in my empty, shrunken stomach. I was glassy-eyed after the first shot. Barely standing by the second.

Willing me into compliance, or an act of compassion, as Jacob knew I'd do what he said anyway.

Nobody wants to be a monster.

But some are still born that way. And others, with bleeding cuts down their arms and enough tequila in their stomachs . . .

Lindy nudged my shoulder, her gaze darting to the corner.

A woman sat there, eyes heavily made up, tube top barely containing her voluminous chest. She was not young and pretty. More like middle-aged and fleshy. A pro, I recognized by now. Because bars like this attracted as many working girls as local drunks.

'Tell her we want to party,' Lindy instructed me. 'We know a place, we have the cash.'

I didn't move. So Jacob shoved me. 'You heard her. Go.'

I staggered back from the bar, having to focus hard to keep my footing. One step in front of the other. Moving past the tables. To the shadows in the corner.

To the woman waiting there.

She eyed me expectantly when I approached. Even for me, it was hard not to stare at all the flesh spilling out from that much-too-tiny top. But I forced myself to find her eyes, to register they were hard and calculating and also brown. Brown eyes. Like her mother's? Like her daughter's?

Everyone is a person.

Only I have become an object.

'Run,' I heard myself say, my voice barely a whisper. Was I speaking to me? Was I speaking to her?

Now was the time. The last moment of truth.

'Girl?' she asked.

'My name is . . .' What is my name? Who am I? Molly. Not Molly. A monster.

'Please, go. Just leave. They . . . they . . .' I needed to say something. Very important. My head was swimming. Too much tequila, not enough food. I was going to be sick.

Suddenly, Lindy was at my side, her hand squeezing my forearm where she'd sliced it earlier. Squeezing hard.

'We're looking for a party,' she practically purred. 'A private party . . .'

The woman agreed to come with us, her gaze going past us to rest on Jacob. The philosophical shrug of a woman who'd seen worse.

All of you? she asked, which nearly made me vomit.

No, Lindy corrected her, just the man. But I want to watch.

The woman shrugging philosophically again.

Don't do it, I wanted to tell her.

But I couldn't find my voice. I couldn't find my will.

I only knew how to survive.

I didn't know how to save anyone else.

Jacob drove. He headed to Lindy's house and then . . . and then . . .

There was muffled screaming. It went on for a long time. There were grunts and groans, smacks and squeaks, all from a place I wouldn't go, a room I never saw.

I sat outside Lindy's house, in the backyard, my arms

wrapped tight around my head, as if that would block the onslaught.

Eventually, I crawled far enough away to vomit up the tequila. Then I dry heaved. Then I picked at the scab on my forearm, if only to distract myself by watching the cut bleed again.

Hours later Jacob walked out wearing jeans, nothing else, his white flabby belly like an obscene growth. He smelled terrible. Sweet and sour. Sweat and sex.

I would've thrown up again if I'd had anything left.

He merely grunted, lit up a cigarette.

'Evening time, we'll take her out to the swamp. Let the gators do the hard work for us.'

I said nothing.

He squatted down, peered straight at me.

'If it hadn't been her, would've been you,' he said.

Brown eyes, I thought. Like her mother's. Like her daughter's.

'Do you have any more children?' I heard myself ask.

He laughed. 'Nah. Just this one.'

'Her mother—'

'Hates my guts. Kept her from me for years. But that's the thing about kids. They grow up. Get a mind of their own. Now, she wants to know her daddy. Can you believe it? All these years later . . .' Jacob grinned in the dark. 'My little girl loves me.'

Jacob rose to standing, stubbed out his cigarette.

'You know things now,' he informed me. 'Got your hands dirty yourself. No matter what happens. You're now one of us. Welcome to the club.'

36

My thin pine shard, meticulously peeled down to slip into the doorjamb, splinters the second I try to use it to jimmy the door latch. I sit back on my heels in the dark, holding the remnants in my hand. I could try again, but what would be the point? The pine is soft and thin. The door is solid and heavy. Using one to pry open the other is never gonna happen.

Behind me, the girl whimpers. I track the sound to the far left corner.

'Yeah, I know,' I say out loud, encouraging contact. I can't see her in the dark, which makes sound more important. Like mine, her hands are now free, her arms unrestricted. God only knows what she'll do next. Jump me from behind. Go for my throat. Just because she's a victim doesn't mean she's innocent. I know that well enough.

Survivors do what survivors must do in order to survive.

'Shut up, Samuel,' I mutter out loud, which makes the girl whimper again.

I rise to standing, stretching out my arms, flexing my wrists, which feels good. Then I contemplate my options.

No sound from outside. No shadowy movements in the viewing window. So far, the girl and I have been unshackled for at least thirty minutes, and there's been no response

339

from the peanut gallery. Evil Kidnapper doesn't realize we're on the loose yet? Or doesn't care?

How did he get pine coffins in here without me ever waking?

How did he snatch me out of my own apartment without me ever fighting?

'Stop it,' I order myself. Now is not the time to analyze the past. Now is the time to move forward.

'Who's out there?' I ask the girl as I roam our dark prison, searching for anything that might make a better crowbar than slivers of cheap wood.

She doesn't talk.

'Did you know Devon?' I ask. It takes me a minute to remember his full name, told to me forever ago while I was sitting in the back of a patrol car. 'Devon Goulding. Bartender. Amazing pecs. Works at Tonic. Did you know him?'

No more whimper. A sharp inhale. Recognition. I would swear it.

'I killed him,' I say, my voice just as conversational. 'I tossed antifreeze and potassium permanganate onto his head and shoulders. Chemical fire. Burned him alive.'

Another shocked inhale.

'Does that make you happy? To know that he suffered. That he's dead. Or do you miss him?'

I don't mean for my voice to sound understanding, even wistful. But these things happen.

'The man's dead?' Her voice sounds hoarse, but at least she's finally talking to me.

'I didn't kidnap you,' I say.

'I don't know.'

'What do you mean, you don't know? How can you not know what happened to you?'

She doesn't answer. I should've stuck with understanding. Compassion is not my strong suit.

'Tonic nightclub. Downtown Boston. Ring a bell?' I've come to the plastic bucket. I pick it up, heft it for weight. A metal handle would've been nice. Even a plastic one might've worked. But I'm not that lucky. Which means there's nothing to harvest as a pry bar. What if I threw the bucket at the viewing window, went for shattering glass? I twist the bucket in my hands, already skeptical. It's too light, the one-way mirror no doubt being heavy-duty. I keep the bucket with me for now, however. If the girl rushes me, I can always use it to conk her over the head, Three Stooges style.

'Tonic,' the girl whispers, as if recalling a name from another lifetime ago.

'Black walls, blue lights, killer bands,' I begin, then halt myself. Black walls. Unbidden, I cross to the right until I hit one of the walls in question. Floor, wall, ceiling, windows all covered in black paint. Could that be coincidence?

Devon Goulding surprised me Friday night. The bartender with the amazing pecs suddenly appearing and taking out my initial target. And yet, regaining consciousness in his garage . . . He felt arrogant and inexperienced to me. A predator, sure, but this kind of predator?

With a blacked-out room, penchant for silk nighties, and elaborate shackle system?

Not to mention, I took him down, and yet here I am.

And yet, and yet . . . A nightclub famous for its blacked-out bar. And a room now covered entirely in black paint. Could that really be a coincidence? Which makes me wonder what else I'd missed Friday night.

Several of Stacey's friends had said they frequented Tonic as well as Birches. Not to mention, the staff at both places were friendly with one another, getting off duty at one club to go grab drinks at the other, given the close proximity. In my mind, that made it worth checking out. After all, the staff at Birches had been cleared in Stacey's disappearance, but what about the folks down the street at Tonic?

Long shot, maybe, but apparently closer than I'd thought.

'Birches,' I say out loud, just to see what kind of reaction I can get from my cell mate.

She inhales again, her official sound of recognition.

'Stacey Summers,' I state.

She doesn't reply as much as she whimpers. Affirmation, denial? What I'd give for the tiniest beam of light.

'Last thing you remember?' I ask her.

She doesn't answer. I search my brain for a better approach. What did I remember in the beginning? Or perhaps, more accurately, what did I allow myself to still know? Because it's not like you magically forget your entire life, identity, the people who loved you. It's more like you box them up, put the images away. Because thinking of such things, knowing such things, is simply too hard. Those memories make you human, which is inconsistent with your current role as an inanimate object.

And just because the police one day spring through the door, black armored beetles toting weapons and shouting orders, doesn't magically open up the mental attic. If anything, I locked down harder, as disoriented by freedom as I'd once been by life in a coffin-shaped box.

I've found the girl. Stumbled upon her, quite literally, in my search for resources. She is curled up in the corner, my foot having tripped over her own. She flinches at the contact. I can feel her recoil, then, when there's no place for her to retreat, make herself smaller.

It tugs at me. Another response I know too well. Tried

so many times myself. Except it never worked. Jacob always got his way in the end.

Until that very last moment, his brains and blood in my hair . . .

I kneel down. I keep my voice soft.

'I dreamed of foxes,' I whisper to this girl in the dark. 'I dreamed I ran with them through the woods. I dreamed I was wild and free. And though I always woke up again, it felt good to dream.'

She doesn't answer.

'It's okay, you know. Survivors do what survivors have to do. Samuel told me that. When we get out of here, I'll introduce you to him. You'd like him.'

Then, when she still doesn't respond:

'You'll have bad nights after this. It's funny. You escape, but you never really get away. You don't realize what a comfort it is to go through life thinking, that will never happen to me, until, of course, that assurance is gone. And every story in the news, every article you read in the paper . . . all you can think is that could be you. I studied. That's what I did. I learned self-defense so next time a fat, sweaty piece of shit couldn't snatch me off the beach. I learned to pick locks so I would never be shackled again.' I rub my wrists, smile ruefully in the dark. 'At least that part worked. What I'm trying to say is, the fear never really goes away, but there are options. You can build a life. You can be a person again. Look at Elizabeth Smart, Jaycee Dugard. There are success stories.'

I'm just not one of them. I don't say that. I don't want to demoralize her. And my failings don't have to be her own.

My goal, my one mission in life, certainly isn't the stuff of happily-ever-afters.

I only spoke it out loud once, five years ago. I leaned down and whispered my promise in Jacob's ear. I told him exactly what I was going to do one day. Right before I placed the barrel of the gun against the top of his head and pulled the trigger.

His blood and brains in my hair.

Not all of my dreams are nightmares.

'Devon Goulding is dead.' I test the waters one last time. 'I know. I personally killed him.'

The girl finally speaks. 'You don't understand.'

'I'm trying to.'

'You shouldn't have hurt him.'

'Had to. It was Friday night.'

'Now, it will be worse.'

'What will be worse?'

'Whatever happens next,' she says quietly, 'it will be much, much worse.'

I leave her in the corner. I'm tired of doom and gloom. What I want is escape. I return to the mattress, encountering the spring coil I bent into my makeshift lock pick. I've been picturing in my head a long, flat object to jimmy open the door. Now, I switch gears. Maybe a mattress coil would work. It's stiffer than the pine. And if I curved the end into the shape of a spoon, or one of those things used to dip hard-boiled eggs into coffee mugs of colored Easter dye . . .

I've got nothing better to try.

I wrestle with the mattress again, removing piles of foam and stuffing with my hands, releasing more musty, herbal smells. I sneeze several times but soldier on. The coils are tied together. I can't see how in the dark, so I have to poke, prod, twist, and turn, with fingertips that are already shredded and bloody. Converting the top of one coil into a lock pick was a far easier operation. This, trying to remove an entire spring, proves nearly impossible. Again, my kingdom for a single beam of light. If I could just see what I was doing . . .

My bruised fingers start to feel heavy, numb. I'm tired. So very tired. I just want to lie down, get some sleep. I find my eyes dragging shut, have to force them open. The stress is catching up with me. I'm hungry again but, without any sense of time, have no idea how long it's been since I last ate.

Hungry. Thirsty. Water somewhere. I should take a nap. Except, of course, I still have to extract the damn coil.

My eyes drifting closed . . .

Fingers latching on to my shoulders, suddenly digging in.

I jolt awake, twisting frantically, tossing back an elbow. But the girl, having finally roused herself, is surprisingly strong.

'The mattress,' she's saying. 'You have to get away from the mattress. Away. Away.'

I try to pull free, but my movements are too sluggish. Then, just as suddenly as she grabbed me, she lets me go. I collapse back, an ungainly beetle with my arms and legs in the air.

I have to blink my eyes, concentrate to right myself. Even then, I feel groggy and I still want to sleep.

'It's in the mattress,' she says.

'What's in the mattress?' I mutter.

'I don't know. But the mattress . . . You'll sleep. It makes you sleep.'

The mattress is drugged, or contaminated or laced with something. That's what she's trying to tell me.

I'd been right in the beginning. The room is booby-trapped, except it's not sleeping powder in the bottled water or some kind of knockout gas in the ventilation system. It's the mattress.

'We need the mattress spring,' I hear myself. 'I got it out. Must be someplace near the top. We need it.'

The girl doesn't answer. She moves, dragging her feet in the dark. Her side, of course. She's still injured and walking must be painful. But she doesn't complain as she shuffles back to the mattress, feels around with her hand.

Then she's back. I feel the wire pressed against my arm.

'I don't understand who you are,' she says.

'A girl, just like you. Except once upon a time, I escaped from the dark.'

'You can get us out of here?'

'Yes.'

'Far, far away? I don't want to ever come back.'

'You're a survivor,' I tell her, tell myself. 'You can do anything.'

'I want to go home.'

'Tell me your name. You want to get out of here? You have to remember who you really are.'

It takes her a bit. I understand. I know how these things work. I've been there myself.

Because it's one thing to survive. It is much, much harder to truly live.

'My name is Stacey Summers,' she whispers. 'And I just want to see my parents again.'

I can't comment. My throat has closed up. There are too many things I want to say, and none of them are enough.

Instead, I pick up the mattress coil. I work it with my poor bloody fingers, looping it around, folding it in on itself, until it's a stiffer, spoonier version of itself. Then I find the door again.

It takes me a bit to wiggle out the pieces of broken wood.

Then the edge is cleared, and it's just me, a jury-rigged mattress spring, and two girls' wildest dreams. Poke, wiggle, push, shimmy. Again, and again.

And suddenly, almost imperceptibly, I can hear it. The tiniest, softest click of the latch suppressing in the lock plate.

I push. Very gently. Almost timidly.

The door moves. The door opens.

I have no idea what will happen next.

37

'We found Kristy Kilker,' D.D. informed her boss, Cal Horgan.

'How certain?'

'Ninety percent. Ben identified a butterfly tattoo on her right shoulder blade. Mother confirmed Kristy has the same. Dental records will be the slam dunk. But we're fairly confident the remains are Kristy Kilker.'

'What about Stacey Summers?'

'I don't know.'

'Wasn't there a second girl? Another license you found in the Goulding kid's bedroom?'

'Natalie Draga from Alabama. Don't know about her either.'

'Flora Dane?' Horgan asked.

'So,' D.D. reported, 'we found Kristy Kilker.'

'And one out of four ain't bad?' Horgan arched a brow at her. She scowled. Her boss switched gears: 'Any theories of the crime?'

'The perpetrator favors glittered hair gel.'

'Seriously?'

'Actually, I have no idea. We're still waiting for the lab reports on our various samples. But we found gold glitter outside Flora's apartment, as well as on Kristy's hair, as well as in the bathroom at the nightclub Tonic.'

'Tonic?'

'Devon Goulding worked there. Same with Natalie Draga until her own disappearance. As for the other missing persons, they have frequented the nightclub, including Stacey Summers. Her friends confirmed they went there on occasion. And two of them shared that information with Flora Dane.'

Horgan folded his hands across his stomach. 'Which would seem to confirm that Devon Goulding was behind all the girls' disappearances, including Stacey Summers's.'

D.D. hesitated.

'Spit it out, Detective.'

'We didn't find anything in Goulding's place to tie him to Stacey Summers. Why keep trophies of two victims but not the third?'

'She was higher profile. And he was caught on tape abducting her. That might have spooked him.'

'I don't think that's how these guys work. I think trophies fall under the compulsive part of their behavior. Plus, where's Stacey's body? Where's Natalie's body? Why did we find one but not the other two?'

Horgan studied her.

'Then, of course, there's the matter of Flora Dane,' D.D. continued, 'who disappeared *after* Goulding died. Except in her case . . . We don't even know that she was abducted. It's possible she simply walked away. Not probable, but possible.'

'What do you know again?' her boss asked her.

'Good news, sir. We found Kristy Kilker's body.'

D.D. was having that kind of day. That kind of case, really. She retreated to her office and the growing pile of paperwork stacking up on her desk. She stared at the reports, tried to tell herself to be a good restricted duty sergeant. Sit. Read. Dot i's, cross t's. Manage. Perhaps somewhere in that mound of files, the next clue awaited. But she didn't believe it. This case didn't give up information; it took away common sense.

Knocking. She looked up from her desk to discover Keynes standing in her doorway, impeccably clad as always and bearing a burnished brown leather attaché. She would never call it a murse. At least not to his face.

'Where's Rosa?' D.D. asked.

'If I were a betting man, I'd say in a kitchen somewhere, baking. Have you allowed her access yet to Flora's apartment?'

'She paid a visit this morning, as I'm sure you know, but crime scene techs aren't ready to release the scene.'

Keynes nodded, moved into her office. He was wearing his cashmere coat. She should stand, take it from him, offer a glass of water. She couldn't bring herself to do anything. She simply sat there, waiting.

'It's the nightclub Tonic,' she stated abruptly. 'Whatever happened to those girls, Tonic had something to do with it. And Devon Goulding. Which reminds me: I'm really angry with Flora. I was peeved when I first arrived at the Goulding crime scene, now I'm pissed. She never should've killed him. Devon alive could answer all of our questions. Devon dead, completely worthless. When we find Flora, I plan on charging her with at least half a dozen offenses, just to feel better.'

Keynes removed his coat. Hung it on the coatrack in the corner. Took a seat.

'My professional opinion?' he offered.

'By all means.'

'The manager, Jocelyne Ethier, had a relationship with Devon Goulding.'

'Seriously? That's all you got? I'm just a city cop and I figured out that much. Woman scorned. Practically had it tattooed on her forehead.'

Keynes shrugged. 'She lied. The question is, did she lie because she was embarrassed, or because she has something more to hide?'

'Yet another question to contemplate in the small hours of the morning. The problem is we have too many questions. We need information. Fresh, tangible clues.'

'Which is why I'm here.'

'You brought me a fresh tangible clue?'

'I brought you information. Regarding Jacob Ness.'

'Jacob Ness is dead.'

'Yes,' Keynes agreed. 'But his daughter isn't.'

'What's relevant about this information is that Flora never provided it.'

'What do you mean?' D.D. asked.

'I debriefed Flora while she was recovering in the hospital. She struck a deal. She would tell her story. One time. To one person. Then, never again. She chose me for the honor. Then she talked. And talked. And talked. Four hundred and seventy-two days. She had much to tell. And yet for every story, every horror, every revelation . . . I would never say I know everything that happened between Flora and Jacob. For each anecdote Flora revealed, I could tell there were others she held back. That's not atypical with survivors. They're traumatized, shell-shocked, and, in many cases, guilt-stricken.'

'Because they survived? Or because of what they did in order to survive?'

Lisa Gardner

'Take your pick. Either way, guilt is guilt.'

D.D. leaned forward. 'The lead FBI agent, Kimberly Quincy, mentioned she still had questions about everything that occurred during Flora's captivity. Something about other traces of hair, DNA belonging to other women, recovered from a box he had in the back of his rig.'

'Flora would not be the first kidnapping victim coerced into helping target other victims.'

'True.'

'Do you know what the hardest part about survival is, Detective?'

'I'm sure you'll tell me.'

'Living with it. Every rescued person I've ever debriefed. They were so sure if they could just escape, just get through the ordeal, they'd never complain, never want, never suffer again. My primary job is helping them understand that won't be the case. Survival isn't a destination. It's a journey. And most of the people I help, they're still getting there.'

'Killing off one perpetrator at a time?' D.D. asked dryly, considering Flora's crime spree.

'Four hundred and seventy-two days. Much of it locked in a coffin. Do you really think you could handle it any better?'

D.D. scowled. She didn't have an answer for that, and they both knew it. 'So, the daughter.'

'The FBI recovered many samples from Jacob's hotel room and his long-haul rig. As SAC Quincy revealed, we found DNA evidence belonging to others. One sample was identified as being female, and bearing markers consistent with Jacob himself. In other words, a daughter.'

'You found DNA from Jacob's own daughter? In the wooden box?'

'From cigarette butts littered on the floor of the rig.'

Keynes lifted his leather attaché, extracting a file. D.D. took it, then, glancing down at her desk, realized she was officially out of room for new paperwork.

'Who is she?' D.D. asked, finally positioning the file crossways on another stack of God knows what.

'We never figured out. The DNA didn't match with anything in the system. Agents ran down birth certificates, et cetera, but never found any records bearing Jacob's name. Of course, it's possible he was never listed as the father. And since we don't have an approximate age, it's hard to be more exact in our search of hospital databases – assuming the hospitals have computerized all their old records. Many small rural hospitals haven't.'

'What about following up with Jacob's known love interests, checking with them about a possible child?'

'The Devon Goulding problem,' Keynes said.

It took D.D. a second; then she got it. 'You mean Flora killed Jacob, meaning you can't ask him for a list of prior relationships. Girl's good at tying up loose ends.'

'Jacob Ness flew under the grid for most of his life. A brief stint in prison. But other than that, he was a loner, driving from state to state in his big rig, his only permanent address being his mother's house in Florida. According to Flora, in the beginning at least, she was kept in a basement room—'

'There are basements in Florida?'

'It's primarily slab construction. Which makes us believe Jacob left the state almost immediately after the kidnapping. He mentioned to Flora that they were in the mountains of Georgia, but we've never been able to pinpoint an exact location. When Jacob worked, his movements were tracked by a computer system used by all long-haul truckers. Jacob was an independent contractor, however, and he spent weeks at a time not working at all. During those periods, we don't know where he went. According to Flora, he had a penchant for crashing at cheap motels in small southern towns. But we've never been able to retrace all of his movements.'

'More questions he can't answer and she won't tell?'

'I don't know if Flora has the answers,' Keynes said bluntly. 'Hard to get your bearings, locked in a box.'

'Good point.'

'We know Jacob moved around. Mostly in the South. We know he *didn't* return to his mother's house during the time he had Flora. But we also know, at some point he met up with his daughter. Happily, unhappily, we have no idea.'

'What's Flora's official position?'

'Jacob was partial to prostitutes. She doesn't know anything about a daughter.'

'He had his own personal sex slave and he was still hiring prostitutes?'

'Jacob Ness was a sex addict. Claimed it wasn't his fault he was a monster.'

D.D. didn't have words for that. She could tell by the hard set of Keynes's jaw that neither did he.

'But you think Flora is lying. You think she knows something about the daughter. Why?'

'Small things. Do you know about the postcards Jacob sent?'

'Some.'

'The messages ran toward irony. Met a handsome guy, when, in fact, Flora had been kidnapped by Jacob. Amazing views, when, in fact, she was locked in a box.'

'Got it.'

'Last e-mail Rosa received: *Made a new friend. Very sweet, I know you'd just love her.*'

'You think that's a reference to Jacob's daughter,' D.D. said. 'Which, if he's describing her as sweet . . .'

'I asked Flora about it directly. She wouldn't respond. Judging by the completely blank look that overtook her face, perhaps she couldn't answer. The more I pressed, the more vehement became her denials. She had an emotional response to my questions, even as she sought to distance herself from the answers.'

'And if there was no daughter, why would she care?'

'Exactly.'

'Given that the cigarette butts with DNA were recovered from the floor of Jacob's cab, that seems to imply a relationship. The woman wasn't stashed in the back in a box but sitting up front, smoking. A meeting of equals. Maybe even father-daughter bonding. Could Flora have felt threatened?'

'Possible.'

D.D. frowned, picked up the file Keynes had brought her, which was painfully thin. A profile of a woman with no name, no address, no known associates. Just genetic markers indicating her half match to a sexual deviant.

'Why are you bringing this up now?' she asked Keynes at last.

'You keep implying I know things about Flora I'm not telling. You also seem to feel Flora's recent disappearance might have something to do with her first abduction. I don't know. Personally, I have more questions than answers at this point. But I am concerned about Flora. And despite what you think, I'm being honest. Anything, everything Flora has ever told me, I have shared. That's my job, Sergeant Detective. I'm not a shrink. I'm a victim specialist. Flora knows this. Which is yet another reason why she never told me about Jacob's daughter.'

Keynes nodded at the file. 'You now know everything I

know about Flora and her time with Jacob. It's not complete. It's not perfect. But I'm hoping, for Flora's sake, it's enough.'

'A virtually empty folder on an unidentified woman?' D.D. picked up the file. 'This isn't a piece of information. It's another damn question!'

'You wanted to know everything. And now you do.'

Keynes rose to standing, retrieved his coat.

'Flora didn't run away,' he stated.

'I know.'

'Meaning if she's gone, someone took her.'

'But not the building inspector,' D.D. conceded with a sigh.

'And not Devon Goulding,' Keynes said, 'who was already dead. Which leaves us with?'

'A connection. Someone who knew the victims, but also knew Devon Goulding.' D.D. looked up at Keynes. 'Someone who either partnered with Devon on the original abductions or was inspired enough to keep on going.'

'A connection,' Keynes agreed.

D.D. stared at all the mounds of paperwork on her desk and realized it was up to her after all. Because she was the central keeper of information. Each detective wrote up his or her piece. It was the sergeant's job, however – D.D.'s job – to study the whole.

'I have to get to work,' she muttered.

Keynes smiled, left her without another word.

38

The corridor isn't lit, and yet is somehow lighter than our shuttered room. Standing with my body halfway behind the door, peering warily down the hall, it takes me a few moments to figure it out. There are no windows, no overhead lights. Hence the relentless gloom. But neither are the walls painted black, enabling some sense of lightness, though maybe mostly in comparison.

I count four doors in addition to mine. One next to this room, two across the hall. The final door is at the end of the hall. Maybe leading to a staircase? All are closed, so it's hard to know.

I don't see any signs of life. Nor do I hear footsteps approaching, noises from other rooms, levels. The hall isn't long; four rooms isn't many.

A house, I think. We are in a house. How many stories there are, which level we're on, I have no idea. If we're still in Boston, most of the construction is triple-deckers. Common living space would be the first floor, bedrooms on the second and third. I would guess we're on the third floor, as far away from the common areas – where neighbors or guests might hear us – as possible. But I don't know anything, and my roommate isn't exactly talking.

Confronted by the empty hallway, dotted with dark

rectangles of shuttered doors, she is shaking uncontrollably, her hand pressed to her injured side.

My first instinct is to get us down the hall to the end doorway, which I'm guessing leads to a stairwell. Over. Down. Out.

Somehow, I doubt it will be that simple.

The girl – Stacey – is staring at the closed door directly across from us. She shakes harder.

Which is when I start to get nervous. What's behind that door? What does she know that I don't?

I wish I had a weapon.

I don't like guns. I still remember that last day, the weight of the .45 in my hand . . .

I don't like guns. But a Taser, pepper spray, even a good old-fashioned baseball bat would make me feel better right about now.

I have a bent mattress coil in my hand. Guess it will have to do.

As I creep silently out from behind the door. Leave my pitch-black prison for the first time in . . . Well, I have no idea.

I don't go left. I don't go right. Instead, responding to Stacey's continuous shudders, I cross the hall, wrap my hand around the doorknob, and pull.

The door opens out into the corridor, just like ours did. It enables me to keep my body positioned behind it, half protected from whatever wild creature might leap from its yawning black depths.

I yank. I step back. Stacey hisses sharply and . . .

Nothing.

No sounds. No activities. No humans or animals appearing from the void. I peer around the door, study the depths more intently.

The room is dark, dark. Like ours was. Same blackout paint job, which makes me wonder what else might be similar. All of my explorations of my room never revealed a light switch. So now I feel along the hall next to the doorway and, sure enough, find the switch out in the corridor. I flip it on.

Stacey shrieks. I snap my eyes shut, my fingers scrambling belatedly to reverse the light process. Off, off, off.

Light burns, burns, burns. We can't handle it.

We've already spent too long in the dark.

I'm breathing heavily. Behind me, Stacey is too. I wait for the sound of pounding footsteps, alerted by Stacey's shriek. The animals are out, have escaped from their cages! Get them!

But the house remains still. Eerily so.

It makes me anxious. No house is this quiet. Just like no room should be that dark. What is this place? And what has happened here?

I'm starting to panic. My breathing is irregular, my heart pounding in my chest. The room in its own way was comforting. A defined void. And, frankly, a fairly luxurious one for a girl once confined to a coffin-size box.

But a house, an entire house with shuttered rooms and unseen levels and unknown quirks . . .

I fist my hand, force myself to focus. Are you tired, are you hungry, are you cold, are you in pain?

No? Then you are okay.

I am okay.

And I'm going to get out of here.

The light went on. The room lit up. What did I see? I try to recall, but I can't. Just an impression of blinding brightness, like a blowtorch in front of my retinas. I take a deep breath. If I'm going to figure out what's in that room,

I'm going to have to flash the light again.

'Look away,' I instruct Stacey. I lower my own gaze, then once again work the switch.

I look sideways first, still blinking hard against even the ambient glow. Behind me, Stacey is doing God knows what. She whimpers but at least doesn't scream this time.

I count to three, then:

I glance up swiftly, register the room, snap the light back off.

Both Stacey and I breathe easier, and now I understand her anxiety about that space. It had contained a thin mattress, plastic bucket, and a length of chain dangling from the ceiling.

I turn to her.

'Was that your room?'

It takes her a moment. She nods. Which makes me glance down the hall, to the two other closed doors.

'And those rooms?' I ask her.

She shrugs, appears more miserable. She is struggling. With evidence of her past captivity, with the hope of new escape, I don't know. But in the gloom, her face is pale and shiny, like a waxy moon.

Maybe she has an infection. Maybe she's dying right now while I stand here and interrogate her in the middle of the hall.

I don't know. I don't know anything.

I keep my ears attuned for any sign of approaching noise, clutch my mattress coil tighter, and advance to the next door.

There are locks on the outside, but near the top of the door frame. I didn't notice on the first door because I hadn't looked up that high. Now I realize all four doors have external latches, placed high. None of them are bolted shut, however.

Why? Why have locks but not use them?

My uneasiness increases again as I approach the next closed door, position myself behind it, and yank it open.

Same pitch black. Some external switch snapped up for a brief, blinding flare of light. Same contents. Bare mattress, heavy chains.

I'm starting to see the theme of this house; it's not a happy one. And now, for the final piece of the puzzle: the closed door next to my room.

Stacey isn't talking. Stacey isn't moving. She simply stands in the hallway, clutching her side, sagging on her feet, as I do the honors.

This is the room with the viewing window. The room where I assumed our abductor liked to hang out, enjoy the show. And now? Is he waiting inside, still one step ahead? I'll open the door and he'll . . .

Taze me, drug me? Laugh his head off at our pathetic attempt to escape?

My hand is shaking. It pisses me off. I don't want to be scared or anxious or intimidated.

I am not hungry. I am not tired. I am not cold, thirsty, hot, or in pain.

I'm okay.

And I'm going to do this.

Door open. Flick light on. Snap light off.

I inhale sharply, exhale fully. Then I shut the door and return to Stacey. No Evil Kidnapper. No bogeyman hiding in the dark. Instead, I saw behind this door exactly what I'd spotted behind the first two. Which brought us to four rooms, counting my own, with four blackout paint jobs, four mattresses, four buckets, and four tethers of chain.

Two of us.

'What aren't you telling me?' I demand.

Stacey looks at me. She opens her mouth. She closes her mouth.

Then, just like a marionette whose strings have been cut, she collapses soundlessly to the floor.

I head straight for the door at the end of the corridor. The exit, most likely to the building's staircase.

I tell myself I'm not running away. I tell myself I'm not abandoning a young girl I've already stabbed in the ribs.

I'm getting out. I'm finding help. It's the sensible thing to do. Come upon an injured person, first thing you do is dial 911. Well, I don't exactly have a cell phone on me. Hence, I'll go out and fetch help.

I reach the door, grab the knob. Heavy, metal. Like a fire door. I twist and pull just as I have three times before.

The door doesn't move.

I pull my gaze up, to where the other doors were latched. But there is no bolt.

At least, not on this side.

How were the doors to the other rooms set up? Locked from the outside. How much do I wanna bet this door is the same? Meaning it opens into the stairwell and is locked inside the stairwell, versus my side of the long, shadowy corridor.

For a second, I can't take it. I hit the door with my open palm. Kick it with my bare foot. My hand hurts; my toes explode. This door is not wood; it doesn't even wobble. This door isn't going anywhere.

Trapped. In a larger venue. For all of my cunning and guile, I haven't gained us freedom at all. Just access to more blacked-out rooms in our prison.

My eyes sting. But I don't cry. Instead, I rest my forehead

against the fire door. I welcome its coolness against my fevered face.

'I'm not hungry,' I whisper. A lie. My stomach is growling.

'I'm not thirsty.' What did I do with the bottle of water?

'I'm not tired. I'm not in pain.' No, but Stacey is.

'I'm okay.' Then, for good measure: 'I am okay. I am okay. I am okay.'

And eventually I'm going to figure this out. I'm going to get out of here. If anything, because the kidnapper's gotta return eventually, and when he does . . .

Unless our abductor really was the bartender with the amazing pecs. Meaning he was already dead. Wouldn't that be ironic?

Except, of course, I got here somehow, someway. I don't care what hurt, confused Stacey thought. I didn't just walk over from my apartment and lock myself in a blacked-out room. Someone did something. And that someone is going to return.

And it will be much, much worse. Isn't that what Stacey said?

I pull myself away from the door. I return to Stacey's form, still sprawled on the floor. I'm not sure what to do, first aid not being my area of expertise. But thinking practically, I do have access to a resource we didn't have before: light. Meaning, I can get a better look at her wound, then do a better job tending it.

She has fallen near the doorway to my room. I untangle her limbs until she is sprawled flat on her back. Then I snap on the light in my former cell. It's easier for me to see using the ambient light spilling into the hallway than to move her directly beneath the bulb. I doubt either of our eyes could take it.

She moans as I move around her, working until the light spills across her exposed abdomen.

The moment I look down, I realize how much the dark disguised before. As hard as I'd worked at feeling out each splinter, I'd barely made a dent. The wound is a long gash. Already I can see lines of dark wood embedded beneath her skin, her flesh red at the edges. Furthermore, her belly is distended. I poke it gently. Hard to the touch.

She's bleeding, I think. On the inside. I'm pretty sure I watched this episode of *Grey's Anatomy*. It hadn't ended well for the victim of the train crash.

And now.

I sit back on my heels. I fist my hands on my thighs. Without a doubt, Stacey Summers requires immediate medical assistance.

And I have no idea how to get us out of here.

39

D.D. was just packing up to go home when her phone rang. She'd already missed dinner with Alex and Jack. If she hustled, she could still make bedtime. So of course, her phone, ringing. On her still terribly crowded, paper-strewn desk. She'd tried – she swore to God she'd done her best – to plow through the piles of reports. But if anything, they seemed to grow before her eyes. Whatever magical nugget of information might be awaiting discovery continued to elude her there.

Phone. Still ringing. According to caller ID, the ME's office.

D.D. sighed. Set down her messenger bag. Picked up the receiver.

'Don't you ever go home?' Ben Whitely asked in his gravelly voice.

'Apparently not. Besides, you're the one calling from the morgue. Who are you to talk?'

'Not the morgue. The lab above the morgue.'

'For most people, that's close enough.'

'I have information,' Ben announced.

D.D. waited. She'd assumed as much. Ben was hardly the type to call to chat.

'I got a prelim on your body.'

'Kristy Kilker. Mom identified the tattoo.'
'Official results will take a few more days, but I got the sense you were in a hurry on this one.'
'Yes.'
'So, unofficially speaking—'
'Bring it on.'
'COD is a heart attack.'
'What?' D.D. sat down.
'Victim had a congenital heart defect. Most likely, she never even knew she had it. Furthermore, her body showed classic signs of starvation: shriveled stomach, atrophied muscles, and enlargement of the liver and spleen. Odds are, the physical stress brought on by her prolonged malnourishment triggered a significant myocardial event.'
'A heart attack. She died of a heart attack.'
'Unofficially, yes.'
'She wasn't murdered.'
'There are marks around both wrists consistent with physical restraints. Also signs of antemortem scars down her arms, back of her legs, most likely made with a fine blade, maybe even a scalpel—'
'She was cut.'
'Yes. Not deeply. But . . .'
D.D. didn't need the ME to say more. Both she and Ben knew some perpetrators liked to play with their food.
'Between that and her level of malnourishment,' Ben continued, 'you can make the legal argument the perpetrator's activities led directly to her death.'
'But he didn't mean it.' D.D. stopped. That statement sounded stupid even to her. Judging by Ben's silence, he agreed. 'I mean . . .' D.D. had to regroup, gather her thoughts. 'Her death wasn't intended. If she hadn't had the heart attack . . .'

'Then she might very well still be tied up, starving somewhere,' Ben agreed dryly.

'You don't understand. We have three more missing girls whose bodies we haven't found. Meaning if Kristy was never meant to die, maybe they aren't either. Maybe they are still tied up, starving somewhere. What can you tell me about time of death?'

D.D. sifted quickly through the stacks of files on her desk, looking for Kristy Kilker, college student, who'd worked nights at Hashtag, just up the street from Tonic, before supposedly leaving to study abroad in Italy, except she'd never signed up for the program. When had her mother last heard from her? Five months ago, Phil had said. And yet at the burial site, Ben had already thought the remains were fresher than that.

'I'm going with a six-to-eight-week window.'

'That recent?'

'Am I on record?'

'No.'

'Then I'm still comfortable with the six-to-eight-week window.'

'Okay.' D.D.'s mind was whirling. Kristy had disappeared in June, but most likely had still been alive in September. Which meant . . .

She'd been held somewhere. Clearly. And not at Devon Goulding's house because they'd torn that place apart.

Meaning there must be a second destination. Someplace large enough to hold multiple victims, given that Natalie, Stacey, and Flora remained missing.

D.D. had been focused on identifying a second person, someone who knew both Goulding and the victims and would've been driven to abduct Flora even after Goulding's death. But given how well that was going, perhaps she should focus instead on finding this second site. After all, how many places could there be in Boston, frequented by Devon Goulding, that were large enough and discreet enough to hide at least four missing girls?

'I'm done,' Ben Whitely said in her ear. 'That's it. All I know for the moment. Now I'm going home, getting some sleep.'

D.D. nodded against the receiver. She hung it up without ever saying good-bye.

She was not going home. She was not getting some sleep.

Instead, she picked the phone back up and summoned the task force.

'We have a significant development.' D.D. stood once more at the whiteboard, dry-erase marker in hand. She had yawning detectives crammed around the conference room table, large pizzas sitting in the middle of it; if you were going to make your people work all hours of the day and night, you had to at least keep them fed.

'COD on Kristy Kilker is a heart attack. Most likely triggered by the physical stress of her captivity. Postmortem revealed signs of prolonged starvation as well as torture with a fine blade. Time of death roughly six to eight weeks ago.'

'But she disappeared in June,' Phil said.

'Exactly. Meaning she was held somewhere for at least several months. Which means our other missing persons' – D.D. tapped each name on the board with her marker: Natalie, Stacey, Flora – 'could still be alive there as well. We need to revisit our theory of the crime. Not to mention our number of perpetrators.

'Let's assume, for a moment, Devon Goulding was involved. He has direct ties to three out of four victims, and based on what Stacey Summers's friends have said, it's probable he encountered her at Tonic a time or two as well.'

'He's big enough to be the guy from the abduction tape,' Neil spoke up.

'And he wasn't working at Tonic the night Stacey Summers disappeared from Birches. Meaning he could very well have been scoping out the scene there,' Carol Manley offered.

'All right.' D.D. tapped the board again. 'We have Goulding. Physically large enough to be our attacker-slash-kidnapper. With at least one known assault, given his attack on Flora. And most likely tied to Kristy's death, given it was the GPS data on his vehicle that led us to her body. Not to mention he has trophies from the first two victims. Put it all together, and I feel it's safe to say he was involved in the first three abductions.'

Around the table her detectives nodded.

'Which brings us to' – she moved down the timeline she'd already written out on the whiteboard – 'Flora Dane. Who disappeared from her highly secure apartment *after* Goulding was murdered. How? What are we missing?'

'A second kidnapper,' Carol spoke up. 'A friend of Goulding's?' She sounded thoughtful. 'Or a follower?'

D.D. nodded. 'Killing teams are rare, but they do happen. Husband and wife. Two males. Relatives, nonrelatives, combinations are endless. What is consistent is there's always one alpha operating with a submissive partner. So, first question, which one is Goulding?'

Phil arched a brow. 'Twentysomething male all pumped up on steroids? Goulding's gotta be the alpha.'

'I don't think so.' Carol again. They all looked at her in surprise. She merely shrugged. 'If Goulding was the alpha, then his death would've ended it. Partner would've run away, or simply broken down, right? Ambushing Flora in her own apartment, kidnapping her . . . That speaks of confidence. Not to mention foresight, planning, and organization. That's not submissive behavior. That's evil mastermind, all the way.'

It truly pained D.D. to say this: 'I think she's right.'

Now all eyes were on her. 'There's inconsistencies with our crimes. Goulding kept trophies of the first two women, but not Stacey Summers. There's blood in his garage, which implies at one time he brought at least one victim there, but the victims must be held somewhere else. Not to mention, he brought Flora to his garage versus bringing her straight to this second location. I think – and I'm going a bit off the reservation here – that the garage is Goulding's domain, but the second location isn't. It belongs to his partner. Meaning, once the girls are there—'

'They aren't his anymore,' Phil finished for her. 'He's turning them over to someone else. Submissive, handing over to the alpha.'

'Evidence would be nice,' D.D. conceded. 'But given that Goulding's dead . . . I wonder if he picked the first two women on his own. Or maybe just Natalie, with whom he clearly had some kind of relationship, to judge by the number of photos. Maybe that first crime was personal and independent. But it drew someone else's attention. Someone who could both add to the adventure – Hey, I got the perfect place we can keep them – but then who also started calling the shots. Leading to Goulding's increasing temper tantrums and his need to snatch Flora and take her to his place first. Because, later, it wouldn't be about him.'

Around the table, detectives eyed one another. Universal shrug. D.D. couldn't argue with that. They were detectives, not profilers. And she really had drifted into the land of conjecture.

'Which leads us to—' she began.

'It's a woman,' Carol interrupted. 'The dominant partner. It's a female. Because there's no way a roid-raging self-perceived stud like Goulding would take orders from another male. But a woman . . . Older, gorgeous, manipulative, she could play him. Start out acting like she was taking orders from him, except next thing he knows, she's the one calling the shots. It's her house they're using. Which would also trigger his basic hardwiring to submit, a house being a woman's domain and all.'

D.D. nodded. 'Yeah. That's what I'm thinking too. The reason we've never found Stacey Summers is because everyone's been looking for the Devon Gouldings of the world. When, in fact, Stacey's most likely stashed with an ice-cold femme fatale. Someone who lives in a stand-alone residence – can't be hiding four girls in an apartment building – somewhere in the Boston area—'

'Downtown?' Phil interrupted with a frown.

'Yeah. If the house was out in the country, why dispose of Kristy's body in the nature center? That kind of disposal was very high risk, and would only be done because they had no other choice. In other words, our perpetrators may have a house suitable for their activities but no land. Hence the field trip to Mattapan.'

'You think the house is in Mattapan?' Phil asked.

'Possible. If I was going to hide four women . . .' D.D. shrugged. 'I'd look for a place in a lower-class neighborhood, where so many of the buildings are boarded up, who would notice yet another triple-decker with plywood over the windows? Where my neighbors are few and far between and, better yet, more inclined to be shooting up than looking out for strange happenings. Where the sound of screams isn't so out of the ordinary.'

'That doesn't exactly limit the possibilities in Boston,' Neil said dryly.

'According to crime stats, if the victims are white, then the perpetrator is most likely white. So we're talking a predominantly Caucasian neighborhood.'

More shrugs from around the table. Given Boston's long history of Irish, Italian, and now Eastern European immigrants, poor white areas of the city were just as easy to come by as those of any other color. Diversity at work. Or just the harsh reality that getting ahead in a strange new city was hard on everyone.

'I don't think we're going to magically find the place through geographic profiling,' D.D. said. 'I think we need to zero in on any known females in Devon Goulding's life. Women he's met on the job, at a gym, hitting the bars at night. Whatever and whoever. To make it even more interesting, it turns out Jacob Ness had a daughter. So if we could tie any of Devon's known associates back to the asshole who first abducted Flora Dane, that would be a slam dunk.'

Around the table, her detectives eyed her blankly.

'I'm just saying—'

'Jacob Ness had a daughter?' Phil asked.

'FBI recovered DNA from his long-haul truck consistent with a daughter. Unfortunately, that's all we know. Literally. A DNA sequence.'

'But she might be in Boston?' Phil again.

'Or Florida, or Georgia, or Brazil for that matter. But given that we're looking for a female . . . it's something to bear in mind. If this daughter had a relationship with Jacob, well, here's at least one woman who'd have some experience with kidnapping and abduction. Not to mention a hatred of Flora Dane. I don't think we can dismiss all that.'

'But how does that help?' Carol Manley this time.

'I don't know,' D.D. said honestly. 'I think . . . First, let's compile a list of Devon Goulding's female associates. We can contact his cellular provider, look at numbers frequently called, texted, et cetera. Then we can run basic backgrounds on likely candidates to see if any of those names match our requirements. We discover that some of these frequently called numbers belong to, say, older beautiful women, maybe even one or two who used to live in the South, and now we've got something. Better yet, one of these names has a house secluded enough and big enough to hold multiple kidnapping victims . . . We have our first target.'

Neil raised his hand. 'I have a different idea.'

D.D. studied him. 'All right, shoot.'

'Goulding's car's GPS. We already used it once, looking through his list of frequent destinations for an area best suitable for hiding a body. What if we did that again, except now we look for the address that best matches our list of housing requirements? Getting a list of frequent callers from a cellular company will take at least twenty-four hours, while running backgrounds and following up with known associates will take yet another day. Whereas I can analyze a list of frequent destinations in' – Neil bobbed his head side to side, considering – 'a matter of hours.'

Around the table, the task force members perked up. Standing in front, so did D.D.

'Neil,' she ordered, 'you and your squad' – she nodded to Phil and Carol – 'are in charge of GPS data. The rest, work on compiling names.' She glanced at her watch. It was 10:00 P.M. now. Which was perfect for her own assignment:

tracking manager Jocelyne Ethier, an older, definitely less than honest female who knew all the players involved, had access to the nightclub's security system, and should even now be roaming the floor at Tonic. When looking at female associates, nothing like starting at the top of the list.

'I'm giving you all two hours,' she announced. 'Whoever brings me the address first gets to lead the charge. We'll go the moment we're cleared. If Flora's abduction was a matter of revenge, God only knows how much time she – or any of the women – have left.'

40

I keep yanking at the locked door. Twisting the knob. Jerking harder. As if this time the heavy metal door will magically swing open. And I will plunge down the stairs, out some side door, and straight into the fresh air of freedom. I'll find help for Stacey. I'll call my mom. I'll get away from an entire corridor of black-painted rooms forever.

The door. The damn door. Why won't it open? I just want out of here.

I pound at it with the flat of my hand. Another useless motion, waste of effort that does nothing but exhaust me further.

I gotta pull it together. I gotta focus. I'm not a terrified kid anymore. I'm the new and improved Flora, who has training and experience and knows better than this.

The windows. It comes to me as I stand, shoulders slumped, forehead resting against the stairwell door. In my room there had been two blacked-out windows. Break them, and I can get a hand out. Call for help. Isn't that what the girl in Cleveland did, got part of the front door open and yelled until a neighbor came?

Okay, windows it is. I leave the locked fire door, force myself to walk away from it, past Stacey's unconscious form, and back into the room I loathe. I snap on the bare bulb, then close my eyes until they adjust.

All my blundering around, roaming from room to room, opening some doors, pounding on others, surely must be broadcasting my newfound freedom upstairs. I don't know if this is a good idea. At any time, maybe the stairwell door will open. And this time, some hulking beast with a gun, a knife, a Taser will come rushing through, and I'll find myself locked up all over again. Someone must still be in the house, right? Someone in charge of the care and feeding of the inmates?

Except maybe that's the point. The person in charge of care and feeding went out for supplies. Hence, no one has been home to respond to all the racket coming from upstairs. Meaning any moment now, said person will return. Walk into his evil lair, catch the first unexpected noise from above, and . . .

I guess I'll find out.

I open my eyes slowly, still struggling with bright light. Remembering what Stacey had said about the sedative-laced mattress, I cross to its mangled form, grab one corner, and gingerly drag it out into the hall. I'm tired and overwhelmed, but this is no time to sleep. I gotta keep sharp.

I have to get both of us out of here.

In the hallway, Stacey's fallen form is illuminated by the slash of light from my room. Her side is puffy and red. Her abdomen appears more swollen. She needs medical attention. She needs me to get help.

Deep breath. Back to the room, which under the harsh glare of the bare bulb looks tired and dingy. The black paint covering the walls and ceiling might be new, but that's about it. And now, more alert, I can catch the faint odor of must and mildew. The house is old. Maybe even abandoned.

Makes sense. You can hardly hold prisoners in a bustling neighborhood surrounded by white picket fences and soccer moms. A derelict building, however, in a not-so-great area of town where the residents are already trained not to report any screams . . .

I trace my fingers around the windows, feeling the plasticky nature of the paint. Thicker than regular paint. More like a spray coating. It reminds me of something, but I can't think of what. I can dent it with my fingernail, so it's not a hard shell. More like rubbery. Breakable, I think, with enough force.

Resources. I have the plastic bucket, the wire coil from the mattress. In the end, however, I decide I am my own best tool. My elbow, to be more precise. Driven in a backward strike, the hard point of an elbow can be a very efficient weapon.

I should cover my elbow with something, to protect it from the breaking glass. I'm still dressed in the ragged remains of a silk negligee, the torn hem and thin straps offering little cover. I could take Stacey's shirt, but I can't bring myself to do it. It's too morbid, like stealing from the dead.

I return to the hall and the shredded mattress. Holding my breath, I reach down with both hands, grab an edge of the worn cover, and tear off the piece of flapping material. Not a huge piece and nearly threadbare, but the best I can do.

Back to the window. I stick the scrap of fabric in the middle of the lower windowpane. Then, I twist around, and moving quickly, before the fabric falls to the floor, I hammer my elbow back.

Pain. Instant and sharp. I suck in a breath, will myself not to scream as the pain ricochets down my arm, turns my hand momentarily numb. I bounce on my feet, bob my head, flex my fingers, and the moment passes. I can breathe again. Better yet, I can turn and inspect the window, which I would swear, beneath the Teflon coating of paint, has started to crack.

It takes me three tries, three little dances of pain, and then I hear it. Sharp, definitive. The glass gives way. My elbow has won.

The paint proves the tougher opponent, resiliently holding the fractured window together. I use my fingers to pick at it, dislodging the first small piece, then, in rapid succession, several larger shards of glass to make a hole.

I'm so excited by this success, I don't notice the obvious. The lack of fresh air. Or sounds from the outside. Or any hint of daylight, streetlights, something.

It's not until I bend down and attempt to peer out my escape hatch that I realize the error in my ways.

I've broken out the glass . . .

Only to discover the window has been boarded up from the outside. Three elbow strikes later, I have exchanged a glass barrier for a piece of plywood.

I am as trapped now as I was before.

Am I hungry? Yes. Am I tired? Very much. Am I thirsty, scared, cold, hot? Sure. I am everything. I am nothing. I'm a stupid girl who once lived in a coffin-size box and now is trapped in a boarded-up house.

I'm a daughter, I'm a sister, who destroyed her family once before, and now is ruining their sanity all over again.

I am a survivor who has yet to figure out how to live.

I'm an overwhelmed person who wants to sink to the floor and feel sorry for herself.

So I do. I let myself sit in front of the boarded-up

window, surrounded by shards of glass. I wrap my hands around my knees. I study the scars on my wrists.

And I think of Jacob.

It's crazy. He snatched me, drunk and stupid, off a beach. He stuck me in a box. He drove me all over the South. He raped me, he starved me, he beat me. He took me out dancing. He introduced me to his daughter. He gave me clothes, and on occasion, he called me pretty.

I hate him. I miss him. He is, and always will be, the most influential person in my life. Other people have first loves, dysfunctional families. I have Jacob. No matter where I go, what I do, I carry him with me. His voice in my head. His smell on my skin. His brains and blood in my hair. He told me it would be like that, and in his own crazy way, Jacob never lied. Even at the bitter end, he warned me I'd never be free of him.

He advised me to kill myself instead.

Now, I picture Jacob and I know he's laughing at me, lips pulled back from his nicotine-stained teeth, hand rubbing his swollen belly. Stupid, stupid girl, he's laughing. Gloating. He always told me I'd be nothing without him. The world is too big, too harsh, for a silly little thing like me. Stupid is as stupid does and stupid is me.

Thinking I would actually be the one to find poor lost Stacey Summers. Thinking I could actually be the hero this time around instead of the victim.

I pick up a shard of glass from the floor beside me. I finger it absently, studying the way the light reflects off the razor-sharp edge.

It's not that I haven't tried, I tell myself. When I first came home, I swore the air smelled sweeter, the sound of my mother's laughter was brighter, my brother's quick grin the warmest sight I'd ever seen. All those days of captivity.

All those nights of horror. And now this. I'd survived. I'd done it. Jacob was dead, I was alive, and I'd never go back again. I'd forget everything. Even that last day. I'd forget it all, the things I'd said, the things I'd done, the promises I'd made.

People told me I was brave and strong and amazing.

Samuel told me I was resilient and to never doubt what I had done. Survivors survive. I am a survivor.

But the air can't stay sweet forever. And eventually my mom stopped laughing and grew more concerned about my screams at night. And my brother stopped grinning and eyed me with open concern. All the things I thought I could forget. I didn't. All the things I wanted to leave behind. I couldn't.

It's not that survivors aren't entitled to happily-ever-afters. It's just . . . After surviving comes living. And in real life, some days are gray. And some nights are hard. And sometimes you cry for no good reason, and you feel sorry for yourself, and you look in the mirror and you don't recognize the girl looking back at you.

Who am I? A girl who once loved foxes? Or a girl scratching her fingers raw against the inside lid of a coffin-shaped box? A girl holding a gun, looking down at the man she despises, depends upon, fears?

Knowing this is her moment. This is it. Just move her finger on the trigger and it will be over.

Feeling herself hesitate. Why is she hesitating? Who hesitates at a moment like this?

'Do it,' Jacob ordered that day, his face a red blubbery mess. 'Pull the fucking trigger. I ain't ever going back, so come on now. End it. Put us both out of our misery.'

My own face hidden behind the cloth he'd tied around my head. Protecting me from the tear gas. The moment the first canister had fired through the window, Jacob had leapt into action. He'd tended to me first.

And now, here we were. Both of us. One bullet from freedom.

Who am I? Who is anyone? We all try so hard. And we all accumulate our failures. From I should never have drunk so much that night, to I never should've fought so hard to live. Seriously. Truthfully. If I had just gone ahead and died in the beginning, other girls might be alive right now. Except, of course, after I died, Jacob would've snatched another pretty young thing. And then she would've died. Or maybe she would've been an even better assistant than me, helping him target and kill even more women.

How do you do the math on that?

How many more predators do I need to kill, how many more potential victims do I have to save, in order to balance those scales?

Five years later, I don't have the answers to these questions. I just know every time I see a case on the news . . . I can't let it go.

Especially after Florida.

The things I don't tell Samuel. The activities I never admitted to anyone, because Jacob told me I'd go to jail too, and Jacob never lied.

So I stay alone with the ghosts that send me out each night, until here I am, trying to save Stacey Summers, and instead am just as trapped as she is.

Now I curl my fingers around the shard of glass. I take a deep breath, and I let myself remember the rest of that final day. The swarming commandos yelling at me to drop my weapon. Jacob screaming at me to shoot.

Who am I? Who is anyone?

I'm the girl who leaned down. I'm the girl who didn't

even recognize my own voice as I whispered one last promise in Jacob's ear. And watched his expression change. As in an instant, I became the one with the power, and he became the one who was terrified.

Then, I pulled the trigger.

Because I'm not just a girl locked in a coffin-size box.

I'm the girl with promises left to keep.

Now, I force myself to rise to standing. I remind myself that I'm not hungry, I'm not tired, I'm not scared, I'm not terrified.

I'm not even okay. I'm more than okay.

I'm a woman prepared to do whatever it takes to complete her mission.

Okay. I can't break a window to go out. I can't open the door to the stairs to go down. That leaves me with one option. I will go up.

Somewhere, there must be attic access. I will find it. I will get Stacey Summers help.

I will live to fight another day.

And then . . .

I will return to my mother? I will live happily ever after? I will never seek out shadows again?

I don't have those answers. I have only my mission.

Time to get to it.

41

Jacob working wasn't a bad man. We'd cruise down the highway, container load in tow, playing the license plate game. Driving, Jacob laid off the beer, weed, God knows what else. He talked instead. About anything, everything. Sometimes he'd rant, about government and politics and all the ways a hardworking guy like himself would never get ahead. But he was just as likely to get fired up about something he saw on the Late Show and wasn't that Letterman a funny bastard.

I got to sit in the front seat. His audience of choice. He'd talk, I'd listen, and then it would be time to pick where we wanted to stop for lunch, and hey, I remembered this cute diner from the last time we passed through, and he'd agree. That was the thing about Jacob. He wasn't opposed to making me happy. He'd even started watching Grey's Anatomy.

Of course, most of these moments occurred as we drove west, away from Florida. But eventually, in the way long-haul routes worked, we'd get a new assignment, sending us back. I would fall silent first. Watching the signs go by, not bothering to read them out loud. Or care if we came upon, of all things, a license plate from Alaska.

Jacob, on the other hand, would become nearly feverish.

His eyes brighter. Hands tighter on the wheel. More sex. Way more sex. Because he was anticipating now, except it wasn't me he wanted.

It was what would happen once we were in Florida again.

I begged him to let her go. She wasn't good for him, I tried to say. She goaded him into more and more dangerous behavior. He already had me. And look, he'd gotten away with it. Why couldn't he be happy?

But he couldn't. The closer we came to Florida.

He would drive to her place the second he delivered his load. Didn't matter if it was forty minutes away or three hours. If we were in the state of Florida, he headed to Lindy's house. Sometimes, she'd arrange to meet in a new location. Had to spread their hunting around to keep the locals from getting suspicious.

'Please,' I would beg, even as he turned in the direction of her house. 'Let's just crash someplace. Have a quiet night. We deserve a quiet night. You've been driving for days.'

'Nah. I'm fine.'

'You're gonna get caught. She doesn't care about you. Second the police catch on, she'll throw you under the bus. Say you made her do it. And the police will believe her. You know they will.'

'You don't understand. You don't have a kid.'

'She doesn't love you.'

'Love me?' He frowned. 'She's my kid. Love's got nothing to do with that. It's bigger than that, better. Love comes and goes. But she'll always be my daughter.'

'She's just using you—'

'Using me? Maybe I'm using her. Ever thought of that? I'm the one who found her first. She didn't know nothing 'bout me. Her mama hates my guts, didn't even include me

on the birth certificate. But I heard rumors. Went looking. First time I saw her, I knew. A father always recognizes his own. I watched her for years, always from afar. Such a pretty little thing. Then one day, when she was eight or nine, a birdie flew into a window beside her. Fell back onto the grass. I watched her pick it up. Figured she'd fuss over it. Maybe cry. But she didn't. No. Not my kid. She picked it apart. Feather by feather. Oh, she's my daughter all right. After that, I knew we'd find a way.

'*I introduced myself to her the first time when she was thirteen. Not sure if she believed me or not. But then her mama came home, saw me standing there. Went into a rage. Told me if she ever saw me again, she'd call the cops. Put me away. She'd do it too. She's that kind of woman.*' Jacob chuckled. "*Course, what she didn't realize was that by hating me, she made me interesting. Lindy might have turned away altogether. But after that . . . each time I came around, Lindy was waiting. She wanted to hear more. She wanted to learn more.*'

'*Her mother hates you?*'

'*Her mama's dead. That house she's in? Used to belong to her mama. But she's gone now. It's all Lindy's and I can stop by whenever I'd like.*'

'*How did her mama die?*' I asked.

Jacob merely smiled. '*Wouldn't you like to know.*'

'*It's going to end badly,*' I tried. But he didn't care. When we were in Florida, it was as if I didn't exist. Jacob didn't care about me.

But Lindy did. She knew I hated her. She knew their evenings together left me sick and shaking and dry heaving.

My revulsion excited her. Sending me trembling and pale into the next bar to help select their newest target turned her on.

Can you miss a coffin-size box? Because I did, I did, I did.

Eventually our time in Florida would end. Mostly because Jacob had to earn money. And paychecks came from the big rig, so sooner or later, he'd roll back into the sleeper cab and away we'd go. Me exhausted and strung out in the passenger's seat. Jacob subdued and chain-smoking behind the wheel.

Neither of us would speak until we crossed state lines. Then, it was as if it never happened. Florida became our Las Vegas. What happened there stayed there, never to be spoken of again.

Eventually, I would call out the letter A. Then he'd find B. And we'd be okay again.

Because that was life heading west. And after enough time, anything can become normal, even hanging out with your kidnapper who's killed three women and counting.

In Georgia we stopped to refuel. Jacob was gone for a long time inside, doing whatever it was he did. I sat. I stared out my window. I saw cars and trees and blacktop. I saw nothing at all.

And I wondered how long a person could live like this. Dying inch by inch. Mile by mile every time she crossed the Florida line.

I pictured my mom. I thought of her for the first time in so long. Not because you ever really forget but because a person can only take so much pain. But now I allowed myself to picture her. Wearing one of her stiff outfits from the press conferences. The sheen in her eyes. The silver fox at her throat.

I wondered what she'd say if she could see me now. I wondered if she'd still beg for my safe return. Or if she would realize, as I had realized, that there are some things a person can't come back from. I wasn't a child from the wilds of Maine anymore. I was the plaything of monsters.

And just for a minute, I wished I could see her again. If only to tell her to let me go. Move on. Be happy. Build a life.

But let me go.

Because then maybe I could let myself go. I wouldn't fight so hard, do such terrible things in order to survive anymore. I'd just fade away.

Surely that would be better than this.

For the first time in a long while, I sent my mother a prayer. I prayed she would never find me. I prayed she'd never see me like this. I prayed that all the things I'd done were things she'd never have to know.

Then Jacob returned and we drove and we drove and we drove. And he found the letter Q and later I found X, and then I started to laugh, and then I started to cry, and Jacob said we'd driven far enough. He splurged for a motel, told me to shower and clean up. He even left me alone after that as I lay curled up in a ball and cried and cried and cried.

For the mother I hoped and begged and prayed would never see me again. For the little girl who'd once fed foxes and now helped hunt humans for sport. For the life I'd lost and for the future I needed to give up. Because I couldn't go back to Florida again. There was only so much you could adapt to and accept.

I'd hit my limit and Florida was it.

Which meant it was time to let go. Give up.

After all those days, nights, weeks, Jacob had threatened to kill me – now I needed him to get the job done. He had a gun. I'd seen it. A single shot through the head. Certainly it would be kinder than what he and Lindy had done to the others.

But how to provoke him? Crazily enough, he seemed to have come to like me. Lindy might be his homicidal partner, but I was his audience. A man liked an audience.

In the morning, I would refuse to climb back into the rig. I would scream. I would scream and scream and scream. Then he'd have to shoot me, if only to shut me up.

In the morning.

I never got my chance. At dawn, just as I was starting to open my eyes, a loud explosion came from the window. Shattering glass. The sound of gunfire. Then a hissing cloud of . . .

Jacob running out of the bathroom, shirt still untucked. He had a towel in his hands. He slapped it, wet and dripping, around my lower face. I didn't understand, not him, not the hissing gas, not the shouts from outside.

Jacob raced to the other bed. Coughing, hacking. I watched his eyes swell, tears streaming down his face, snot flooding from his nose. His hand under the pillow pulling out his gun.

I remained sitting, mesmerized behind my dripping face mask as the door of the motel room flew open and black-clad men poured into the room.

Jacob falling to his knees. Moaning. Groaning. Sobbing pitifully. He stared straight at me, reaching out with his hand.

Offering me his gun.

So I took it. Hefted its weight, felt its heaviness.

While black-clad men continued to stream in and yell words I couldn't compute.

This wasn't about them. This had never been about them.

This was about Jacob and me.

His lips were moving. He was begging me to shoot him. No, he was ordering me to shoot him. Just do it. Pull the trigger.

The black-clad men came to a halt. They stood all around us. They didn't seem to know what to do.

Because of me, I realized. Because I was holding a gun and they didn't know what to expect. No doubt they had instructions to shoot Jacob, his murderous ways having finally caught up with him.

But me? No one knew what to do about me.

For the first time in four hundred and seventy-two days, I was the one holding the gun. I was the one in power.

'Do it,' Jacob commanded. 'Pull the fucking trigger. I ain't ever going back, so come on now. End it. Put us both out of our misery.'

Then, when I still didn't move: 'Hell, save a bullet for yourself. Why not? Once they hear what you've done, think they'll take it easy on you? Think you're really any different than me?'

I knew what he was saying. I understood completely.

'You'll never get over me. You'll never forget. I'll always be inside your head. Every night you wake up, you'll reach for me. Every time you drive down a highway, you'll look for me. Any man you'll meet, you'll wish he was as tough as me. There's no coming back. So just pull the trigger. Fucking end it.'

He was right, I thought. But he was wrong.

I was not who I was, and yet I wasn't who he wanted me to be.

My mother. Stiff clothes, silver fox charm. My mother begging to see me.

'I'm sorry,' I said. But I wasn't talking to Jacob. I was talking to my mother, who had no idea she was about to

get exactly what she'd wished for, which, if memory served, was a kind of ancient curse.

I placed the gun against the top of Jacob's head. Then I leaned down and I whispered in his ear:

'I'm not going to die. I'm going to stay alive. And someday, when I'm strong enough and skilled enough, I'm going to head to Florida. I'm going to track down Lindy, and then, I'm going to kill her. There will be nothing of you left, Jacob. You, your daughter, the "strong ones". I will kill you both, and it will be all your fault; you never should've snatched me from that beach.'

His eyes widened. A look of fear, not for himself but for his precious Lindy.

'I will never think of you again,' I promised, swore, lied.

Then I pulled the trigger.

A fine mist. Blood and brains in my hair. The men in black surging forward.

I won, I thought.

I lost, I already understood.

Then a woman was standing there. 'Flora, it's okay. Flora, Flora! My name is SAC Kimberly Quincy. I'm here to take you home.'

I felt sorry for her because I already understood that the Flora everyone once knew and loved would never be going home again.

There was simply me.

And I didn't even know who that was anymore.

42

By the time D.D. arrived at Tonic, the nightclub was in full swing. Music so loud the blacked-out walls vibrated with the beat of the bass. A dance floor crowded with writhing bodies. Strobing blue lights casting everything into a surreal glow of moving parts.

D.D. cut through the line outside by virtue of her badge, then worked her way around the outskirts of the dance floor until she came to the hall leading to the manager's office. Sure enough, Jocelyne Ethier sat inside wearing the same black top and black slacks from earlier. Except she was not alone. Across from her sat Keynes.

D.D. drew up short. And not because the victim specialist had finally traded in his trademark suit for some ridiculously expensive designer jeans, but because there was no good reason for Keynes to be here. As in, what the hell? As in, what was he once again not telling her?

'Evening,' she drawled from the doorway.

Ethier looked up, pale face shuttered, which only heightened D.D.'s tension.

Keynes, on the other hand, smiled. Contained. Mysterious. D.D. hated that smile.

'Didn't realize you were into the club scene,' she said pointedly.

'I was in the area.'

'Funny, me too.'

'Would you care to join us?' Keynes waved a hand, as if inviting her to his party.

In contrast to Ethier, his expression was open. D.D. didn't buy it for a moment. She stepped into the room warily. Her left hand drifted automatically to her hip, where once she'd carried a sidearm. Except she wasn't permitted to carry anymore. She was a restricted duty desk sergeant out on her own.

'I had some follow-up questions,' Keynes said.

'Really.' D.D. eyed the manager. 'So do I.'

Ethier sighed, appeared less than happy. 'If both of you could come back tomorrow—'

'It'll only take a minute,' Keynes said.

'Only a minute,' D.D. echoed.

'A minute? Have you seen the bar? This is peak hours. Look, I don't mean to be rude—'

'Then don't,' Keynes said. He was staring right at the woman. And just for a moment, D.D. saw Ethier hesitate. As if responding to the power of a handsome man's gaze? Or as if receiving an unspoken signal?

Once again, her hand drifted toward her hip. Once again, there was nothing there.

Keynes caught the motion. And she would have sworn he knew exactly what she was thinking.

'I was just asking some more questions about Natalie Draga,' Keynes said. 'The first victim.'

'She implied she didn't know Natalie very well,' D.D. murmured.

'I don't—' the manager began.

'But perhaps someone on your staff does,' Keynes continued smoothly. 'A fellow bartender, best friend. It's important. The sooner you find that person for us, the sooner we'll be out of your hair.'

Ethier scowled, shifted from side to side. 'Larissa,' she stated abruptly. 'She's another bartender. She and Natalie often took their breaks together.'

'Is she working tonight?' Keynes asked.

'Yes.'

'Then why don't you fetch her for us.'

Ethier hesitated, clearly reluctant. Then, when Keynes continued to stare at her: 'Fine. I'll get her. But keep your questions short. It's Killer Band Night – can't you see how busy it is out there?'

The manager rose, pushing her way past D.D. A second later, she disappeared down the hall, leaving D.D. alone with Keynes.

She was already turning on him when he spoke first.

'Something about our first conversation with her kept bothering me,' he said.

'You mean other than her obvious lie about her relationship with Goulding?'

'Yes. Because covering up a past relationship with a suspected rapist is a logical thing to do. Not necessarily a sign of guilt.'

'Whatever.' D.D. kept her voice hard. She remained suspicious. And something else . . . frightened? No. Wary.

'Five years,' Keynes said abruptly. 'Jocelyne Ethier said she'd been the manager here for the past five years.'

'So?' Except then D.D. got it. 'Five years, as in exactly how long Flora's been home.'

'It could be a coincidence,' Keynes said.

'Sure.'

'Except I did some digging. You know where Ethier worked five years ago?'

D.D. shook her head. It was an obvious question, and no, she and her team hadn't gotten that far.

'She managed another bar. In Tampa, Florida.'

Now, D.D.'s heart accelerated in her chest. 'Florida, as in Jacob's home state?'

'Think it's still a coincidence?'

'No. But why did you send her out of the room?'

'So we could compare notes. I could tell you were suspicious—'

'You *sent her away*! As in, how do you know she's coming back?'

Keynes's eyes widened.

D.D. didn't bother to wait. She was already bolting down the hall.

43

Stacey moans again in the hallway. In search of attic access, I pause, kneeling by her side, uncertain of what to do.

Her side looks terrible, a mass of bloody flesh and wooden splinters. Infected, inflamed, why not. But I don't think that injury alone would cause her this much distress. My best guess remains that something more has gone wrong, some kind of internal damage I can't see. A slow bleed? Invisible but deadly?

I consider moving her out of the hallway. Sooner or later, the stairwell door will open, our captor returning from wherever to come storming down the corridor. Enraged at our escape. Prepared to cow us once again into submission. Or exact further revenge.

It's only a matter of time.

Stacey moans again. I need to think quicker, act faster.

If she has some kind of internal damage, chances are dragging her from room to room will only make things worse. Instead, I bring the shredded mattress over to her. I prop her head onto one corner. Maybe the sedative-laced foam will put her to sleep. Maybe she'll be grateful for the escape.

The musty, grassy odor teases at me again. A sense of déjà vu. I should know what this is.

Then, it comes to me. Standing in a bar. Drinking a beer. Hops. The mattress smells of hops. Reeks of them really.

I'd read about hops while researching various herbal remedies and basic first aid. Hops have been used as a sleep aid since medieval times, when people realized the workers in the hops fields had a tendency to fall asleep on the job. Now, some companies even sell hops pillows for better sleeping, that sort of thing. The science behind it is still sketchy, but I read one report that said if the hops are distilled down to a strong enough extract and then mixed with viburnum root, it boosts effectiveness.

So that's the trick then. The mattress has been treated with hops and viburnum. Easy enough to do if you have access to hops.

Say, Devon Goulding, bartender extraordinaire.

Coming to get me from beyond the grave?

I killed him, I remind myself. Which seems to be my theme for the day. I killed Jacob. I killed Devon. And yet here I am, kidnapped and locked away with a dying girl.

For someone who keeps killing people, I am just not getting the job done.

The thought angers me, kick-starts me back into action.

I leave Stacey on one side of the hall, head on the hops-soaked mattress; then I start my search for the attic in earnest. Room by room, eyeing ceiling panels.

Boston is known for its triple-deckers, three-story homes built narrow and deep, perfect for wedging into skinny rectangular lots. This floor's layout, hallway in the middle, bedrooms either side, is consistent with that. If my assumption is right, the hall should end in a common room with front-facing bay windows, but maybe that part has been walled off. As for which level I'm on, top level makes the most sense. More isolated, no one above to be disturbed by the screams below.

I start by going room to room, gazing overhead.

The bedrooms are tough. The rubbery black paint obscures everything. I'm not studying a ceiling as much as trying to dissect a Teflon pan. I can't see anything. I return to the hallway, where the waterstained drywall is just as disappointing.

Stacey is still moaning, moaning, moaning.

I rub my temples. Feeling a rising tide of stress and anxiety.

I'm trapped. We're trapped. Four rooms and a hallway. It doesn't matter the size of the cage. Quantity of real estate makes little difference when there's still no way out.

I should return to the broken window. I'll finish removing the glass. Beat against the plywood. Maybe I can knock it loose.

With what? A ramming mattress? A tightly coiled spring? An elbow that is still bruised from my last attempt?

Think, think, think.

My apartment. Top corner of my landlord's triple-decker. Where the attic access panel is at the landing at the top of the stairs.

And that quickly, my heart sinks. Because I'm pretty sure I know where the stairs are: on the other side of the locked metal fire door.

Stacey's head is thrashing from side to side on the mattress. She is dying from my stupidity.

Boarded-up window it is.

Except at that moment, I hear it. A sound. Not the thundering of my own heart or Stacey's labored breath.

A creak from down the hall. On the opposite side of the door. There it is again. And again.

Someone is coming up the stairs.

44

D.D. had just made it down the hall when Ethier appeared, pulling a tall blonde with puffy hair and a micromini in her wake. D.D. drew up short, hand on her hip, feeling, if anything, more bewildered than before.

The manager stared at her questioningly. 'Larissa Roberts,' she said, introducing the blonde. 'I think it will be easiest to talk in my office.'

She passed by D.D., and then Keynes, who was halfway down the hall. He exchanged a glance with D.D. Both fell in step behind the manager and her charge. Neither said a word.

'So you knew Natalie Draga?' D.D. said at last when they'd all returned to the very tight office. She was trying to regroup, uncertain whom to study hardest. Jocelyne Ethier, who she was pretty sure might be Jacob Ness's long-lost daughter, or the new girl, Larissa, who apparently had been friends with the first victim.

She did her best to split her attention between the two, mostly interested in Ethier's reaction to anything Larissa had to say.

'Natalie and I were friends,' Larissa volunteered now. 'Hung out together, that sort of thing. But Natalie, she wasn't big on the personal stuff. I always had the impression this place was just one more stop along the way. When she didn't return, I wasn't surprised.'

'Where'd you two . . . hang out?' Keynes asked.

'Well, during work hours, in the break room. But after hours, we might go out, grab a drink, that sort of thing.'

'Favorite places?' D.D. asked.

'Birches. Hashtag. There's lots of bars around here. We'd wander.'

'Devon ever join you?' D.D. kept her gaze on Ethier, determined to catch some sign of jealousy, rage.

'Sure. Devon liked Natalie. Anyone could see that. She was gorgeous, of course. But she could be edgy, you know? She played him. Would offer a smile one second, then cut him down the next. She called him her puppy dog. Definitely didn't take him seriously. But as for him . . . I think he thought it was all very serious. And the more she rebuffed him, the more determined he became.'

'He wanted her. She didn't want him,' D.D. filled in, still watching Ethier. The manager appeared bored. Nothing here she didn't already know? Or she was that good at wearing a mask?

'Oh, I wouldn't say that. I came upon Natalie with Devon a couple of times in the supply closet. Natalie might have liked to look down her nose at him in public, but behind closed doors, apparently even the Buff Bot would do.'

Ethier had turned her attention to the computer screen, was frowning at something on the monitor. So far, details of Devon Goulding's affair with another woman seemed to mean nothing to her.

'How long did they know each other?' Keynes asked Larissa.

'Not sure. I mean, most of the time Natalie worked here,

Devon was chasing her. But . . . she didn't stay that long. Couple of months? Like I said, she was just passing through.'

'What brought Natalie to Boston?' D.D. asked.

'Change of pace. She said she was tired of Florida. Though how you can tire of sun and sand . . .'

'Florida? I thought she was from Alabama?'

Larissa shook her head. 'I never heard her mention Alabama. And while she did have a bit of an accent . . . Not Alabama. Nothing as heavy as Alabama.'

'Is that how you knew her then?' D.D. asked abruptly, attention zeroing in on Ethier. 'Natalie came here looking for you, didn't she? She felt comfortable asking for a job after her time working for you in Florida.'

Ethier looked up from the monitor, blinked her eyes. 'What?'

'Florida. You worked in Florida before moving here. Why didn't you mention that before?'

'You never asked.'

'What brought you to Boston?'

'A promotion. This is a better job.'

'Did you read about Flora Dane?' Keynes now, piling on. 'Her story was in all the papers. Her return home to Maine. At least in the beginning, the talk of her returning to school in Boston.'

'I have no idea—'

'That must've rankled.' D.D. now, pulling the manager's attention away, keeping her disoriented. 'She kills your father, and everyone hails her as a hero. Strong, brave girl who saved herself.'

'What the hell are you talking about?'

Larissa shrunk back, clearly wanting out of this sudden change in conversation but having no place to go.

'When did you first sleep with Devon? Big hunky guy

like that. Must've felt good to wrap him around your little finger. Until, of course, Natalie showed up. Took his attention away from you. Is that when you decided she must pay? And to make your revenge that much sweeter, you forced Devon to help.'

'Wait a second—'

'She didn't sleep with Devon.' Larissa, suddenly speaking up.

D.D. and Keynes both paused, stared at her. The blonde flushed, fiddled with the hem of her skirt.

'Jocelyne was never involved with Devon, if that's what you're asking. She was involved with me. At least, when Natalie first arrived, Jocelyne and I were together. I'm the one—' The girl paused, looked down. 'I'm the one who messed everything up. Not Natalie. Not Devon. They had nothing to do with our breakup. That was my fault. All my fault.'

D.D. frowned, studied the manager, who was now bright red with embarrassment.

'Management is not supposed to get involved with staff,' Ethier said tightly. 'If my bosses found out . . .'

'You were never involved with Devon Goulding?' D.D. asked.

'Needless to say, not my type.'

'And Natalie Draga?'

'Well, more my type, but to be honest' – Ethier glanced at Larissa – 'I prefer blondes.'

'How old are you?' Keynes asked abruptly.

'Thirty-four.'

'And your parents?'

'Roger and Denise Ethier. Live in Tampa. Do you want to call them?'

D.D. looked over at Keynes. 'I don't think she's the one.'

'No,' he agreed.

'And yet all roads lead back to this bar. The victims, Devon Goulding.' She stared at Ethier, stared at Larissa, willing them to help her. 'What aren't you telling us? For the sake of Natalie, Stacey, and Flora, what are we still missing?'

45

Glass shard. I still have it in my hand. I wipe my palm on my bare leg, then tighten my grip. Studying the door, calculating which way it will open.

The lights. I've turned them on in all the bedrooms to aid with my search. Now I jog quickly down the corridor, snapping off switches before they can give me away.

Stacey is muttering, twitching. No time to hide her.

But maybe her presence in the hall isn't a bad thing. The noise will distract our captor. While he peers down the hall, trying to figure out who's moaning, what's going on, I can make my move. Attack, then evade. It's as good a plan as any.

I'm ready.

I focus on the door, breath held, ears tuned for more footsteps. My efforts are soon rewarded: A floorboard creaks right on the other side of the door. He has reached the landing.

I crouch low, glass shard in hand. I keep my eyes peeled on the barely visible doorknob, a slight silver gleam in the now darkened hall.

The door will open toward me, into the corridor. Plan A, trip up my attacker and dart through, yanking the door shut behind me and leaving my captor as trapped as I had once been. From there, I'd have smooth sailing down the stairs, out into the free world, where I could flag down help.

Plan B, fight like hell. I have surprise, training, and a shard of glass on my side. Wars had been won with less.

The door rattles slightly. I hear the rasp of a metal bolt being pulled back. Unlocking the door from the outside. And now . . .

The handle turns. I will myself to be lower, smaller, invisible in the dark.

As the door pushes open. One inch, two, three. Enough that I could get a foot in to block it.

The door opens. A figure fills the void. And then . . .

I spring forward, clutching the glass dagger close to my chest as I lash out with my foot. An *oomph* as the person falls, not forward into the corridor as I'd hoped but backward onto the equally dark landing.

No time to think, no time to redirect. The heavy metal door is already swinging shut as I suck in my stomach and slide through. A dark void to my left. Stairs, I think, twisting toward them.

Just as a hand snaps around my ankle.

A woman's voice sings out. 'Molly! It's been so long.'

Stacey Summers has been telling the truth all along. Outside our locked rooms, things are much, much worse.

'Tell us about Natalie Draga,' D.D. said at last. 'She was the first victim, and the one Devon kept the most photos of. You were her friend.' She turned to Larissa. 'What should we know about her?'

'I don't know. She was pretty. But kind of dark, really. Her sense of humor, it could be cutting. Honestly, I thought that was one of the things Devon liked about her. She was one of those women who even when you had her, you didn't know where you stood. She'd say something awful to him one minute, then throw her arms around him the next.'

'She talk about her personal life? Time in Florida?'

'No.'

'Mother, father, brothers, sisters, family?'

'Never.'

'I have her file,' Ethier spoke up. 'But to be honest, there's not much in here either.'

D.D. reached across the desk for it, discovering inside the required government paperwork, a sheet of personal information, and a check dated nearly nine months ago, confirming that Natalie Draga had left her job one day, never to return.

As the manager had warned, the sheet of personal info was scant in its contents. The top of the page contained Natalie's full name, in looping script. After that: emergency contact, which was blank; then a phone number, which, according to Ethier, was disconnected; followed by a physical address that took D.D. only a moment to place as the official location of the Massachusetts State House in downtown Boston. She glanced up at Ethier, who shrugged.

'We're only required to ask for an employee's information, not to verify it. Around here, lots of people are new to the city or just passing through. As long as they show up on time and work hard, it's good enough for me.'

D.D. went back to the file, the top of the form where Natalie had scrawled her full name. Natalie Molly Draga. Middle name Molly. Which rang a bell. She'd recently heard the name Molly. Who'd she been talking to . . . ?

It came to her. And when it did, D.D.'s gaze went straight to Keynes.

'Molly. That's the name Jacob Ness gave to Flora,' D.D. stated.

'After Jacob served time for raping a fourteen-year-old girl, Mahlia – Molly to her friends.' Keynes took the file from her. 'She could've had a child. Certainly, she'd have good reason not to include Jacob's name on the birth certificate.'

D.D. got out her phone; she dialed Phil first, who was her expert on database searches. Keynes provided Mahlia's full name. Phil did the honors of searching hospital databases in Florida.

He came back in a matter of minutes. 'Mahlia Dragone. Gave birth to a daughter, same year as the sexual assault. Oh, and get this. A year later, I have a record of Mahlia legally changing her last name to Draga. Her mom did as well. How much you wanna bet the whole family was looking for a fresh start?'

After Mahlia gave birth to Jacob Ness's child. Who at this stage of her life would now be an older, manipulative female. Her father's daughter. Recently moved to Boston to do some hunting on her own.

D.D. turned to Larissa.

'Tell us. Right now. Where does Natalie live?'

'I don't know. I never went—'

'She had to have mentioned something. Come on. Think. Where did Natalie go at the end of your "wanderings"?'

'The T station. Wait! I can tell you the line. Oh, oh, oh, I know which subway line she took!'

46

I don't think. I move. I hear her voice, Lindy's voice, for the first time in years, and it triggers an immediate wave of horror, rage, guilt, terror. I don't have to think about it. I kick hard, connecting with the side of her head.

Her hand loosens around my ankle.

I flee.

No thought. Blind panic. I thunder down the stairs, heart racing, pulse pounding. In the back of my mind, an internal voice is yelling at me. Stop. Take a stand. Fight. This is the moment I've dreamed about. Even imagined during every single self-defense or target-shooting class.

Finally coming face-to-face with Lindy again. Except this time, I'd get it right. No more dropping the kitchen knife. No more being pinned to the floor while she sat on my chest and outlined what she was going to do with me.

No, in my wildest fantasies, I slayed the beast. I did what I should've done years ago.

A woman with promises left to keep.

Except the truth is, five years of training later, I still haven't headed to Florida in search of Lindy. Because five years later, she still terrifies me.

She's laughing. The sound drifts down the stairs behind me as I round the first landing and keep on trucking. Beneath my hand, the railing is wooden and wobbly, clearly in need of repair. Old home – I was right about that.

I have to find the door. Make it to ground level, locate the front door, and flee into the night.

Leaving Stacey Summers behind with Jacob's beloved daughter and favorite partner in crime.

I hit the bottom. No more stairs. Just a dark enclosed space. With no lights, it's hard to get my bearings. I think I'm in a small foyer, not unlike the one in my apartment building. As my eyes adjust further, I can make out an open doorway to my right, where I can peer through to the lighter shadows of other rooms. Then I identify another opening to my left, leading to yet another corridor. This confuses me. I've been picturing a traditional triple-decker layout in my head. In that case, the stairs should be at one end of the building, not in the middle. Meaning this probably isn't a triple-decker. Meaning I have no idea where I am after all or where the front door might be.

Play the odds. Doors have a tendency to lead directly to the stairs, hence straight across from me should be an egress. At least that's the best place to start.

I approach with my arms outstretched, feeling for a doorknob. Behind me, I hear groaning wood as Lindy begins her descent.

Come on, come on, come on. There must a door. Any kind of exit. Come on!

I feel wood panels, then to my left the thin outline of a hinge. My hands fly to the right, and lo and behold. Knob. I have located the doorknob. I twist, yank, and . . .

Nothing. The door doesn't open. Doesn't budge.

It's locked.

My fingers fly around the knob, searching for latches to twist, bolts to undo. I find one, then two.

A second twist, a second yank.

The door moves, rattles in the frame. But it doesn't open. Something is still connected, a bolt, a chain, something I haven't found yet.

I remember the doors of the upstairs rooms, then stretch up, up, up. And sure enough. I find it. Them. Two more bolts latched tight at the top of the door frame.

I whimper. I can't help myself.

The stairs, creaking right behind me.

I'm running out of time.

And then . . .

She's here.

'I got a T line,' D.D. announced to Neil over the phone. Ethier and Larissa had vacated the office, given D.D. and Keynes space to work. She rattled off the information to Neil, heard the scratching sound of him taking notes. 'Combine that with our other requirements, plus frequent destinations on Goulding's GPS, and give me the address.'

'It doesn't help,' Neil said.

'What do you mean, it doesn't help?'

'I mean, nothing makes sense!' Her favorite redheaded detective sounded frustrated. 'I've been over and over the vehicle's list of frequent destinations. None of them match our location profile, with or without subway lines included.'

'But that doesn't make any sense,' D.D. said.

'Told you so!'

'He had to have used his vehicle, right?' She paused, backing up and revisiting their original logic. Across from her, Keynes nodded encouragingly. 'The night Goulding abducted Flora, he knocked her out, loaded her in his vehicle, drove her home. Right?'

'He knocked her out,' Neil supplied. 'Meaning she didn't know how he transported her home; she was unconscious.'

'But you can see that trip in his car, right? It would be his last drive.'

'Hang on. Okay, Friday night, car journeyed from downtown Boston to home address.'

'His abduction of Flora. Where, of course, he used his personal vehicle for transport. It's not like you can take an unconscious girl on the T, or dump her into a taxi. So he's gotta be using his vehicle for at least the initial kidnapping.'

'Okay,' Neil agreed.

'Parking garages,' Keynes mouthed across from her.

D.D. nodded, then repeated the words into the phone. 'If Devon's driving someplace all the time, he'd need to park. What about parking garage passes, memberships, something like that?'

A pause. She could hear Neil talking to someone, most likely Carol, on the other end of the phone.

'No monthly payments to a parking garage,' Neil reported shortly.

'Really? But that doesn't—'

'Make any sense?'

Both she and Neil sighed heavily. They were close. D.D. could feel it. Just one last connection, deduction, and then . . . Flora and Stacey Summers at the mercy of Jacob Ness's daughter. D.D. shuddered just thinking about it.

'Oh. Oooh,' Neil said suddenly.

'What?'

'Carol has a point. Maybe it's not separate.'

'What do you mean?'

'The location, maybe it's not unique. For example, we

wouldn't notice him driving to work, right? Because that's his job, of course he's going there.'

'He's not holding four women in a nightclub,' D.D. said, though her gaze drifted up to the black-painted ceiling.

She shook her head. She was being ridiculous. They'd been here during the day, when the nightclub had shed its blue lights and was a tired but definitely very busy shell. Given the number of people passing through at any time, cleaning up, restocking, prepping, no way three kidnapped girls would go unnoticed.

'So not his job,' Neil was saying, 'but another logical destination no one would think to question.'

D.D. got it: 'Gym. He's always working out. And most of those huge twenty-four-hour fitness clubs—'

'Are located in South Boston, near the water,' Neil filled in. 'Where in the name of gentrification half of the area is being demolished and the other half rebuilt. I got an address for the gym. Even better, Carol says it's right by some of the boarded-up tenement houses which are still waiting to be torn down.'

He rattled off the gym's location.

'Thank you, Neil.' Then, not even grudgingly, 'And you too, Carol.'

D.D. hung up the phone; then she and Keynes were on the move.

47

'I've been looking for you,' Lindy singsongs as she pads across the landing, through the right-hand doorway, deeper into the building after me.

I flee first. Forcing myself away from a locked door into the rest of the building. I think I'm in a living room. I can just make out the shape of a sofa, table, chairs. Maybe a ground-floor apartment, long and narrow. I try to create some kind of blueprint in my mind to guide me as I creep deeper into the gloom. The windows here must be boarded up as well. It's the only way to explain the total darkness.

I make it through a second doorway into another shadowed hall. I halt on the other side, my back pressed against the wall. I still have my shard of glass from the broken window. I clutch it to my chest and try to get my breathing under control before the sound of my own panic gives me away.

Time to focus. Time to pull it together. I'm not Jacob's terrified little mouse anymore.

I'm a woman with promises left to keep.

'I read all about your last day with my dad,' Lindy is saying now. Her voice comes from behind me, in the first room, I think, near the sofa. 'Bullet through the head. Did he beg for you to do it? I knew if they caught him, he was never going back.'

I don't say anything. Deep breath in, deep breath out.

I'm not tired. I'm not hungry. I'm not cold.

I am okay.

'I worried in the beginning. Thought the police might come looking for me. So I disappeared for a bit. Spent some time in Texas, Alabama, California. Saw more of the country. I figured Jacob would approve.'

Her voice is closer.

Deep breath in. Deep breath out. I can do this.

'But you didn't tell them about me, did you, Flora? You kept our time together to yourself. Our special little secret.'

I squeeze my eyes shut, bite my lower lip to silence the whimper. She's right. I never told. Not that piece of the puzzle. The shame? The horror? I don't know. But all survivors have their secrets. Things we can't say out loud because that makes what happened too real, not just to other people but especially to ourselves.

Samuel suspected something. He dangled bait during our initial sessions. But I never gave in.

No one wants to be a monster.

And certainly, no one wants to talk about it later.

'I thought I would let you go,' Lindy continues now. She's drifted to the left. Not moving forward, but now into the kitchen area, prowling around the table and chairs.

'But I just couldn't. The fact you were still alive and doing well, while Jacob . . . I don't expect you to understand, but I know that you, of all people, realize just how special Jacob's and my relationship was. No one ever knew me the way he did. And no one ever accepted him the way I did. He was my father, and I was his Lindy, a special nickname he made up just for me, first time he saw me. Natalie belonged to my mother. But Lindy . . . I was his. And you, little bitch, had no right to take him from me.'

Her voice so close it's nearly in my ear. She's right behind me. Other side of the wall, I realize. No more breathing. I suck in all the air, hold it in my lungs, will myself not to make a sound.

'Last year, I decided it was time to get serious; I came looking for you. Paid a visit to your mother's farm. She was easy enough to track down using the Internet. Did she ever tell you that, mention an old friend who stopped by? She's a tight one. No matter what I tried, she wouldn't answer any questions about you. Best I could get is that you lived in Boston. So I decided to move here too. Why not? Nice change of a pace for a southern girl like me. I got a job, prepared to settle in while I continued to look for you, and then . . .

'I met him. Devon. A man who didn't even know what kind of man he was. But I knew. I recognized him immediately. And then, it was easy enough to bring him along. I set up the house, I let him make me its first occupant. Then I sent him in search of more playmates. Because a girl like me has certain appetites. As you know better than anyone.'

I shake uncontrollably. I hate the response. Primal. Visceral. But the more she talks, the more it all comes back. Those terrible nights. The noises, the taste of bile.

I'm not okay, I'm not okay, I'm not okay.

I'm Molly again, and I'm not going to make it.

'You killed him too. Didn't you? I went to Devon's house Saturday morning. He never stopped by after work, never called. I knew he was getting restless. I had told him he had to lie low after getting caught on video. Sloppy! We had to rein things in, keep it tight. But that's the problem with trained dogs – sometimes they fight the leash. So I went to

Devon's house to check up on him, and what did I discover? All those police cars, the crime scene tape. You. I saw you sitting in the back of the patrol car, garbage smeared all over your face. And just like that, I knew what you'd cost me. Again.

'Did you really think I'd just let you go? Walk away a second time? That I wouldn't follow you back to your place? That I wouldn't hang out on the fire escape, waiting until your landlords had stepped out to come back down, pick the lock to their apartment, and steal the master keys? Then, when all was quiet, I unlocked the door and walked straight into your apartment. A little chloroform cocktail to disorient, a quick shot of sedative to knock you out completely, and that was that. I replaced the keys in your landlord's apartment, then hustled you down to my own personal taxi. I drive it at nights. The perfect way to earn extra cash while cruising the streets for fresh opportunities.

'No one notices a taxi driver. No one even questions one loading a stumbling, disoriented woman into the back of the cab. Poor thing is drunk; good thing a taxi is taking her home.

'Now, everything is exactly as Daddy would've wanted it to be. You and me together again. Except this time, I'm the one with the gun, and you're the one who will never leave.

'You're mine. You'll always be mine,' Lindy whispers, and just like that, she's in the doorway, right beside me. I don't need light to know there's a smile on her face.

No more thinking. No planning. No preparation.

She might have found me first, but that doesn't mean I didn't know this day was coming.

I slice the piece of jagged glass across her face.

She screams.

I turn and bolt down the hall.

D.D. drove. In terms of distance, it wasn't far from the nightclub to South Boston. Through narrow winding streets and way too many red lights, she careened, fishtailed, and flashed her lights. Keynes gripped the oh-shit handle above the door but didn't say a word.

She found her way to the tenement housing from memory. Once upon a time, in the days of Whitey Bulger, this section of Boston had belonged to the Irish. It had been a hub of gangland activity, drugs, and poverty. In the 1990s, however, rent control had ended, forcing many low-income families from the area while the demand for waterfront real estate led to a nearly overnight gentrification. But before there could be progress, first there had to be demo. Which had been long and ongoing, with at least one stretch of boarded-up former tenement houses shuttered away behind a chain-link fence, still awaiting its fate.

She came to the fencing first. Drove around looking for a gate, discovered two other patrol cars already parked in front. An officer looked up as she pulled in. He held up a chain in front of her headlights. Enough for her to see the padlock was missing.

Meaning they weren't the first people to be accessing the property.

D.D. killed her lights; then she and Keynes climbed out of the car, approached the other officers. She could hear sirens in the distance, other units responding to the call. She frowned.

Currently, Natalie Draga was holed up with at least two kidnapping victims. Broadcast the police's approach and she might spook, leading to a hostage situation or worse.

This would have to be a stealth operation all the way. Like the SWAT team raid against Jacob Ness, who hadn't had a clue until the first tear gas canister shattered his motel window.

D.D. got on the radio, made the call. Thirty seconds later, the distant sirens cut off abruptly, and only the sound of the approaching engines remained. Better.

She gathered the four officers. One of them reported having found an abandoned taxi just up the street. Otherwise, all appeared quiet and they had yet to see anyone enter the property.

D.D. nodded. The abandoned housing project was large. Six, seven massive brick buildings, all featuring boarded-up windows and crumbling facades. God knew about structural integrity, let alone what else they'd find inside. Squatters, drug addicts, rodents of all sizes. This would take finesse.

'We'll work in teams of two. Start at the perimeter, work your way to the center. Classic grid search. Look for any trace of light coming from the edges of a window, footprints in the dust, recently disturbed entrances, picked locks, that sort of thing. Don't approach on your own. Just recon. We have at least two victims trapped somewhere inside, and a suspect with nothing to lose. We need to control the situation first, not escalate.'

Officers nodded, snapped on flashlights, and prepared to enter.

D.D. walked back with Keynes to her vehicle. She kept her voice low. 'Want to wait in the car?'

'No.'

'Got a vest?'

'I'm hoping you have a spare.'

She paused. 'You have any fieldwork training?' she asked.

'Yes.'

'Because, um . . .' She stumbled over the words, couldn't help herself. 'I'm on restricted duty. I don't have a sidearm. I can shoot, though. I mean, I've been practicing. Just the standard two-handed stance is a little tricky with my shoulder right now. But straight on. I can do it. I can.'

He seemed to understand what she saying. 'I have a backup piece. Thirty-eight.'

'Trade you for my shotgun?'

'Makes sense.'

She popped open the trunk of her vehicle, where she had supplies for tactical situations, including an extra vest and a gun locker.

'So,' he said conversationally, as they geared up, 'a wounded detective and a federal PhD.'

'Best cavalry ever,' she assured him.

'We'd better get it right because the paperwork alone will make us both wish we were dead.'

D.D. smiled, tried to pretend her hands weren't shaking. What had Phil said, she needed to rely more on her team? Well, she'd communicated. This wasn't her entering alone. She had officers in front, a feebie at her side, and backup on its way.

She was learning, adapting.

Still, taking Keynes's .38, a gun that used to feel so natural in her grasp . . .

She pictured Jack. She pictured Alex. She promised herself she'd return home to them soon enough.

Then, she followed Keynes into the abandoned housing complex.

48

The first bullet wings over my shoulder. I duck reflexively, veering right as drywall explodes to my left. A second shot, third, fourth.

She's laughing as she pulls the trigger. Maybe not even aiming, but enjoying the show as I dart right, then left, then right, flinching and ducking. I resist the urge to look over my shoulder, to see how close I am to impending death. Instead, I keep on trucking, bare feet pounding down the debris-littered corridor.

In self-defense class, a teacher had advised us to flee if ever confronted by someone with a gun. Apparently it's astonishingly difficult to hit a moving target. At least, your odds of survival are higher running from a shooting gunman than, say, getting into a car with him and driving to a remote location where he can do exactly what he wants.

So I sprint. Chest heaving. Elbows tucked tight, head ducked low, trying to make myself a smaller target. My foot hits something sharp, then something stabbing. There's no time to pause, pick out slivers of wood or, worse, pieces of glass. I keep on running, transitioning from a relatively domesticated section of the building to some kind of construction zone, the smell of dust and neglect heavier in the air. The hall is too dark for me to see where I'm going or adjust my footsteps to avoid the sharpest objects.

More shots fired.

I run for my life.

Doorway to the right. I careen through it without a second thought, intent on getting out of the line of fire. Only afterward does it occur to me it might be a bedroom or, worse, a bathroom. A room with no exit where I'd be trapped.

But in this case, it appears to be yet another common room. I've given up on my theory of being trapped in a traditional Boston triple-decker. The structure is too vast. Too many hallways, too many rooms. Not a warehouse or commercial building because the rooms are small. Maybe a group home? Abandoned, undergoing renovations, something.

I should stop, get my bearings, but I can't think anymore. I sprint down dark hallways, leap through dark spaces, like a deer through the woods.

I might be crying, which is stupid. Last thing I need to do right now is make any undue noise.

I crash through another doorway, step on something sharp, and feel it slice deeply into the ball of my foot. I can't help myself. I draw up short, hopping on one leg, biting my lower lip against the scream.

Belatedly, I flatten myself against the wall. Will myself to stand still.

Breathe. Think. Breathe.

I can't keep running pell-mell through a maze of sharp objects and unknown spaces, waiting to become trapped, shot, killed. I need to come up with a strategy. Something worthy of taking on a homicidal maniac armed with a gun.

A woman who's been waiting five years to destroy me.

Though, to be fair, I've been waiting five years to kill her too.

My breathing is ragged. I force myself to inhale deeply, try to smooth out my racing pulse so I can listen for the sound of approaching footsteps.

Then, I concentrate on thinking.

Lindy. She's here. In Boston. She tracked me down. Visited my mother's farm. Found me at Devon Goulding's house. Then followed me back to my highly secure apartment, where she broke in using my landlord's keys. Neat trick, that. It had never occurred to me that for all my extra bolts, my landlords would remain the weak link. But yes. Their own approach to locking up is haphazard at this stage of their lives. And once she had their keys . . .

Lindy. In my apartment. Lindy bringing me back here to finish what Jacob had started.

I want her dead. The flatness of the thought, the direct, compelling need, grounds me, further calms my breathing.

I've hated her since the first time I saw Jacob watching her. Since she threw her arms around him in welcome. Since they sat on the sofa, heads nearly touching.

Then, her forcing me to go out, approach that woman in the bar.

I don't think about that night, or any of the others that followed. I don't talk about her, Jacob, what they made me do. No, I save those memories for my nightmares, where all these years later, I still wake up screaming.

Jacob made me roll the bodies from his rig to the marshy grass alongside the road. Then he made me sit and watch till the gators discovered the unexpected treats.

He never said a word. Just watched me with eyes that

told me someday this would be my fate. Except Lindy would be the one to roll my body out the door, and she'd be clapping gleefully as the local wildlife came to feed.

Lindy. Here in Boston.

Lindy. Somewhere in the dark behind me.

When I took the first self-defense class, I'm sure my mother assumed it was the Jacobs of the world I was practicing taking down. I never corrected her. Never told her that every time I blocked and kicked, it was a slightly older, astonishingly beautiful opponent I pictured in my head. That when I handled my first firearm, it was her face I imagined as the target.

I've been practicing killing Lindy for five years now. Each time I set out on a mission, I even told myself that if I could pull this off, maybe it would mean I was ready for Florida. Except, of course, I never quite accepted that answer. There was always one more thing for me to attend to up here, then, of course, Stacey Summers. I couldn't just leave Stacey Summers.

Now, here I am. I don't have to find Lindy after all. Lindy has found me.

And I'm a shaking, quivering mass all over again. She has a gun. I have a jagged piece of window glass. She is . . . Lindy. And I'm . . . not Molly, I have to remind myself. Not Molly, not Molly, not Molly.

Except, of course, I feel that helpless all over again.

I need a plan. Kill Lindy, slay the beast, and maybe, maybe, I can come home again.

And bring Stacey Summers with me.

I don't think of the motel room anymore. I don't think of that final day, the weight of Jacob's gun in my hand, the echo of my promise in his ear, or the sticky feel of his brains in my hair.

I picture my mom. The way she looked standing in my kitchen the other morning. Proud and resigned, caring and reserved. The mother who still loves me, even knowing her daughter has never truly returned.

I want to go home now. I want to throw my arms around my mother and her ridiculous flannel shirts. I want to hug her, and even if it doesn't feel like how it felt before, I want to appreciate how it feels now.

I don't want to survive anymore.

I want to live.

There, I hear it. Footsteps, slow and shuffling down the hall behind me. Lindy is approaching. No doubt with the gun held before her, finger on the trigger.

Resources? I have a sharp piece of glass, already wet with her blood. I have elbows and knees and an excellent kick. Glancing around the shadowed space, I don't see any sign of furniture but dark piles of random garbage. Which could prove interesting. After all, trash has saved me before. I pull myself up, prepare to sort through the piles.

I have it together now.

I'm not tired, I'm not hungry, nor cold, nor in pain.

I'm okay.

And I'm about to do what I do best: whatever it takes to survive.

D.D. pulled up short, her hand on Keynes's arm as she turned toward the sound.

'There,' she whispered as the sharp crack sounded again. 'Gunfire.'

'Second building to the right,' Keynes murmured.

She illuminated it with her flashlight, a hulking structure of faded brick and boarded-up windows. She didn't see any light peering around the plywood eyes, but then, just as she was about to turn to the next building, three more shots in rapid succession.

'Definitely that building,' she agreed.

She adjusted her grip on the .38.

They made their approach.

49

Did you ever hear the martial arts master's brag: I know ten ways to kill someone with a drinking straw, twelve if you include the paper wrapper?

According to my instructor, this is more hyperbole than fact. What's the point of being the master of anything if you can't sound very, very scary?

A plastic straw, however, can be a useful weapon. I found one in the pile of garbage closest to me. I bent it in half, then tucked it between the index and middle finger of my left hand. Folded, the straw is sharp enough and rigid enough to make a decent jabbing weapon. Catch an opponent in the eye or, better yet, slam into the hyoid bone at the front of the throat, and you can inflict some damage.

How much, I'm about to find out. I can hear Lindy creeping down the end of the corridor. So close, I can make out the sound of her breathing.

I picture her smiling, happy to be on the hunt once more.

I never understood the full dynamics of her and Jacob's relationship. He loved her. I could tell that just by watching. And Lindy?

She was excited to see him. But love? I don't know. I think of Lindy as a sleek, dark panther stalking the night, aroused by the scent of blood. Does such a creature truly love?

I think she loved how special Jacob made her feel. How powerful and strong. When he appeared, hunting was twice the fun.

I guess she thought the same of the bartender with the amazing pecs. Devon Goulding. The guy I watched burn to death in front of my eyes.

The memory of which makes me feel powerful and strong.

No one wants to be a monster.

And yet here we are.

I expect Lindy to lead with her weapon. The gun will appear first, followed by her arm. And in that unprotected moment, I will lash out with the glass, aiming for her wrist, the back of her hand. One deep slash, she'll reflexively drop her firearm, and then we'll be on a level playing field.

Of course, she's too smart for that.

When she finally appears beside me in the doorway, she has her elbows glued tight to her ribs, gun tucked to her chest. A human wall, presenting only the side of her shoulder for attack. Even if I got her with my glass dagger, it would be a glancing blow, nothing serious.

I hold my breath, will her to take one more step into the room. Then, I'll kick out with my left foot, go for the side of her knee.

I am not tired, not hungry, not cold, not in pain.

I am in the zone.

Where I can kill another human being and feel just fine about it.

I think, in that moment, it would be best if my mother never touched me again. Because the daughter she misses is a happy girl who loves foxes. And I am someone else.

I am something else.

Lindy steps into the room.

I kick just as she twists toward me, her teeth flashing white in the dark. She's already bringing the gun forward, clearly having known exactly where I was standing, exactly what I was planning.

What neither of us can predict, however, is that my missed kick throws me off balance, sending me careening into her, collapsing onto her form.

We crash to the floor and I have a weird sense of déjà vu.

We are in her dingy little house. I have the kitchen knife.

Gun, gun. She has the gun, trapped between us. Pointed at her, pointed at me. I'm not sure either of us know. I can't afford to roll away, which would give her the room to aim. But tangled up in each other, I can't effectively jab or stab. We wrestle instead, her determined not to drop the gun, me determined not to lose my broken glass or plastic straw.

I smell blood. Hers from her slashed cheek. Mine from my lacerated feet.

Then: pain, sharp and piercing. Her teeth biting into my ear, grinding, pulling, tugging. In response, I twist my right hand, rake the shard of glass down her side, then twist it cruelly.

Neither of us gasp or scream or cry out. We are intent. This is serious business.

But just for a second, I think I hear something in the distance.

She bites me again. Chomps, chews, does her best Mike Tyson. I can't afford to care about her teeth. The gun is the problem. I need to get the gun away from her.

Rolling across the dusty floor. Trying to bring my left hand up. I still have the bent straw wedged between my fingers. Now, I punch it best that I can into her throat. We're too close, inside each other's kill zones. Once again, I dig in with my makeshift weapon. Even if I can't take a backswing for effective strike force, I can poke, press, scratch, and claw. She gurgles as the straw jabs deep into her windpipe, interfering with her ability to draw air. I shove harder, determined to capitalize on the advantage.

She wedges both hands between us, forcefully shoves me away. I fall to the side. Realize immediately I gotta move, move, move. The slightest twist on her part, a single pull of the trigger . . .

I thrust with my right hand, scoring the shard of glass down her arm, the back of her hand.

Us on the floor, fighting for the kitchen blade . . .

She gasps, flinches. I slash again and again, my fingers growing slippery with blood.

And she laughs. Breathlessly. Excitedly. Because this is what she likes. This is what she wants. There's no pain for her, only pleasure.

I am merely Flora 2.0.

She is . . . She is . . .

Beyond Jacob. Beyond any of us. The monster other monsters fear.

She will get the kitchen knife. She will drive it deep into my chest, but only after having some fun first. Then my body will be fed to the gators. Never to be recovered. While Jacob goes out, snatches another girl, and starts the whole process all over again.

Stacey Summers, collapsed upstairs in desperate need of medical attention.

My mother, no doubt standing in my kitchen right now, baking, baking, baking, while she once again awaits word of her daughter.

I don't want to die in this house any more than I wanted to die in a coffin-shaped box. I accept that I'm not a good person, or a happy person. I realize I can't find peace walking through the woods of my childhood. I understand that I no longer know how to return my mother's hug.

But somewhere deep inside, I still believe that one day I might be that person again. That just because I've turned into a monster doesn't mean that one day I won't change back again, and be the girl my mother and brother both miss.

Someday, I might find myself again.

Noises. In the distance. The groaning wrench of plywood, hard pounding footsteps. Beside me, Lindy stills, listening as well. Her gunshots have drawn notice. Others are coming. Most likely the police, SWAT officers with tear gas. If I can just buy time, they will save me again.

Except . . .

Lindy twists back at me. I stare at her.

And we both know what has to happen next.

Because this isn't about outsiders. This is, has to be, about her and me.

My right hand slashes down with the shard of glass.

Her arms pop up, absorbing the strike just long enough to level the gun.

I follow with my left fist, plastic straw still tight beneath my fingers as I punch it hard into the side of her neck.

Her wheezing gasp. A suspended moment of time.

'I told him I'd kill you,' I whisper. 'That last day. Tears and snot smeared all over his face. I told him I'd kill you next.'

She opens her mouth. I think she's going to laugh again.

Instead, she pulls the trigger.

I hear the sound as if from far, far away. I feel the impact, an explosion of pain.

I am rocked back. I fall back.

Just as twin beams of light come dashing into the room. 'Police! Drop your weapon!'

The words are hard to hear through the ringing in my ears, but I think I recognize the voice. The female detective from Saturday morning, the one who doesn't like me.

I try to call out a warning. That Lindy's armed and more than capable of killing again.

But it turns out the detective doesn't need any advice. Lindy turns toward the beams of light. She wheezes, probably the closest she can come to a laugh. Then she points her gun just in time for the cop to open fire.

I watch Lindy collapse on the floor beside me. I think there should be gators. They should come and drag her body away, never to be recovered.

Then Samuel is there, peering down at me with concern. 'Hang on, Flora. Help is coming. Hang on.'

I whisper back: 'Stacey Summers. Upstairs. Help her.'

Then the gators do come. Except it's me they carry away.

50

Keynes sat on the floor in his ridiculously expensive jeans, holding Flora's hand while D.D. called for EMTs, then for additional officers to search the complex.

It took them a good fifteen minutes to work their way through the vast space. Devon Goulding, Natalie Draga had created quite the nest in the middle of the abandoned building. D.D. discovered a kitchen where the plumbing had been jury-rigged with an illegally tapped water pipe and stocked with various food supplies and alcohol bottles, obviously pilfered from the Tonic nightclub. Same with a downstairs bathroom, that, yes, contained tubes and tubes of glittery hair gel.

The team spread out, searching room by room, floor by floor, until at last, an officer discovered Stacey Summers collapsed in an upstairs corridor, clearly in critical condition. More calls for medical assistance; then they had both Stacey and Flora whisked away to local hospitals.

Keynes went off, talking on his cell phone to Flora's mother, while D.D. finally made the middle-of-the-night phone call the Summers family had been waiting three months for.

Then, she paced.

Keynes hadn't been lying. The paperwork for this kind

of incident would be something else. D.D. was required to remain on scene to answer preliminary questions from independent investigators regarding her use of deadly force. As a restricted duty detective, not even cleared to carry a firearm, she would face further scrutiny, perhaps even disciplinary action.

Maybe Phil would yell at her again. For behaving recklessly. For not trusting her team. For once more walking into a darkened building, whether it was a good idea or not.

She should feel anxious. Stressed. Contrite?

But she didn't.

She'd called for backup. She'd organized a team of officers to assist. She had approached the situation with the goal of containment, not confrontation, as befitted a supervisor. Then, when the situation had escalated to the point of immediate action . . .

She'd performed as she'd been trained. Regardless of her injured left shoulder and physical limitations, she'd eliminated the clearly visible threat and saved a victim's life.

She felt . . . strong. Capable. Self-sufficient.

She felt, for the first time in months, like herself again.

She called home. It was 3:00 A.M., but Alex was familiar with middle-of-the-night conversations. Truth was, she needed to hear his voice. After a night like this, she wanted to feel at least that close to him.

'I'm okay,' she started the call.

'Good. Where are you?'

'I killed her. Jacob's daughter, Natalie. I shot and killed her in the line of duty.'

A pause. 'I'm sorry.'

'Me too. She pointed her gun right at me, I had no choice.'

'You had a weapon?' Alex had always been a smart one.

'I borrowed one, to enter the property. We heard shots fired. We went in prepared.'

He didn't say anything, because going in prepared wasn't the same as going in cleared for duty and they both knew it.

'I was scared,' she whispered. 'I've never been scared before. It's always been just part of the job. But this time . . . All I could think about was my stupid shoulder. Could I aim fast enough, would I be strong enough . . . I did what I had to do, but I was scared.'

'Cal Horgan—'

'Is going to ream me a new one.'

'With good reason?'

'I don't want to be scared. And sitting at a desk, that feels like hiding to me. Being on restricted duty, that's being frightened. I want to be cleared. I want to be the detective I used to be.'

'Honey, your injury—'

'I did what I had to do. A suspect leveled a firearm at me in a life-and-death situation and I performed under pressure. I won't be scared again, Alex. And I won't stay chained to a desk.'

'So, you're not calling home to tell me I can get out the bubble wrap, roll you up, and keep you safe with me forever?'

'I'm going to face disciplinary actions.'

'Probably.'

'I'm going to need your support.'

'You have it.'

'Then . . . I want to pass my physical. I want to be cleared for full duty.'

'Is it okay if I'm scared? Because this call right now, my wife just faced an armed gunman, not my favorite middle-of-the-night conversation.'

'I want to be the detective I used to be.'

'D.D., I fell in love with the detective you used to be. I married the detective you used to be. You don't have to change for me, or for Jack. We know the detective you used to be.'

'Okay.'

'Are you crying?'

'Detectives don't cry.'

'But a restricted duty supervisor . . .'

'Maybe.'

'Thank you for still being alive.'

'Thank you for having my back.'

'Did you find the missing girls?'

'Both Stacey Summers and Flora Dane.'

'That's great! Are they all right?'

D.D. told him the truth: 'We don't know yet.'

I wake up to bright lights. I'm staring at white ceiling panels high overhead, a scratchy sheet tucked tight around my chest, metal bed rail clearly visible. I turn my head just enough to see Samuel sitting slumped in the chair, head in his hands. No suit this time, but a jet-black dress shirt and dark jeans that would be more appropriate for a nightclub than a hospital room.

My mom is on a plane, I find myself thinking, then have to catch myself.

I'm not in Georgia. I'm in Boston. And I haven't just escaped from Jacob; I've escaped from Jacob's daughter. For a moment . . . there are so many thoughts in my head. So many memories, emotions. I'm not sure where the past ends and the present begins. I'm not sure who I was, and who I will ever be again.

I'm in limbo.

It's not the worst feeling in the world. All the promise of a fresh start without the pain of actually attempting it.

My shoulder aches. My head is fuzzy. My mouth is dry.

Lindy with her gun. Me with my broken glass and plastic straw. She pulled the trigger. So did the detective. And we all fell down.

She's dead. I don't have to ask to know. Lindy must be dead. It's the only way to explain me being alive.

I got out. I'm free.

And just the thought makes me start to laugh, though it's not a happy sound coming from my throat.

Samuel appears immediately at my side. Offers me water, fusses with the edge of the blanket. I don't see my mom yet, but she must be in the hospital somewhere. Even if she hates me, is heartbroken, furious, devastated, she's not the type to back down from a fight. I guess I get that from her.

I'm laughing again. Or crying. Because here I am, except who am I? A killer? A woman only comfortable in the dark?

A woman with no promises left to keep. Except who is that exactly?

I wish I could scrub my brain. I wish I could bleach my eyes. I wish I could take my entire body and empty it out. No more memories of coffin-shaped boxes, or Jacob's tobacco-stained teeth, or exactly how it smells when human flesh bursts into flame.

I would give it all up. Remember nothing. Know nothing.

I would be simply a girl running through the woods of Maine, sneaking pieces of cheese to the foxes.

Samuel is holding my left hand, as my right shoulder is heavily bandaged.

'You're a survivor,' he's saying. 'You're strong. You can do this. You are a survivor.'

'Stacey Summers?' I hear myself whisper.

'Thanks to you, we found her and got her to the hospital in time. You did it, Flora. You did it.'

I find myself smiling, but again, not the happiest look. Because I know better than anyone that this moment, right now, is the only easy one. This one second, where Stacey gets to wake up, finally free, with her parents by her side. And they cry, and she cries, and everyone is so relieved. Their wildest dream has just come true.

And the other moments? Tomorrow, the next day, the one after that?

She will need help, I think.

And then . . .

She will have it. From me, from Samuel, from my mother. We all started this journey together, each in our own way. I would finish it. If Stacey would let me, I would be there for her. I've fought enough alone in the dark. It might be nice to try working together with someone to find the light.

The next question I ask Samuel with my eyes because I can't say the words out loud.

'She died at the scene,' he offers simply. 'It appears she and Devon Goulding kidnapped at least three girls together. Kristy Kilker died. But you, Stacey Summers. You two made it.'

'I didn't know Lindy was even in town,' I murmured. 'I went to Tonic Friday night because Stacey's friends said they went there on occasion. Lindy . . . Jacob's daughter. I never knew she was in Boston. Never even suspected.'

'You met her when you were with Jacob.'

I understand the question he's really asking. Why didn't I ever talk about her, alert authorities? I tell him the truth: 'No one wants to be a monster.'

'You're not a monster, Flora. You're a survivor.'

'It's not enough. You think it will be. But it's not.'

'You saved a girl's life.'

'I killed a man.' And that quickly, I can feel the darkness rushing in again. 'I watched him burn and didn't even care. I stood alone in the void. I'm always alone in the void!'

'Then make a different choice, Flora. No one said living is easy. You're still going to have to get up each morning. And you're going to have to make decisions. It's been five years, and here we are again. Do you really want to keep making the same choices?'

I don't have an answer. He's told me similar things before. First, you survive. Next, you have to stop feeling like a victim.

It all sounds so simple. And yet, and yet . . .

My mom appears, hovering uncertainly in the doorway, trapped in her own version of déjà vu.

Her sad, determined face. Her terribly ugly flannel shirt.

The silver fox charm nestled at the hollow of her throat.

So many things I should tell her. So many apologies I should make. I want it to be as simple as Samuel makes it sound. I want the same happily-ever-after Stacey Summers surely deserves.

I want to tell the truth, and hope that it sets me free. I pull my hand from Samuel. I hold it out to my mother.

'I'm sorry,' I say.

'You don't have to—'

'I blamed you,' I hear myself say. 'I didn't mean to. But you wanted me to come home so badly. I would watch you on the news, begging for my safe return. So I survived for you. Even when it would've been better if I hadn't. Even when I wanted to let go. I survived because I didn't want to let you down.'

She doesn't say anything, but I can tell from her expression that she already knows. She glances at Samuel.

This is something they've discussed. They realized, even if I didn't.

'Jacob had a daughter. They forced me to go with them to bars. They forced me to help pick up women to kill. Three times. Three women dead because of me. I can't change that,' I tell her honestly. 'Even now, with Stacey Summers. It still doesn't balance the scale.'

'It's not your scale to balance. The crimes are on them.'

'I watched him burn, that crime is on me.'

'Flora . . . I don't know what you want from me. I'm your mother and I love you. Even now, even after you're telling me these things. I'm your mother. And I love you.'

'I don't know who I am,' I say.

'No one does. Everyone spends their lives figuring that out, even people who've never been kidnapped.'

'I still miss him. And that's wrong. That's twisted. I hate him for being inside my head.'

'Then welcome him. Thank him for helping make you strong. Thank him for dying so you could go home. A man like that, he has no defense against gratitude, Flora. Welcome him, and he'll leave on his own.'

'That's new age crap.'

'That's the basics of turning away from hate. Sooner or later, you gotta give it up if you're going to live again.'

'Do you hate him?'

'The police thought Jacob would kill you that day, Flora. Their best experts predicted he'd shoot you, then kill himself. I choose to be grateful he didn't.'

I have to think about it. It takes one kind of courage to face down an armed opponent. A different kind of courage to live again.

I say: 'This is Flora. This is all of Flora, finally waking up.'

My mother hugs me. It hurts my bandaged shoulder. It terrifies the rest of me.

But I return her hug. I focus on the feel, the smell, the complete experience. My mother. Her hug. Our embrace. Four hundred and seventy-two days. Five long years.

This is Flora, finally going home, I think, and I squeeze back as hard as I can.

Acknowledgments

This book started with an article I read online about the FBI's Office for Victim Assistance. I'd never heard of a victim specialist, and was immediately captivated by the idea that victims and their families require support above and beyond our traditional concept of happily-ever-afters. As Flora can attest, rescue isn't the end of an ordeal but the beginning of an entirely new one. My thanks to the FBI's Office of Public Affairs for arranging for me to interview two victim specialists and, of course, my gratitude to everyone for sharing their time and expertise. Dr Samuel Keynes's involvement in Rosa's and Flora's lives exceeds the norm, naturally, and I hope you will understand the fictional license. Of course, all mistakes are mine and mine alone.

Next up, thank you to retired BPD detective Wayne Rock for getting D.D. back on the job! I couldn't just leave her sidelined, so I reached out to Wayne. Once he explained the nature of restricted duty, it sounded so torturous for someone with D.D.'s temperament, how could I resist? Thanks, Wayne!

SAC Nidia Gamba assisted me with procedural details for tracking down the evil Jacob Ness. I consider her the real-life Kimberly Quincy, only better. Thank you for taking time out to assist with catching my fictional bad guys, and thank you even more for taking down the real ones.

My favorite local detective, Lieutenant Michael Santuccio, also helped save the day, mostly by answering my frantic text, *Quick I gotta kidnap someone, how would you do it?* While my pharmacist of choice, Margaret Charpentier, came up with the hops-and-viburnum-laced mattress. As Flora mentions, while hops is a herbal sleep aid dating back to medieval times, the science behind its effectiveness remains sketchy. For the purposes of fiction, however, why not?

D.D.'s squad owes their new unit member, Carol Manley, to Carol's son, David Martin, who made a very generous donation to the Conway Area Humane Society in return for his mother's name being included in a novel. I hope you both enjoy, especially the shout-out to Carol's dog, Harley.

Congratulations to Kristy Kilker, who won this year's Kill a Friend, Maim a Buddy sweepstakes, earning herself a grand end. Also, Jocelyne Ethier nabbed the right to be a suspicious nightclub manager as winner of the international edition of Kill a Friend, Maim a Mate. Thank you both for sharing in this fun and definitely unique contest.

For my good friend Lisa Mac, thank you for yet another brilliant forensic insight – this time the value of glitter as trace evidence, which helped me forge ahead when I needed it most. Yep, I owe you another dinner. Or perhaps we're up to a year's supply of meals.

Fellow suspense novelist and doctor C. J. Lyons provided some fun medical details on the physical effects of starvation. Thanks!

Finally, like writers everywhere, I owe a huge debt of gratitude to my family, who actually has to live with me while I gnash my teeth, mutter at people who don't exist, and curse my novel regularly. My daughter, well trained at this point, spent the final week of my deadline baking cookies and shoving them at me. I really like her.

Surviving is not a destination but a journey. To survivors everywhere, this book is for you.

If you love

LISA GARDNER

Go to www.headline.co.uk to discover
more of her chilling books

  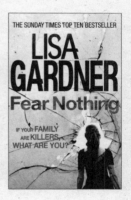

headline

Look out for Lisa Gardner's
next spectacular novel

RIGHT BEHIND YOU

Out early 2017

Thirteen-year-old Sharlah Nash knows that the first time her brother killed eight years ago, he did it to save their lives.

Now retired FBI profiler Pierce Quincy and his wife Rainie Connor have offered Sharlah a new life of safety. She desperately wants to believe this is her shot at happily ever after.

Then two people are murdered in their local convenience store and Sharlah's brother is identified as the killer.

Telly Ray Nash is on the hunt for Sharlah and as the death count rises it becomes clear that nothing and no-one, including Pierce and Rainie, will stop him getting to her.

Now, Sharlah has one chance to take control.

She can run for her life . . . or turn and face the danger right behind her.

headline

THRILLINGLY GOOD BOOKS
FROM CRIMINALLY
GOOD WRITERS

CRIME FILES BRINGS YOU THE LATEST RELEASES FROM
TOP CRIME AND THRILLER AUTHORS.

SIGN UP ONLINE FOR OUR MONTHLY NEWSLETTER AND BE THE FIRST
TO KNOW ABOUT OUR COMPETITIONS, NEW BOOKS AND MORE.

VISIT OUR WEBSITE: WWW.CRIMEFILES.CO.UK
LIKE US ON FACEBOOK: FACEBOOK.COM/CRIMEFILES
FOLLOW US ON TWITTER: @CRIMEFILESBOOKS